ALBERTA
BOUND

Thirty Stories by Alberta Writers

Edited by Fred Stenson

NeWest Press   Edmonton

First Edition

Canadian Cataloguing in Publication Data

Main entry under title:

Alberta bound

ISBN 0-920897-04-5

1. Short stories, Canadian (English) - Alberta. * I. Stenson,
Fred, 1951-
PS8329.5.A4A42   1986   C813'.01'0897123
C86-091528-X   PR9197.32.A42   1986

Credits

Cover design: Bob Young
Typesetting: Mary Albert
Printing and binding: Hignell Printing Ltd., Winnipeg

Financial Assistance

Alberta Culture
The Canada Council

NeWest Press gratefully acknowledges the assistance of The Alberta Foundation for the Literary Arts, whose generous grant made this publication possible.

NeWest Publishers Ltd.
Suite 204, 8631 - 109 Street
Edmonton, Alberta, Canada   T6G 1E8

Contents

Contents

Introduction

The book you are about to read—breathlessly and cover to cover, we hope—brings together the short stories of thirty Alberta writers. There was a time, and not so long ago, when thirty Alberta short story writers would have been hard to find. Not so, today. Except for the problem of creating a book of ungainly size, *Alberta Bound* could have contained the stories of many more writers and still have come up against no shortage of quality work. To give some indication of how many Albertans do write creatively, the Writers Guild of Alberta presently has a membership of over five hundred. Thirty-two books, written by Albertans and published in the previous year, vied for that organization's annual awards in 1986. When a national journalist recently wrote that, if you drill a hole in Alberta, a writer is likely to pop out, it was with some justification.

A surprising thing about the thirty writers in *Alberta Bound* is that not one of them is making his or her debut here. For a few, this is the first time between book covers, but all have appeared in print before. On the other end of the spectrum of experience are the likes of Henry Kreisel, W.O. Mitchell, Sam Selvon, Merna Summers, Jan Truss, Aritha van Herk and Rudy Wiebe, writers with impressive lists of publications for which they have been awarded the highest literary honours in Canada, as well as top prizes earned abroad. In other words, the well-known are side by side with the soon-to-be well-known; the top names of today with the top names of tomorrow.

Alberta, in many ways, remains a frontier, its economy as variable as its weather. We always seem to be setting records for the fastest growing this and the most swiftly declining that. Riding that fulcrum, the population lives on the edge, on the jump and, when we sit down to write, there is a tendency to refuse contentment and to search for something new. As you read this collection, I believe you will feel that restlessness, the sense that the writers are in motion; Alberta bound but not quite satisfied that the destination has been reached.

Fred Stenson
Calgary

ALBERTA BOUND

Patterns
W.O. Mitchell

Often on a Saturday night, when he found himself badly blocked in a sermon, Mr. Cameron found release in tying dry flies; it was a solitary and mesmerizing occupation which somehow freed his mind and imagination. The loose feathers lifted and slid over the desk top under his gentle breath; the completed flies increased one by one, resting high and light on their hackle tips at his elbow. With each fly the tension loosened more and he experienced a little of the satiety that attended the netting of a trout itself. Rings slowly widened and spread to grassy banks; sunlight disked and danced on green water; clear bubbles and foam were borne slowly circling; mosquitoes whined thin; grasshoppers leaped clicketing; and he had broken off for himself a warm and humming fragment of August.

Plato, he felt, would have approved of dry-fly tying; the feather filaments were so spirit-light they could lift and float the heavy dross of the material hook, ideal camouflage raying from the barbed and lethal matter. These were classical flies to ride bravely down summer streams, drifting like waterborne stars on their tantalizing course over slicks and riffles where hungry rainbow lay.

The minister leaned back in his chair and poured himself another cup of tea. Somehow tonight the fly tying did not soothe—certainly not enough to rid his mind of the thought of a Rory Napoleon missing for three days. And why was it that he must always be so concerned for the

Napoleons? He was too practical a man to imagine he could bring them spiritual nourishment. They were not members of his congregation, though that would have been impertinent if they had been in actual want. To his knowledge they never were; they were warm; they were fed; they were clothed; their goats and their 80 weed-infested acres and Rory's job as town garbage collector seemed to take care of their material needs. Their health was the continuing concern of Dr. Fotheringham, who made sure they got to the clinic once a month.

The minister could understand the doctor's interest in the Napoleons; he could also appreciate Mr. Oliver's concern. The police magistrate was the tidiest man in town; proprietor of the Oliver Trading Company General Store, law was only an avocation with him but it was his first love, all the same. In the impeccability of the lawn about his house, store window displays, grocery shelves and counters, one could see that order was Mr. Oliver's passion. His interest, the minister felt, might simply be an attraction to an opposite. Mr. Cameron could not so simply explain his own fascination, a disturbing one dating from the time that he had first come to his charge in Shelby ten years ago. Deliberately then he had set out to discover all he could about the Napoleons; Dr. Fotheringham had been a most fertile source of information.

In Rory Napoleon's veins, the doctor thought, flowed the blood of Brittany tinted with some Basque and min-gling with one-quarter Piegan contributed by his maternal grandfather, Chief Baseball, who had signed the Blackfoot Crossing Treaty in 1878. These had been given Rory by the French half-breed mother, who had met and loved under lodge-pole pines a remittance cowhand in 1908, so that Rory as well boasted the proud blood of the line Mac-Crimmon, composers of pibroch and pipers to the chiefs of Scotland. Mame, his common-law wife, was ten years younger than Rory; like Ontario cheddar she was pure Canadian. Their offspring: Buster, Byron, Avalon, Evelyn, Ester, Elvira—living—and Violet, Herbert, Calvin and Clarence, who had died at birth or in infancy, carried the Breton-Basque-Piegan-Scot-Canadian blood.

Town legend had it that Byron had been born on Dominion Day and on top of a ferris wheel at the thirty-ninth Annual Shelby Fair, Light Horse Show and Rodeo. This was not precisely true, Henry Fotheringham explained to the minister.

"Byron was born exactly nine months after Dominion Day," the doctor said. " 'I always been fussy about the ferris wheel,' Mame told me. 'Fair was almost over an' I told Rory I'd like one more ride before we went home. Ferris wheel broke down. We never did get a good type of ferris wheel at our fairs you know. An' there was Rory an' me with the motor broke down an' our seats swingin' from the top of midnight for a good hour. What else was there for us to . . .' "

A slight, dark and insouciant man with a rather wild eye, Rory could be seen daily in the Post Office just before mail time. He wore a faded blue jacket, its breast pockets lined with a battery of fountain pens and pencils. Usually he took up a position, leaning against the wall near the door and under the WANTED posters and the civil service examination notices. He had no mail box so that when Mr. Fry lifted the frosted window and swung in the brass grill, Rory took his place in line with those lesser individuals whose mail came in a lump under the initial letter of their surnames in General Delivery.

Mr. Fry at the Post Office handed him out regularly: the Shelby *Chinook*, both the Calgary dailies, the Regina *Leader-Post*, the Winnipeg *Tribune*, Nor-west *Prairie Farm Review*, the *Country Gentleman*, *Maclean's*, *Star Weekly*, *Saturday Evening Post*, and Dr. Wine-singer's

Calendar Almanac. "I see by the papers today," was Rory's unfailing gangplank to conversation. He was unable to read or write.

With their herd of 47 goats the Napoleons lived just at the edge of town and next to the farm of Dan Sibbald. Year after year of goat trespass had thinned Mr. Sibbald's patience until an afternoon in the Maple Leaf Beer Parlour just three months before, when Rory had laid open Dan's head with a beer bottle. Mr. Cameron had talked it over with Mr. Oliver, the police magistrate, before he visited the Napoleons.

He found only Mame at home, accepted her invitation to a cup of tea, and came directly to the reason for his visit. "Mrs. Napoleon, I've called to see you about Rory."

"Uh-huh."

"And about Dan Sibbald."

"Did you?" There was little warmth in the red-rimmed eyes.

"Something has to be done, Mrs. Napoleon."

She turned away, took down a brown teapot from the wooden board that formed a shelf above the stove. As she began to shake tea into it she said, "What?"

"I've talked it over with Mr. Oliver . . ."

"Him!"

"And he's had a talk with Dan Sibbald . . ."

"Might have known Oliver'd get into it with his big flat English feet . . ."

"Mr. Oliver has been very just about . . ."

"Always had it in for the Napoleons—can't leave us alone!"

"Mr. Oliver! Oh, I don't think so . . ."

"Well, I do."

"But why would he have it in for . . ."

"I don't know why," Mrs. Napoleon said, "but he always has—always will—stubborn—he was to drownd they'd find his body upstream!"

"But Mr. Oliver is willing to give Rory a chance. That doesn't sound as though he . . ."

"What kind of a chance?"

"He is willing to use his influence with Dan Sibbald—persuade him not to press charges against Rory either for trespass or for assault."

"Is that right?" Some of the coldness had vanished from Mrs. Napoleon's eyes. "Don't sound like Oliver."

"But it is."

"Don't sound like Dan Sibbald either," she said. "What's Rory got to do—apologize to Dan?"

"That would help, Mrs. Napoleon—to begin with."

"What else has he got to . . ."

"It's not Rory who has to do something else—it's you."

"Me? How?"

"I'd like you to have Rory interdicted—for his own good—for your own—for the children . . ."

"An' if I don't put Rory on the Indian List?"

"Then Mr. Oliver will have to let the law take its course."

"That sounds more like Oliver."

"There'll be a summons tomorrow."

"An' Rory'll have to go up before Oliver."

"Yes."

She tipped the boiling kettle over the teapot.

"I'm sorry, Mrs. Napoleon," Mr. Cameron said.

She set a cup before him. "I believe you."

"I wanted to talk it over with Mr. Napoleon but Mr. Oliver said it wouldn't be a good . . ."

"He's right. Wouldn't have a chance if Rory got tipped off first." She sat down in the backless wooden chair by the table. "If it's gotta be done—I'm the one's gonna do it."

"Will you do it for us?"

"I won't do it for Oliver."

"Will you do it for Rory?"

She shook her head. "Kids has it bad enough without Rory goin' down to Lethbridge for a couple months. I'll do it for them. Drink your tea while it's hot. And I'll do it for you."

Now, in his study, Mr. Cameron set aside his empty teacup, stared at the half-tied grey hackle held in the slant nose of the fly-tying vise. It had been so much easier than he had anticipated it would be—and persistently successful; to his knowledge and to Magistrate Oliver's. Rory had put in a sober three months; the goats had stayed in their pen on Napoleon land. Pangs of conscience had come more and more infrequently to the minister as he assured himself that the man's loss of drinking privileges had benefited his work for the town, his wife, his children. Of course there had never been any questioning the desirability of the end; it was the means that had disturbed Mr. Cameron. He would have felt so much better if he had talked it over with Rory first, given the man a chance to agree. It just wasn't right to push people about—even for their own good, for in a way then it stopped being their own good, nor was it such a satisfactory good. There was a comparable difference between a rainbow taken on bait and a rainbow taken fairly on a dry fly.

Obviously with the man missing for three days, it hadn't worked out so well after all. For three months he had deluded himself. Behind the drily casual facade the Napoleons presented to the world, the minister had always sensed a faint threat, but exactly what was threatened or to whom, he had never been sure. He knew only that the threat was there—vaguely ominous—persistent. Somehow—tonight—the minister told himself as he leaned forward over the fly vise—the Napoleon threat was the strongest it had ever been; in the heart of some dark place a hidden Rory waited—had always been waiting—but now was almost through waiting.

For three months Rory Napoleon had waited; for three months his tongue had stuck to the roof of his mouth and his throat had got stiff for the tickle of beer and the earth taste of beer. But Cameron and Oliver and the law had said God Save the Queen to it and that was all there was to it—he couldn't do a thing about it. Couldn't go in the place even. Well, send the law victorious didn't know beer was glorious! Beer never hurt him—never hurt anybody. Let everyone suck beer down and not a drop for him!

At the end of three months he had called on Artie Buller, black-mailed the taxi man into selling him five jugs of wine improved by the addition of grain alcohol to the mother catawba. Artie had resisted making the sale until Rory had threatened to inform Mr. Oliver that Artie had many customers among Napoleon relatives still resident on Paradise Valley Indian Reserve. Rory left Art's Taxi building with his five jugs of Artie's Own; among his cousins out at Paradise Reserve it was more familiarly known as Old Wolverine.

There was one thing to be said about being interdicted for over three months, Rory Napoleon decided: when a man did get hold of the stuff it had gained in muzzle velocity, increased its range, and improved penetration power. He had quite soon achieved a holiday state of total anaesthesia, reclining on sweet clover hay in a corner of the pole shed south of the goat pen. Three days and four and one half jugs later he awoke chilled, in dusk musty with the smell of mould, aslant with dust-vibrant bars of late-afternoon sunlight.

He teetered out of the shed and across the yard to the goat pen. He made a place for himself by pushing aside the brush that Byron had piled on top to keep the goats from leaping to freedom and Dan Sibbald's land, then climbed up and hooked his heels on a lower pole. He stared down upon the 47 goats below. It might have been a matter only of common clues in eye and jaw and nostril; Rory was not interested in the perceptual why; he only knew that now he looked down upon the citizens of Shelby, members of Shelby Rotary, the Activarians, Knights of the Loyal Order of Homesteaders, the town council, North Siders.

"You—Mrs. Fotherin'ham," he addressed the white nanny just beneath him, "can go spit up a rope, for I ain't emptyin' another can for you. I'm human same as anybody else, ain't I? Don't that mean somethin', Oliver?" He was speaking to the billy behind Mrs. Fotheringham, a one-horned ram with a glassy wall eye fixed upon him. "Don't it mean somethin' if a person's a human? Ain't it more important to be a human than to be a horse or a dog or a goat? It's a head start, Oliver!"

But Mr. Oliver had turned and was making his slow way through the herd to the opposite side of the pen. Rory was suddenly filled with uncontrollable anger against Mr. Oliver—all of them. He half rose from his perch.

"I was born human!" he shouted after Mr. Oliver. "I'll die human! I eat human! I drink human! I am human! I'm me! I'm Rory Napoleon!"

All the assembly had turned their attention up to him, but they were just goats now. 47 plain goats. "I am a human," he explained carefully to them. "What's more I am the only human on this whole earth, which is Rory Napoleon."

He grabbed the butt end of willow brush by his thigh and wrenched it loose from the pile; he attacked the rest furiously, flushed with wine, elation and exertion. It was only a moment till he had the top of the pen cleared of the brush that had been piled there to keep the goats inside.

"All right—all right now!" he yelled at them, "you can come up outa there—nothin' to stop you now! High-yuh!" he shrilled as they huddled together at the far side of the pen, blinking up at him in the astonishing sunlight.

"Get your lazy nose out of it, you shag-anappi-spring-heeled, china-eyed English bastard, Oliver! Hough-hough-hah-hup-yaah, Mrs. Tregillis an' Revrund Cameron! Hell's about to go out for recess!"

In 30 seconds the goat eruction was complete.

Rory Napoleon had selected a Saturday night precisely right for the outrage that followed his release of the goats. It was the Saturday night of the month on which the Shelby and Greater Shelby Emergency and Disaster Relief and Civil Defence Committee met. It was as well the night that the Cameo Theatre was exhibiting to its only packed house since the advent of television to Shelby, a vista-vision religious spectacular showing the slaughter of 5000 Christian extras and 9000 animals in the Coliseum as well as the crucifixion and the sack of Rome. The Russians had just shocked the world with the announcement of another successful satellite; ten days ago a 200-yard section of the Trans-Canada Pipeline had exploded 29 miles east of Shelby; Northern Lights the night before had tented the entire sky with frightening brilliance. The day, the week, the month, the year were unique in a chain of chance fragile with coincidence which might have parted at any line short of the final anarchy.

As soon as Rory Napoleon had herded his 47 goats to the head of a brightly lighted and teeming Main Street, the Saturday night traffic came to a halt and quickly bottled the street back in both directions to the ends of the block. The goats left the street itself and took to the sidewalk, trotting as far as Oliver's Trading Company General Store, where Mayor Frazer (goat) caught sight of the fresh vegetable display and led a splinter group of seven through the open door. Eleven others followed Mr. Oliver (goat) to the front of the Maple Leaf Beer Parlour, where one of the outgoing patrons obligingly held open the door. To any of the Napoleon goats a doorway was a familiar phenomenon and now in their frightened bewilderment they automatically sought the security of a confinement they'd known for three months.

Nettie Fotheringham (goat) took her diminished retinue of 28 as far as the Cameo Theatre where the double doors stood wide for the changing of the show. They entered the darkened interior just as Alaric's Visigothic hordes breached the outer gates of Rome. Mr. Cameron (goat), a dissenter from Mr. Oliver's (goat) Maple Leaf Beer Parlour group, trotted to the corner, went up a side street and out of the business section entirely. Three blocks away he came to the shelter of a vague cluster of buildings and stopped to clip the dry grass there.

Within the Maple Leaf Beer Parlour the banter and laughter and friendly argument had changed to curses, grunts, shouts and roars as beer-inflamed men and sober goats mixed together in bleating, butting, kicking, struggling nihilism over a floor awash with spilled beverage, broken glass and chairs and overturned tables. The concussion of the fray vibrated the common wall the beer parlour shared with Totecole's Hardware next door, and Morton Totecole, looking after the store during his father's coffee break, took down the double-barrel ten-gauge from the shotgun rack and slipped in two number-four magnum shells.

Torches had been touched to the Palantine Hill; gladiator and Goth battled against the leaping technicolour flames; Cameo Theatre patrons in outside seats were aware of numerous rustling, moving shapes tapping along the darkened aisle.

Unable to dislodge Mayor Frazer (goat) and his

grazing council from the fresh vegetable and fruit counter, Mr. Oliver (human) admitted failure and phoned Millie Clocker, asking her breathlessly to ring for the police and as well have Fire Chief Alsop turn out a couple of available men. In his excitement he did not explain to Millie that there was no fire and that the men were needed for extraordinary duties. Millie set off the fire siren first and then plugged in for the Mounted Police.

Mr. Cameron (goat) had been grazing, minding his own business, when the fire siren on the fire hall beside him set up its scooping wail. He catapulted to the roof, picked his way along the ridge, at the end of which he could discern a towering skeletal structure; his hooves clanged as he soared upward and came to brief rest before climbing to the top, high over the town buildings.

On hearing the fire siren Cross-cut Jack Brown (Rescue and First Aid), Malleable Jack Brown (Flat-Bottom Boats and Flood Control), Pipe-fitting Jack Brown (Shelter and Alarm) went to the Main Street window of the Ranchman's Club smoking-room where they were holding their meeting of the Shelby and Greater Shelby Emergency and Disaster Relief and Civil Defence Committee. They saw the Mounted Police cruiser wheel around the Royal Bank corner with red light flashing, sensed the confusion in the street below, and heard the rioting uproar from the Maple Leaf Beer Parlour. Pipe-fitting Jack Brown ran to the phone and gave Millie Clocker the blue alert. She signalled the red, however, which would sound the siren again, ring St. Aiden's Church bell, warn the hospital staff, summon Dr. Fotheringham with stretcher bearers, and flush out Ollie Pringle—with ambulance and Pulmotor.

Morton Totecole stood before the Maple Leaf Beer Parlour with the loaded ten-gauge in his hands; he had no intention of using it as he had seen sheriffs and their deputies do on CBC; he was simply waiting to hand it to someone older and much braver than he. The fury within the Maple Leaf had abated, for Taffy had gathered his waiters and some of the patrons at the bar end of the parlour, formed them into a slowly advancing line of men facing a slowly retreating line of goats. Taffy himself stood to one side of the door, ready to throw it open at the strategic moment that the goats were close enough to recognize the triangular gestalt of themselves/the door/freedom.

On the street before the Maple Leaf, Morton Totecole heard the sounds of two new sirens; the one on the fire engine racing south on First Street, the other on Ollie Pringle's ambulance racing north on First Street. St. Aiden's bell began to tongue the night. The fire siren gave three preparatory whoops before it took up the sustained ululation of the red alert.

The church bell penetrated the stirring darkness of the Cameo Theatre where skinned barbarians were garrotting fine old Senators with their own togas and carrying shrieking Roman matrons through falling marble columns and burning rubble. The scrambling in the aisles and the elastic hysteria of three sirens instantly convinced all patrons that the theatre was ablaze.

It was as though the downtown section of Shelby had become the toy of some idiot giant child and was now activated by a great hopper trickling alarm that filled each heart with a cargo of dread till it ran downhill, was tripped, spilled, only to be refilled again, this time with grains of consternation, the next with fright, then terror, and finally panic. As Cameo patrons erupted from the theatre they thought was burning, the herd burst out of the Maple Leaf. Ollie Pringle's ambulance reached Main and First Street at the same moment as the fire engine. Morton Totecole went down in a smother of goats. Mr. Cameron (goat) put out a moist and inquisitive nose to the thing of gleaming glass and metal cable before him. Morton's hand convulsed on the triggers of the ten-gauge goose gun, discharged both barrels at a distance of eighteen inches from the 26-foot plate window of his father's store. The shotgun blast coincided with the superb head-on collision of the ambulance and fire engine as well as with the crackling detonation that signalled the electrocution of Mr. Cameron (goat), who had grounded the power plant transformer with a Queen's Birthday fountain of sparks and a sheet of violet light that winked up the town and the district as far as the correction line. Citizens of Khartoum heard the explosion; those of Tiger Lily said they had.

In the pitch darkness of Main Street there were too many people and too many goats. Humans stamped blindly toward the Royal Bank corner and were brought up against the barricade formed by the fire engine and the ambulance. They swept back through the lightless night, driving the goats before them. Some sought safety in cars, others in stores. Those in cars and trucks turned on their headlights so that a grotesque magic-lantern show of goats and humans was projected against the flat faces of the stores; it was neither vista-vision nor technicolour, but the sack of Rome had been pale by comparison.

Within the stores kerosene and mantle lamps, flashlights and candles were brought out, but they had hardly been lit before full light came on from the town's auxiliary power plant. Some order was reasserting itself, for many now knew that there had been no fire, invasion, earthquake, pipeline explosion, falling Russian satellite—just the Napoleon goats. Except for Maple Leaf cuts and bruises now being treated by Dr. Fotheringham there had miraculously been no serious injuries. Right after he had turned the goats into the top of Main Street, Rory Napoleon had gone back through Hepner's lumber yards, retraced his steps over the CNR bridge, made straight for home and the feed shed. There he fell upon the hay, reached down for the last of his jugs of wine. He finished it.

Slightly after midnight Constables Dove and Clarkson entered the shed. One took Rory by the legs, the other by the armpits. They carried him out, a snoring hammock, between them to the cruiser, headed for the town and the barracks.

The Reverend Cameron finished whipping the head of the last grey hackle, touched it with a bead of black enamel, released it from the vise and laid it down by the others. He had intended going to bed by eleven, but with the power break which had put out the lights, it had taken him till now to tie the dozen flies he liked to complete at one sitting. He leaned back in his chair and as he sighed, three flies drifted over the varnished surface of the desk. Fly patterns—Plato's patterns—God's patterns—man's patterns —oh, so terribly fragile! Always the Napoleons to destroy them; that was the Napoleon threat indeed.

Half Past Eight
Edna Alford

Tessie Bishop took her tube of "Scarlet Fire" lipstick and removed the lid. The lipstick was old and stale and had that sickly sweet smell peculiar to the cosmetics of the aged.

The mirror on the dowager dresser was adjustable, swung on ornate brass hooks, and Tessie tilted it so she could see as much of herself as possible. She wished she had a full-length mirror like the one she had hung on the bathroom door of the apartment she lived in before she had to come to the lodge, before the money ran out and the time with it. She wanted to check the hem of her dress, get the overall effect of the outfit she was wearing to the Stampede Parade.

The mirror on this dresser was tarnished and wavy—like all the others in the lodge, Tessie supposed. Her image was distorted in this mirror, unreal in the bronze shimmer. She couldn't believe she really looked like this, her skin old and wavy and discoloured, mapped with cracks. But what could you expect, she thought. Time passes, doesn't it, and all things considered, she had held her own, didn't look nearly as old as she was, she assured herself, in spite of the mirror.

Mirrors weren't trustworthy, regardless of the fairytales. "Mirror, mirror on the wall, who is the *oldest* of us all?" she mocked the white-haired woman trapped in the yellow glass. Then laughing she said, "See, you can't tell, you silly old bitch. You don't know a goddamn thing—

and in a few minutes you'll know even less."

She stretched her lips thin, into a false smile. Then she slowly, meticulously spread a thick, bleeding layer of lipstick horizontally across her mouth, right to the tapered corners—first on the top lip, then on the bottom. She replaced the lid on the tube and laid it on the dresser top. She took a piece of Kleenex and patted her mouth several times, gingerly.

Next she took a round clear plastic container from a small top drawer of her dresser. The brown-stained label on the bottom read "Pomegranate Blush." She unscrewed the lid and dipped the tip of her right index finger into it. Then she smeared a round high blotch of "Pomegranate Blush" on each cheek.

The rouge was pink and had the same sweet sickening odour as the lipstick, like rosewater and glycerin gone rancid in sun and age. The bright pink cheeks clashed violently with her "Scarlet Fire" lips and together with white, heavily powdered skin in wrinkles, made her look like a clown.

She applied eyebrow pencil in thin black arches over her almost browless eyes and in conclusion, brushed mascara thickly on her short white lashes. It dried lumpy.

When she had finished, she smiled with satisfaction at the mirror. She began to hum to herself. She went to the long window of her small dark room and was delighted to see the summer sun already climbing high and hot in the eastern sky. There were only a few roguish tufts of cloud drifting easily through the blue whiteness.

She had been hoping for weeks now that there would be no rain today. She and Flora Henderson had crossed their fingers in unison yesterday—at the supper table, in the tea room, and at prayer meetings where everyone else was singing "Rock of ages cleft for me, let me hide—" they would both look out at the sky, then back at each other, hoping the weather would hold for the parade.

The weatherman on CFCN Radio last night had reported that a fine day *was* expected for the parade, that there were clouds moving in over the Rockies but they weren't expected to reach Calgary till late tomorrow. Tessie put her face close to the warm green shimmer of the window screen and breathed a satisfied, and at the same time, excited sigh of relief.

She had on her best summer dress, a flowered cotton print with huge pink and red and orange mums with black stems and leaves frolicking all over it. A thin black patent leather belt sat squarely on her hips. A very classy number, she thought. A perfect dress for a parade. She wore a navy straw hat with a small brim and last week she had bought an orange chiffon scarf to lace through the brass holes in the hat and tie pertly under the chin. The scarf perfectly matched the orange mums in the dress print.

When she brushed her hair, she flipped a small white curl on either side of her face to fall sultry against her cheeks. Her hair looked exactly as she had worn it in what she called her "hey day," in the early twenties. Tessie had been one of the first to bob her hair and she wore it now in the same short-cropped style. Admiring herself in the wavy mirror, she remembered that she had been a very beautiful young woman. Everyone had told her so and she herself had thought that it was true.

When she was finished putting on her make-up, she put the lipstick along with her comb, some Kleenex, and her clutch purse in a small black bag she had crocheted.

Although she could barely make ends meet on the small pension she got from the Veterans' Affairs Department, she had managed to save a little over twenty dollars for today. It hadn't been easy but she had cut down on wool for crocheting last month and she made do with the meals at the lodge which, she thought, was a sacrifice, to say the least. And she hadn't bought a drop of liquor in all that time.

One good thing about today was that she didn't have to worry about Flora. Flora was game to go and always had lots of money. In fact, she was more excited about the parade than Tessie, could talk of nothing else. You'd never know she was eighty-six. Nothing could keep her down— a lot like me, thought Tessie. Age meant nothing to her, which was probably why they chummed around together, not because of the drinking, which was the opinion of most of the old biddies who lived here. And Flora always paid her own way.

There were all sorts of rumours about Flora. Some said she won the "Pot of Gold" at the fair one year and that was why she could stick her old age pension cheques under her mattress and not worry about cashing them. But Tessie knew that Flora and old man Henderson had owned a hotel up north in British Columbia and that they had catered to the men from the logging camps. Flora spent a good deal of her time supervising the girls on the top floor. "There was good money in them girls," Flora told Tessie confidentially.

Today's the day, all right, Tessie thought. Today we'll go out and see the parade and eat and kick up our heels for a change.

Leaving her bed unmade, she picked up her straw sun hat, her black bag, and a sweater just in case. She locked the door, trying the lock afterward and then walked down the hall and knocked on Flora's door, number twenty-three. She frowned down at her brown oxfords which were not beautiful and didn't match her dress. But they were sturdy, she thought, for all the walking they would have to do today.

Flora opened the door a crack. Then, finding it was Tessie, she flung the door back against the jamb. "Yah, come on in," she bellowed.

Flora, too, had high rouge blotches on her cheeks and her hair stuck pin-curl fuzzy out from under a wide-brimmed mannish straw hat. For all her money, thought Tessie, Flora might at least buy a new summer hat. That one, Tessie was sure, must have been old man Henderson's fifty years ago.

Flora wore a long-sleeved, shapeless dress of grey-striped arnel her daughter-in-law had helped her pick three years ago. But she had new shoes, handsome sturdy white sandals. Tessie felt a slight twinge when she saw them.

"Good day for a parade, eh Flora?" she said. She was not about to let on to Flora how envious she was of the new sandals.

"Good day for a parade, eh Tess?" Flora hadn't heard Tessie speak. That was another thing that irked her about the older woman. She was partially deaf. But at least she wasn't afraid to go. So Tessie smiled patronizingly at Flora. I may not have fancy sandals, she thought to herself, but at least I'm not deaf—yet.

Flora smiled back, picked up her purse and sweater, and they left the room, Flora locking the door of room twenty-three behind them. She tried the lock twice.

They passed several ancient ladies with canes, shuffle-feeling thick routes along the walls of the hallway on their way to breakfast. The hoyer stood in the middle of the lower hallway outside Miss Bole's room and Tessie edged her way around it as if she were afraid it were alive, as if it might reach out and grab her. But Flora stuck out her foot and gave the hoyer a shove and sent it rolling into the wall, clanking when it hit the baseboard, its canvas straps swinging foolishly.

"You'll never get me into that goddamn thing," she bellered at the metal hoist used to transport bedridden lodgers to and from the bathtub. "Goddamn stupid nurse,"

Flora continued, "leaving that contraption out in the hall so's one of us'll fall and break our bloody hips. No more of a nurse than a pig's foot," she yelled. "She hasn't got the brains she was born with. I wouldn't hire her if ya paid me, Tess."

Tessie raised her eyebrows and smiled. Flora guffawed. "Oh Christ, Tess. She ain't fit for that kinda work!" Tessie giggled.

At breakfast Tessie and Flora had to sit with Mrs. Morrison and Mrs. Popovich because there were no spaces left at the other tables by the time they got there. Tessie had hated Helen Popovich ever since the fight over the big brown rocker on the sun porch. Tessie had lost that one, but only because Helen Popovich called in the matrons. And Mrs. Morrison wasn't much better—"Yes Helen this" and "Yes Helen that"—a spineless old bat if there ever was one.

But she tried to ignore the other two women and she and Flora talked about their plans. Would they take the bus as far as the stadium or would they walk while it was still cool? Better take the bus, they decided. No sense risking being late and missing the Parade Marshall. Tessie would definitely be upset if she missed Prince Charles.

Mrs. Popovich's forehead furrowed cynically. "Why you'd want to fight them crowds is beyond me," she clipped the remnants of a fractured voice, "and on a day like this! Good Lord, Flora, you'll shrivel up in the heat. What if you have an attack? Things aren't like they used to be you know. Nobody'll pick you up from the street now—they just leave you lying there. I know an old woman who lay for five hours, I say, on the street and her leg was broke and nobody helped her. She died too."

"We all do," Flora interrupted, "but Tessie and me ain't dead yet." She winked at Tessie and Tessie winked back.

"We won't strain ourselves, Helen," Tessie compromised. "We're just going to have a look. We don't plan to be gone long. After all, we're not going to be on the street you know. We do have seats in Mewata Stadium and we do have our hats."

"Suit yourself," Helen clucked with finality. She didn't speak to them again but when Tessie and Flora gathered their things together and strutted out of the dining room, Tessie whispered loudly, not only for Flora but so Helen could hear.

"You know what they say, Flora—mind your own business, eat your own fish—not to mention the dog in the manger." She looked around to make certain Helen had heard her and smiled with satisfaction. Helen was staring furiously at the porridge in the thick porcelain bowl on her plate. She was jabbing it viciously with the wrong end of her spoon.

Outside the building and walking on the sidewalk toward the bus stop, Tessie and Flora were a peculiar and somewhat amusing couple. Flora, although eighty-six, was still tall and raw-boned, her heavy body lumbering like a large grey-striped animal from side to side with each step. Tessie, on the other hand, was a little like a bird, very small and colourful beside Flora. The steps Tessie took were Lilliputian and energetic which produced a kind of hopping effect as she dodged Flora's large body, like a bright pecking bird on the back of a hippo.

When they boarded the bus it was already packed with an uproar of parade people. Tessie and Flora had to cling desperately to the chrome rods along the top of the seats because there was no place to sit. They didn't mind, except when the teeming vehicle lurched.

"Take it easy you old sonuvabitch," Flora called up to the driver, although he couldn't have been a day over fifty, Tessie thought, and not half-bad looking. To Tessie's embarrassment, Flora continued heckling, "I been in bloody buckboards made better time than this and was smoother too, yah, you bet—they give a better ride!" Some of the passengers nearest them giggled or muffled their laughter but one man laughed right out loud.

"What the hell's the matter with *you*?" Flora turned on him. "Ya drunk or just off your rocker?" The man laughed again and so did Flora this time.

Tessie inspected the clothing worn by the other passengers, mentally rated the parade outfits on a scale of one to ten. A zero, she thought, that one is definitely a zero. Pausing tentatively, her eyes scanned a young girl from the waist down. "If I had legs like that," she said to Flora, "I wouldn't be caught dead in shorts, even if I was sixteen-years-old."

"Yah, you bet," said Flora, "she'd be scrubbin' floors in my place." She winked at Tessie. "Not like you Tess," she added. Tessie blushed and cupped her hand over her eyes, pretending to look out the window to see where they were.

The ride to the stadium wasn't long but when they slowly and awkwardly disembarked all the while jostled and shoved by the swarming young, the two old women were relieved to breathe more deeply, even though the air was full of exhaust from the back of the bus. By now the near-noon sun was very high and the heat wafted around the women. But instead of making them sluggish or uncomfortable as it did most old folk, the heat only served to increase their excitement. Along the way to their seats, Flora openly rebuked the rude, both drivers and pedestrians. She broke a ten-dollar bill to buy them two Revels and two paper cups full of Orange Crush. "Why don't you watch where you're goin', ya dirty bugger," she cursed when a young man bumped her elbow, making her spill the drinks so that her hands were sticky when they arrived at their seats.

From where they sat they could see the whole spread of the city centre—the Calgary Tower, a dull one-legged crane with a red crown, half-surrounded on one side by tall lean office buildings, the head offices of banks and oil companies, like confident prehistoric monsters with thousands of glass eyes glittering in the high hot sunlight. For a while they both stared at it, intently, as if their city were a foreign country they had never set foot in—they were not afraid, but were not exactly sure what they could expect.

They were soon distracted. Tessie first heard the off-key din of horns and the tremor of drums in the air as the great parade wound its way along farther up the route. Flora, being hard of hearing, had to be told that it was very near the stadium and then they both fidgeted, straining to catch their first glimpse of the leading entourage.

Finally the Parade Marshall rode into view. He was none other than Prince Charles himself, the Crown Prince of England. He was mounted on one of the magnificent dark R.C.M.P. stallions, just as his Uncle Edward had been so many years before. It didn't seem that long a time ago. Tessie tallied the years in her head. No doubt about it. Fifty. Half a century. It hardly seemed possible, but there it was.

Prince Edward was a doll and she hadn't been the only girl who thought so. And Charles was a fine looking young man, too—but just a boy really. Nevertheless, Tessie was impressed. He carried himself well, exactly the way Tessie thought the Crown Prince of England should. From the time he was a baby, Tessie had kept a scrapbook of newspaper clippings, pictures and stories about his arrivals and departures all over the Commonwealth. That was how she learned he was going to lead the parade. There had been big spreads about him in the newspapers, both the *Herald* and the *Albertan*, several weeks before.

Tessie was more than impressed. Other than Edward, there had been only one Marshall who had excited her more and that was Bing Crosby. He rode in a low, sleek convertible, but because Tessie had watched that parade from the street, she had been almost close enough to touch the man with the dreaming voice as he passed. "Where the blooo of the night / Meets the gold of the day (babababababa-baba) / Someone—waits for—meeee," Tessie crooned. In her memory, Bing had waved directly to her and at the very thought of it, she could feel a warm flow of blood flush her pomegranate cheeks. Flora never could get too worked up about the Royal Family and Bing Crosby seemed somehow after her time.

Behind the Crown Prince rode the Royal Canadian Mounted Police. To Tessie they looked like a flock of red birds, flag wings fluttering. There were white hats scattered all along the parade and the hats looked like white gulls on dark waves. And there was the waving of hand wings from the procession to the crowd and the wing-waving back from the white-hatted bleachers which to Tessie looked for all the world like an island of white birds in the middle of the city.

There was a wide assortment of Indians with red and yellow and white and blue beadwork. Riding and walking, they looked like beautiful and mystical doomed birds, leather headdresses swaying on their backs and feather plumes totter-waving from the tight headbands.

Among them walked a riderless horse with a sign hanging on its side. The sign identified the horse as the one Nelson Small Legs should have been riding. He was the young Indian man who had just taken his own life, Tessie remembered, the young man who couldn't go on with his battles with bureaucracies and reservations, the newscaster had said. Tessie pointed his horse out to Flora and reminded her who he was. "Yah, yah, yah, I know," Flora replied in a sad low voice.

Tessie hoped the riderless horse wouldn't dampen Flora's spirits. She always liked the Indian section of the parade best of all and looked forward to it every year. Tessie remembered their talks about the Indians in the North who sold their beaded moccasins to the loggers who came to the hotel. And Flora talked especially of a raven blue beauty who had worked in her house, on the top floor of the hotel. Tessie thought there was more to that part of the story than Flora let on by the far away look in her eyes when she spoke of the girl. Tessie had been around too. Flora didn't need to think she could pull the wool over *her* eyes.

But Flora soon perked up and the two old women quickly became intoxicated with the colour of the parade and the sound and with the smell of fresh horse droppings randomly and indiscreetly released by the great beasts on the pavement. The hot sun ricocheted off the trumpets and the cymbals of the strutting bands and off the majorettes' batons thrown high and gleaming into the summer sky.

Floats of paper flowers glided miraculously by themselves, dream-like, their tractors hidden under more paper flowers. Flora and Tessie both disagreed with the choice of the judges as to which floats should win the first and second prizes and they argued with each other about the way it should have been.

They drank the spectacle whole and undiluted while the sun played on their gleaming wrinkles which collected small droplets of sweat in the heat. Tessie's mascara ran and blackened the already prominent bags of skin under her eyes.

Long after the last float had passed the stadium, they sat watching the crowd clear, watching the parade trail away along the route. They were sorry it was over and only after a cleaner arrived pushing his long-handled bristle broom down their aisle, did they stand laboriously and gather their things. They started down one of the aisles of the bleachers. There were only a few people wearing white stetsons left, picking up thermoses, cushions and left-over lunches.

When they got down to the street Flora said her tongue was stuck to the roof of her mouth—that's how thirsty she was. And Tessie agreed. "You have to take it easy when you get to be our age, Flora," she said, "dehydration, you have to be careful of dehydration at our age." Flora looked shocked. "I *mean*, Flora, that we old folks need a lot of rest—and liquids—say at the Palliser Hotel, for example."

Flora laughed. "Yah, you bet, Tess. This here Rimrock Lounge—now that's what I call a nice quiet place. We should have brought the other old dames with us, Tess. Be good for 'em." Tessie hailed a Yellow Cab and they set off toward the city centre.

In the old days, Tessie remembered, the Palliser had been the tallest, most impressive building in the city, a testimonial to the indisputable might of the Canadian Pacific Railroad. But in recent years it had been dwarfed by a six-hundred-foot concrete tower which hovered over it, and by the sleek new shopping complex which appeared to be nudging the old hotel slowly toward the curb, toward the subway. She remembered when the tower had been built by the Husky Oil Company. At first it was called the Husky Tower but they had already renamed it the Calgary Tower. Why, Tessie didn't have the faintest idea, but they had done it, down in City Hall she supposed. Anyway the tower looked to Tessie like a man's you know what and she couldn't resist telling Flora that it was the biggest one she'd ever seen—and she had seen a few in her time.

The heat was beginning to work on the women as

they climbed and their feet grew heavy and slow. Inside, the hotel was large and cool and bright. An enormous old chandelier glittered with amber light near the high ceiling of the lobby. The two women went directly to the Rimrock Lounge and sat down in luxuriously upholstered red velvet chairs at a small round table. Tessie ordered a Shanghai Sling with a red maraschino cherry and a piece of pineapple on top and Flora ordered a shot of whiskey, straight.

After their second drink an old man in a brown straw cowboy hat, a western tie and a big belt with a large brass horse-head buckle came over to Flora and Tessie's table. The ladies were boisterous by now and asked him to join them. He swept his cowboy hat off his head, harlequin-tipped it to the ladies and introduced himself as Hank. Hank had a lumpy hooked nose like the warted beak of an old hawk. He bought two rounds and Tessie, especially, was grateful.

"Well wha' did you ladies think of it this year?" asked Hank.

"Stacks up, I'd say," said Tessie. "Better than last year's if you ask me."

"Didya ever see so much *horseshit* in all yer life?" Hank shook his heavy hawk head.

"*Never*," Tessie replied, emphatically.

"Seems to me it don't all come from a horse's ass neither," Hank continued. "Every bloody politician in the city was there and some come all the way from Ottawa to ride over the turds—" he paused. "On second thought," he said, "maybe some of it *do* come from a horse's ass."

Tessie covered her mouth with her hand and laughed till her face turned red. Flora just threw her head back and let the laughter roll up from her belly. Her hat fell off and landed on the carpet behind her chair. Satisfied with the effect his commentary had on his new companions, Hank stretched out his legs and clasped his gnarled brown hands behind his head, slowly lifted one enormous, scuffed Texas boot and crossed it deliberately over the other boot.

"I'll tell you what I like," he drawled. "I like them majorettes with their baa-tons."

"You mean their legs don't you, Hank?" Tessie volleyed.

"Yah, you bet," said Flora who had her hand cupped to her best ear and had caught the word "legs." "Not too bad, not too bad at all. You and me, Tess, if we had a couple of them peaches, we could buy and sell that Pine Mountain hole ten times over. Get ourselves a fair-sized house, one of them old fellas across from Maunley Park. We'd live on the first floor and set up shop on the second. Whadaya say, Tess?" Flora's voice, low and hoarse, rumbled along like an old train.

"Why *not* Pine Mountain?" snickered Tessie. The "not" was high-pitched, a little girl's squeal. She put her hand on Hank's arm and said, "That's where we live, Hank, in the lodge," and turning to Flora, continued, "God knows it's old enough—lots of rooms. You and I could live in the Maunley Mansion, Flora, in style, like the matrons."

"Yah, you bet. Be nice and quiet. The girls could take the fellas out inta the park, under the trees—be nice in the spring, eh Tess?" She winked at Tessie and Tessie winked back.

"One small problem," said Tessie, "what do we do with all those old ladies? As you would say, Flora, they sure as hell ain't fit for work."

"Yah, you bet," Flora laughed, "as far as I can figure half of 'em don't even know where they are. Seems to me things could go on pretty much as usual, Tess, and nobody'd know the difference—but for the matrons, I guess. We might have a little trouble bringing them around."

Hank, who had finally come to appreciate the nature of Tessie's and Flora's plan, rolled his eyes toward the ceiling, then bowed his head and, tipping his hat low over his brow, drawled, "Ah-haa—I didn't know you was that sort of ladies." Then he raised his head and stared directly at Tessie who blushed and looked down at her drink. Gingerly, she slid the maraschino cherry from its plastic green arrow and popped it into her mouth. It was sweet, deliciously sweet.

Late in the afternoon the three tottered into the hotel dining room and ordered steak sandwiches. Tessie ate too much and had stabbing gas pains for some time after the meal. Flora had trouble chewing the meat with her false teeth but she enjoyed the blood beef flavour and ate everything on her plate.

When they finished their meal the three went back to the bar. Flora had to stop at the washroom on the way. There was a line-up and Hank and Tessie could hear Flora cursing from all the way across the lobby. Once in the bar they drank beer from pitchers and sang along with a man who played a honky-tonk piano in a dark corner of the lounge. The words of the songs were projected on a white square of wall and a little ball bounced from word to word along the lyrics so they could know where they were and what to sing.

"Roll out the barrel," Flora bellowed, "we'll have a barrel of fun," not always in tune or in time with the piano.

Tessie's hands fluttered and she leaned her old body, covered in orange and pink and red mums, languorously toward Hank as they sang together and whispered ripe jokes which Flora couldn't hear but laughed at anyway.

Once, while asking "What'll the ladies have?" when buying another round, Hank slapped Tessie's thigh and left his hand on one of the large orange mums that clung to the cloth of her dress. He left it there for what seemed a

very long time to Tessie and she felt the blood rise to the
rouge on her cheeks. She winked at him. Flora didn't see
any of this and Tessie didn't let on to her what had happened.

After awhile, Flora began to doze and snore intermittently. Twice, she nearly fell off her chair. The second
time, she almost tipped the chair over and that seemed to
startle her, perk her up. Tessie had to admit she was a bit
disappointed in Flora for petering out so fast, but then she
was so much older than Tessie.

Hank had just come back from the washroom and had
poured himself another glass of beer when Tessie felt the
hand on her stocking, moving up her thigh. She leaned
toward Hank, then straightened abruptly. Both of Hank's
hands were occupied—a half-full glass of beer in one and
a Player's cigarette in the other. She had just watched him
light it. She turned on Flora.

"Jesus H. Christ, Flora!" she yelled. "That's the limit!
We're going home!" She blushed. The people at the next
table all turned and looked at her as if she'd lost her mind.
Hank was looking at her that way too.

"Oh come on, Tess," Flora cajoled, "I didn't mean
nothin' by it. The party's just beginning."

"I say it's over, Flora. Come on." Despite Hank's
slurred protests, Tessie went out to the lobby and called a
cab. When she came back, she picked up Flora's hat and
their purses and they left. Hank walked out to the lobby
with them. Before Tessie passed the doorman, she turned
and pretended to look back at the glittering old chandelier.
But she couldn't see Hank. He must already have gone
back into the bar.

Tessie was furious with Flora, plunked the older
woman's hat on her head, put her in the back seat of the
cab, and climbed into the front with the driver. But after
they had been driving for awhile, she began to calm down.
No point in looking back, she thought to herself. She
shouldn't have done it. It never worked. And there was no
sense spoiling the whole day because of what Flora did,
not over a little thing like that. Flora was drunk. That was

the problem. But they'd gotten drunk together before and there was none of this nonsense. Must have been the parade, thought Tessie, all those bloody majorettes and all those Indians. She thought about that for a moment. Well, at least Flora would go with her, wasn't afraid of a little fun, and there was no harm done after all.

Instead, Tessie began to worry that the matrons would be up, or that the night nurse would catch them coming in. With any luck Mrs. Tittler would be asleep, but if she wasn't—. Tessie sighed deeply, then belched. Her stomach was full of gas again because of the beer. Not only that, she was pretty sure she would be hung over in the morning.

Flora began to sing in a subdued, broken voice, "Roll out the barrel, we'll have a barrel of fun——," then stopped abruptly in the middle of the first verse as if she had just remembered something vitally important. She laughed and launched into a rollicking chorus of a different song, sung to the tune of "The Dark-Town Strutters' Ball"—

OOOH—there's gonna be a ball
the mother-fuckers' ball.
The witches an' the bitches
gonna be there all.
Now honey, don't be late
'cause we'll be passin' out
pussy 'bout half-past eight

The cabbie tipped back the brim of his hat, looked over his shoulder and grinned. "That's a new one on me," he said. "I thought I'd heard 'em all."

"Huhaw!" Flora guffawed. "Do I look like I'd be singin' a new song?"

That wasn't very likely, Tessie thought, regarding her old friend with amusement and a fair amount of admiration, but then Tessie had never heard the song before either—and she had been around.

"Oh yah, we sung it in the bar all the time, years ago, up North in my old man's hotel." She paused, remembering. "Yah," she said quietly, "that's an old dog."

As they climbed the steps toward the dark building, Tessie could hear the roll of thunder in the black west. She smelled something dank, like mildew, in the air. That's all right, she thought. Let her come down in buckets—all night if she wants to, and all day tomorrow. As long as it didn't rain today.

At the top of the steps, Flora rattled her throat, dragged up a patch of phlegm and spat it into the flower bed beside the lodge where it hung white and bubbly on a purple petunia. Tessie winced. They snuck in through the sun porch door which, luckily, had not yet been locked. In all likelihood, Mrs. Tittler had completely forgotten about it again, Tessie thought.

In the feeble light of the porch, Tessie noticed that Flora's straw hat sat awry and saucy on her head. Someone might get up. Maybe Mrs. Tittler would come out and see the tilt and suspect. "Stand still a minute will ya, Flora," she said. She reached up and straightened the hat and fuss-tucked the fuzzy grey strands of hair under the brim. Flora pretended to stand at attention.

But no sooner had they started up the hall when Flora began to wander from one side to the other, banging on each door and roaring, "Wake up ya deaf old coots! C'mon now, outa the sack!" Then she began to sing—"Oh, there's gonna be a ball, the mother—"

"Shshshsh," Tessie pleaded, her right index finger poised dramatically stiff and vertical over her red-crusted lips. "You'll wake 'em up for shhure, you crazy old drunk!"

"What's a matter with ya, Tess?" Flora bellered to the lodge of aged sleeping ladies. "I'd rather be fuckin' drunk than this." She wheeled and staggered, raised her right arm, waved it around in the air and, fisting the fingers, resumed weaving back and forth across the hall, banging on bedroom doors and singing—

"The witches and the bitches
gonna be there all.

Now honeee, don't be late
'cause we'll be passin' out—

"Jesus Christ," she interrupted herself, "most of these old dames don't even make it to seven-thirty let alone half-past eight—and the worst of it is they wouldn't know what to do with it even if they could get holda some."

Tessie, who was now standing in the stairwell at the other end of the hall, stopped tapping her foot. Though she was half-hidden in shadow, her moon white face appeared to project itself out of the dark, like a mask on a stick. Her eyes were rimmed in black where the mascara had run in the hot afternoon sun and met the thin black arches pencilled on her brows.

Prima Vera
Caterina Edwards

"The doctor," Cesare would say on his way out, "told me you must get more rest," picking up his lunch box and thermos, pulling on his gloves. "Go. Sleep," his last words before he wound his scarf around the bottom half of his face and turned to the door.

And Maria would obey him. That is, she would try. She would stretch out on their bed and close her eyes. Sleep, she would tell herself. Sleep. But then she would think of all the things Cesare had said the Doctor had said. Toxemia, preclampsia, Cesare had looked the words up in the Italian-English dictionary, but they weren't there. High blood pressure. She understood that. She could feel the blood running through her veins, pushing too hard. Her heart beating too fast, too loud. She couldn't lie on her front; her stomach had got too big. If she tried her side, she had to fiddle with the pillow. She was forced to lie on her back, her stomach protruding, forced to lie as if already laid out. And her hand, each time, strayed to her chest or throat. Her fingertips counting the beats. Runaway heart. And she couldn't get away. Runaway heart, and she was stuck to this miserable house, to this small drafty room, to the coming child, to the approaching day.

If she could be home in this time of waiting. If she could be with her sisters, her father. If she could see his faded blue eyes, feel his large knobbled hands on her hair, enter again his smell, lime and pipe tobacco. Home again. Then, she would not be afraid, then.

"How can you send me away—so far? How?"

And he had pulled away from her.

"He's your husband. Your place IS WITH him."

Her place. What a place. Even in the panic of those last days before she'd left her home to come and join Cesare, even then she had imagined it better than it was. So this is my America, she'd thought when she first saw the house: the paint chipped and patchy, the front stairs cracked, the tiny front yard littered with old tires. "*Mia casetta in Canada.*" None of the houses in her village were as flimsy as this one. Nor had she imagined how confined she'd be to the house, locked in partly by her lack of English and her not being able to drive but mostly by the never-ending winter. A prisoner of this cold country. Month after month. Her very thoughts were freezing into the shape of the rooms and the furniture. And she could feel the fragile walls trying to hold off the snow, trying to keep back the cold. She could feel them buffetted, weakening.

The ice was pushing in at the windows, at the corners. Reaching for her.

How could she sleep? She hauled herself onto her side, feet on the floor, pushed up with a small grunt to a sitting position. She was enormous; the Doctor was right about that. Though she hadn't liked his tone when he'd said, "Tell your wife not to eat so much spaghetti." She had told him, told him through Cesare, that she wasn't eating much. Couldn't. Three quarters of what went in came right back, from the first day onward, all eight months. But he hadn't paid attention. Just spoke louder. "Less spaghetti." So she didn't tell him that they, Veneti, rarely ate the stuff.

The baby shifted, lurched. Maria, who had just got herself into a standing position, smoothed down her dress. That doctor could make all the accusations he wanted; she knew.

"It's feeding off me, sucking out my bones," she'd
said, smiling to Cesare. By the time it's born, there'll be
nothing left of me." He'd looked at her then, examined her
face closely, trying to gauge the level of seriousness
behind the light tone and light expression.

He'd said something noncommital. Then added his
usual reassurance. "Everything will be fine. We're not in
your village now. We have doctors—and a good hospital."
But all evening his eyes had returned to her face. As if he
suddenly wondered who this woman he'd chosen for a
wife really was.

"So far and to a man I don't know."

"You will," her father had said, "you will know each
other."

Cesare's old, open slippers slapped on the linoleum as
Maria crossed the kitchen to the living room. She could no
longer wear any of her own shoes. Her feet were swollen,
doughy. Sometimes they were numb or prickly, and
always she had to will them to move, pull them along. Her
feet that used to run up the hill to her house, that used to
fly, so it seemed, over the fields to her special spot, her circle of trees.

Maria sighed as she lowered herself carefully onto the
battered sofa, then arranged her feet on the arm. Cesare
was right. She was getting worse. Thinking things she
shouldn't think. What had Beppi said? "Think beautiful
thoughts. Concentrate on what is good and sweet and the
baby will flourish."

Maria stared out the window at a bare tree, grey
against the white snow and sky. She must think of spring.
If she could concentrate hard enough. *Primavera*, she
could call back that first truth. The scent of new grass,
prima, the snowdrops at the base of her trees, *vera*, the

buds on the branches, fresh and green and lacey.

She could see herself, hyacinths filling her arms, a hyacinth in her hair, buoyed by the sweet perfume. And beside her, in the gentle spring night, a gentle young man speaking soft words. She was floating on the scent and the language and the touch of the breeze on her skin.

"So far. And to a man . . . "

Not that she would ever have put flowers in her hair. Not when anyone could see. She would have been too embarrassed. And when was there such a smooth-faced and smooth-tongued young man? Her suitors were of a rougher mold. Except for Maurizio, her godmother's son. He'd come to visit each time he was home from university. He brought flowers, sweets. It was understood. Everyone agreed it was understood. Only she hadn't acquiesced to the understanding, to his languishing glances or his moist, plump fingers casual and proprietorial on her arm. Even in the piazza, his hand around her shoulder or on her elbow, guiding. His words had been not so much smooth as spongy. Maria'd felt she could sink into them without ever encountering a central core of meaning. "I don't under-stand. What do you mean?" she would say to Maurizio as they ambled on a Sunday afternoon walk. And he would smile. "Well, you wouldn't."

Cesare, he had been different from the beginning, hard-edged in his straightforwardness. "I've come back to Italy to find a wife," he'd told her father on his first visit to the house. "I had a fianceé. That is, I thought I did. But when I got home everything had changed. And I only have three weeks left." He'd come to bring news of her oldest brother, who didn't live in the same city as Cesare did but whom he knew, nevertheless. "Two hundred miles is noth-ing there," he said. "The space—the room—it's fantastic."

If only she'd understood then how "fantastic" it was. Of course, she hadn't been thinking at all at the time. How else could she explain it? She'd looked at this dark, quick moving stranger in a too tight suit and hair that stood straight up like a rooster, and she was dazed. He had the brightness of the sun at noon shining on the sea, hurting her eyes.

And the stranger, Cesare, watched her from across the room, and in two evenings he chose. "I was desperate. I had so little time left," he told not only her but all the *ragazzi* one Sunday dinner. "I had to have a wife. I couldn't return without one. I would have taken anyone. Even a whore if she was willing."

"Thank you." She couldn't look at the others.

Cesare laughed and passed his hand roughly over her cheeks, in and out of her hair. "I'm just amazed with what I got. My own little snowdrop."

"A mountain flower indeed," Lucio added.

"Special. And as pure—"

"Enough."

He'd chosen and she, well, she had found herself in the town hall, embarrassed as Cesare shouted at the official who insisted the papers couldn't be done on such short notice, mesmerized as his fist pounded the shiny desk over and over. She found herself in her cousin's wedding dress, found herself repeating the hallowed words. And when Cesare was gone and she was released from the force of his choice and began to think, it was too late.

"I don't know him. He's a stranger and Canada is so far—"

"It's ever thus in marriage. You will know him. After your years together, you'll know. And you are his wife. Before God."

His wife before God. Before. The child flailed. Before.

A sudden sharp sound. She lay still, waiting, her feet still up. What else could she do? But it was only Nico, lunch-bucket in hand. She didn't like his seeing her so laid out, but to start thrashing around to get up would be worse. She'd always felt more awkward with him than with Lucio or Mario or Beppi. He rarely said much, and the paucity of words together with his stockiness and jaw-heavy face gave him a sullen, hulking presence.

"Is there any mail?" It was always his first question. Though, of course, it was the primary concern of all the *ragazzi*, no matter how politely the others might first inquire after her health.

"Not for you. There's a letter for Beppi." She started to hoist herself to a sitting position. Nico did not offer a helping hand but continued to stare down at her. A bit irritated, she said without thinking, "It has been a long time since she wrote to you. Maybe you should start worrying."

His expression didn't change. "Twenty days." He suddenly put out his hand to her.

In the kitchen she began the supper preparations. She felt even more clumsy and misshapen than usual before him. Not that Nico was watching her. Each time she turned from the counter or sink, he was staring down at his hands. He had never sat with her before. Normally he stayed in his room. He had a record player and many 78's of operatic arias. He played them for hours, *Vesti La Giubba* and *Addio Gloria* infiltrating the whole house. He did sit in the kitchen some evenings, but only when all the *ragazzi* were there. He liked to play cards and to harmonize on an impromptu song. He particularly liked to be coaxed into giving a solo. He had a good baritone voice, with only a slight tendency to shout.

"I didn't know you used cans."

Maria nearly dropped a can of chicken broth. "I don't. Only the natural, of course. Everything homemade. But now," she could feel her face flushing. "I can't stand the smell of it cooking. Makes me ill. Tomato sauce too . . . You do understand? You won't say anything?"

Nico murmured an "of course" and went back to staring at his hands.

What did he want? She disliked cooking at the best of times, and being watched made it worse. Maria hadn't known how to cook when she got married. That first night she'd arrived in Edmonton, on top of her disappointment with the house, her shyness with Cesare, on top of her grief at leaving home, the crowning touch was the realization she was expected to care and cook for not one man, but five.

Cesare had noticed her expression. He immediately guided her into their bedroom and sat her down. "We can ask them to leave. It's up to you. I won't impose them on you." And when she didn't answer, "I know it's hard. I remember what it was like for me four years ago. Did I ever tell you that after the first six weeks, I made up my mind to go back? I thought cold country, cold people. It's not the place for me. I was on my way to buy the ticket." His arm crept around her shoulder. "But Mario and Beppi, they walked all the way to the ticket office with me, trying to persuade me to stay. I was at the door when what they were saying began to sink in. Friends make all the difference in this place. You'll see. Surrounded as we are by strangers—just to come home and hear the sound of our dialect." He paused and turned her head so that she faced him. "It makes me feel not so far from home." His touch on her face was assertive. "And they do pay me well. It's a way you can help. We can get back home faster."

At the end of the three days she'd asked for in which to decide, she told Cesare they could stay. It didn't take much to understand that otherwise with Cesare working at two jobs she would be almost always alone. The *ragazzi* helped keep the ice from her heart. The teasing, the laughter and the songs were insulation against the winter winds.

"We thought you were *in servizio*," Mario had said quite soon after she arrived. "We counted on it."

"I was." Maria was indignant. "But I never cooked. I was the children's nursemaid. I was in service to the Count and Countess Cicogna. I certainly wasn't expected to cook."

"What about at home?" From Beppi.

"My stepmother did it all. And before her, my older sister . . . I was never interested."

"Ohho," Mario, as usual, was smiling. "And what feasts we dreamt of. When Cesare told us you were coming. Such banquets. After my days in that wretched house with only a hotplate. I thought what luck. Now—now— everything will be put right. Cesare, you should have thought of this. Given each prospective bride a test."

They'd all laughed. Except Maria. Though it didn't take her long to see that it was no use getting offended. They did, indeed, need those meals, reproducing as closely as possible what they had eaten at home.

Lucio, the one with the best profile and the big dark eyes, gave her lessons in the basics: broth, minestrone, sauce, and so on. He spoke Italian with her rather than the dialect he used with the others, and that, with his deliberate, slow movements and his formal manner, "now one measures out," gave a ritualistic tone to those lessons. The slicing, the frying, the boiling, *the* preparation of the meal.

"I've been laid off." Again Nico's words, after the long silence, startled her. He was staring at her, waiting.

"It's so cold working outside now. Maybe it's for the best. You have enough stamps for unemployment, don't you?"

"Barely enough. But, you see, the less I earn the longer until I can ask Milvia to marry me." His cheeks were flushed. "I'm tired of waiting . . . I need a wife."

The need for a wife, Nico, Beppi, Mario, Lucio, they all came back to that, over and over. At home, they had had mothers, aunts, sisters, friends. There were ex-schoolmates and the girls that walked the *passeggiata* in the evening. But here, except for Maria, their daily lives were womanless. They ogled any girl they saw, of course; there was a convent school near the house and Mario in particular would stand beneath the dormitory windows and call up. But there was never any real contact. And they hadn't been raised to be the type of men who went to whores, not unless they were desperate. A wife, she could replace all the women each had felt he had lost. She could take care of and care for him, certainly; but more, she could save him from losing himself in this land of indifferent eyes. Woman, she could protect him from the brute state he felt he could be so easily reduced to: beast of burden, lustfilled animal.

That evening, as, with Lucio's help, she cleared the table, they began again. Beppi was smoking and complaining, complaining and smoking. Gina, his fianceé, had announced that she wouldn't come to Canada unless he promised that they stayed no longer than five years. "Ridiculous. Five years. And she expects me to sign a legal document. No trust."

"At least she writes to you. At least you have it fixed. You and Lucio are the lucky ones." Nico poured himself another glass of wine.

Mario picked three oranges from the fruit bowl still on the table. Pushing his chair back a bit, he began to juggle and hum the old song, *Femmena*.

"Why do I fool myself about Milvia. She doesn't

write any more. It has been so long . . . " Nico was drawing
the bottle towards him again.

Mario missed an orange. It fell, plaff. "I may have the
solution for you." But he kept on with the remaining two.
"Did you notice that little dark-eyed sweetie in church the
last two Sundays?" He had all their attention now. "Tiny.
Brown hair. And a white coat, I think."

"I thought she was here to marry one of the Neapoli-
tans."

"She was. But she'd never met the groom. And when
she got here and saw him, she refused to go through with
it."

"I don't see now this can help me. And how do you
know anyway?"

Mario was easing himself into a standing position,
still juggling.

Maria began to bend over to pick up the orange. Her
stomach tightened as it had many times in the last week,
but this time there was an undertow of pain.

"The supposed brother-in-law-to-be works with me at
the packing plant. He's indignant of course."

"But why," Beppi asked, "would she be interested in
Nico?"

"So pretty," Lucio added.

"Think. She's from the South. If she went back, there
would be a scandal."

"But how do I start? How do I approach her? Where's
she staying?"

Mario began to dance around the table. He swiveled
his hips and pretended the oranges were mariachis.

"Ma tu sei guaglione
Non conosci femmena."

Her abdomen tightened again, and again there was
pain. "I have to lie down."

They all focused on Maria. "Are you tired?" "Do you

think it's starting?" "What's wrong. You're very pale."
"Your stomach?" "It's not time yet is it?" "I thought the
spring." "Late March, Cesare said." "What is it?"

"I don't know. I don't know what it's supposed to
feel like. No one told me. I don't know."

"We'll call Cesare."

"It comes and goes."

"That's it, I'm sure of it. Go and phone, Lucio."

"Some wine?"

"Breathe deeply."

Her whole body was clenching. The *ragazzi* were still
asking questions, but their voices were a background roar
to her. She was frozen to her chair, unable to move.

Her runaway heart was speeding, the blood pressing
against the pain. If she could run away, if she could escape
the pain that came not from within but without, escape the
alien force that was squeezing, squeezing the baby out.

If she could get home, if she could see her father's
eyes, faded and blue, if she could smell . . .

"So far and to a man I don't know."

Cesare was with her now, his eyes wide with emotion. "Calm. Stay calm," he kept saying but in a sharp, loud
voice. He rammed her feet into his boots, pushed her arms
into his parka. He was still so unexpected, so strange to
her.

"You will know him."

Papá no, Mamma. It was her mother's eyes, those
first eyes, that she needed. Though she couldn't remember
them, not as they were. When she tried to conjure them,
she saw the steady gaze of a black and white photograph.
She could recall her presence, her arms and lap, being held
in a darkened room. But that was all.

To call Mamma was to long to see again the well-tended grass in the cemetery on the hill behind the village, to long for the scent of oleanders Mamma, she had been told, planted along the front of their house. To call Mamma was to long for the primary comfort that should have been.

In the car, shivering partly with cold, Maria stared out at the dirtied streets. "What do they do with the coffins? Do they keep them stacked up somewhere?"

"What do you mean?"

She gestured at the piles of snow in the yards, glinting under the streetlights. "The land is too hard. How could they dig a hole?" She wanted to say more, much more. But she held back. Cesare was so quick to anger, and she didn't want to be called 'stupida', not again.

In fact, Cesare didn't answer her. He kept staring straight ahead. Only after the next pain, when she'd forgotten that she'd said anything, did he glance at her. "Everything will be fine. We're not in your village now. And you're not your mother." The words and the voice, a quiet voice he'd never used before, broke through to her.

For the first time, she began to cry before him. "I'm afraid."

"No need."

"I'll . . . I can't do it."

"Of course you can." Then, in a different tone, "Come, we're here. It's time to go in."

"Time . . . " Maria stared at the brightly lit emergency entrance. Cesare opened her door and extended an arm. She didn't move. He reached in and pulled at her legs.

In the last months the house and the car had both imprisoned and protected her. Now, outside containment, in the moments of unrelieved winter and in the many hours of corridors and hospital rooms, she was exposed. She had already lost much that she was in leaving home. Now the nurses took away her clothes; they sent away Cesare, a small blond one unlatched her fingers from his arm. They prodded and palpitated. They gestured and jabbered. The small one flashed a long rubber hose in front of Maria's eyes. She was commanding her to do something but what? Her pursed little mouth barked at the aide. Immediately hands were upon Maria, shoving her on her side, spreading her buttock cheeks. She had been crying silently but could no longer hold back. "Mamma," she called, "Mamma." Being helped to the toilet, being washed, being shaved, two aides holding her, one on each leg. "Mamma."

"SSHhush," said the blond nurse, her freckled face scrunched in disgust. "Italians!"

Maria understood that. She wished she had the strength to sit up and punch her in her flat stomach. She did try and lift a leg. But now the nurse was talking to someone in the corner. The doctor floated into view. He was pulling on rubber gloves—inspecting. Not her face. He never looked at her face or into her eyes. He thrust his hand inside her. "Big," he said over her stomach to the nurse and then something, 'spaghetti'.

But the pain was blotting out the room, the doctor, and the nurse. It was tearing up time, tearing up any pause. It was tearing her apart. "Mamma," a prick on her arm and she no longer heard her own cries. More hands. "Mamma," she was whispering. The pain was no alien force. It was her very centre.

She was in another room with shiny walls. A bright light shone in her eyes. The nurses were masked. And her doctor—she recognized his icy eyes though. Finally, she must be close to the end. A rubber mask was handed to her. She understood "gas", a solid word in a stream of sounds.

The pain no longer possessed her. A still terror had

beaten it off. A frozen sea, a still sky, icebergs. Where was this place? What was happening? She was floating in the icy whiteness. There was no up or down, no signposts and no sounds. Only the relentless white. And she was falling, slowly spiralling down, ever down. She thrashed against the fall, stretching her hands to catch onto anything that might be there. Where was she? More, who was she? But her mind was as white as the featureless world. She was lost.

But, as suddenly as the fall began, her hands were no longer grasping at air. She was holding something solid. The whiteness was separating into colours and shapes. She could make out murmurs, metallic sounds. Her baby was in her arms. Perfect to see, to smell, to touch. Maria's head was still spiralling, still confused, but her boy had been grounded. Indeed, though she was not to know it for many years, his pudgy body was her first connection to the hard, foreign land. She was saved and she was bound.

Passage by Water
Joan Clark

Emily didn't see the face of the night nurse though the same woman came into her hospital room three nights in a row and shone a flashlight at her. The round blinding arc swept through the dark, across the metal bed, a searchlight tracking a lone prisoner in a night compound.

The first time the night nurse came into her room Emily was hallucinating. Ten days before she'd had her bladder repaired, a necessity after child-bearing. Before the operation it had flopped down loosely, shapeless as a collapsed balloon, which meant she spilled urine whenever she jumped, ran or sneezed. Now her bladder was sewn to her pubic bone, so tightly stitched into place that it felt like an old leather shoe that has become wet then left to dry stiff and hard in the sun. Its muscles had stopped working. Here she was a thirty-seven year old housewife unable to pass water. She wanted to disown her body. She felt foolish, helpless as if she was inhabiting a baby's body. Except that any baby was born being able to do what she couldn't. Babies came into the world screaming anger, wetting themselves freely. Emily could do neither.

Before Emily had gone to sleep Mrs. Schoenburg, the afternoon nurse, a soft-spoken motherly woman, had brought Emily new pain killers, two round green pills. She took the pills eagerly. Her stitches were hurting and the tube the doctor had inserted through her stomach wall into her bladder was uncomfortable. The tube had a miniature white plastic tap on it as tiny as one on a dollhouse sink.

The other end was connected to a plastic canteen, a Uripac, into which her bladder was emptied.

Mrs. Schoenburg emptied the afternoon's urine into the stainless steel kidney pan, poured it into a pitcher then wrote 800 cc's on the record sheet.

"That's only 800 cc's for the day." She frowned.

"But I drank five cups of tea, four glasses of juice and two cups of coffee and it was emptied this morning!"

"Ah well. Never mind," Mrs. Schoenburg consoled her. "Perhaps the morning nurse forgot to put down her entry." She checked the record sheet. "Yes, that's right. There's nothing down for this morning. That accounts for it."

Mrs. Schoenburg reached over and switched off the light.

"Do you think I'll be able to go tomorrow?" Emily's voice was wistful.

Mrs. Schoenburg patted her arm comfortingly. "It's early yet. Usually it takes a week or two to get going. Every woman's different. Some women are tricklers going a little more each day until they're back to normal. Other women are gushers—they just pass water all of a sudden. My guess is you'll be that kind, though it's hard to say. The important thing is to push fluids and relax. That's the secret. Now you get some sleep."

Emily's hallucination began with the night light, an orange cube recessed into the wall at the foot of her bed. When she came out of sleep, her eyes focussed on the orange cube. It glowed queerly in the dark. Emily blinked. The orange light sparked, flickered, became two. Emily closed her eyes. She heard a rush of whirling air near the door. She blinked again and saw something dark by the wall, something that whirled and spun like a top, an elongated top, a column, a pillar of black, mummy-bandaged. As it whirled closer the bandages unwrapped themselves, lengthening, snapping off ceilings and walls. The mummy whirled around the foot of the bed then veered toward the window, spinning. Suddenly it tilted itself and came straight toward Emily, there was no mistaking its intent, its attack on her. Its orange eyes narrowed to glowing slits, its black bandages flapped across her feet, her legs, her chest then up to her face slapping at her nose, her mouth, smothering her. Emily's hands went up to tear them away. She opened her mouth to scream, to protest, to breathe. No sound came out.

The white arc of light swept across the bed, incurious, routine. Emily sat up in its glare shaking her head to free herself, pawing the air. Her chest was heaving, sweat was running down her back. Thin strips of black snaked around her arms.

"A bad dream?" the night nurse asked from the doorway. Her voice was hollow like it was coming through a long metal tube.

"Not a bad dream. It was worse than that. It was an hallucination. I think." Emily said slowly. "It was terrifying."

The night nurse didn't ask for details but kept the flashlight trained on Emily's face. All Emily could see of her was a low stocky shape blocking the doorway.

"It must have been the green pills," Emily went on. "They must have caused it."

Still the night nurse stayed where she was: one of her hands holding the door open, the other the flashlight.

Emily wanted to shout, "Get that light off my face!"

But she couldn't say it, just as she'd been unable to scream.

"I'll make a note of it on your chart," the night nurse said and, snapping off the flashlight, went out the door leaving it ajar.

A corridor of yellow light, shining water, open sunny fields shone bright and warm beyond the door. Emily kept her eyes on the warm light listening for sounds—the ringing phone, tapping oxfords, murmuring voices—the nursing station was right across from her room. Finally as she was sliding into sleep, gently this time, a narrow letter being eased into a wide envelope, she heard a voice. It seemed to be coming from a valley far away past the fields and shining water.

"Miss-us," the voice called, plaintive, needing rescue, "miss-us."

It was the old Italian lady two doors away in 310, six weeks in hospital with a gall bladder operation. Emily heard her every night calling the nurses: she never used the buzzer. Sometimes she called for an hour before the night nurse finally went to her.

In the morning Emily drank a glass of juice, a glass of milk and two cups of coffee from her breakfast tray. After she had bathed and powdered herself, she pinned the offending Uripac to the inside of her nightgown where it didn't show except as an unnatural bulge on her hip. She imagined she resembled a diseased tree whose trunk was distended, the sort she saw in front of people's houses, varnished and hung with signs and lamps. Emily thought they made obscene use of deformity.

She went into the corridor, crossed to the kitchenette, opened the fridge and forced down two glasses of apple juice. Then she began to walk. Down one side of the wing past bare walls painted buttercup yellow, across the end of the corridor where the colour changed to turquoise, then along the other wing where the walls were bubble gum pink. The colours were so determinedly cheerful, so garishly bright, they looked like they had been chosen from a package of Easter egg dye. Although the floors were unblemished by scuffs or stains, a uniformed man was

buffing the shining tiles with an electric polisher. He kept
his head down, avoiding the string of women trailing past.
One woman, a day out of a hysterectomy, staggered past,
pale, unsteady, holding onto her metal intravenous stand
for support. Clear fluid dripped down a tube into her arm;
she looked like a prisoner of war surrendering to some
ingenious method of water torture. Other women, three or
four days out of surgery, walked gingerly, one hand on the
corridor railings, the other holding their stomachs. Some
women managed to do this unobtrusively as if they were
merely intent on keeping a hand pocketed; others were
more careless, beyond modesty, boldly pushing hands
against their incisions.

Though her stitches pulled, Emily walked straight,
hands at her sides. She walked and walked, stopping at the
end of the corridor where there was a large picture window. Sealed behind the glass she heard no outside noises,
saw no sign of movement except smoke from chimneys
curling upward toward the low forehead of winter sky.
The city was locked in white Siberian silence, in square
straight bars of concrete, plate glass and pavement. Emily
kept walking. Until she thought the morning fluids had
worked themselves into her bladder. Until she felt the urge
to have a bowel movement. That was important, Mrs.
Schoenburg had said, some women went by doing the two
together.

Emily was sitting on the toilet with a magazine
propped up on top of the disposal can, reading, trying to
keep her mind off going. The tap was carefully adjusted to
simulate a gentle flow of water, a small brook falling over
stones. In Emily's lap was a basin of warm water in which
she held her hands. She couldn't figure out why keeping
her hands in warm water should induce the urge to go but
it did. She felt her bladder muscles pull in slightly. But the

sensation was so weak that it had no effect. She tried to relax by forming a mental picture of herself as a sleek jet flying at cruising speed, moving effortlessly through the air, coming in for a landing, coasting onto the runway, stopping, opening up the baggage compartment, the suitcases dropping out, one by one.

She had a bowel movement but no urine came with it. The bathroom had a rich fecund smell that was comforting. At home she used Pine Fresh to get rid of the odour but since being in the hospital she'd grown more appreciative of the powerful smell of her own feces. She was reassured by it like a baby proudly filling its diapers.

The door burst open abruptly almost knocking the basin of water off Emily's knees. A fat arm reached in, jerked up the lid of the disposal tin, yanked out the white plastic liner and pulled the bag through the crack in the door. The magazine fell to the floor. Emily couldn't bend over to pick it up. There was no point anyway. The woman would be back again with a new plastic liner. There was also no point in resenting the intrusion. There were no secrets in this ward: sanitary napkins hung in gunny sacks on doors, enema syringes and douches were thrown into wastebaskets for visitors to see, nurses and nurses' aides burst into the room without knocking, bringing in clean sheets, thermometers, catheters, medication, meal trays, water jugs. It was the same with the housekeepers. They started in the corridor at seven in the morning and kept coming into the room in erratic thrusts of energy: to dust, to mop, to clean the bathroom sink, disinfect the toilet bowl, empty the disposal can.

Both the housekeeper's arms and legs came into the bathroom this time as a new plastic bag was inserted into the disposal can. Emily recognized the fat limbs as belonging to Jessie. It was Jessie's voice she heard every morning outside her door first and loudest. Grousing about the

nurses. What they expected. It wasn't *her* job to pick up
dirty laundry. It wasn't *her* job to carry out meal trays.
Those nurses were always trying to get you to do work for
them. You had to stand up to them, that's what you had to
do.

Jessie disappeared again. Emily stood up, added more
hot water to the basin, picked up the magazine, sat down
and concentrated on choosing something to read. Most of
the articles were about women who seemed freer than herself: Do-It-Yourself-Divorces, The Advantages of Being
Bisexual, Adoption for Singles, even the titles depressed
her. She was so far behind the times, there seemed no hope
of her catching up or even understanding what was going
on.

The bathroom door was flung open again and there
was Jessie in full glory, her fatness encased in a mint green
uniform, her frizzy hair framing puttyish skin. Jessie
shoved the mop between Emily's legs. Or tried to. Emily
resisted. The least the woman could do was ask her to
move her feet.

Jessie poked the mop under the sink, whanging it
roughly against the tiles.

"You still on the can?" She grinned raw friendliness
at Emily, showing a wide band of purplish gums above her
dentures.

Emily nodded but kept her eyes on the magazine.

Jessie tilted her head to one side and leaned on the
mop bunching up her heavy breast.

"Tried beer yet?"

Emily looked up. "Why? Is beer supposed to work?"

"Work! I'll say it works! Some of them younger doctors prescribe it. Maybe your doctor don't know about it."

"You can't have beer in the hospital."

"Ha! That's what you think. I know two women
down in chronic keep wine in their closets. You can bet

your bottom dollar their doctors know about it. There was a woman here last month in the same fix as you. She had beer." Jessie leaned over conspiratorially. "Kept it in her shower."

That would be a good place to keep it all right. Emily wasn't allowed showers yet so the plastic curtain remained closed.

"See what's good about beer," Jessie went on, "is it goes right through you so fast. Works like a charm."

"Maybe I should try it. I've tried everything else."

"That's the spirit. You get your hubby to bring you some beer next time he comes and you'll pee all right." Jessie stabbed the corner with the mop then closed the bathroom door, satisfied. Emily could hear her in the bedroom banging the mop against the baseboards, the closet door, the waste can.

Lena Whynaugt was a big bold girl who was Emily's seatmate in grade three at Harbour Mines Elementary back when there were two to a desk. Lena lived in a shack on the outskirts of town with nine other kids and smelled stale as if she ate, slept and played inside a breadbox. In November Lena came to school with impetigo: yellow oozing crusted sores spotting her arms and legs. She was sent home and never came back. But before she left, she sat through one of Miss Frazee's lessons on manners. Halfway through the lesson, Lena put up her hand.

"Please, Miss, I got to pee."

Miss Frazee suspended the chalk over the blackboard where she had been writing down different ways of answering the telephone. She smiled encouragingly.

"That's not what we say, Lena."

Lena put a hand to her crotch.

"Please, Miss, I got to piss."

The smile remained fixed.

"What we say, Lena, is we have to go to the bathroom."

Even toilet wasn't good enough for Miss Frazee. An English teacher, Miss Frazee constantly exhorted them to refine their speech. The English language must not be corrupted with vulgarisms.

"But we have a privy, Miss!" Lena said, looking around the class, enjoying the audience.

Only then did the chalk touch the blackboard, the smile disappear.

"All right, Lena. You may go. I'll see you after school."

The grade two teacher, Mrs. Fairweather, had made them hold up either one finger or two and say aloud number one or number two. Emily didn't know why it mattered for the whole class to know which you had to do until Squirt Layton told her. If you put up two fingers Miss Fairweather didn't question how long you were gone from class whereas you were allowed only five minutes for one finger. Most of the boys said number two until Miss Fairweather caught on and questioned them closely in front of everybody threatening to write notes home to parents, making sure the big jobs, as she called them, were done at home.

The nurses called it passing water, the doctor voiding. Emily's husband, Don, said taking a leak and crap. When they were younger, her children said wee-wee and poop. Since then Emily had taught them to say urinate and B.M. She had taught school herself, social studies, so she had more leeway than Miss Frazee. Emily was no longer sure of these words. Choosing the right word had become important to her. She had the idea that if she came upon a certain arrangement of words, it would have the power of a chant and the muscles of her bladder would magically open like the doors of Ali Baba's cave. She remembered how effective schoolground chants were in exorcising tattlers.

> *Tattle-tale tattle-tale*
> *Tie you on the bull's tail.*
> *When the bull begins to pee*
> *We will have a cup of tea.*

Jody Strom was a little girl who used to play with Emily's ten year old daughter, Megan. Until Emily caught her with her pants down defecating under the spruce tree on the front lawn. When Emily asked her what she thought she was doing, Jody simply pulled up her pants and walked home leaving Emily staring down at droppings lined up like a row of sausages in front of the tree. No dog would do that. The child must want attention. She'd better tell Marg Strom. Since the divorce Marg had gone back to university to study social work. She was away all day. Jody must be trying to tell her mother something.

Emily waited until she thought Jody would be in bed before she crossed the street. Through the window she could see books and papers spread over the kitchen table. Marg came to the door wearing reading glasses.

Emily tried to be brief.

"I hate to bother you Marg, but I think you should know that Jody's been defecating on our front lawn. Judging from the number of droppings it looks like she's been doing it for a couple of weeks." Emily felt this was a reasonable beginning: a statement of fact.

But Marg was annoyed. "Come off it, Em. Did you come all the way over here to tell me about a few turds? I've got a term paper due tomorrow."

"Well, if it was *my* daughter doing it, *I'd* want to be told."

Emily didn't know why she felt it necessary to explain this.

"You and I are different. I don't let details like that

bother me. I've got better things to do with my time."

Emily wasn't about to let this pass.

"Perhaps you'd better spend more time with your daughter instead of at the university. I mean it is social work you're taking, isn't it? What better place to start than at home!" The bandages flew out of Emily's mouth like tongues of fire. "Maybe you should take the time to see what your daughter's done to our lawn. And when you come, bring a shovel!"

After she had stormed home, Emily felt terrible to have said so much or to have said it the wrong way. There were two other children besides Jody. It must be hard raising them alone. The next morning she went to the florist and bought a white rose in a bud vase, getting Megan to take it over, to show Marg she was sorry. Marg never acknowledged it. Which Emily took as further proof of her failure to speak her mind without going too far.

It had reached the point where she would avoid making a complaint even when it was justified. She did this with her family: day after day she picked up dirty clothes, wet towels, newspapers, wiped up spilled milk and mud tracked as far as bedrooms, saying nothing: There was no one around to say anything to anyway, they were all off to work or school when she set to cleaning up, muttering, shaking her head. Then one day she would burst open angrily: the whole family: Don, Tom, Megan, Jimmy, came under fire. She overstated her case, played the martyr, exaggerated the wrongs until she became disgusted by her dramatization, her inability to be casual and matter-of-fact.

"Maybe you should go back teaching," Don said to her after one of these sessions. "I don't think you're cut out to stay home."

Contrite, determined to reform, to become the all-giving earth mother, Emily would scrape off Don's windshield, start his car for him, pick up the children's clothes, take out the garbage, begin the cycle all over again.

Emily had been drinking beer for two days averaging three bottles a day. She had one after her nap, taking the bottle with her into the sitz bath. She ran two inches of water as hot as she could stand and sat in it drinking beer. The idea according to the nurses was to pass water in the water. To Emily this was tantamount to going in the sea. She tried to recall those lazy summer days as a child when she lay like a fish in a tidal pool at Ingonish. She leaned back in the bath, closed her eyes, the beer making her light-headed and tried to hypnotize herself into thinking she was a fish that rested in the shallows, the fluids of its body moving with the tide. It didn't work.

She had another beer with Don during evening visiting hours. After he had left she tried to squeeze in another. It was really too much. One night, a Saturday after Don had gone home early to watch the hockey game, Emily took a bottle of beer with her into Gina's room. She had taken to visiting the old lady in the evening, thinking if she got more attention she'd be less likely to call out during the night. Whenever she visited Gina, Emily took something with her: a flower, a chocolate bar, a magazine.

The first time Emily went into Gina's room she'd been appalled by its starkness. When she walked past other rooms she saw bouquets of flowers lined up on window sills: roses, mums, carnations done up with ferns and bows. There were boxes of chocolates, books, magazines, and always a new pastel coloured bathrobe folded across the foot of the bed. The old lady had nothing. Except for the empty water glass on the night table and the woman herself sitting in the corner chair with a blanket over her knees to cover up what the blue hospital gown did not, the room might have been unoccupied. Gina had the abundant white hair and sad brown eyes of a defeated matriarch. Even the sagging tea-coloured jowels couldn't disguise the strong cheekbones, the thrusting jaw. There was no smile whenever Emily entered the room, only a nodded acknowledgement that another brief distraction had come her way like the feather of a migrating bird fluttering into her lap.

Tonight when she came into the room, Emily asked the old lady if she would help her out by drinking some of her beer.

"I like wine, Missus," Gina said, "but I take beer."

Emily poured a glass full of beer and handed it to the old lady who took it with a firm hand.

"How's it going tonight?" Emily said.

"Terrible. The doctor says I go home tomorrow."

"Why that's wonderful."

Gina took a swallow of beer and eyed Emily balefully.

"Maybe for you. Not for me. My husband have bad heart. Can't help me to bathroom. My son works."

"Isn't there someone who could help you, a V.O.N. nurse?"

"Maybe. I like to get woman in but my son won't pay. He wants me to cook for him. I'm not wife. Too old. He should get wife. He stay with us because he wants house. My husband and him build it a long time ago. When my husband die, my son put me in place for old people." Gina shook her head. "In Italy my mother turn over in grave."

Despite or maybe because of Gina's pessimism, Emily couldn't resist the urge to patronize.

"I'm sure once you get home, things will work out for the best."

"Maybe Missus," Gina said sourly, "maybe." She finished the beer and held the empty glass up for Emily.

Emily took the glass to the bathroom, rinsed it out and brought it back three-quarters full of water. The old woman waved it away.

"Is there anything I can do for you before I go?"

"No, Missus. No." Gina said. "Nothing."

Her sad eyes dropped to her lap. Emily's visit was no more, no less than she'd expected.

Emily had been in bed an hour staring into the dark. As usual her door had been left ajar. But the corridor of yellow light no longer shone bright and warm beyond her door. She could hear a storm: chill laughter and word gusts coming from the nursing station. She remembered it was Saturday: the nurses must be having a party. She got up, unpinned her Uripac from the bed and padded across the bare floor to the door.

"Missus! Missus! I need you!" With all the commotion in the nursing station Gina's plaintive voice might have been coming from the bottom of an abandoned well.

"Missus! Come quick! I need you."

Obviously no one was going to help the old lady. Emily put on her slippers and padded down to 310. When she pushed open the door, Gina whined, "Oh Missus, you came. I got to go bad," and assuming Emily was the night nurse, said, "That lady, she gave me beer."

"I'm not the nurse. I can't take you," Emily said, "but I'll ring for someone."

She went over to the bed and pushed the buzzer.

The old woman grabbed hold of Emily's arm. Emily tried to pull away but the grip tightened as Gina began to lever herself up with Emily's arm.

"Please, Missus. You take me. That night nurse mean. She won't come. She hates me."

Emily jerked away.

"No! I can't lift you or I'll pull my stitches. I'll go up

to the desk and get you a nurse."

When she stood in the doorway of the nursing station, simply stood there until the laughter subsided and they noticed her, she was aware how strange she must look, at least to herself if not to them. They were used to women whose nightgowns were hitched up by plastic tubes exposing white legs and shaved pubic hair. One of the nurses came forward and Emily knew by the stocky shape of her that she was the night nurse. She was unprepared for the youngness of the face, the childish snub nose, the wide flatness of the eyes. She didn't look mean or hateful, only untouched by experience.

"The old lady in 310 needs to go to the toilet," Emily told her.

"She's always saying that," the night nurse said. "When we get her up, she doesn't go. Later she wets the bed."

"I'm sure that happens," Emily conceded, "but the fact is she definitely has to go now."

She didn't stop there. She knew they might think she was interfering but she didn't care. She was going to say it anyway. She looked at the night nurse. "You know," she said, "it wouldn't hurt to remind yourself that you might be eighty-four someday and needing attention."

Then she stomped across the hall, got into bed and went to sleep.

Two hours later her bladder woke her up. The sensation to go was so strong she got up too quickly and was pulled back by the tube pinned to the bed. She bumped into the night table. It banged against the wall. Fumbling with the pin she tried to free herself. She couldn't manage it. She yanked the tube clear, disconnecting the Uripac from her bladder. Not bothering to turn on the light, she followed the well-worn path to the bathroom. As she was settling onto the toilet she kicked over an empty beer bottle she'd forgotten to put back in the shower. It clattered into the corner.

The night nurse opened the bathroom door and shone the flashlight on Emily's face.

"I heard banging. Are you all right?"

"Of course I'm all right," Emily said. "And don't shine that flashlight in my face."

The flashlight beam swung to the floor and circled the bottle.

"It looks like you've been drinking," the night nurse said.

"That's right," Emily said triumphantly. "And I'm peeing too."

"You're what?"

"I'm PEEING!" Emily shouted it out. *Open Sesame.* The proud rush of yellow fluid came warm between her legs.

Mrs. Schoenburg had been bang on: she was a gusher all right.

Harris
Shirlee Matheson

When I was five I used to listen to "Kindergarten of the Air." It did not prepare me for beginning Grade One in a one-room Ukrainian country school in rural Manitoba.

They were so big, those Ukrainians. Two girls, Annie and Mary, sisters, were respectively thirteen and fourteen years of age in Grade One. They were retarded but in those days such children were not sent to the city to attend training schools. They were of too much use on the farm. They worked like men, tucking their large breasts into wraparound "waists", as we called them, getting them out of the way. In men's pants and boots they worked in the fields until dusk; pitching hay, stooking, shovelling manure; killing and plucking chickens, twenty at a time.

I liked Annie and Mary. They were my friends among the big kids, the normal ones who tormented me with threats of a timber wolf lurking in my fields, who baited me in a language I did not understand. Annie and Mary could always be counted on to stand beside me, cross-eyed Mary who had to be led to the front of the room, big Annie with her long woman's legs jutting out each side of the tiny fixed double desk. The Province of Manitoba made it mandatory for each child to remain in school until he reached the age of fifteen. Annie and Mary remained in Grade One until they were released by their birthdays, wasting six hours of every day when they could have been slaving on their father's farm. The Province of Manitoba was Annie and Mary's best friend.

They wore babushkas in class and flowered house-dresses, thick brown stockings and rubber boots. Annie's hair was naturally curly and hung shoulder length in the back under the babushka. Mary's was straight, cut blunt at ear length. With her short bob, bright babushka and crossed blue eyes, Mary looked like a lopsided dutch doll. Hands heavy with work and dirt, the two girls laboriously copied into scribblers: "See Spot. See Puff. See Spot and Puff." It made no sense.

"Mudder and Fadder vurk," they'd read in faltering men's voices laden with an accent I envied. The accompanying picture would show blonde mother and shirt-and-tie father raking leaves. That was 'vurk'? Why weren't they out stooking? Killing the winter pig? Cleaning the hen house?

"See Spot. See Puff. Spot and Puff run. Dey run to Sally. Run, Sally, run." For seven years each Annie and Mary stumbled around with Spot and Puff and cute baby Sally. By the time they left school they were ready to have baby Sallys of their own. But they were patient, Annie and Mary, never getting frustrated and throwing the book at the stern Ukrainian teacher, who each year slammed their fingers with the ruler, hit them over their flowered babushkas with the Puff books, humiliated them until their faces turned bright red with shame. Mary sometimes cried, looking to Annie for support, but Annie could not protect her.

Harris Latosky got it too. Harris wasn't retarded, just slow, and from a dirt poor family that lived with their pigs, like their pigs. The Latoskys used a trap door in the floor of the kitchen as the bathroom during the winter it was said, something that made sense initially. They had a baby girl named Lassie.

Harris wasn't mean. He was a pinch-faced boney little boy with long hair that hung in his eyes. He wore too-large overalls and heavy wool shirts and his lunch kit was

regularly picked over by the bigger boys who stole his
meagre desserts—unless it was announced that Harris had
lice on his food. On those days Harris was made to choke
down his lunch in front of everybody.

"Look, look, Harris is going to EAT it! Harris is eating lice!"

Harris was an easy target for the teacher, a woman
newly abandoned by her man in an area and at a time when
it was a disgrace. She had been forced to go back to teaching to support her own children. A city-bred Ukrainian,
she looked with loathing on the simple-minded peasants
she must work with, and Harris caught the lash of that
loathing from the start. He couldn't learn. In vain, he
struggled with the black signs in the book that the teacher
said were words.

I can still see the sweat standing out on Harris' upper
lip, his hair falling into his eyes to be swiped back again
and again as his mouth works furiously to make sense out
of the signs. He tries valiantly to *remember* what the
teacher said they were, but there are so many! Each one
different. He can't remember. SMACK! The long ruler
comes down on Harris' head.

"Sound it out, Harris!" I can hear Mrs. Leschuk
screech. "Sound-it-out."

Harris' eyes brim, his eyelids blink rapidly. Silence.
His mouth works furiously, but no sound comes. SMACK!
Again I hear the ruler connecting, watch his hair flying up.
No sound.

"Say something, Harris. Do you remember your own
name?"

Titters from the rest of the room, from some of the
braver Grade Ones up to the brawny and boorish Grade
Six's.

"What's your name, Harris?"

Laughter. Harris looks up through the protective

fence of hair. A whisper.

"What? I'm not deaf, but I can't hear that!"

"Harris." It comes out in a whisper, a mere passing of air through quivering lips.

"Well, Harris, as you know that, why can't you learn anyone else's name? S-P-O-T. That spells 'Spot.' That's the dog's name."

"Just like Lassie," one big boy whispers loudly.

Mrs. Leschuk turns around quickly in an angry sham at catching the offender. "Alright. S-P-O-T. S-P-O-T." Each time getting louder, until she screams out the letters. "S-P-O-T. *Now* do you get it? *Now* can you read it?" Her face is an angry welt.

The rest of us Grade Ones stand in line, readers held tightly, eyes closed. Harris stands immobile, his eyes downcast on his offending book.

"S-P-O-T," he mumbles.

"Don't parrot the letters, read the *word*!" our teacher screams.

Harris stands, petrified into silence, his eyes staring glassily at the floor. Mrs. Leschuk suddenly lunges forward, her book clattering to the floor, and grabs Harris by his long forward-hanging mane.

"Spot!" she screams, giving it a shake. "Spot! Can't you learn even that?"

I can recall the vision yet, seen as through a blurring lens, the teacher tugging at Harris, unbalancing him, throwing him backward. His body hangs suspended from her hand. Back and ever back she throws him, knocking his fragile body against the desks, against the out-turned knees of the big boys, now shocked into silence. "Spot!" she screams as she flings him, kicks him, knocks him to the back of the school. With one tremendous effort she opens the back door, throws Harris out through the porch where our coats hang, and, jerking open the outside door,

heaves him down the steps into the snow. She slams shut
the door and comes inside.

I can remember screaming, running to the back.
Annie and Mary lumber after me. Harris is sprawled on the
ground, covered in snow, humiliated. Annie picks him up
and just stands there on the ice-covered step hugging
Harris to her big woman's bosom, as he shivers and sobs
into her flowered breast.

I stand there useless but wanting to be outside rather
than in the school, wanting to help, to cry the tears freely
that Harris tries to choke back in. Mary stands with me, so
close her cow-smelling warmth creeps into me and com-
forts me too.

One of the big boys comes out to get us, his usually
arrogant face now soft and calm. "You'd better come back
in," he says quietly, holding open the door. "You'll
freeze."

We file inside.

Mrs. Leschuk sits at her desk, holding her head in her
hands. Her harsh breathing can be heard throughout the
whole room. We stand at the back, Annie still holding
Harris, her big arm around his hunched shoulders, Mary
still standing protectively near me, her crossed eyes looking bewildered around the room, gone so silent that the
only sounds are the harsh breathing of the teacher and the
snap and crackle of the wood in the corner stove.

"School's over for the day," Mrs. Leschuk mumbles
from the sanctuary of her crossed arms. "Get on your coats
and go home."

Not a word is exchanged as we file into the small
back porch and claim our heavy coats, leggings, scarves,
hats, mitts. No one gets his belongings mixed, no one
pushes or shoves. No one threatens me with tales of the
timber wolf behind our straw stacks. Silently as soldiers
we march down the steps, the snow creaking beneath our

feet, past the barbwire fence of the school, down the long road.

I turn to take the short-cut through my field, the tip of my house roof peeking above the horizon one mile distant. I walk stiffly, dumbly, past the strawstacks, not even caring if the wolf waits, over the hump that brings my house into full view, through the fence into the barnyard. My dog runs to meet me, but I cannot speak.

I remember telling my mother the story, then repeating it in turn for my big brother and my dad. Three times I tell it, numbly, without expression. My dad goes out and I hear him hitching our mare to the cutter. Mom starts peeling potatoes. I sit in the big woodbox in the corner of the kitchen, on top of the high pile of wood, enjoying the sharpness of the bark as it pierces through my pants, ridging my bottom, pinching my legs. The pungent smell of the wood fire slowly settles around me, chasing out the cold, the cruelty of the outside world.

Belinda's Seal
Helen Rosta

Belinda is squatting on the bedroom floor. She is dressed, except for one sock, and as she lifts her foot to pull it over her stubby toes she hears her father's voice: "Are you sure you don't want to come?" But the voice is funny—incomplete—as if half of it had stayed in his throat. Belinda stops, one leg suspended in the air, the white sock barely touching her toes, waiting for her mother's answer. When it arrives, the words do not surprise her.

"No, I have too much to do here."

Belinda heaves a sigh of resignation. Absentmindedly, she draws the sock over her foot and slips into her shoes. She wishes her mother wouldn't lie. She knows when they return, she'll glimpse, through the picture window, her mother slumped on the chesterfield—just staring—although she'll spring up and make a show of dusting the furniture the minute the door opens.

It's been that way since Harvey died. Except at first, when her mother would suddenly rush out of the house, jump into the car and roar away.

As Belinda steps into the hall, a sudden blast from Gail's record player drowns out the voices from the living room. Belinda pauses at her sister's doorway. Gail is sprawled on the bed, stomach down, gyrating her long legs in time to the music and poring over a magazine propped on her pillow. She does not look up.

In the living room, Belinda's father is standing at the picture window, hands in his pockets, looking out, and she can't read from the set of his back whether he is angry, disappointed—or what.

Her mother hurries over and worries Belinda's hair, tugs down her tee shirt, hikes up her jeans. Belinda bears these things stoically. She lifts her head and searches her mother's face, trying to meet her mother's eyes.

The hands perform a final adjustment; her mother straightens and turns to Belinda's father. "With the long weekend, there'll be so many people out, I worry she might get lost in the crowds. I want Gail to go with you."

"Has she ever got lost when she's with me?"

"You haven't taken her to the zoo before—."

"Mamma!" Belinda grabs her mother's arm. "Mamma, teacher takes us to the zoo all the time and I never got lost."

Her mother doesn't hear. "There are all those ponds about. What if she slipped away from you and fell in? Gail can keep an eye on her."

Belinda's father makes a huffing sound, a fierce sound, and Belinda cringes between the two of them. Still, she wants him to put his foot down, to say that Gail can't come. When she has to look after Belinda, Gail says mean things, things like, "Bill you need a haircut." And then people think that Belinda's a boy.

Her father turns from the window and shouts, "For God's sake, Christine, I'm quite capable of keeping an eye on her." He draws a deep, hissing breath through his teeth and holds it for a moment.

"All those animals—."

He speaks quietly now, slowly. "It's a little kids' zoo. She's just going to look at some perfectly harmless animals and ride on the merry-go-round."

"Gail!"

The volume of Gail's record player immediately escalates and when her mother calls again, the voice has shrill, ragged edges. Like right after Harvey died. "Gail! You get in here."

The music stops abruptly but Gail doesn't appear. Belinda imagines her rising languidly from the bed and appraising herself in the dresser mirror, head tilted, eyes half closed, smiling. Belinda has even seen Gail kiss her own reflection.

Her father opens his mouth and Belinda fixes on it, waiting for the words, but he closes it without saying anything and, as he does, his face seems to close against her mother. Perhaps against Belinda too.

Her mother anxiously rubs her hands together. "It's so easy for a child to get lost in a crowd." And then, as if to herself, she says, "A man never sees anything."

She means the man who killed Harvey, the man who didn't see him when he got off the bus and ran across the street.

Belinda knows the man's name—John Talbot—it's burned into her mind by repetition. She's seen the car that killed Harvey—"How can he bear to drive that car?" Knows the terror that seized her when her mother caught sight of it in traffic, the desperate pursuit, screech of brakes at stop lights, her mother's shrieks, "Murderer! Murderer!"

That was when her mother still drove. When she still left the house. "If it depended on you the child would never go anywhere," Belinda's father says in a hard voice. "So don't get started on another crazy—." He breaks off and as he turns again to the window, he looks so sad that Belinda feels like crying. She wishes her mother would just sit down and let them go.

Gail shuffles through the doorway and lounges against the frame, scowling. "Whatdaya want?" She scowls a lot lately. Except when she's with girls her own age. Or boys. With them she smiles and holds her head as if there were a kink in her neck.

Before Belinda's mother can answer, her father says over his shoulder. "Your mother wants you to come with us to the Children's Zoo."

"The Children's Zoo," Gail says, making the words sound dirty. "The Children's Zoo. You gotta be kidding."

"I want you to help look after Belinda."

Gail turns a sullen face toward her mother. "Why don't you go and look after her? She's your kid, not mine. It's about time you got out of this stinking house."

"That's enough," Belinda's father snaps, but he doesn't give her one of his "I mean business" frowns.

Belinda sends Gail conciliatory glances but, really, Belinda wishes she were invisible. Or better yet, grown-up. Then no one would have to look after her.

"You're going with them."

"But I promised Debby—."

"I said you're going."

Belinda's father makes an angry, impatient noise. "Damn it," he snaps, "If we stand here wrangling all day, the place will be closed by the time we get there."

"Do I have to go?" Gail whines.

Now he gives her the frown. "Get out to the car."

Belinda scrambles into the back seat. As they pull away from the curb, she turns to wave to her mother who is hovering behind the picture window. Like a goldfish brushing against the side of its bowl.

Once they are around the corner—out of sight—Belinda lets the trip begin. It's marred only by Gail's complaining.

Belinda's father is driving slowly with both hands on the wheel, acting as if he doesn't hear.

In fact, he couldn't have: he interrupts Gail's whining about her ruined day—her ruined life—to ask in that incomplete voice what she had planned for this afternoon.

"Before your mother commandeered you."

Gail whirls her head toward him, revealing to Belinda an exasperated roll of the eye and a petulantly raised eyebrow. "That's what I've been trying to tell you. A bunch of us were going to study at Debby's. I've got a math exam coming up on Tuesday. Now, I'll probably flunk." She droops against the seat, limp, wilted, like an expiring flower. "I could just die."

"Die." Belinda writhes. Gail shouldn't say that word. Harvey died and that's why Mamma drove around screaming at the bad man, and when she finally gave that up she never wanted to go anyplace again.

But Harvey didn't really die; he went to heaven to be an angel. Belinda presses her face against the window. He's up there in the clouds, watching the car move slowly down the street, piercing the metal with his angel eyes, seeing the three of them, and behind them the house where he used to live. With Mother in it.

The car picks up speed so suddenly that Belinda is jolted away from the window and bumped against the back of the seat. Her father has taken one hand off the wheel and his head is inclined slightly toward Gail. "Flunk?" he says. "My goodness, I wouldn't want to be responsible for that." His voice sounds serious but underneath there's the lilt he uses when he's teasing.

Gail shoots him a glance. Then her shoulders straighten and she turns her head, slowly, delicately—like a flower following the sun—to stare out the windshield. There's an alert, waiting attitude about the set of her head and shoulders.

"You'd certainly be better off spending your time studying than trailing us around." Belinda's father pauses and then says, "I'll drop you off at Debby's."

"Oh Daddy," Gail squeals and throws a rapturous arm around his neck. "Oh Daddy, you're wonderful."

"Wow, take it easy. Now listen Gail." His voice becomes stern, commanding. "I don't want one word of this to your mother. I don't want to worry her. Understand?"

"You think I'm stupid or something." Gail jerks her head toward the back seat. "It's little Lindy-Lou who's likely to spill the beans."

"Never mind Lindy," her father says as he pulls up in front of Debby's house. He glances at his watch. "I'll be back at 5:30 sharp. Just see that you're ready."

As soon as Gail is gone, Belinda climbs into the front seat. Her father pulls out from the curb and steps on the gas. He looks relaxed now, leaning back, smiling slightly.

Belinda kicks her heels against the seat and clears her throat to get his attention. "I didn't want Gail to come with us."

"What's that Lindy?"

"I didn't want Gail. She's mean when Mamma makes her look after me."

He glances sharply sideways. "Mean? Does she hit you?"

"She calls me names," Belinda pouts. "Like Lindy-Lou and Bill."

Her father laughs and speaks lightly. "It's a stage she's going through, Lindy. She really loves you."

"Why doesn't Mamma ever come with us anymore?"

He doesn't answer for a moment. "I guess she's got work to do at home."

"She never goes anywhere anymore," Belinda says and then an idea occurs to her. "Maybe she wants to stay home to think about Harvey."

"Maybe you're right."

"How old was I when Harvey died?"

Her father brushes a hand across his forehead, rubs his temple. "It's been two years now . . . you were just coming four."

"Why did Harvey get killed?"

"I don't know." He reaches over and gives her shoulder a quick squeeze. "Look ahead now, the zoo's coming up. See any animals?"

Belinda braces her hands on the seat, lifts her body and cranes to look out the windshield. Over the tops of parked cars, she sees only the arched sign above the gate. "Daddy," she scolds, "we're too far away."

Her father wheels the car around and around in the parking lot, trying to find a vacant stall. "If we hadn't spent all morning wrangling," he grumbles, "we'd have been here before the place filled up."

At last he noses the car into a spot, turns off the engine and rubs the palms of his hands on his trouser legs. He takes out a handkerchief and wipes sweat from his face. "I thought we were going to have to turn around and go home."

Belinda is methodical. When her teacher takes the class to the zoo, they always start with the seals—then to the monkey house, on to the red barn, the bears' pit, the aviary, stopping just the right amount of time at each until everyone is ready for the ride on the merry-go-round and finally, before boarding the bus for the trip back, hot dogs and pop.

Belinda hears the seals. She grabs her father's hand and pulls him toward the hoarse coughs; counts, as they approach, the sleek, black bodies cleaving the water.

Over the pond the air is cooler. Moist. Belinda slides her hands along the damp rail and looks down, following a liquid form to where it rises and clamours awkwardly onto a rock. The seal lies momentarily sunning itself, darkly gleaming, before sliding under the water to emerge— miraculously—beneath the spot where Belinda stands. First, the sharp nose splitting the surface, then the elegant head lifted toward her, the eyes, shining like lamps, looking directly into her own.

She feels the tug of her father's hand but holds back.

"Come on Lindy."

They pause at the monkey house. The monkeys chatter and play, hanging by their tails from tiny swings, hurtling themselves through the air, halting abruptly to scratch themselves with narrow brown hands and stare quizzically out of round, yellow eyes.

Belinda counts. "Five," she announces triumphantly.

She feels impatience in her father's hand. His grip tightens, moving her away. "We'll come by again," he says, all the time looking about, turning quickly this way and that.

The crowd divides and swerves around them, pressing so close that Belinda is engulfed in a sea of legs. She tugs at her father. "What do you want to see, Daddy?"

No answer.

"We could go back to the seals."

"Ah!" he exclaims. "The merry-go-round. Over there."

"Daddy," she protests. But he is walking rapidly now, cleaving a path through the crowd and she is carried in his wake. They stop suddenly in the circle of merry-go-round music, the blur of happy-coloured horses; her father is standing in front of a tall woman who is wearing a white blouse and a billowy blue skirt.

"Carol," he cries out. "Imagine meeting you here."

The woman laughs and extends her hand. "David."

"David." Startled, Belinda looks up at her father, the unfamiliar sound of his name making him seem a stranger.

"Lindy." Her father sets gentle hands on her shoulders and manoeuvers her in front of him. "Lindy, this is Mrs. Heywood and that handsome young fellow back there is her son, Rick."

Mrs. Heywood reaches behind her and pushes Rick forward. He's the same height as Belinda, but broader. He pulls his baseball cap over his eyes and stares at Belinda from under it.

"So this is little Belinda." The woman bends and places a fingertip beneath Belinda's chin, forcing her face upward and gazing seriously into it. Her own face is out of focus, palely amorphous. Her scent billows like a cloud of face powder and Belinda holds her breath. "You and my Rick are the same age." The woman drops her hand and straightens, smiling at Belinda's father. "She's so sweet. I just know she and Rick are going to be great friends."

Belinda is sorry they ran into the Heywoods. She doesn't want to be "great friends" with Rick; she wants to see the animals.

Belinda isn't ready for the merry-go-round but she forgets she isn't the minute it starts. She glances at Rick. He is sitting nonchalantly on his gold-coloured horse, oblivious, it seems, to the mounting excitement, the hurdy-gurdy music. Her horse is lifted on a swell of sound, dropped, lifted again. She looks back to where her father is standing with Mrs. Heywood. Then they are left behind, swept from view, until—her horse rounding the circle—they come in sight again and Belinda seems to be riding straight toward them.

Her father buys hot dogs and pop which they carry to a grassy slope overlooking a small pond. The sun is hot and the smell of bruised grass mingles with the sharp tang of mustard and relish. Ducks and swans swim on the water below, the swans gliding regally, proud necks arched, unmindful of the capricious ducks—their agitated runs across the water, the sudden updendings.

Mrs. Heywood and Belinda's father talk quietly, so softly that the words flow into one another and their voices become one with the background of zoo sounds, the drone of insects.

Then Rick begins to devour his hot dog in huge bites, making gulping sounds—like a dog. Mrs. Heywood lays a hand on his arm. "Take it easy. You aren't starving."

Belinda's father intercedes in an unfamiliar voice. "A growing boy has a big appetite. Isn't that right Rick. You want another hot dog?"

Rick angrily shakes his head, takes a deep breath and heaves the last bite of his hot dog toward the pond. A duck which has been sunning, one-legged, on a rock, flaps its wings, snakes out its head, and flounders after the morsel.

Belinda laughs and stuffs the rest of her hot dog into her pocket. She will save it to throw to the ducks.

Her father reaches out and touches Rick's arm. "You sure you don't want another?"

Rick jerks away, jams his hands into his pockets and glares into space.

"Now don't sulk," his mother admonishes.

"You're not sulking, are you Fella?" Belinda's father says in a loud, hearty voice. "Come on Rick, let's show your mother the kind of stuff you're made of. How about a little wrestling match?" Half-crouching, he advances, wraps his arms around the boy, flips him to the ground and tickles his ribs.

Rick wriggles and squirms, legs flailing the air. His face turns crimson and he emits a squeal which becomes high-pitched frantic laughter.

Belinda's father is laughing too, boisterous belly-laughs that shake his body. Belinda is astounded to see him rolling on the ground, carrying on so with this stranger.

Her father jumps to his feet, grabs Rick under the arms and sweeps him high into the air. Rick's body stiffens and his mouth opens on a piercing scream. He kicks frantically at Belinda's father who promptly sets him down and rocks back on his heels.

"My god, Carol," he cries out. "I didn't hurt him, did I? You aren't hurt are you Ricky? Here let me look at you."

Mrs. Heywood throws out an arm, blocking him. "Not now David." She rushes over and gathers Rick in her arms. "There, there," she says, patting him on the back. She looks over Rick's shoulder at Belinda's father. "He's frightened, David, that's all—just got carried away by the game. He's not used to roughhousing with a man. Maybe I coddle him—there let's dry those tears, Rick. That's a big boy."

Rick pulls away from his mother, picks up his cap and tugs it onto his head. He digs the toes of his shoes into the turf and gazes belligerently around him.

Belinda's father looks crushed. "God, I'm sorry Carol."

"David. David. It's all right." Mrs. Heywood watches Rick for a moment before going over and picking up a paper napkin from the grass. "I've got some scraps left here," she says brightly. "Rick, you take Belinda down to the pond and feed them to the birds. Won't that be fun. And afterwards," she says, raising her eyebrows at Belinda's father, "we'll have some icecream." She gives Belinda a light shove between the shoulder blades. "Run along with Rick, Belinda."

Belinda jumps forward eagerly. With the bun she's got stuffed in her pocket and Mrs. Heywood's scraps the ducks will go crazy. Also, she wants to make amends for her father's weird behaviour. "Come on Ricky," she says, holding out her hand.

Ricky shoves his hands into his pockets and wordlessly follows.

Standing at the edge of the pond with the toes of her sneakers softly sinking in the green scum, Belinda crumbles the remnants of her hot dog in her palm and says, "I'm sorry Daddy made you cry, Ricky." She fixes her eyes on the opposite side of the pond and mimics her mother's voice. "I just don't know what got into him."

She is totally unprepared for Rick's assault, ram-hard fists pounding her stomach, nauseous waves cartwheeling her into the muck. Stunned, she feels the wet ooze on her skin, smells the stench of rotten weeds and duck droppings, tastes slime and salt-blood in her mouth.

Above her, she see's the V of Rick's legs straddling her body. His arms are silhouetted against the sky, the fists savagely knotted.

Belinda opens her mouth and screams. And screams.

At the first service station, Belinda's father stops and washes her off.

He rinses the tee shirt in the basin and wrings it out.

"We'll hang it out the window," he says as he brushes the mud from her jeans, "and it'll be dry by the time we pick up Gail. We won't say a word about it to anybody. Mamma won't let you visit the zoo again if she knows you had an accident." He opens the car door, "You want to sit up front, Lindy, till we pick up Gail?"

Belinda shakes her head and climbs into the back seat. As they drive away her tee shirt is waving like a flag from the car window.

Belinda folds her arms over her sore belly and watches her father's—David's—back. She tries to remember if he ever wrestled with Harvey. She can't remember. When she's with her mother in the house, it's like Harvey's right there with them, out of sight, but present—perhaps in the kitchen getting a drink of water or playing behind the closed door of his room; he's that real, even though Belinda knows that now he lives in heaven.

But at this moment, when she tries to bring him to mind, to picture him, she can't. He's just a name and a photograph on Mamma's dresser.

The car comes to a sudden stop. Belinda's father jumps out and takes down the tee shirt. He crawls into the back seat and pulls the shirt over Belinda's head, smoothing it with the palm of his hand. "It's all dry, Lindy. Just like Daddy said it would be." He holds her against his shoulder, pats her tenderly. "Poor little Lindy." Runs his fingers gently over her belly. "Doesn't hurt now, does it Baby? Rick said he was sorry and he'll never pull that kind of stunt again."

At Debby's house, he reaches back and brushes Belinda's hair from her temples, examines her face. "We'll go to the zoo again, just you and I." His hand slides down Belinda's cheek. "But remember, we don't want to worry Mamma," he says and his thumb and forefinger close over Belinda's lips, pinch them together, "so we won't say a word about Gail's not coming with us today. Will we, Belinda?" The pressure increases. As Belinda moves her head from side to side; the fingers relax and the hand falls away.

He seems to slump then and his face wears the same unhappy expression she saw that morning—the one that made her want to cry.

"There's Gail now." Belinda's father straightens and glances at his watch as Gail slides into the front seat. "Sorry we're late."

"No problem, Daddy. All the more time to study, y'know."

"And how were the studies?"

Gail tosses her head and her hair swirls around her neck. "Great, Daddy. Just great." She shifts to look over the back seat at Belinda. Her eyes are bright and her cheeks flushed. "And how was the zoo, Lindy-Lou? See anything interesting?"

Belinda hugs her belly and deliberates. Finally, she says, "I saw a seal."

For Mrs. Hallett,
Best wishes,
Cristine Bye

Box Social
Cristine Bye

Miss Brenner announced just before Christmas that our Grade 5 class would have a box social to raise money for the Red Cross. The girls would provide the boxes. Because we had three more boys than girls in our class, Miss Brenner said she would supply lunch for those boys who ended up with no box.

For days, Robby Anderson pestered me about how I was going to decorate my box. I said: "That's for me to know and you to find out." Robby, whose dad farmed south of town, wore green plaid cowboy shirts and a belt buckle with a Hereford bull's face on it. His hair was short and blond, like stubble, and his ears stuck out. Whenever he got excited, they turned vibrant red.

I had no intention of sharing my lunch with Robby. It was Devlin Williams I had in mind. Devlin had curly dark hair with eyelashes to match. He was a town kid, very tall and sophisticated. He actually had a dimple in his chin. Every girl in class considered him breathtakingly sexy— "sexy" being the newest, most titillating word in our vocabulary. To attract Devlin, my box would have to be extra special.

The night before the social, I set to work at the kitchen table. First, I wrapped the bottom part of a shoe box in shiny green paper and then covered the lid with banks of snowy cotton batting. I cut eight reindeer out of brown construction paper, being careful to leave tabs on their feet so I could glue them upright on the box lid. I linked them together with string. Finally, I built a sleigh in the cotton batting and tied the string leading from the reindeer onto Santa's scarlet mittens.

The next morning, I danced excitedly at my mother's elbow as she packed the shoe box with four wrapped pieces of fried chicken, two identical plastic tubs of macaroni salad, two dill pickles, two miniature cans of apple juice and two plastic forks. For dessert, she added a cluster of her homemade cherry surprise cookies. My favourites. When Devlin saw all this, his heart would melt.

After gently setting the lid on the shoe box, I went to the cellar-way and searched among the cardboard boxes that my mother brings groceries in from town. I picked out a box which had a picture of a puppy on the side and said "Perky: Your Puppy's Favourite Food." Into this, I lowered my masterpiece. The bigger box was important so the reindeer wouldn't get crushed during the bus ride to school, and also because I didn't want the other kids to see them before the social started. Miss Brenner had insisted the box owners remain anonymous until their boxes were auctioned off.

At school, I placed my Perky box in Miss Brenner's closet with the other lunches and squirmed in my seat all morning, waiting for noon to arrive. Finally, Miss Brenner said to close our arithmetic scribblers, that it was time for the bidding to start. The room rustled as the kids straightened up expectantly. I could feel Robby shooting eager glances at me from his seat across the aisle, but I refused to look at him. My eyes were pinned on the back of Devlin's curly head, two seats in front of me. Miss Brenner took the first box out of the closet and held it up in front of the class.

"How much am I offered for this lovely box?" she said. "Don't be timid, boys. Do I hear 50 cents?" A hand waved hesitantly from the back of the room. "Good. One dollar, anyone?"

The box was wrapped in white tissue paper and decorated with a plastic poinsetta, rather bedraggled-looking. Some girl sure hadn't taken much trouble. Devlin wouldn't go for that one. Sure enough, he kept his hand down. Robby, meanwhile, drilled his eyes into me.

"Is this one yours, Georgina?"

I pursed my lips and tried to look icy. Robby shifted nervously in his desk, but didn't raise his hand.

"Sold! For one dollar and 50 cents, to Garth Barnard. Now, will the girl who made this box stand up, please?"

Peggy Johnson, who stooped and wore black-rimmed glasses, pulled herself up. "Thank you, Peggy," said Miss Brenner. Robby looked relieved.

More boxes were auctioned: several wrapped in plain Christmas paper, one box covered with pictures cut out of Simpson's catalogue, one draped in gingham and tied with braid. Pretty original, some of them, but not that great.

As each box emerged from the closet, Robby grew increasingly agitated, rubbing his palms on the thighs of his jeans. Several times, he stared at me searchingly, half-raised his arm, then let it drop.

I, too, was getting more and more jittery. When was Miss Brenner going to bring out my box? What if Devlin had already bought one by then? He hadn't been bidding so far, but almost all the other boys already had boxes perched on their desks. I figured there were only five lunches left in the closet. Devlin might settle for a second-rate box, just so he wouldn't end up being one of the left-over boys who got no box at all. Around me, the girls whose boxes were sold giggled and waved at their prospective lunch partners. I bit anxiously into my thumb and tried to concentrate on Devlin.

"Now, this is a beautiful box," said Miss Brenner. "Someone has put a great deal of effort into it."

In Miss Brenner's hand was a hatbox wrapped in lilac-coloured tissue paper. On top, posed on a paper doily, sat a Barbie doll wearing a lilac crocheted dress and matching muff. I chewed my thumb vigorously. The box, I was sure, belonged to Charlene Myers the banker's daughter, who wore pastel dresses and pierced earrings and had a tinkly laugh. I thought Charlene's box looked mushy. But there was no telling what the boys—and Devlin—would think.

"Shall we start the bidding at 50 cents?" said Miss Brenner. Two boys flung up their hands. "One dollar. One dollar and 50 cents." The bidding was rolling fast. Robby's ears were a delicate crimson shade. His whole face was flushed. He ran his fingers through his crew-cut and leaned across the aisle.

"Is this it?" he whispered in a loud, painful voice. Several kids swivelled to look at us. My cheeks flared.

"Two dollars," said Miss Brenner. "Two dollars and 50 cents. My, this is the highest we've gone yet. Three dollars! Why Devlin!"

There it was. Devlin's long, handsome arm, coolly hoisted over his head. I stopped working on my thumb and began to gnaw my knuckles. There was still hope. Another boy might outbid him.

"Georgina!" Robby was almost falling out of his desk in his desperation to peer into my face. "Is this it? Is this the one?"

His pink, pleading face, his horrible whisper, were more than I could bear.

"No!" I hissed, though it occurred to me later I should have lied.

"Three dollars is our last bid," said Miss Brenner. "Three dollars once, three dollars twice. Sold! To Devlin Williams. And this box belongs to . . . ?" Charlene Myers rose and smiled daintily in Devlin's direction. He gave her a brief, nonchalant nod.

I wilted in my seat, trying hard not to cry. My knuckles hurt. I pulled my fist out of my mouth and numbly examined the teeth marks. Now what would become of my box? Only the creepy boys were left. Maybe no one would buy my box at all.

Three more boxes trickled past. Shabby things. She's saving the ugly ones for last. And then I realized. My box. She's saving mine, too.

Through a curtain of tears, I saw Miss Brenner hold the Perky box aloft. I was crippled with shame. I couldn't even speak, couldn't lift my arm to say, "Look inside!"

"Um," said Miss Brenner. "Who would like to bid on this box?" No bids rang out. I heard a stifled laugh. From the side of the box, the Perky puppy smirked at me. Tears trickled from the end of my nose. If only I could shrink down, down and crawl inside my desk.

"Five dollars!" a voice exploded from across the aisle.

"Five dollars?" echoed Miss Brenner, as if she hadn't heard right. I turned to look. Robby was beaming exultantly at me, practically standing up in his desk so he could stretch his arm even higher than it was. His ears blazed.

"Yes, well," said Miss Brenner, recovering herself. "If there are no more bids," she paused tactfully, "then the box is sold to Robby Anderson. Thank you very much, Robby." She deposited the box on Robby's desk. "Oh, and whose box is this, please?" She scanned the room.

I burrowed further into my seat but her eyes found me. I swallowed and shuffled to my feet.

"It's mine," I croaked.

"Thank you, Georgina," said Miss Brenner, as I hid in my seat again. "Now, class, I want the boys to move their desks beside the girls, so you can eat your lunches together."

Robby bumped his desk up to mine.

"I figured that Perky box was yours," he said,
" 'cause it was the last one. I was keeping track. Everything worked out great, eh?"

I couldn't look at him. In the corner of the room,
Devlin was seated next to Charlene. She was laughing at
something he was saying. Tinkle, tinkle.

Robby handed me the Perky box. "Your box is
really—it sure looks—well, it's big!" he said.

Slowly, I lifted the reindeer box from the Perky container.

"Oh, Georgina." Miss Brenner's voice was gentle as
she touched my shoulder. "I'm sorry. I didn't even think to
look inside the dog food box."

I sponged my dripping nose with the back of my hand
and tried to say something, but nothing would come.
Robby stretched out his hand to wiggle one of the reindeer.

"Wow!" he said reverently. "This is neat."

The Party
Jan Truss

My Dad pressed a good crease into the trousers that went with his navyblue suit and he put a clean collar on his white shirt. He was taking me to the party—four o'clock to six—because the invitation stated that the child must be accompanied by an unemployed father.

The day was damp and raw so, although I was too big, he held my hand to keep it warm. The other one I made into a fist and pulled up inside my sleeve. As we set out on the long walk, stores were already lit up, making the narrow city streets glow friendly in misty blurs. Inside butchers' shop windows there were pigs' heads smiling with oranges in their mouths while outside fowl hung by the feet from high hooks ready for Christmas; ducks, pheasants, geese, turkeys, all plucked pimply naked except for ruffs of their own special feathers left with the dead heads at the ends of their long stretched necks. Pastry shops smelled warm with hot crusty bread, custard tarts, clove-spicy mincemeat, and rich fruit cake. Sweet shops had coloured lights that turned jars of candies into caves of jewels. "I could just eat a caramel. I dream about having a cream caramel in my mouth," I confided to my Dad.

"Imagine it," my Dad said. "Imagination tastes better than anything."

I believed him because he was my Dad.

We walked past factories whose tall fat-bellied chimneys spewed black smoke, and from whose grimy windows came sounds of machinery, and men's and women's chatter, and laughter.

"They're lucky in there to have jobs," my Dad told me.

Long before we reached the railway bridge the lamp-lighter was lighting the street lamps with his long pole. Boys and girls, as though called by magic, came shouting to play in the golden islands of gaslight. With the mist and the lights, and the long walk, it seemed like night-time already when we dodged the traffic under the bridge at the main street crossroads while a train rumbled and rattled above us. Ahead we saw jolly signs with arrows pointing to the Town Hall, telling us where to enter for the children's party.

My Dad and I went inside, up a curving marble stair-way, out of the cold, still holding hands because the build-ing was so immensely grand, like the inside of castles in story books; and so importantly silent around the noise of the people. On the second floor my Dad told me to look down between the bulbous marble balusters to see the great crowd of children coming up the wide stairway hold-ing hands with their unemployed Dads. My Dad said, "It's a spectacle you'll want to remember."

I thought it was a spectacle when, at exactly four o'clock, we were let through heavy oaken doors into the biggest room I'd ever seen. Rows and rows of tables were covered in white, with thick white cups, saucers, and plates set out, and by every setting a red Christmas cracker. At the far end of the room the stage had TWO Christmas trees on it, heavily garlanded with loops of glistening tinsel. Underneath and around the trees were mountains of gift parcels, fat squares and thin oblongs wrapped in plain colours; green, red, blue, yellow.

At first only the children were let in. I left my coat for my Dad to hold and followed where men and ladies with paper hats above their big smiles showed us where to go.

"Fill up the next space," they called as we edged our way with bent knees between long benches and trestle tables. Before anyone told us we might, we started pulling the crackers, shouting, and getting the paper hats on our heads, red, yellow, green, or blue crowns. Little gifts came out of the crackers but mine got lost under the table. We had to wait until everybody had a seat and the tables were full before the party really started. A man dressed as Santa Claus made a space in front of the parcels on the stage and stood there shouting for us to be patient.

When all the children were in, our Dads were let in to stand round the sides of the hall to watch us. I waved to my Dad. He looked very small. All the Dads looked small. They didn't have paper hats. Most of them kept their workmans' caps on.

When the Dads were all in, we passed our cups to one end of the table to be filled with milky sweet tea from big jugs while, from the other end, white paper bags were passed down to us. "One bag per child," the men and women in the paper hats kept calling while our Dads watched. A beautiful pastry shop smell and flavour came out of my bag when I opened it. I closed it quickly to keep the glory in, but the boys on either side of me spread everything from their bags around their plates. "Everybody's got the same," the word went from child to child. "Five things."

We were supposed to eat the five things while our Dads watched. Some children ate everything but quite a lot took only one bite out of each thing and left a mess on their plates. The men and women were happy to fill up the cups as many times as we liked. They smiled when we asked for more, so I had four cups of tea, but I ate only the bread bun because there were five—counting me—in our family.

Then it was time to go. The tables that came in last

now went out first, the Dads going with the children. On the way out three Santa Clauses on each side, six altogether, gave out the gift boxes. Every age got a different colour. The sevens got green oblongs. I was seven. I knew there was a board game inside by the way the box rattled.

The long walk home with my Dad was lovely, moonlit, starlit, lamplit and storelit. The roofs were wet and shining.

When we got home I gave my Mum the white bag I'd kept so tightly closed. One by one she took out the currant bun, the cupcake with white icing on top, the chocolate cake with the brown icing, and the red lollipop, setting each one on the table, then shaking her head sadly at them.

"Four stale cakes! Yesterday's cakes and a penny lollipop! Could they spare them!" She bit on her lip to stop herself from crying.

My Mum didn't even catch a whiff of the pastry shop glory I'd saved for her.

I, however, kept very secure in the bag of my memories, the biggest party I was ever to see, with *two* Christmas trees and *six* Santas, where men and women with shining faces under paper hats had a lovely time doing something for the children of the poor.

Clues
Diane Schoemperlen

Every Friday just after lunch, Linda Anderson went out to their wheezing blue Chevy in the driveway next door and sat there honking for me—a ritual which irritated my mother marvellously and made me feel like I was going out on a heavy date. We were going grocery shopping.

Once in the car, I would admire Linda's new lilac skirt, multi-coloured sandals, or glittering earring and brooch set. She made the jewellery herself from little kits she got every week through a special mail order club in the States. She was always wearing something new and flamboyant to, as she cheerfully put it, "perk myself up a bit. I know I'm plain." Even then I could see that this was true. Linda was one of those young women I've often seen since on buses or trains, pale and rabbity-looking with slightly buck teeth and round eyes, baby-fine hair, light brown or dirty blonde depending on how you look at things. One of those young women destined to be unhappy, unhealthy or alone.

In the Safeway store I pushed the cart while Linda joyfully loaded it up, tossing in items from either side, checking her list, flipping through the fistful of discount coupons we'd been dutifully clipping from magazines and newspapers all week. This did not take on the stingy penny-pinching quality it did when I was forced to go grocery shopping with my parents on Saturday. Then, my mother led the way, my father pushed the cart, which was invariably one of those balky ones with the wheels going in all directions at once, and I lagged along uselessly behind. My mother didn't even need a list. She bought exactly the same things every week. You could count on it.

The Safeway on Saturday was full of disgruntled men and hectic children. But on Fridays the shoppers were mostly women, moving smoothly and courteously through the aisles, sure of themselves, experts in their element.

Linda flipped her purchases one by one into the cart. Kraft Dinner, cream corn, brussels sprouts, dish soap. Gallons of milk. "Neil's a real milk-drinker."

Green beans. "Neil hates green beens but they're on sale."

Macaroni. "Neil just loves my macaroni and cheese."

I felt I was collecting clues, learning everything there was to know about Neil Anderson and so, by extrapolation, about men in general. Neil, like all the other desirable men in the world, was swarthy and slim, brooding, sensitive and hard to please.

More items were checked off the list. Tomato soup. "It always comes in handy."

Fish for Friday. "We're not Catholic, but still, it's nice."

Cheese slices. "Last night I made this new casserole with sausage and cheese slices and was it ever good."

Linda was always trying out new products, new dishes. She had a whole shelf of cookbooks in her kitchen, from which she liked to read me recipes out loud: Apple-Ham Open-Facers, Inside-Out Ravioli, Lazy Day Lasagne. She prided herself on both her cooking and her shopping. Being seven years younger, I was immensely interested in the entire procedure, confident that this was one of the inevitable things which lay in store for me—shopping and cooking for my husband and our eventual children—they would love everything I served them.

We waited at the meat counter while the butcher in

his bloody apron sliced four chops off a big chunk of pork. The vertical blade whined through the flesh, silver teeth grinding on bone. The man in line behind us, wearing tinted glasses and a uniform of some kind, said, "That's just how it sounds when they cut the top of your head off to do an autopsy." Now the butcher was spearing slabs of dripping liver with a pointed wooden stick. Linda smiled and nodded, dropping the chops into the cart which I was already pushing away.

On the way to the checkout stand, we had to stop at the candy counter to pick up something for Neil, licorice pipes or jujubes or a chocolate-covered cherry. "I have to get him a little treat or he'll be mad at me," Linda explained coyly, making her husband sound like a spoiled child or maybe a snake she had managed to charm, but just barely.

The Andersons had moved into the house next door on the first of July, newly married, just come to Hastings from Newberry, a dumpy little town to the north. Jobs were easier to come by then and, within the week, Neil was working at the same paper mill as my father.

In the beginning Linda came over to our house several times a week. She could sit at our kitchen table all afternoon just chatting and drinking coffee with my mother. We soon knew all about her.

Her maiden name was Jessop. Her family had been in Newberry for decades. They owned both the dry goods stores and the funeral parlour now, though they'd started out with nothing just like everybody else. Linda was in the middle, with two older sisters and two younger brothers. There had been one older brother, Lance, but he was dead now, beaten to death outside the Newberry bar by a jealous husband from a neighbouring town. The husband had then driven home, on a tractor no less, and killed his wife with a pitchfork. "As I see it," Linda said, "he knew he'd get caught so he figured he might as well finish the job."

Linda and Neil had been childhood sweethearts. "His family is basically no-count," she admitted. "Oh, don't tell him I said that, he'll kill me." As if I would. She was drawing me into a womanly conspiracy, lush with the promise of fat secrets and special knowledge.

But they were good at heart, the Andersons. In fact, one of Linda's brothers would soon be married to one of Neil's sisters. "It's a real family affair."

They were renting just until they could afford to buy a house in one of the new subdivisions. They planned to have three children and were getting busy on that right away. "I can't afford to wait too long," Linda confided. "Both my sisters were cut open for cancer when they weren't much older than me. So I suppose it'll get me too, in a few years."

Linda's life, past, present and future, was endlessly interesting to her, and to me too. But my mother wasn't much for socializing or sitting around gabbing all day. After the first few visits, she developed the habit of drifting inconspicuously back to the dishes, the dusting, or rolling up socks. Linda hardly seemed to notice her defection and I was flattered to think that it was really *my* company she sought.

Once, after Linda had finally gone home to start supper for Neil, my mother said viciously, "That girl's a feather-brain!" and threw the dish towel across the kitchen after her. "And don't you go getting any crazy ideas, young lady." I could not have said exactly what she meant—ideas about what? men, marriage, babies, cancer?—but I knew, grudgingly, that she had a point of some kind.

Linda had other stories besides her own—a repertoire of alarming gruesome tales which, for a time, I neither doubted nor forgot. But I didn't repeat them either. There was the one about the man who murdered his son and his dog with an axe. The woman found strangled in her car beside the Number One highway. The man who chopped up his wife and kept the parts in the freezer, all packaged up and labelled.

Such things happened all the time, in California, Paris, Vancouver, Brazil, but they could happen to anyone anywhere. There was no reason to think that you would be spared. You could no longer know what to expect of people, especially men, in this crazy world. There were so many of them, all equally unpredictable. Most of the time there was no telling what they might do. According to Linda, the men were depraved savages who might run amok at any time and the women were helpless obvious victims, dying all over the place. The best and the worst of her stories were those in which the killers were *never caught*.

One afternoon Linda asked, "Did you hear about those kids?", casually stirring more sugar into her third cup of coffee. My mother was defrosting the fridge with pots of hot water.

"No," I said. My mother sat down at the table, wanting, I suppose, to hear the news in spite of herself.

Linda settled in to tell the story. "This couple took their four kids to an arts and crafts show at the community centre. When they left, two of the kids, a boy and a girl, went on ahead. But they never got home. They found them the next day, strangled, side by side, in a field not far from the centre."

"Here in Hastings?" I asked, for lack of any other response.

"Yes. Right here in Hastings."

My mother jumped up from the table, knocking her chair over backwards, and stomped out the door, muttering, "Garbage, garbage!" Which could have been either what she was going to do, put out the garbage, or her opinion of Linda, her story, or both.

That night after supper I went through the newspaper page by page, hoping that no one would ask what I was looking for. On the second last page, I found the small headline, KIDS FOUND DEAD, above a half-inch story. Two children found dead in a schoolyard in Caracas, Venezuela. They'd been left at home alone and discovered missing when their parents came home the next day.

I was both disappointed and relieved. Linda, in her hurry to tell us something horrible that we didn't already know, got the story all wrong. She was looking for proof that she was justified in her cheerful expectation of tragedy. After this, there were many times when I suspected her of lying, trying to make me as frightened as she was. This did not immediately make me like her less, although it probably should have and would now.

I was soon spending more time at Linda's house than she did at ours. My mother had succeeded in making her feel, if not exactly unwelcome, then certainly unappreciated.

The Andersons' house was just the way ours had been before we renovated. We called them war-time houses. They were single-storey squares with dugouts instead of basements, small cosy or cluttered rooms all opening off the kitchen, and wooden steps front and back.

When we were too hot and miserable to do anything else, Linda and I sat out on her front step in our shorts, watching the traffic and sipping pink lemonade till we felt pickled in it. Occasionally a carload of boys would slowly cruise by, whistling as we stretched and admired our legs in the sun. We were feeling like sleepy cats and ignored them.

My legs were a deep reddish-brown, so dark by August that my mother said, "You look like a little Indian." Linda was fair-skinned but neither burned nor tanned, remaining all summer long a marbled, bluish white. "Too much sun is bad for you anyway," she said. "It'll give you cancer." I didn't believe her and continued to cultivate my colour. I couldn't help but notice that the blue veins in her thighs were beginning to bulge and break.

When it was cooler or raining, we sat inside, usually at their stylish new breakfast nook which Neil had built himself and Linda had wall-papered in a blue and orange pattern featuring teapots and coffee mugs.

While Linda talked, polished her salt and pepper shaker collection, or fussed and cooed over Twinky, the blue budgie in his cage by the window, I took careful note of everything in the house. The teapot clock, the ceramic Aunt Jemima canisters, the hot pot holders which read, "Don't Monkey With The Cook," the plastic placemats with kittens, roosters or roses on them—she changed them once a week.

Every detail was important to me, an avenue into the esoteric intricacies of married life, a state of being which seemed to me then divinely blessed, glamorous, intimate but clean. I needed to know exactly how you achieved such a permanent and inviolable state of grace. As far as I was concerned, their perfect happiness was a foregone conclusion, stretching sanguinely out to embrace infinity. Any connection or resemblance between their marriage and that of my parents was remote, if it existed at all. It did not occur to me that either my parents had once been like Linda and Neil or that Linda and Neil would one day be like my parents, solidified and decidedly unromantic.

Linda, herself still quite convinced of the powerful magic of homemaking, was more than happy to answer my nosy questions. I was digging for information, especially about Neil and what it was like to live with a man.

"How do you make an omelette? What TV shows do you watch? Does Neil help with the dishes? How often do you vaccuum? What time do you go to bed? Do you ever stay up all night? Which side of the bed do you sleep on?" The questions I was afraid to ask were the most important.

Their bedroom door always stood proudly open, displaying a dainty doll in the middle of the white chenille bedspread, her voluminous pink skirt spread around her in layers like a cake. At home the bedroom doors were always shut tight, a concession to privacy, shame, or not having made the bed yet.

One rainy afternoon Linda had the bright idea of rearranging the living room furniture to surprise Neil when he got home from the mill. The aqua-coloured couch and chair with arms at least a foot wide were unwieldy but simple enough once we threw our weight into it. Before moving the TV set we had first to take down the dozens of photographs in different sized filigree frames which completely covered its top. This was a lengthy procedure which involved the identification of every person in every picture, who took which shot, and what the special occasion was and at whose house it was held that year. Dismantling the china cabinet where Linda kept her salt and pepper shaker collection was even worse. She estimated the collection at two hundred pairs but it seemed more like eight or nine hundred to me, every set different, from cupids to corn cobs, from Santa and Mrs. Claus to Paul Bunyan and his blue ox, Babe. By the time Linda was finished fondling and explaining them, I was so bored, impatient and somehow embarrassed for her, that I went home, leaving her sprawled on the couch, sweating and self-satisfied.

The one thing we had not touched was Neil's gun collection. Arrayed in wooden racks against the wall, the smooth metal barrels were perfectly, endlessly polished, cool to the touch even in this unbearable heat.

I did not go back for several days and, when I did, found everything once again in its original position. Neil, obviously, had not been impressed. I was obscurely pleased, meanly imagining that he'd made her put it all back by herself. No one was going to push him around, least of all silly, fluffy Linda. It served her right. She could be so tiresome. Some days—mean, sulky days—I'd taken to wondering how Neil—quiet, sensitive, so handsome Neil—could even stand her. I was beginning to understand why she had no other friends. And if I was too young for her, as my mother repeatedly pointed out, then she was certainly too old for me.

I didn't spend all my time that summer with Linda. In fact, I seldom saw her in the evening and never on weekends. I usually wanted to stay inside and read, but felt obligated to go out and suntan. I would spread myself on a beach towel in the backyard, armed with baby oil, radio and a pitcher of water to sprinkle on intermittently, believing this would speed the tanning process. I was bored and uncomfortable but lying there made me feel more normal, doing exactly what I supposed all the other girls my age were doing or wanting to.

On weekends I lay there by the honeysuckle hedge hoping that Neil Anderson would see me and want me and go back inside and holler at pale gabby Linda. Whenever I heard a sound from that direction, I couldn't open my eyes for fear that it would or wouldn't be him.

I could not have said when I began to feel this way about Neil. It was all Linda's fault anyway, I reasoned. She had made him seem so desirable, so serious and important, so perfectly male, the only man worth having. How could I help myself? I no longer wanted to be like

Linda. But I did want everything she had, including her house and her husband. Linda, I imagined, was the only obstacle which kept him from me. Now I fantasized about their divorce.

Evenings were usually spent with my best friend, Mary Yurick, who had a job in the kitchen of a nursing home downtown and so was not available to me during the day. I was not yet allowed to work and envied her mightily, foolishly brushing aside my mother's wise words: "You'll be working for the rest of your life—so what's your hurry?"

Mary and I passed the time at her house or mine, watching beauty pageants and variety shows on TV, playing Scrabble or poker, sipping lemon gin from her father's well-stocked liquor cabinet whenever her parents were out for the evening. When the night was too warm, too long, too inviting, we went out and we walked, restless and uneasily innocent.

We headed downtown, past those boring plump houses just like ours, with flowers, families and fat dogs in the yard. Downtown where the dangerous young men were hanging in restaurant doorways, draped potently over parking meters or the hoods of hot cars, watching the bright street where something might happen to jerk them awake, something electric and clarion, like a siren. We were already aware of their power but not yet of the need to protect ourselves from it. We thought we could become part of it, did not know yet of the danger, of how they would use it over and against us, never offering a share.

We browsed through the record store which was always open late and peeked through the glass doors of the Hastings Hotel bar, longing. Once there was a fight out in front, two men thumping bloodless and silent on the sidewalk. Once a young woman lay face down on the curb, stinking. But nothing could deter us. We walked the nights on a leash that summer, Mary and I, all dressed up and tingling, daring each other to be disgusted. The summer was almost over and we had wasted it.

Some evenings I stayed home and read, not wanting to know. Alone in the hot house, I curled up on the couch in my nightgown with a new novel and just one light on, feeling safe and relieved. All the screens were up, hoping to catch a breeze, and I could hear June bugs hitting against them, falling to the ground on their backs. From all up and down the block came voices, thin music, the hum of sprinklers and lawn mowers. Once in a while I could hear someone else's phone ringing faintly.

My parents were out in the yard cutting peonies and roses just as it grew dark, their voices young and strong in the twilight. Sometimes they sat out front in the lawn chairs, citronella candles smoking in a circle around them to keep the mosquitoes away. I wondered what Linda and Neil were doing, wished I had never met them, would never be like them. Wished I could stay home here forever, here where they did not draw blood, here where you knew exactly what they expected of you, here where my father was coming in through the door and putting his arms around me for no reason. Here where I wanted to cry.

Friday night the week before school started, Linda called and invited me over.

"Neil's gone out again, I'm all alone. We could make popcorn, I'll do you hair." She was begging.

I was hard-hearted. "No, I can't. I'm going out with Mary." I wanted to hurt her. I wanted her to know that I had better things to do and was nothing like her after all. It was Friday and I was feeling frisky, thinking of what I would wear, who we might see, how late I could stay downtown without pushing my mother over the edge.

Grocery shopping that afternoon, Linda had been careless and preoccupied, missing half the items on her list, spending her money instead with desperate extravagance on T-bone steaks, fresh asparagus tips, a precious can of lobster. Her dirty blonde hair was greasy and her out-of-style pedal-pushers were held together at the waist with a big safety pin. She perked up only once, just long enough to tell me the story of a marine in Michigan who had murdered his wife and three children and then turned the gun on himself.

"It was a real bloodbath. You can imagine," she muttered with grim satisfaction, fondling a sweet-smelling canteloupe before tossing it into the cart. "All I really want is one of those little gadgets you make melon balls with."

I was barely listening, absent-mindedly examining the onions, not thinking of anything else in particular, but not allowing myself to be interested either. Linda, I had decided, no longer needed to be listened to. Her grisly gossip was merely her way of reassuring herself that things could be and probably would be worse. Everybody needs to be certain of something.

In my smug, soon-to-be-undermined adolescent superiority, I pitied her. But I was shutting her off, cutting her out, moving glibly away. We could not do anything for each other anymore.

On the way home we took a detour downtown, cruising several times slowly past the Hastings Hotel so Linda could squint intently at the doorway, looking for clues. Neil Anderson, I knew from eavesdropping on my parents, was in trouble for drinking at work (this from my father) and sometimes stayed out all night without Linda (this from my mother who liked to keep track of things). I was interested but only mildly surprised. Linda was one of those women who expected the worst and got it. Neil was clever, sly and volatile, capable of anything.

Linda attempted to confide in me. "I just don't know what to do," she began and then stopped.

She tried again. "I just can't believe that Neil would—." I was holding my breath, afraid to look at her. What did she want from me anyway? She was older, married, she wasn't supposed to have problems anymore. I would not be drawn into her miseries. I would not talk about Neil behind his back anymore. It felt now like a betrayal or a shameful admission of helplessness.

Downtown that night Mary and I hung around the Exchange Cafe for a while, spending our allowances on chocolate milkshakes and chips and gravy, and then we gravitated wordlessly towards the Hastings Hotel. We perched on the wooden bench out front where the winos slumped in the sunshine and sometimes slept under newspapers at night. The police would be by in half an hour or so, telling us to move along. We sat there smoking cigarettes stolen from Mary's mother and talking, mostly about how easy it would be to sneak inside and have a beer. We were all dressed up, trying to look older in earrings and, despite the cooler nights, new white tank tops selected to show off our silky suntans. But we both knew we wouldn't try it, not yet.

The boarded-up bar door opened—someone had kicked in the glass again—emitting a belch of boozy laughter and a country and western chorus.

Neil Anderson came out with his arm around the waist of a blonde woman wearing skin-tight slacks and white cowboy boots. She was quite stunning in an ornamental sort of way, smiling all-inclusively around her, proud of herself. Neil was just drunk enough to be expansive and flirtatious, not at all the way he was around the neighbourhood, not at all the way Linda made him out to be.

He came right up to me and threw his other arm

around my neck, kissing the top of my head. "Hiya, honey!"

Mary was impressed. Neil patted through the pockets of his black leather jacket, as if looking for matches or a gun. Exposing a gleaming buck knife strapped to his belt, he produced a mickey of rye.

"For you, ladies!" he said and swaggered away.

The bottle, of course, was a bribe, so I wouldn't tell Linda. As if I would. I probably should have been indignant or afraid, but instead I was feeling privileged and ripe with our secret, winking and wanting to go with them. I was aching for adventure and convinced now that Neil, more than anyone, knew where to find it.

Ronnie So Long at the Fair
Merna Summers

There was absolutely no reason to smoke that he could think of, but it seemed that he was determined to do it. He lay on his bed, his cigarette on a jam-can lid beside him, and watched the smoke rise and form a layer between bed and ceiling. He was seventeen, past the age where he ought to have done such things, and he didn't want to be a laggard at the table of life.

So he was thinking, and congratulating himself for procrastinating no longer, when he heard the voices at the back door. He leapt from his bed, he who had thought that the only way he could get up was very, very slowly, and picked up the dirty shirt and began to fan it toward the window. Before the voices he had had one problem; now he had two.

"It's not worth it," he said to himself, meaning the smoking. "I'm going to give it up."

The truth was that he was having a hard time getting it started, that smoking made him dizzy, that he had to take to his bed to do it. But he was practising, and it seemed to him that he was making progress. He might have finished this cigarette if his mother hadn't come home. He had smoked two-thirds of it already and he still had some smoking capacity left.

The voices in the kitchen reached him over the sound of his shirt flapping. His mother's voice, complacent. "We *do* get along pretty well." And Mrs. Warner's, congratulating, flattering. "I should think you do. There's a lot of mothers would envy you."

He realized that they were talking about him, registered the fact without much interest. Then his mother spoke again. "When Ronnie was just a little fellow he used to say, 'You're my best friend, Mum.'"

Hearing this, Ron felt his skin move over his body as if it were trying to dissociate itself from the rest of him. Mostly, as his mother said, they did get along pretty well . . . but he wished she would stop telling people things he had said when he was a little kid. And he wished she would stop calling him *Ronnie*.

He dribbled some Kool-Aid on top of the cigarette butt in the jam-can lid and then poured the whole mess out of the window into the petunia bed. His clothes would smell of smoke, he realized. He had to go through the kitchen to get out of the house and his mother and Mrs. Warner would smell him.

Let them smell him, he thought. He was old enough to do as he pleased. There wasn't a thing his mother could say to him.

But when he was dressed and ready to go it seemed to him that there was no point in making a big thing of it and so he made a run for it, speeding through the kitchen and calling "Sorry, I'm late" over his shoulder. Then he was outside and one problem was behind him.

What was ahead of him wasn't exactly a problem but a party . . . which amounted to the same thing, Ron thought. He was going to a party. He didn't expect very much of it. He didn't expect very much of any of the parties he went to.

Parties in Willow Bunch never seemed like *real* parties. They seemed like poor makeshifts, like imitations of the kind of parties that people would have in other places. He wouldn't have gone to them at all if he hadn't needed the practice, and felt that the practice you got at imitation parties was better than no practice at all.

One of the things he needed practice with was girls; he didn't know how to get started with them. It seemed to him that if he could get started he would know how to carry on, but he didn't know how to get started. It was one of the things he would have liked to ask his father about, if he had had a father to ask, but his father hadn't come home from the war.

That was the way they always said it: that his father hadn't come home from the war. It was the phrase that was used for men who had been killed overseas, but his father hadn't been killed overseas. He had simply decided not to come back to Willow Bunch when the war was over.

"He's tom-catting around somewhere in England," Ron had overheard his mother telling Mrs. Warner. "Well, good luck to him. I'm sure I wouldn't want to hold him back."

His mother hadn't sounded bitter or unhappy. She had a light girlish voice and she spoke briskly, as one disposing of an inconvenient fact, putting it in its place. And Ron, who was twelve then, had not known what tom-catting meant. He had thought that it must be the code word for some kind of secret mission. He had imagined his father coming home when the mission was over, had imagined how impressed people would be. Platforms would be decorated and medals presented, he had thought. "Sappy kid," he thought now, remembering. But the memory made him uncomfortable, as if it were not a thing that he had thought long ago, but recently.

He was supposed to call on Preston Blackwell, but Preston was waiting for him in the lane, his portable record-player in his hand. "Christ we're late," he said as Ron came up.

"I'm in no hurry," Ron said.

They walked along together in silence for a while.

Then, "Do you think there'll be any new girls at the party?" Preston asked.

Ron had already considered this. If it were two weeks later and the summer holidays, some of the girls might have had cousins or pen-pals staying with them, and brought them to the party. But the last week of school?

"Not much chance," he said.

He began then to think of the girls who *would* be at the party—Lorraine Fenske, Shirley Larson, Derry Drake—and it was as if each of them had a question mark behind her name. He always thought of girls that way: as if they had question marks behind their names. One of them was going to mean something to him, he thought, but he had no way of knowing which one that was going to be.

They turned a corner and came into sight of the church hall, where the party was being held, and Ron felt a sudden reluctance to go any farther. "Shall we stop for a smoke?" he asked.

Preston looked impatient. "Can't you wait?" he said. "We're late now."

Ron shrugged. "I guess I can sneak out later," he said.

There were as many boys as girls at the party, but the room seemed to be full of girls. They fluttered around in their light summer dresses, twice as noticeable as boys; you couldn't not notice them. The way they dressed, the perfume they wore, the way they talked: all these things were meant for noticing. Beside them the boys seemed to colourless, smell-less, soundless. It seemed to Ron that even a girl would have a hard time finding anything about most of them to be interested in.

Preston took his record-player up to the front and busied himself with setting it up, and Ron went to stand beside Walter Hafner, a farm boy he chummed with when he was on Uncle Ross's farm. "I wondered if you'd changed your mind about coming," Walter said.

Ron nodded, acknowledging the possibility. "There was nothing else to do," he said. "There never is in this burg."

He felt better when he had said that, as if he had put himself on top of the situation.

The girls were talking in voices higher than they needed to be heard. They were standing in a group at the other side of the hall, but the centre of their group was not a girl and he was not standing. Alf Henderson, older than the rest of them and working now, was sprawled on a seat, almost sitting on his spine, drooping his eyelids as if to say that it was going to take something pretty special to interest him. As far as Ron could see, Alf behaved in exactly the way his mother had taught him that you didn't behave around girls, but the girls clustered around him as if he were candy. Which went to show that you couldn't believe everything that you were taught, Ron thought, that if there was anything useful to be learned, you were going to learn it from your own generation.

Walter was watching too. "Dames," he said with disgust.

"Yeah," Ron said.

After a while Alf stood up, and there was a blatant maleness about the way he did it. He hoisted himself from the belt, the way Ron had seen truck drivers in the coffee shop do when they stood up.

"Look at him," Walter said. "Lifting his nuts. He's got to make sure they're still there."

"Yeah," Ron said.

Ron hadn't expected much of the party, but afterwards it seemed to him that he had got more than he expected, and that this party was more real than other parties he had been to. What made this party different was that he went out on the porch for air with a girl. He was dancing with Derry Drake, and it was hot, and when the dance ended, Derry suggested that they go out for air.

Ron was glad that it was Derry who asked him. Derry wasn't the prettiest girl at the party—Derry's face wasn't really *pretty*—but she was perhaps the most striking. Blond hair drew your eyes to a girl, and Derry's hair was so blond that it was almost silver. Besides that, there was an air of imminent happenings about Derry. She leaned forward when she talked, as if she couldn't wait to get where she was going, and you felt that her life had more excitement in it than most people's. Derry's father was a lawyer and Ron was impressed by this, although he didn't know why he should be.

On the porch Ron reached into his pocket and took out his pack of Exports. "Smoke?" he asked.

Derry shook her head. "I would, but I don't like the smell," she said. "You go ahead, though."

Ron put the cigarettes away. "Actually, I'm trying to quit," he said.

After that Ron didn't know what to do, but Derry asked him what he was doing in the summer holidays and he told her that he always worked for Uncle Ross and it seemed to him that she looked at him with admiration. Then she asked if he was going to the Vermilion Fair and he said he was thinking about it and she said, "Maybe I'll see you there, then."

It wasn't a date, Ron told himself later, you couldn't call it a date. But still, *something* had happened. He only wished that he had thought to ask Derry what day she was going to the fair.

The water in the wash-basin was almost mud. Ron grinned, pleased that all this dirt had come off his face and hands. On the farm he did a man's work and he felt like a man. Stacking bales or driving the big Minnie, he was conscious of power, his own and the machine's. Of its own accord his body took on a man's way of moving, a way of moving that took up space, too much space for his mother's little house in town.

"I thought you were going to take a bath," Uncle Ross said as Ron dumped the dirty water and filled the wash-basin again.

"I am," Ron said. "I'm just taking the rough off. I don't want to get my bath water dirty."

Under Ross whistled. "It sounds like a heavy date," he said.

Ron grinned again. He was going to the fair with Walter, but he and Walter *might* pick up a couple of girls, he thought. They might see Derry and one of her friends, and tie up with them, or they might meet some new girls. He had a strong feeling of possibility. There were times when he felt inspired with knowledge about how to act with girls, and today had been one of those days.

This feeling increased as he and Walter drove across country to the fair. It was early evening, and summer was at its height, and it seemed to him that the world itself was giving him messages about how to conduct his affairs. He looked at the fenceposts sending shadows across the wheat and barley fields, shadows long in the long light of evening, and he listened to the song of a meadowlark rising from fencepost to sky. *Reach*, these things said to him. And he breathed in the scent of newly made hay, of purple clover blooming in the ditches, and felt himself instructed by their fragrance. *Touch* was what they told him.

They parked the car on the road outside the fairgrounds. Ahead they could see the Rollo-plane circling and diving, the Ferris wheel drawing circles of light against a still-bright sky, and Ron's feeling that this was the night, that something was going to happen, grew. The

fair was a different world, a world where the ordinary
rules didn't apply. You might not know how to get started
other places, but here you would know how to get started.

Ron and Walter passed through the Exhibits Building
quickly. Other people might come to the fair to look at the
winter wheat and the red currant jelly, but they weren't
among them. They spared not a glance for the vibrating
chairs or, outside, the avenues of green farm machinery.
They did stop for a minute to look at a Holstein cow standing in a pen under a striped canopy. *Alcartra Gerben, The
World's Champion Milk Producer*, a sign in front of the
cow said, and seeing it, Ron felt a stir of pride, of
confirmation. The Vermilion Fair might only be a little C
Circuit fair, he thought, but it had managed to get a
World's Champion here. That must mean something.

Then they were on to the Midway, with its smell of
frying onions, its booths of kewpie dolls in feather skirts,
its plumed hats with bands that said *Hubba Hubba*. This
was the heart of the fair, and Ron felt as if he had come to
a place of testing. That was what the fair was, he thought: a
kind of test. You could test your skill, or your luck, or your
strength. And what else were the rides but a kind of test?
You went on the wild ones the first time to see if you could
take it. And afterwards you felt more of a man for it.

There was a concession where people shot ducks on a
moving belt. The girl who ran the concession was about
Ron's age, but she had a tattoo on each bare shoulder. Ron
was looking at her, thinking that she looked as if she
would be interesting to talk to, when he heard a little
squeal and turned to see where it had come from. Then he
saw the girls—Derry Drake and Lorraine Fenske—and he
wondered why he hadn't seen them sooner. They were
dressed to stand out in a crowd, Derry especially. She had
on white slacks and a paddy-green blouse, and a crazy hat
with a long plume on it. She looked like a tap-dancer, or

like somebody who might belong to the fair.

Walter saw the girls too. He didn't say anything, just motioned in their direction with his head. And as he and Ron moved forward together Derry turned and Ron saw that she had seen them first and was checking to make sure that they had seen her.

Ron hadn't seen Derry since school ended. He had thought about her, had made stories about her and himself, as he sometimes made stories about his father and himself. He didn't know very much about either of them, outside of the way they were in his stories, but it seemed to him that if you imagined a person a certain way, they probably were like that. But at the same time, he knew that Derry was the girl in his stories because she was the girl he had gone out on the porch with; if something had happened with another girl, he would have thought about her instead.

"Well, look who's here," Derry said.

"This is your lucky day," Walter said.

They stood around for a while then, joking, and then Ron said, "I guess we might as well take a stroll around and see what there is to see," including the girls in the invitation. He felt expansive saying it, liked the way it sounded coming out.

They set off paired, Walter with Lorraine and Ron with Derry, and with Ron thinking about the commands he had been getting about reaching and touching. There was a poem in a book at school about young people at a fair, seeking out the bypaths and kissing bridges. It occurred to Ron that the Vermilion Fair was a little short of both. If he wanted to touch Derry he was going to have to reach out right in the middle of the Midway, where the whole world could see if she moved away.

But then he thought of the rides. The rides could have been invented for this. On the Tilt-A-Whirl or the Loop-O-Plane, touching would be all but inevitable; centrifugal force would be on your side.

He felt pleased with himself for having thought of this, and pleased when the rides turned out to have precisely the advantages he had foreseen. On the Tilt-A-Whirl, Derry's small body leaned against him and his leaned against her. On the Silver Streak he discovered that the only way two could sit comfortably in the narrow seat was for him to put his arm around her. And by the time they got to the Ferris wheel, to the top of it, he felt able to kiss her, and did, but not very well. It wasn't that their noses collided or anything like that, but he felt as if he wanted to kiss her in a place that wasn't high and swinging, at a time when they didn't have a sickening lurch down ahead of them. He wanted to be able to concentrate.

Immediately he began to think of Walter's car, of how, if they could get to it, they could kiss there.

Walter must have been thinking of the same thing. When they got off the Ferris wheel he said he was hungry, suggested a hamburger. But he said that he wanted to go to the Exhibits Building to get it, that they made better hamburgers there.

Ron was full of admiration. When you were at the Exhibits Building you were half-way to the car. And when their hamburgers were eaten Walter remembered that he had left his sweater in the car and they all set out with him to get it, walking purposefully through the darkness, the Midway lights behind them reflected in the hoods of parked cars.

They got to Walter's car and Walter and Lorraine got in the front and Ron and Derry got in the back. Ron's excitement now was intense. He didn't have time to wonder if he would know how to get started touching Derry. As soon as they got in the car he was doing it. Derry was there, in the handiest place for kissing, and he kissed her. And you couldn't very well sit kissing a girl as if she was nothing but a pair of lips and so he held her.

He didn't expect more than that: a kiss, a touch. It hadn't occurred to him that there could be more. He was not, for instance, expecting to touch anything so personal as a breast. But it somehow happened that Derry's breast was against his hand, and the feeling of it there, soft and warm and thrusting, was almost too much for him. He groaned, heard himself groan.

"Easy back there," Walter said.

Ron remembered then that they were not alone, and took his hand away. But as soon as he had done it, he felt its exile, wanted it back. He was trying to figure out a way of getting it back there without Derry noticing when he realized that he had another problem: Derry was mad at him. She pulled away from him, turning her head, as if he had done something.

He didn't know what to do. After a minute he put out a hand and touched Derry tentatively, and it seemed to him that Derry moved back a little, that she was not quite as far away as she had been. He kissed the back of her neck, which was the part of her that was closest to him, and then it was as if Derry forgave him for whatever he had done because she turned and began to kiss him urgently, her breasts pressing against his chest. It seemed to Ron that this was an accident, but he accepted it gratefully. Derry must not feel things like he did, he thought. It occurred to him that he liked everything about Derry, but that this absent-mindedness of hers was the best thing of all. He betted he could touch her all over and she wouldn't notice at all.

The thought made him feel like groaning again, but this time he did not groan. He was learning, he thought, and at a rate he would not have believed possible.

All the time he was thinking these things he was kissing away like crazy. It seemed to him astonishing the way he could think and do at once, that the harder he kissed the faster he thought, and the more daring his thoughts became. He decided to try putting his hand on Derry's breast again, and it was just as he thought: she didn't notice it there at all, but just kissed him harder than before. He thought of how much there was of Derry that might be touched, and goodness knows what part of him or of her might have got into the touching next if Lorraine hadn't spoken from the front seat. "My God," she said. "It's 11. I'm going to get killed."

It turned out that Derry and Lorraine had come to the fair with Lorraine's parents, and had to go home with them. But Derry didn't move away from him, didn't shrug his hand off her breast, until Lorraine opened the front door and the car light came on. Then his hand dropped of its own accord.

They walked the girls back to the Midway. Later, walking back to the car, "How did you make out?" Walter asked. And then, not waiting for an answer, "You know that little short blouse that Lorraine was wearing? Well, I had my hand on the skin at her waist."

Ron felt like laughing. "Kid stuff," he could have said. But he wouldn't say it, because then Walter would know how far he had gone with Derry, and he didn't want Walter to know. He realized that now, when he dreamed, it would always be about Derry. And he wanted to protect her, he felt that she needed his protection. Because if she had known what was happening, it wouldn't have.

There were two main smells in the kitchen. There was the smell of Uncle Ross's Sunday morning coffee, laced with rum, and there was the smell of chicken gravy, rising from a roaster on top of the stove. His mother was stirring the gravy, if stirring was the right word for what she was doing. Lumps had formed in it and she was attacking

them, threshing against them with the back of her spoon.
She looked angry.

Ron and his mother had been to church. Ron seldom
went in the summertime—it was one of the masculine
privileges of being part of Uncle Ross's bachelor estab-
lishment that nobody expected you to—and his mother had
been surprised when he had turned up this time. He hadn't
told her his reason: that Derry was arranging the flowers
for the service, that Derry was, she said, "very interested in
flower-arranging."

Sitting beside his mother, Ron had thought that the
flowers looked fine. But they must not have looked that
way to Derry, because just before the service started, she
got up and went into the sanctuary to make some last-
minute adjustments, moving a snapdragon here, a bachelor
button there. She made a pretty picture doing it, with her
hair so blond that it was almost silver, and her eyes as blue
as the blue skies over Uncle Ross's hayfield. Ron thought
that you could look at a blue wall or a blue dress and it
didn't do the same thing to you as a blue sky did, but
Derry's eyes were different. He felt the same soaring of
spirit looking at them as he did looking at a sky.

Derry finished her adjusting and returned to the middle of the altar. She stopped there and bowed deeply,
reverently, and there was a look of purity about her.
Unbidden, there came into Ron's mind a picture of himself
and Derry, years hence, sitting together in this same
church. He did not want to get married, he knew that it was
years too soon for him to think about getting married, but
the picture that formed in his mind was a *married* picture.
He saw himself and Derry going home from church for
Sunday dinner with "the folks," Derry's parents, Mr. and
Mrs. Drake. He saw the white damask on the table, saw
Mr. Drake standing at the end of it, carving the roast. That
was the way things would be done in the Drake household,

he thought: white linen and the carving done at the table.

Derry turned to rejoin her parents in their pew and as she did so, Ron could tell that her eyes were going to move toward the pew where he was sitting with his mother, and they did. But it was not his eyes that Derry sought out, but his mother's.

Ron's mother gave up on her gravy and got out a strainer and grimly began to push it through. Watching her, Ron had the feeling that there was something that he ought to make up to her, but he didn't know what it was. And he wondered how he was going to tell her that he was practically going with Derry Drake, wondered if he had to tell her, or if he could just wait and let her hear about it from somebody else.

But as they sat down to dinner, "What was Derry Drake doing parading around the sanctuary before the service started?" his mother demanded.

Ron answered stiffly. "She was arranging the flowers. She's very interested in flower-arrangement," he said.

"Is that what she calls it?" his mother said. "*Flower-arrangement*?"

The way she said it made Derry sound pretentious, but before Ron could think of a way to reply Uncle Ross had spoken. "Watch it, Wilma," he said. "I think somebody's got a sweetie."

"Ron?" his mother said, and her face grew red. "I should hope that Ron has better things to do with his time than go mooning around over some little *flower-arranger*."

"Derry and I are going to the ballgame this afternoon," Ron said. "Uncle Ross said I could borrow the truck."

"Really, Ross," his mother said.

But Uncle Ross returned her gaze calmly. "Most natural thing in the world, a boy taking out a girl. You'd better get used to it, Wilma," he said.

For a moment Ron thought that his mother was going to say something else, but then he could see her struggling to bring herself under control. Finally, "You'll have to excuse me, Ron," she said in her light voice. "Of course you want to take out girls. The more the merrier."

Ron relaxed then. His mother was usually pretty good about things. Once in a while she flew off the handle, but usually she could be persuaded to see things your way. And she had a nice feminine way of apologizing so that whatever the disagreement was, she let you come out of it feeling good.

All that summer, when Ron came to town from the farm, he went to see Derry first and then to see his mother. And often when he came home he was singing a song that he and Derry sang together.

> Honors flysis
> Income beesis
> Onches nobbis
> Innob keesis.

A half-witted girl had sung it in a show they had gone to together, and that song had been the key to the whole movie. You could sing it:

> On horse, flies is
> In comb, bees is
> On chest, knob is
> In knob, keys is.

Only it was more fun to sing it the other way.

The first time his mother heard him sing the song she asked him about it and when he explained it, she said, "It's something like *Hutsa Brolsin on the Rilla Ra*."

Hutsa Brolsin on the Rilla Ra was a song his mother sometimes sang. It seemed to Ron a silly song, something left over from years ago when his mother was young. "It's not like that at all," he said.

"I guess not," his mother said, but she looked hurt. It occurred to Ron that she was old now, and out of things, and he felt sorry for her.

His mother had apologized after the Sunday that Derry had arranged the flowers, taking all the blame for what had happened on herself and making it clear that she really liked Derry, that if she had been bad-natured it was because there was something else bothering her and she had got the two things mixed up. "I feel sorry for you men," she had said, and given her light little laugh. "Having to put up with poor creatures like us."

And Ron had had to smile. She could charm him, his mother could, but he saw no harm in that. Especially since she had made up her mind to charm Derry too.

"Now you be sure to bring Derry over for cocoa afterwards," she would say whenever she knew that he was taking Derry to the show, and sometimes Ron did that. He had never brought his friends home much. When he was a little kid he had learned that if he had fights, it was best not to let his mother know about them. She took his part too strongly, went to see the principal, or the other boy's mother. And she was almost as bad about his friendships. When boys came to the house she got out all his toys and lined them up, as if to show the boys what they would be missing if they didn't play with him. She baked little cakes and fussed over them and made everyone uncomfortable. But it was different with a girl. Girls liked to be fussed over. "I think you mother's just charming," Derry said, and his mother was. Derry and his mother got along like a house afire.

One night, when he and Derry had been to a musical, "I think that Ron looks just like Dick Haymes," Derry announced when they were back at the house.

Derry didn't think that, Ron knew. She was only trying to make him feel good.

But his mother took it one step further. "I think that Dick Haymes would be very flattered to hear that," she said. "I think Ron is *much* better looking than Dick Haymes. Don't you?"

And Derry had looked embarrassed, but a minute later she managed to turn the whole thing into a joke. "Now if he could just *sing* like Dick Haymes," she said.

When Derry knew they were coming to see his mother, she would twist her long hair into a bun at the back of her neck and borrow her mother's brown and white spectator pumps to wear. "They just look like your mother," she said when Ron asked her about it.

They didn't. His mother liked clothes that were feminine, not sporty. What they looked like was Derry's idea of the way she should be for his mother, the self that Derry thought was the right one to show. Derry had many selves, Ron was discovering; she changed her *self* the way other people change hats, taking one off and putting another on to see which was more becoming. She would be sedate, a lady, having cocoa with his mother. But then Ron would walk her home and she would either kiss him passionately or else fight with him. It seemed to Ron that whenever he and Derry weren't kissing, they were fighting, and he tried to keep those times as short as possible.

Finding a *place* to kiss was really not a problem, even when the summer holidays ended and he didn't have Uncle Ross's truck any more. The town was full of places you could kiss, dark places where there wasn't somebody going by every five minutes, and it was as if Ron had been filing away information about these places all his life, against the day of need. Most of their kissing, however, was done in Derry's backyard, on the dark side of the Drakes' back porch, because Derry's house was the last place they went every date. Ron would walk Derry home thinking that they weren't going to be doing anything that they couldn't do at her back door, and then, of course, they would do it.

By now Ron knew that Derry was not unaware of what went on when they kissed, that she felt it too. But whenever they were going a little further than they had gone before, she would slip into the same absent-mindedness. And, while Ron didn't really want things to go much further—he wanted to show Derry that he respected her—somehow things always went ahead, they never went back.

At the very first, theirs was an above-the-waist expression of affection. But then somehow Ron understood that anything that he did with his hands was all right. Derry didn't tell him that—they didn't talk about what they were doing, pretended they weren't doing it—but that was what it amounted to.

Ron was grateful. At first he thought that he wanted no more than to feel Derry's body, warm and trusting under his hands. Her body was like a continent and his hands were like two explorers. Here come Lewis and Clark, he thought. Make way for LaVerendrye. Only he really didn't want LaVerendrye getting into it. He had all he could handle now.

But he did, of course. He wanted more. He didn't want everything, but he did want more. When Derry let him touch her *there*, he wanted her to touch him *there*. That was all, he thought, just a touch.

But Derry turned out to be reticent about this. She would let his hand go wherever it wanted to go, do whatever it wanted to do, and sometimes she even showed him the way. But she would not touch him. It was as if what her body did didn't count, because *she* wasn't doing it, but her hand was different. There was a chastity, a purity, about her hand, and Ron respected this. He was almost sick sometimes, respecting it, but he asked for no more than more of the same sickness. Being with Derry could be an agony, and he felt that if he didn't find some way of increasing the agony he would die.

Sometimes he thought that they ought to give the whole thing up. But even if they could have, they couldn't have, because whenever they weren't touching each other, they were fighting. Sometimes Ron would see the telltale signs that Derry intended to pick a fight with him even when they were with his mother. Then he would have to get her away fast to someplace where they could kiss and all the rest of it. None of this, of course, was anything that his mother could know or even suspect.

When Ron thought of the future, he thought of it as a time when all the pain would be gone and all the joy left. There would never be any limit to their capacity to feel, he thought, but he and Derry would one day come past the place of hurting. He saw them as together always, and one of the things he wanted was for them to have mementoes of all the stages they had passed through along the way. He thought of Valentine's, when he would give Derry a card a foot high, the kind that comes in a box instead of an envelope, the kind that has a red satin heart and *To My Sweetheart* on it. When he learned that Derry's birthday was in the fall, that he wouldn't have to wait till Valentine's or even Christmas to give her a present, it seemed to him like a great opportunity.

As soon as he saw it, Ron knew that it was what he wanted. The box was shell-shaped, and it was covered with embossed silver paper and lined with pink satin. Inside was a dresser set: a comb, hairbrush, and handmirror, all with pink mother-of-pearl backs. A compact would have done, perfume in an atomizer bottle would have done, but this was perfect. This was a tribute to femininity.

It cost $17, more than he had ever thought of spending on a present for anybody, but he didn't hesitate. And he found it gave him a fine feeling to pull the money out of his pocket to pay for it. You weren't a boy any more when you bought a present like that, he thought; you were a man.

He hadn't intended to show the present to anyone before he gave it to Derry, and if he had remembered to buy wrapping paper for it, he wouldn't have. But when he asked his mother for some wrapping paper and she asked to see it, he couldn't think of any good reason to say no.

"Oh, my," his mother said when she saw it. "Oh, my."

Uncle Ross was there too. "That's some present," he said.

Ron was pleased. "You like it?" he asked.

"You want to watch it, giving presents like that to girls," Uncle Ross said. "They'll be throwing themselves at your head."

But Ron saw that his mother's face had taken on a doubtful look. "You don't think it's a little too much?" she said. And then, "You *know* I want Derry to have a nice present," she said. "You know how much I like Derry. It's just that I'm afraid it's not in good taste for a boy to give a girl a present as elaborate as this."

Ron felt his spirits fall. With a girl like Derry, with parents like hers, taste had to be considered, he felt.

"You do understand that I want Derry to have a nice present, don't you?" his mother said. "It's just that I couldn't bear to have you give her a present so . . . so . . ."

"So feminine?" Uncle Ross suggested.

"Yes," his mother said. "I mean no. It's just excessive is all. It's not in good taste."

"What do you think Ron should give her?" Uncle Ross asked.

"Oh, a jigsaw puzzle. A box of handkerchiefs."

Ron almost laughed out loud. A box of handkerchiefs! For a girl like Derry!

His mother saw her mistake. "Well, not a box of handkerchiefs then. But something nice. A bottle of toilet water, maybe. Something that is both nice and in good taste."

Afterwards Ron wondered if his mother might have persuaded him if Uncle Ross hadn't been there. "I don't see very much the matter with this," Uncle Ross said.

Suddenly his mother was angry. "You wouldn't," she said. "You men. You're all alike."

And for no reason at all there came to Ron's mind a parade of presents: the presents he had given to his mother over the years. Fancy bread-boards he had given her, and cushion covers to embroider, and a picture of a moose to hang on the wall. But never a piece of jewellery, never a bottle of perfume. Never a tribute to femininity.

He would make it up to her, he thought.

Then his mother, no longer angry, gave a light, girlish laugh. "Do as you like," she said. "But if Derry doesn't like it, don't say I didn't warn you."

"I'll chance it," Ron said.

As it turned out, Derry did like it. She accepted it with delight, and Ron came to think of the moment he had given it to her as a kind of sacrament they had celebrated together.

It was two weeks later. They were standing on the dark side of her parents' back porch and Derry had her hand inside his pants. It was the first time she had had it there, and it was only tentatively there, as if he were an electric fence that might come on at any minute, as if she might at any minute fly away. By an effort of will Ron kept himself from moving against her. But then, when her hand stayed where it was and then curved around him, he began to move, carefully at first, and then faster. It was unlike anything he had ever experienced before, to do this with someone else, in some ways not quite so good and in other ways a hundred times better.

Afterwards he felt as if there was nothing he could do to show Derry how he felt about her. He would have liked to get down and worship her. He felt that she had proven her love—realized for the first time that girls *did* prove their love when they did this. They *gave* themselves to you. Bodies that have touched are not like bodies that have not touched. When a thing like this had happened, it couldn't unhappen.

He would never do Derry any harm, he promised himself; he would never do anything that could possibly harm her. But even as he was promising, his mind was going to the thing that he would not do, that he didn't want to do, and the pictures formed in spite of him.

They wouldn't do *that*, he promised himself. But there was something else. He had been sure that if Derry would just touch him *there*, he wouldn't ask for another thing. But now he knew that there was just one more thing he wanted. He wanted to feel his maleness between Derry's legs. Not inside of her, never inside of her until they were older and had some way out of it. Just between her legs. He wanted to feel his *there* against her *there*.

His power had returned to him almost at once and he began to move, putting himself where he wanted to be, and from the way that Derry arranged her body he could tell that she wanted it too. But when he got to where he wanted

to be, he stopped. Because when he got there he was half
scared of being even this far. It seemed to him that they
had gone too far too fast. Maybe another time they would
want to go further and then he would have to fight with
himself, but for now, he was scared.

Derry began to move and soon he began to move too.
But it didn't feel like he wanted it to. Standing like this,
they couldn't move enough, and they couldn't move in the
right places. Ron's legs began to cramp from the way he
had to stand.

Then suddenly Derry moved away from him and Ron
saw that for no reason at all she was going to be mad at
him. "I wonder what your mother would say if she could
see us now," Derry said brutally. "Boy, would I like to see
the look on her face."

And Ron recognized that from this end of the evening, with the touching over, there was nothing he could do
to make Derry feel better. He cleaned himself up with his
handkerchief and went home.

He was gone for one weekend and when he came back it
was all over. There was absolutely nothing that could
have enabled him to predict the breakup.

He went to see Derry, and she came out on the back
porch for a minute, but she wouldn't go out with him.
"I've got something to tell you," she said.

She told him that her parents didn't think that she
should go out with just one boy, and she thought they were
right. It was one of the things she had said before, pretending reason, when they were fighting. But Ron knew that
while girls in other places might go out with more than one
boy at a time, girls here didn't. Here it was off with the old
love before you were on with the new. And Derry was his
girl.

Then Derry told him that she had gone out with Alf

Henderson.

Ron felt as if there was a space of time between the time when Derry told him and the time when he heard it, a time when he could feel its meaning travelling toward him. Derry out with Alf Henderson. He felt there were things that he could not bear to know.

At first he thought that Derry meant to keep on going out with him too, but then he discovered that she did not. What had happened was final, she said. "Some men can make a girl do whatever they want," she whispered. "I'm sorry, Ron."

Ron looked at her, knowing, but unable to comprehend. Just last week when they had been clinging to each other in an anguish of longing, Derry had moaned over and over, "I love you. I love you," and Ron knew that she had meant forever. Now it seemed that she was unable to remember what she had felt then, honestly unable to do it. It was past and she felt it no more. If Ron had reminded her of her feeling she would have denied it and believed that she spoke the truth.

What was a man supposed to do? When a girl liked him one day, couldn't keep her hands off him, and then wanted nothing to do with him the next, what was he supposed to do?

If there had been anything he could have done to get Derry back, Ron would have done it. But he saw that there was nothing. And Derry let him know that there was no question of him overlooking what had happened, made it clear that she would think less of him if he made light of it by accepting it.

There was nothing he could do. Getting mad wouldn't help, and neither would crying. He was powerless. All that Derry asked of him now was that he be on his way, get out of her life. Her voice, which had been sympathetic at the beginning, was already growing impatient, with hard edges in it. He felt that she wanted to laugh, that she wanted to say to him, "Run on home, little boy."

There were no words for the pain he felt as he walked home. He felt a need to be sick, to be in bed, with his mother bringing him things, or to be cut, broken, so that he could be bandaged. He did not tell himself that he should take it like a man. He wasn't sure that he could take it at all. When he got home he crawled into bed, not intending to stay there, but needing a place to hide. But once he was there it was as if his capacity for rising had left him forever. To stand upright, to walk on the earth, seemed like impossibilities.

He did not tell his mother about his breakup with Derry or that Derry was going out with someone else. Instead, three days later, his mother told him.

"Yeah," he said, confirming it. He was still in his bed, and he felt that he might never move again.

"I'm sorry," his mother said, and he could see the compassion on her face, and he realized that he had been needing to see it there.

His mother talked to him then, comforting him, but he heard only part of what she said. He heard her say that it appeared that Derry was not the girl they had thought her to be, that there were no two ways about it, Derry had treated him badly. He understood that while she had always liked Derry, she liked her less now. And Ron wondered if Derry deserved to be liked, the way she had treated him.

With the thought, the anger, he felt the tiniest wisp of energy run through his body. But he lacked the will even for anger.

And he felt that he shouldn't need his mother's sympathy as much as he did. He tried to tell his mother that he could handle it, but the words wouldn't come.

It wasn't that day but the next that his mother asked him if Derry had given him his presents back.

Ron, still lying on his bed, shook his head. He had given Derry only one present, the dresser set, and she still had it.

His mother widened her eyes. "I don't believe it," she said, meaning that she did. And then, "A girl is *supposed* to give a man his presents back when she stops going out with him."

Ron remembered having heard something of the kind. It wasn't a thing he would have thought of on his own, but he did remember hearing it. But the thought of the dresser set was almost more painful to him than the thought of Derry herself. He didn't want to think about it. "Let her keep it," he said. "I don't want it."

His mother sat down on a chair beside his bed and it was a moment before she spoke. "I understand how you feel," she said. "But Derry shouldn't be let get away with a thing like that. She ought to be shown."

Ron shook his head. "No," he said.

His mother gave her head a little shake, as if to say that Ron hadn't understood what she meant. "I don't want to tell you what to do," she said, "but Derry would respect you a lot more if you *didn't* let her get away with it. If you asked her for it back. It would be the manly thing to do."

Ron said nothing, but he was listening.

But when his mother spoke again it was as if she had changed her mind. "At your age nobody would think anything of it if you didn't do a thing," she said. "A man wouldn't put up with it, but nobody would think anything of it if you just walked away from the whole thing."

Ron saw then that asking for his present back was a thing he should do, that his mother would think less of him if he didn't do it. And it seemed to him that he would think less of himself.

"It isn't a thing anybody else can do for you," his mother said. "There are some things in this life that you've got to do for yourself."

That seemed to Ron very right and very true. You couldn't argue with it. And what was the tiny feeling of unwillingness that he had but a kind of cowardice? There were duties a man couldn't shirk no matter how much he might want to.

He walked to Derry's house not really thinking, just putting one foot in front of the other. But as he opened her front gate and started up the walk to her house, the Derry he pictured ahead of him at the door was the Derry he had always seen there, and he was in practice at loving Derry, not at showing her something. What if this was not the right thing to do? What if there was some flaw in his mother's thinking?

But he couldn't bear the thought of uncertainty. Start thinking this way and he would be back in bed again, unable to lift his head off the pillow. He had thought about it and made his decision and now he had come to the time to act upon it. He knocked at the door. Derry's eyes widened when she heard what he had to say, and he saw both hurt and disbelief in them. But this turned quickly to contempt, a contempt that seemed to be endless, and he understood that his mother's belief that Derry would respect him for this was not true, and that it never could have been true. It seemed to him that this was something that he had to do something about.

But the thought did not stay with him. Derry came back with the dresser set and, in despair and a last-minute attempt to undo what he had done, Ron said, "Look, keep it. It's yours. I want you to have it."

But Derry's look of contempt only deepened. "I wouldn't touch it with a ten-foot pole," she said.

Then Ron was back on the street, with a shell-shaped

box in his hand, and no place to go except home. He walked along remembering that he had something to do, but he couldn't remember what it was. He only knew that there was something still waiting to be done, and that whatever it was, it was still ahead of him, waiting for him to do it.

The Biggest Tent in the World
Shirley Black

"But it's the biggest tent in the world," I pleaded. I handed my Grandmother the newspaper. "I've just got to go."

"Julia you know I don't hold with revival meetings." My Grandmother looked at the big tent and the headline *Homar Grant World Renown Evangelist*.

"Barbara asked me. She's been to lots. She says they're really fun."

"Fun!" My Grandmother raised her eyebrows.

"Yes, fun. They do healing and everything."

"Well I wouldn't call that fun." My Grandmother folded the newspaper and placed Homar Grant face down on the table.

"Please."

"Oh, all right. But just this once." My Grandmother reached for her curling tongs. "Just remember you are not to go forward when they ask you."

"I won't." I sipped my tea and unfolded the newspaper so I could look at the big tent once more.

"And remember you've been saved."

"When?"

"On the first Good Friday and you tell anyone who asks you just that."

"Okay." My nostrils twitched at the smell of burning hair.

"And if you must use the public washrooms don't sit on the seat." Don't go forward, I've been saved, don't sit on the seat. I hoped I'd remember all these instructions.

Five o'clock found me waiting at Barbara's door. My collection ten cents in one pocket, a wad of toilet paper in the other, just in case the public facilities ran short, and a little brown bag of hard candies in my hand, sermon candy, we called it. Homar Grant might be long winded, my Grandmother had said, so she'd given me ten candies, five for each of us.

"I can hardly wait," I said to Barbara as we started out the gate.

"You'll like it. They're fun."

"Have you been often?"

"Lots of times with my girlfriend from the old neighbourhood."

"Will she be there?"

"She and her mother never miss a revival meeting. They're very religious."

The big tent had been erected on the Stampede Grounds. As we got closer, the smell of the rodeo barns surrounded us. The river was high and muddy looking. There were oodles of people around, all heading in the same direction we were. It was almost like Stampede week except the people passing Barbara and I called "God bless you" and "Praise the Lord."

"Will you go forward?" I asked Barbara.

"Of course, I always go forward. I've been saved six times."

"Well I won't. My Grandmother won't let me. Anyway I've been saved once and that's enough." We were almost there, almost in the shadow of the most colourful, prettiest, biggest tent in the whole wide world—*Homar Grant World Renown Evangelist* written on a banner that stretched right across its front. Both tent and banner flapped in the wind. People were still coming from all directions. Some on crutches, people in wheelchairs, blind people being led, even beds with wheels on them. Most were women but there were some older men and a few in uniform.

"Are you sure this is the revival meeting?" I questioned Barbara.

"Well, of course. Can't you read the banner?"

"It looks more like a hospital tent to me." We pushed inside and Barbara looked around eagerly, hoping to see Ellen-Sue and her mother.

"There they are." Barbara dragged me forward across the sawdust floor to a straight backless bench where an old-fashioned girl sat with her mother. Both of them looked very religious.

"This is Ellen-Sue," said Barbara, introducing me to a pale prim and proper girl with mousy coloured hair and a funny tam pulled down over her ears. Her skirt covered her knees. She wore cotton stockings and sturdy black oxfords.

What a drip, I thought, as I smiled and said hello.

"And this is her mother, Mrs. Jones." Ellen-Sue's mother put forth a damp hand and said how glad she was that Barbara had brought me. She was sure I'd enjoy it.

"What church do you go to, dear?" she asked.

"Anglican," I proudly replied.

"Oh my. Well it's better than being a Jew or a Catholic."

Two men and two women were standing on the platform singing:

> *There is a fountain filled with blood*
> *Drawn from Emmanual's veins*

Some of the people joined them. Their singing filled the tent as more and more people squeezed in. I was glad that I was sitting on the end of the bench; I didn't want any sick person sitting next to me. I was a little bit afraid of sick people.

A blind lady bumped me as she was being led down the aisle. "Sorry," she said, looking down with sightless eyes. A shiver went through me and I wished I hadn't come. Her friend led her to the bench right in front of us. She put her hand down beside her and murmured, "Empty." Then she turned to her friend and said, "There'll be a lot of empty seats when this war is over."

The tent was almost full. People were standing in the aisles. A young boy, a little bit older than Barbara and I, stood next to me, his hands on the back of his mother's wheelchair where she sat slumped, her chin resting on her chest. His father stood next to him. Both of them looked very sad.

Suddenly the quartet began to sing:

> *Jesus is standing in Pilate's hall*
> *Friendless, forsaken, betrayed by all.*

A short ruddy-faced man with red hair walked onto the stage.

"Is that him?" I asked Barbara.

"I think so."

"Oh." I was really disappointed. I thought he'd look like Roy Rogers. Instead he looked like Mr. Rice, our school principal.

"He's not much to look at."

"That doesn't count." Barbara turned back to Ellen-Sue.

Homar Grant's voice boomed out as he sang. Some of the people stood up and called out, "Praise the Lord." Everyone seemed so joyful, so happy to see him. I began to wonder what was the matter with me.

Finally the singing stopped and Homar Grant called out, "There's Jesus, friendless, forsaken, betrayed by all.

That brothers and sisters is why you're here tonight. You're here to give your lives to Jesus. Yesiree, you're here to give your lives to Jesus."

"Amen," said the people. "Praise the Lord," they cried out.

"You ask me, how do I give my life to Jesus? I'll tell you how. You forsake your worldly ways—dancing, drinking, moviehouses, all things of the devil. You just put them all behind you and you come forth. Come forth, you hear."

Barbara poked me in the ribs and asked for a candy. My bag rattled but no one seemed to notice. The boy beside me put his hands under his mother's chin and held her head up so she could see the stage. He was the best looking boy I'd ever seen and I wished that I could know him.

"Once I was a sinner too," yelled Homar Grant. "And then one day I was working in my field and the Lord called me—'Homar Grant, follow me'—and I climbed off my tractor and I've been preaching the Lord's word ever since. Just like that I was called and it can happen to you, oh yes, and you and you." Homar Grant pointed at first one person then another. "But you have to give up your worldly ways." Here Homar Grant's voice became a whisper.

"Ellen-Sue's never been to a movie," said Barbara, leaning towards me.

"Never?"

"No, they're very religious."

"Can we still go?" After all we were following a serial at the Saturday afternoon matinee.

"I'll have to think about it." Barbara looked very righteous.

"Yesiree," said Homar Grant. "Whosoever is a friend of the world is an enemy of God. The devil lies in wait for you and you and you."

"He's pointing right at me," I said to Barbara.

"Oh he is not," she replied.

The boy next to me took his hands gently away from his mother's chin. Her head fell against her chest again. She looked so uncomfortable slumped down like that, but I just knew how much they loved her and I sure hoped that she'd be healed.

"Pray, brothers and sisters, pray that you might be saved. Read your bibles, brothers and sisters, for the grass dies, the flowers wither but the word of the Lord endures forever."

"How much longer do you think it will be?" I offered Barbara a candy. Our supply was dwindling.

"How would I know?" she said.

"And let me leave you with one last word, brothers and sisters; any of you that convert a sinner from the error of his ways shall save a soul, you hear. Now we'll be here all week so you have time to bring your friends. Wouldn't that be something if you could save a sinner? Yesiree, that sure would be something."

Suddenly it seemed as if everyone in the tent was standing up. Many had their hands above their heads. "Praise the Lord!" "Amen!" "Bless you, Jesus!" It echoed from all sides and the big tent swayed back and forth with the wind.

Homar Grant stepped forward. He asked us all to pray for forgiveness. The tent was getting dark. I wasn't supposed to be out after dark.

"My Grandmother's sure going to be mad if this goes on much longer," I said to Barbara.

"Well, she shouldn't be. It's a revival meeting."

Finally, Homar Grant looked up from his silent prayer and said it was time for the sinners to come forward and give their lives to Jesus.

"Unless a man be born again, he shall not enter the kingdom of heaven and I beseech you to declare yourselves unto the Lord." Homar Grant stared out at first one side of the tent, then the other.

Quietly the quartet began to sing:

Softly and tenderly Jesus is calling.

People began to get up off the hard benches and slowly, very slowly, start up the aisle.

"Are you going?" I asked Barbara.

"I think so." She didn't look too eager.

Mrs. Jones got up and pulled Ellen-Sue up with her, then stopped in front of Barbara.

"Come along," she said. Barbara started out of her seat.

"Julia, come along, dear."

"No thanks, Mrs. Jones."

"But you really should be saved. Wouldn't you like to give your life to Jesus?"

"Yes. But I've already been saved thanks, Mrs. Jones."

"When was that, dear?"

"Friday. A Friday long ago."

"Really? Well you can't be saved too many times." She grabbed me by the upper arm as though to pull me up.

"My Grandmother said I can't go forward," I blurted it out. She released my arm, shaking her head and muttering something about Anglicans under her breath.

"Sissy," said Barbara as the three of them started up the aisle.

Homar Grant looked taller as he stared over the heads of the kneeling sinners. His eyes looked bright. His mouth was set in a hard line.

"Once more I ask you to come forward, brothers and

sisters. Not for my sake but for your own. Come forth and witness for Jesus. Let's show the devil who's boss," he said.

A few more people got up and started down the aisle. The blond boy and his father stood silently beside me. I wished that I could talk to them or even stand beside them. Barbara's fair head was just a speck. Mrs. Jones and Ellen-Sue were hidden by the crowd.

Homar Grant shook his head sadly as he looked at the few of us left sitting. Then, suddenly, he walked around the kneeling sinners and came straight down the centre aisle.

"I can't help you if you won't help yourselves," he said, pausing at the bench four rows ahead of me where five or six people were still sitting.

"We're just onlookers," said a man in uniform.

"Onlookers!" roared Homar Grant. "Will you just be onlookers on that final judgement day?" His face was red. His eyes looked angry as they darted back and forth across the tent.

"And what's your excuse young lady?" His eyes bored right into me. I just looked the other way hoping he'd think I was deaf.

"Do you not have an answer?" He moved along the bench until he was directly in front of me.

"No," I replied, making crosses in the sawdust with the tip of my shoe. I was afraid to look at him. In fact I was just plain afraid of him. I wanted to cry.

"Well, you should. You had just better get ready to answer to the Lord." He continued down the aisle, stopping briefly beside the lady in the wheelchair, patting her hand gently.

Several more people followed him to the front. I kept hearing my Grandmother's voice—*don't go forward*—then I'd think of Homar Grant—*you had just better get ready to answer.* I didn't know what to do so I just sat there, listening, as the wind howled around that great big tent.

After what seemed like an hour, people began to trickle back.

"We prayed for you," said Ellen-Sue as I put my knees out to let them pass.

"Thanks a lot," I replied turning to Barbara.

"How was it?"

"Same as ever." She shrugged nonchalantly.

"Homar Grant came down here."

"Did he save you?"

"No, he just bawled me out." I sniffed back a tear.

"See, you should have come," said dull old Ellen-Sue, picking away at the folds in her skirt.

Homar Grant raised his hand for quiet.

"And Jesus said, take up your bed and walk," he called out. "Let's just see how much faith we have here, yesiree, let's just see how many of you go home healed."

"What do they do with the crutches?" I asked Barbara.

"I don't know. I've never seen anyone throw them away."

"Sometimes they put them on church pillars," I told her.

"Who said that?" asked Ellen-Sue.

"I saw a picture. It was a Catholic Church. Yes, I'm pretty sure it was a Catholic Church." I hoped Mrs. Jones could hear me.

The blond boy turned his head to look at me. I kept trying to remember the name of the Catholic Church just in case Homar Grant didn't cure his mother.

"Now any of you wishing to take part in the healing, just step forward," said Homar Grant.

The blind lady and her companion stepped out into the aisle. People with canes and crutches hobbled forward. Many of the people looked as healthy as me but they joined the group. The blond boy began to push his mother slowly forward. His father walked by her side, his hand on the arm of the wheelchair.

A man stepped in front of Homar Grant. He could walk and talk, he looked fine to me.

"What is your affliction, brother?" asked Homar Grant.

"Pardon?" asked the man.

"What's troubling you?" Homar Grant raised his voice.

"I'm deaf," replied the man.

Homar Grant put his hands on the man's ears and asked the Lord to give him back his hearing. The man stood very still, his eyes shut. Finally Homar Grant took his hands away and turned the man towards the people. Stepping behind him, he yelled "Can you hear me?"

"Yes, I can!" yelled the man.

Homar Grant stepped farther back. "Can you still hear me?"

"I can, I can! Praise the Lord!" shouted the man. He shook Homar Grant's hand then ran down the aisle.

"You should have brought your mother, she's deaf," I said to Barbara.

"She wouldn't come in a million years."

"Well I'm sure going to tell my Grandmother about this." We looked eagerly to the front of the tent waiting for the next miracle.

Our blind lady was standing in front of Homar Grant. He placed his hands on her eyes and prayed—but nothing happened.

"Can you see me?" he asked.

"No, I can't." Her friend led her back to her seat. She

didn't look really sad, just resigned. Homar Grant's hair was falling on his forehead. He slowly removed his suit jacket.

The next lady suffered from headaches. She was healed instantly.

"You have headaches," said Barbara.

"Sometimes." It was true. I did have headaches sometimes. My Grandmother said I suffered from bilious attacks.

"You should go up."

"I haven't got one now. How would we know if they were cured when I haven't got one now?"

"Well if you had enough faith." She turned to whisper to Ellen-Sue.

Homar Grant took out a white handkerchief and wiped his wet forehead. His eyes surveyed the sick people still waiting. He looked tired, small and sad. The blond boy pushed his mother to the front. His father followed behind.

"Keep your fingers crossed," I said to Barbara.

"I will," she replied.

The blond boy and his father towered over Homar Grant as he placed his hands on the mother's head and prayed for her healing.

"Let there be a miracle here tonight, Lord," he said. "Let these people have faith. Hear us, Lord, please hear us."

"Homar Grant's sure trying."

"She's pretty sick," said Barbara.

The lady still sat with her chin against her chest. There wasn't a flicker of movement in her entire body.

"We beseech you, Lord," prayed Homar Grant. Still the woman sat slumped in her wheelchair. Finally Homar Grant knelt in front of her and gently, oh so gently, lifted her chin so he could look in her eyes.

"May the Lord grant you peace," he said. The boy took hold of the arms of her wheelchair and pushed his mother quickly down the aisle. The knuckles of his hands were white. He was biting his lower lip. Tears rolled down his father's face as they walked through the flap of the tent. That's that, I thought, I'll never see them again.

Homar Grant looked at all of us. He said he was very tired. Would the people mind coming back another night.

"We've seen a lot of miracles here tonight," he said. "A lot of you have been saved, yesiree, a lot of you have seen the light. I hope you'll all come back every night for the next week. Come back and bring your friends."

Barbara and I said goodbye to the others. We walked out into the cold windy night. Our short skirts whipped against our bare legs and we clutched our sweaters close to our bodies.

"Wasn't that fun?" said Barbara.

"No, and I don't ever want to come again." I was anxious to get home. We followed a more subdued crowd out past the barns.

Then I saw the blond boy picking up an empty wheelchair and placing it in the back of a station wagon. He slammed the door and was heading around to the passenger side when he saw us. He looked and looked again, then got into the car and they drove away. Barbara and I stood watching until the tail lights disappeared.

Homestead Crescent
Ruth Krahn

My mother's house is at the edge of town and the view
from her kitchen windows is of long pale fields and
scrubby trees and grey light-filled sky. Late in the day
when I go outside to get dill from the garden the air smells
of smoke, a long snake thread of it drifting over from the
town dump: bags of garbage soggy with coffee grounds
and orange peel, the edge of an old striped mattress
smouldering away on this cool silent day. I have come
home for the funeral of my Great-Aunt Anna, a relative I
hardly knew.

  I make stew for supper. When my mother gets home
from her job at Lakeview Home for the Aged the house
smells of herbs and spices. She walks into this haven of
warmth and domesticity, the bubbling stew and the six
o'clock news and a daughter setting the table. After
supper we stack the dishes in the dishwasher, go for a brisk
walk, the two of us burning off calories on the dirt road
outskirts of town. We head in the direction of our old farm
but it is too many miles away and we turn back somewhere
around the cemetery. When we get back to the house she
suggests we play table games, Scrabble or Sorry or
Memory. We sit at the dining-room table where a dim
chandelier shines down on our heads, our reflections small
and bleak in the black front window where the drapes have
been tied back. Around ten, her friend Liz drops in for coffee before going on her night shift at the hospital. The two
of them talk and laugh like two schoolgirls and at five to

eleven Liz hurries out to her ancient Buick with no muffler and my mother locks all the doors and starts putting out lights.

And then I feel what I often felt as a child on Sunday evenings at home—that sad sharp loneliness that came from having spent the day in limbo, torn between the thrill of no school, no having to go anywhere or do anything, and the waiting, the waiting all day long for something— anything—to happen, anything to break the routine of no routine. My father inexplicably pulling on good shoes after his nap on the sofa or the sound of a car miraculously gearing down on the mile road, a neighbouring farmer navigating the ruts to the field in his pick-up, the ringing telephone—anything held hope in a day as calm and monotonous as a cow swatting flies. All that time floating by, all those hymns from religious radio programs wafting through the house. Toward evening, straight from Pasadena, California, came the fretful grating voice of Doctor Michaelson: "Greetings my dear friends in the name of the Lord Jesus Christ . . . " and when he was done, the sweet breathy voices of the background choir singing, "He Leadeth Me." As if this wasn't enough, a mass choir—hundreds of voices—signed off at midnight with "Abide With Me", a tune that pulled you right up into the heavens with its power. I would remember that my father had had trouble climbing the steps to his choir conductor stand that morning in church, that he had collapsed one day not long ago on the narrow path between the house and the barn, "blacked out" my mother said. I would think of the girl on my schoolbus who, for a whole year, was dying of cancer.

There are no radio hymns floating through my mother's house now. She has her T.V. on most of the time, watches reruns of *Laugh In* and *M.A.S.H.*, *Three's Company*, *Barney Miller*. Sometimes, before she goes to bed, she does exercises. I hear the dull thump-thump, thump-thump of the trampolene, the small round rubber bouncer, on which she leaps in the next room.

It gets very stormy at night; wind and rain drive against the side of the house. I wake up because a door is slamming open and shut. The back deck is dry because of the new green plastic roof my mother has had put on; the rain bangs tinnily on this roof, a hard unpleasant sound. Like a flicker of distant lightning, a short uneven memory of my parents appears (this would be back on the farm) the two of them running around the yard, closing car windows, garage doors, the day turned suddenly dark and ominous. My mother grabbing sheets off the line, yard debris dancing along the ground until it hits the fence. The flash of lightning, the heavy rolling thunder, and then the rain coming down in waves. All of us, Willy, Jen and I, our mother, holding pillows to the windows on the west side of the house, the ground white in a matter of minutes from the hail beating down. And, in all of this, our father somewhere—outside?—angry, yelling, shaking his fist in despair. Don't be such a fool, woman, where's your head? Why was he yelling at her? But I'm half asleep now, this must be something I'm dreaming, or imagining.

"Do you remember the year we got hailed out?" I ask my mother at breakfast. The air is sharp this morning and smells of wet earth. We have opened the patio doors to let in the fresh air.

"Do I remember," she says, reaching for some toast. "That year was a nightmare. Oh I shouldn't have bread, should I. I've been doing so good."

"Did you have hail insurance?"

"Oh we never had hail insurance, we couldn't afford it! Who could afford hail insurance those days? It was all we could do to keep you kids fed and clothed. Hand me that paring knive, will you? I'm allowed as much fruit as I want. Barb gained two pounds last week and that was with cutting down on fruit. I lost two eating apples all day long. It's a scientifically worked out diet, you know. You are best off following it exactly the way it's written down."

She's wiping her hands at the sink, leaning toward the window, trying to see who's driving by.

"I remember that time we got hailed out," I say. "How old would I have been?"

"You? Oh I'd have to think. We were married twelve years, you'd have been about grade four, old enough to remember. Darn it, I promised Barb I'd give her a call this morning. What time is it? Do you want to go uptown with me, go have coffee with Barb and the girls over at The Bright Spot before I go to work? I only start at eleven this week."

"The Bright Spot?"

"Yeah, it's that new place over near the IGA. Terrific pastries, not that I can have any. We might as well, tomorrow's out with the funeral and all."

But The Bright Spot is full, a few men from Lakeview Home for the Aged at one table, a few women in brown uniforms at another, and the rest occupied by farmers with their farm caps on, all drinking coffee, gossiping and joking—Jake had a flat goin' out to Miller's. Did you see that car Bill's wife is driving now?—turning red baleful faces in our direction when we come in. "Oh, Bert Lowe," says my mother under her breath. She turns around and goes out the door. "To heck with them," she says outside. "I see enough of those old farts at work without having to drink coffee with them too." But where else is there? We walk down the street, past the hardware store and the post office, the Shopper's Drug Mart and the Bank of

Montreal. We end up at Lakeview Home half an hour before my mother starts work, sitting in the staff room with the other 'girls', whose ages range from late forties to early sixties. "Sarah!" they call happily when they see my mother. "You're early!"

"Wait 'til you hear what old Ida's been up to this morning!"

"Did you tell Mrs. Pankratz she should get a perm today, Sarah? She's been pestering the girls doing rooms all morning!"

Poor old Anna, they say. Isn't it a shock? Such a nice woman, such a good kind person. They'll miss her around here. I just did her hair Monday, says Edith. The family was in this morning, says Barb. I've seen that one girl on TV, I think, looks just like her father. Poor old Jacob, such a nice man. He won't last long without her, that's for sure. How did you do yesterday? they ask my mother, meaning her diet.

Most of them are on the same diet but today—what the heck—they all have seconds of crumb cake, hot out of the oven.

"Yeah," sighs one of the older women. "I wonder sometimes if it's worth it working here. Every time you turn around it's someone else."

Barb's got her grandchildren coming for the weekend. Elaine had to work. Marcie's bringing her kids too, says someone else. God, was Steve furious last night, says one of the cooks. He thinks I'm passed out in the bar if I'm not home by eight. That's men for you, says Edith. How's Anna Peter's brother taking all this? Poor man, he's going to go any day now too. Maybe they should move him into the south wing, so it would be easier to keep an eye on him.

They look reflectively out the tall cathedral window, watch Mr. Dyck, the caretaker, drive by on the lawn tractor. Muriel, the head cook, tells a story about a couple she knew who were on a winter vacation somewhere— Hawaii, Acapulco, Palm Beach, one of those—and the husband just up and died one day when they were walking along the beach and the wife had to cross the continent in the middle of the night with her dead husband beneath her in the cargo hatch.

I make a green salad and boil eggs for supper. My mother tells me a story about old Aunt Anna, how the day after her wedding in a small village in Russia, soldiers came to the bridal couple's new home and wanted Anna to hand over her gold wedding ring. And how Uncle Jacob, small and meek, picked up a brick and told them to get out and they did.

I want my mother to elaborate on this story, and others like it; I want her to embroider the facts—just a little—give me some idea of how things once were, what certain people were like, how they behaved toward one another. Some colourful images, some clues, anything. But she only told that story to demonstrate Uncle Jacob's tough streak, hidden under all that gentleness. "The kids are the same," she says. "Those girls. Your Dad couldn't get them to sing for him in the choir for anything. Too stubborn. They've all got minds of their own in that family." And now she wants to talk about The Home instead, to tell details of tricks they played today or yesterday or last week on unsuspecting 'guests' and on each other too, of course. What they had for dinner, who complained. So and so's migraines. Mrs. Baker's terrible relatives waiting for her to die so they can back up to her door with their truck.

"Jeez, I could have killed myself laughing at Barb today," she says, crunching into some celery. "Laugh?"

Like a child I drag her back. "Remember that story

about someone having to hide their son on the boat when they came over to Canada? Because he had lice or something?"

"Oh well, that was your father," she says.

"What happened?" I ask. I know it was my father.

"What happened. Well nothing happened. He had lice is all. They wrapped his head in a kerchief hoping nobody would notice and it worked. Do you want some more salad?"

"Wasn't there something about him almost having to stay behind?"

"Oh, that," she says. "Yeah. You mean where they were in England waiting to get on the boat. If they would have found out about the lice he would have had to stay behind."

"What? And the parents would have left without him?"

"What choice did they have?"

"They wouldn't have gone without him."

She doesn't answer. *Why talk about that*, I can feel her thinking. Soon she is in the middle of a complicated account of Mrs. Ida Parker's recent attempt to switch places at the dining-room table with Mrs. Lana Baker, just so she, Ida Parker, wouldn't have to sit next to that piggish old Bert Lowe any more.

"Crumb was I mad," she says. "They'll do anything to get their way, you wouldn't believe the conniving that goes on. Not that I blame Ida. That Bert Lowe has terrible manners, slurping his food and burping and complaining. We finally gave in and moved her to a table with Mrs. Stewart. Well, Bert Lowe walks up to this table at supper. I was so pissed off, excuse my language. He knocks over a glass, he crashes into a chair . . . "

The mother whom we pitied, the silent mistreated farm wife; fat, meek, self-conscious in her dark flowered print dress, trundling up to the choir loft every Sunday because he told her to. Humiliated by her weight, singing alto in the second row centre. We saw her face up there, her held-in shame, how she avoided looking anywhere, at him making a spectacle of himself. He was dancing on the stand, bug-eyed, whispering loudly. "Come on! Show some gumption! All of you! What are you, a bunch of ninety-year-olds?" And on the way home in the car. "What's wrong now?" he'd say, laughing. "Wasn't I respectable enough for you?" But she wouldn't answer. And in the barn at night, furious with complacent cows, "Move! Move your arse, you rotten bitch!"

"Stop it!" she'd say finally, spitting her words, almost whispering. "Don't you care what your own children think?" Ha! He'd laugh, "Don't show your ignorance, mamie." "Mamie," he'd say again, caressingly, watching her face. "You can sing a hymn before dinner," she said, "curse like a heathen before the sun goes down." He had an old farm cap with flaps that he pulled comically over his ears, so he couldn't hear her. He whistled and he sang. Move your big arse, Betty. Sang some more. After supper he said, "Well I guess we better go to evening service." She stared at him as if he were crazy. Then she hurried to get ready, slapping us around, trying to get us into decent clothes again. Sometimes he changed his mind when he saw her all ready—her hair neatly combed, nylons, high heeled shoes, a brooch on her silky ample flowered breast.

But why talk about that, my mother would say. This evening we eat in the family room. My mother carries her supper in on a tray so she won't miss *M.A.S.H.*.

11:15 p.m., Air Canada. I drive to the airport to get Jenny. We haven't seen each other for six months. Her coming home now is my idea, something we arranged by phone (the funeral is only an excuse).

"So she's not sitting around the house moping or feeling sorry for herself?"

"Not quite, Jen. She's having the time of her life."

"Well that's fair enough, isn't it?"

"Yes," I agree heartily.

This first evening the hours stretch into morning, the first streaks of light in the sky when we go to bed. This is what we did when he died, years ago. (Years ago . . . so it has become something that happened long ago.) We would sit up night after night, a time of year when it was dark for only a few hours. The sight of a pale streaked sky at this early hour reminds me of that time.

Coming home and expecting him in one of the usual places, in that certain chair in one corner of the living room near the green fern. Always surprised that he wasn't in the room with all the other people who were there, who had come to offer their condolences, silent embarrassed people doing their best. I would hear him talking in the room; I knew he was in there. I went into rooms where he could have been and put on all the lights so that no dark hiding places existed.

The first night I was afraid to go downstairs to the room where the piano was kept.

In the morning Jen and I drive our mother to work. She is wearing a white uniform of which she is proud, white shoes, white stockings. After we drop her off, Jen says, "Did you see her underwear? She's wearing bikinis now. You could see the flowers right through the uniform! Remember the kind she used to wear, those great long bloomer types?"

We drive in the country down the old familiar roads, turning automatically down the one that leads eventually to the farm where we grew up. There are shiny silos in the yard now, a new sprawling bungalow.

"Remember when we came out here last summer? With Mom?"

Jen doesn't remember. "Last summer?"

"Yeah, last summer. We even packed a lunch to take along? No?"

I remember. It was Jen who kept getting excited about all the old landmarks, the old wreck of a barn, the chicken coop, the outhouse. "Oh look!" she wailed. "The path to the creek!" as if it was her favourite thing, our mother standing to one side and waiting for us to be done with our foolishness. She was cold, bored. She was wearing a flimsy summer jacket and the wind was making her skirt flap around. She did not want to be here; she thought the new owners would return at any moment and find us trespassing.

"Let's go."

There is a lovely sky today, the thin washed blue of it behind high wispy clouds. We turn, as we knew we would, down the road leading past the cemetery. The front of this cemetery is pleasant, with large deep green spruce trees as a border and pools of shallow reflecting water everywhere; at the back of the cemetery they have taken down the fence and extended the graves into a farmer's field. Here there is quite a lot of dry stubble, deep hard ruts at the edge of the field. In summer the sun beats relentlessly on this patch of land, no trees or bushes to break the flat monotony of it. Here, at the back, is where my father is buried.

The last time I saw him was three months before he died. He and my mother took their first plane ride ever, crossed the country and landed in the small eastern city where I lived that year. Crossing the tarmac they looked small and nondescript. I felt a rush of protectiveness toward them. My father was having trouble breathing. He tried to go off by himself. He was going to get the luggage, he said. He did not want us to witness his struggle for air.

Sometimes now I imagine what it must be like to be short of breath, how it would feel, what you'd wait for. Could you forget about trying to breathe? Or maybe that's a sentimental question. He had lost his gumption.

We drive over to the old Esso station on the highway to get gas and on a whim decide to go into the coffee shop. We sit down in one of the big faded vinyl booths near the front window, order coffee and laugh, thinking of ourselves sitting here years ago. We watch people drive up for gas, try to figure out who they are. It's quiet in here, not much business on a weekday morning; they've got a radio going in the back, in the kitchen, or maybe the music's coming from the garage. Voices from the kitchen. An old coke sign. My father could walk in through the front door. I wouldn't even have to turn around to look. The screen door would give that flat snapping sound and he'd be over at the cash register paying for gas. Then he'd make a joke with the girl behind the counter. He'd have to do that.

On that last visit he wanted to know if I needed money.

"No," I said, pretending surprise. "Why would I need money? I've got a good job, remember? I was telling you last night."

He cleared his throat and said, "Well, we've sold the farm now . .

He wanted to get going on the long story of how they finally had enough to live on and could now afford to help out their kids. "Why save it all up for the future?" His eyes were preoccupied, afraid. "Later on you won't need it." He waited for me to respond. I think he wanted me to acknowledge what he knew was happening to him, but I couldn't do it.

"I don't need any help," I insisted in a light voice. I was stacking the dishes, or putting them away in a cupboard, doing anything to avoid a locked-eye encounter

with him, in which he would tell me he didn't expect to
live much longer, maybe a few more months, until spring?
Another summer?

"But here I go again, right?"

"No," says Jen thoughtfully. "You probably needed to
get it out of your system."

So I don't say any more. The woman who brings us
our bill has had one breast removed, the only thing I know
about her, the kind of information that does you no good.

After supper Jen and I go over to the church to prac-
tise the song we have been asked to sing by the family. It's
wonderfully lit up inside, a warm orange glow from the
sunset. We wander around like children; we go behind the
pulpit and look down on where the congregation will be.
We sit in the choir loft and end up talking until it is nearly
dark. Neither of us can remember much about Aunt Anna.
She was my father's cousin; she was someone who raised
children. We don't know the children well. They are all
much older than we are. None of them stayed around here.

If you drove by the cemetery now, at night, you
would see the red glow somewhere near the back, in the
new part. The red coals, used for drawing frost from the
ground, glowing softly in the dark.

Aunt Anna had pitch black hair until she turned
sixty-five. She leaves to mourn four daughters and her husband, sad old Uncle Jacob.

There's a note stuck on the fridge door when we get
back. "Back around ten. Went over to Liz' for coffee." At
midnight we realize she's not home yet. We start worrying
when we remember Liz goes to work at eleven.

"Liz Messier? Tessier? Try that."

Oh she's there all right. I can hear the party going on
in the background. They're playing Kenny Rogers on the

record player . . . *Four hungry children and a crop in the field . . . You picked a fine time . . .*

"I'm leaving this minute," she says, like a contrite child. "I didn't realize it was so late. Liz isn't working tonight."

When she gets home her eyes are merry, she's had something to drink. She flings herself on the couch, smiling, sits up defensively when she realizes we are both watching her. "That Liz is a scream," she says. "We're doing a play for Talent Night and she's the main character. Laugh?!" And she launches into an explanation of the play.

Jen pages slowly through a photograph album. "Who's this, Mom? This guy with the moustache?"

She leans over, squinting. "Oh, him," she says without interest. "That's one of that Peters family, I can never tell them apart. He was a friend of your father's. Do either of you want anything to eat? I can still have a fruit tonight."

She comes back from the kitchen with her orange, wraps an afghan around her shoulders and settles back to watch Merv Griffin.

The sky is grey on the day of the funeral. Jen and I drive over to the church around noon to go through our song one more time. Jen's voice cracks accidentally on a high note and instantly we lapse into our long ago imitation of familiar voices. She does an aunt notorious for her croaky swooping soprano; I join in as our mother, the rich slightly forced contralto. We hold the last note for as long as possible; Jen ends with a flourish of rolled chords on the piano. We have barely settled down when a door slams and two of the Peters girls walk in, carrying flowers. Rebecca. Mary. They are cheerful, healthy, rosy cheeked. Grey haired. They lead the conversation, their prerogative on this occasion, and it's about weather, what Jenny and I are up to these days, the flowers someone has placed on the piano; but nothing about themselves or their mother whom they loved. There's still an hour to go before the funeral so we go home, leaving them to be alone.

In the house, my mother is lying down. She is in her bedroom and has the drapes pulled, is lying flat on her back in her black dress and Sunday shoes. We approach her cautiously on either side of the bed. She sits up quickly, says, "Is it time?"

People's clothes smell damp. Everyone is very sober, nodding, checking to see who's here, who they recognize, trying not to look like they're doing that. Bev Dyck's playing Bach on the piano, very unusual; it must have been requested by the family. Around here it's usually the soft tremulous vibrato of the organ. "Safe in the Arms of Jesus" or "In the Sweet By and By." Despite the greyness of the day, the church is filled with a cool bright light, like looking at a sea shell. The piano melody seems to shift and go up, right up to the ceiling; the melody is a high thin thread.

So why do I hear my mother's alto voice? There it is, there she is, in the second row of the ladies' choir, up in the choir loft. Humming her rich choir alto not quite on key along to the piano prelude. The way she does in restaurants waiting for her meal to arrive, in a grocery store line-up, humming along, unaware of what she is doing. Jen and I exchange looks, a dangerous thing to do in this stifled atmosphere.

But a little later she seems to have stopped, maybe because the music has changed into something more subdued or because the grieving family has just walked in. They have come in like soldiers—briskly, businesslike, no tears. A few of the daughters are smiling cheerily.

And there's old Great-Uncle Jacob, the new widower. I had forgotten about him. A small older man, small and sad, like a child would be sad, without considering his effect on anyone. His suit looks rumpled, as though he has already joined the ranks of all those old sad neglected men who don't know how to look after themselves, whose Sunday suits bear heavy dark grease stains, smell of damp, or have ripped out underarms.

There's the woman whose husband went across the field one day carrying his shotgun in plain view of everyone, went into the old grey barn where his kids played all summer long, where long grey slats of roof were missing, revealing white sky, and shot himself. The man sitting beside me had a daughter who was killed in a car accident this past year. He picks with his hands at the cuffs of his sleeves. I expect him to sigh deeply, or wipe gruffly at his face, something, but he looks only bored, as though he is here out of duty and has no thoughts to fall back on.

My sister is looking at me and I realize we're supposed to sing, stand in front of the congregation, present them with our calm familiar version of a comforting hymn. It's easy to do, accompanied by the pouring rain outside, the hum on the roof. And something else. She wouldn't. I can't turn around to look. Is she singing along with us or is it an acoustic trick? Maybe I am finally sounding like her when I sing, a further nightmare, every daughter's in some form or another.

The whole congregation is singing now, standing, filling this place with sound. My father, sweat on his forehead, cajoling, pleading with them to "Sing! Sing!" Reluctant farmers, prim wives, ashamed daughters, all of them singing resentfully, hating him.

My mother says there were times when he didn't want to lead the congregational singing anymore. I never knew that. His dizzy spells. He was afraid he would lose his balance, topple to the floor, an ignominious heap in front of everyone. This is not an aspect of him that I remember. I thought he was immune to personal embarrassment or why the spectacle he made of himself at other times? I asked her that this morning but she kept that indifferent expression on her face, that look that said she would not be drawn into further conversation about him. Then the phone rang and it was Liz, releasing her. The look on her face was that of a surly teenager's confronted by parents wanting answers.

We shuffle slowly out of the church, past the open coffin, one last look at old Aunt Anna made up with powder and lipstick to look the way she never looked in life.

This was the moment, the building in which, five years earlier, my mother cried out like an animal in pain. For three days she had been calm, doing everything she had to do: phoning across the country to her children, making arrangements and dealing with people, even mouthing the words to the hymns during the service. But now she called out to him as if he heard her; she tried to grab him, to make him understand her need for him, her love. He had never been indifferent. Pale men in black, used to these outbursts, took her firmly by the shoulders and led her away.

Outside, it is still raining lightly but the air smells fresh and clean. People are relieved to be out here, ties are being loosened, umbrellas opened. Well, hello, hello! Haven't seen you for years! It's all over, only the family left with the dead person behind closed doors.

My mother gives me the car keys, motions for Jen to get in the front with me, slumps down in the back seat. "There's no point in us going to the cemetery," she says. We work our way along in the procession until we see the Homestead Crescent sign.

After supper we play Hearts. My mother is competitive when she plays, gives all her attention to the game, doesn't like it if Jen or I are slow about taking a turn. She wins most of the games. Around ten, Liz phones and says she can't make it tonight, she has unexpected company. "It's probably Melvin," says my mother knowingly. "I'll bet you anything it's Melvin. I'll get it out of her tomorrow."

It's our last night so Jen and I stay up until four in the morning. Our mother shuffles out of her bedroom when she hears us in the hallway, a wild-looking middle-aged figure, half asleep, bewildered.

"Is it time?" she says.

"What do you mean?" says Jen.

"I thought I heard something. Did he say it was all right?"

"Who?"

"Well, your father. I thought if I didn't say anything he'd let you go." Her hair stands straight out from her head on one side; on the other side it's pressed flat. "I must have been dreaming," she says finally. "What a dream. You were in it, both of you."

"What?" I ask reluctantly.

"Oh it's not worth repeating," she says, puzzled. "On top of everything else the two of you were taking me shopping. You wanted me to buy a housedress for some reason. Crazy."

It's not really a dream. Just before I go to sleep an old friend, my first friend, a good and true cousin friend, is calling me. Urgently, anxiously calling my name.

I am supposed to help him do something. He is handing me sandbags which I am supposed to place in a certain spot. Behind him is a square patch of light. There is someone else here, a woman, and I can see a corner of her dress, the telltale quaint print of it. And a man, a small older man. We are all handing down sandbags. We are handing down bales, that's it, wouldn't you know.

A faint smoke smell in the air (burning day down at the dump), a thin blue haze filtering out of the trees. We carry our luggage to the car. I'm dropping Jen off at the airport first, then the long drive home.

In the house it smells like fried eggs and bacon. My mother is quickly scraping the breakfast plates. She's wearing her white uniform already, even though she doesn't have to be at work for an hour. Muriel's coming over for coffee before they both have to go to work.

Jen and I wander around the house one last time, looking at the wall full of family photographs. We have framed ourselves to give to her. There's Will and his family, in Australia now (maybe things would have been different if he'd wanted to farm); there's the aerial view of the farm just before it was sold five years ago, her collection of spoons with *Alberta, Canada* written on them, *Chilliwack, B.C.*, *EXPO '67*. Jen pokes her finger into the dirt of a plant and says, "This needs watering."

In the kitchen, my mother is rinsing the spatula, having just iced her Pineapple Slice, a weightwatcher dessert she's put together from tins. She's humming along to a hit parade song on the radio. I know what's in store for me. Some day I will stand somewhere, in a line-up at a supermarket or in someone's fluorescent-lit bathroom, some cold impersonal place, a living room in which there is too much designer furniture, too much talk of dry whites, and hear that off key voice, stunned by how near she has come. Even though now she exasperates me, irks me beyond words.

She is telling a long story about how she had to spend half a day last week chasing around town for Bert Lowe's hat, an old fur thing, "a rag," he had misplaced. How she had to phone the hospital, tear over to the post office in the middle of the afternoon, check the IGA where he had gone for cigars.

"Imagine me," she says, mildly indignant, "tearing around town, phoning doctors and nurses about an old cap, honestly."

We're ready to leave, have our suitcases in the car, keys ready.

My mother puts a deck of cards and a plastic two-litre bottle of diet ginger ale on the table, beside the Pineapple Slice. "Oh," she says, "I didn't know you were ready." She wipes her hands on a tea towel and follows us out to the car. She's looking past us, over our heads, and, sure enough, here comes Muriel, burning up the crescent in her son's Firebird. "Okay," says my mother. "I won't keep you. Have a good trip. Bye."

Cache Reward
Cathy Reininger

It was two days before she could open her mouth. She drank frothy water from a pail using the hollow cattail stem she had cut and dried to make music. The worst damage had been done with the heavy belt buckle when he swung it at her face. She was glad it had missed her teeth. That it had struck her cheekbone and blackened half her face and that the bottom half of the initials for Hudson's Bay Company were now etched deep into the soft skin below her eye did not matter. What mattered was that he had not broken any of her teeth. The Grey Nuns had framed a picture of an Indian, sad, hollow eyed and smiling with a puckered toothless grin. She had vowed to keep her teeth even though she was six at the time. Now she struggled to keep her life.

On the third day she made her way to the creek. Swirling fog which seemed to begin and end inside her pounding skull blurred her vision and made her nauseous. She held her arms folded across her belly as if she were afraid something might fall out, but in her left hand she stubbornly clung to a hunting knife. Neither the quivering hare in the alders nor the fat porcupine snuffling down the trail feared her now. She too was an animal, wounded and struggling through the black spruce forest after water, groans coming from her dry mouth when a root or branch jarred her aching body.

At the sight of the stream she lunged forward and fell to her knees. She tilted slowly forward and dipped her whole face into the sparkling cool liquid. Not once had she unfolded her arms but, rising, she did so with great care. Steadying herself she aligned the tip of the knife with her sternum and drew the blade through the bloodied dress. It fell away like a split chrysalis and she stepped away from it naked and watched it float slowly away.

That blue dress and her house with its lace curtains and small china cups—anything not Indian, anything white—had brought her to this. Was it really less than three years since that day outside the post on her fifteenth birthday?

"What is it you want?" he had asked her as he heaved supplies and traps into his canoe. She had pointed to the doctor's wife all in blue. "A dress like that."

His laughter had filled her with a cheerfulness she had not felt since the death of her father and brother in the heavy spring runoff of the year before.

"Come with me and I'll buy you a dozen." And she had gone.

Now she watched what was left of that illusion float away. When he first struck her she thought it was the result of drinking. She had seen how alcohol had torn families apart in her village. But the worst attacks began when she had first told him she would have his child. His rage was endless. The words he screamed at her she did not know but the tone she recognized. There had once been a man in their village who had fornicated with the lead bitch of his husky team. Afterward he had suffered such self-loathing that he had ranted nights like one possessed and then impaled himself on his knife. This trapper felt the same way about her, yet he could not curb his yearning. She could not understand. When she told him she would have his child she hoped it would change something and it did. His brutality knew no bounds. He had hammered her with such methodical and vicious blows to her breasts and abdomen that her breasts became hard and blue and her body convulsed and expelled the unfinished infant in a sea of blood.

His comings and goings from the cabin were marked upon her body and mind. Long ago she had stopped accompanying him to the post. Her people had turned their backs when she approached. They had warned her he would reach into her living flesh and try to capture her spirit. She had scorned their warning and they had called her lost, mourned her passing because to them she was already dead.

Now, standing alone, naked and afraid, she understood. Understood that he would return again and again and that his blows would never kill her. He had broken some law in his heart and he could placate his demon by beating her. She had wished for the peace of death but she knew now that it would never come, and worse yet he might come to own her soul. He was cold, methodical and savage when he hurt her. Sometimes she thought that on his face there was the same pleasure as when he lay with her. In the dreams she saw him tear into her flesh and drag her still-pulsing spirit from her.

This could not be. He had taken enough. She began a plan.

It took many tries but finally she brought down a deer. Painfully she struggled to drag the quartered carcass home but failed. She built a fire where the animal fell and dried the meat. This she brought home and pounded again and again. She made a paste from saskatoons and mixed them with rendered fat. Then she went to the forest in search of the main ingredient of her survival. Among the ferns and mosses in damp cool places sheltered by rotting logs grew countless mushrooms. She sought one very white and special one. No insect ever violated the perfection of the mushroom she carried home. To her pemmican, except for one small portion, she added this forest fruit. Carefully she packed the pemmican into folded hide parfleches.

On recent visits he had taken the furs from the small trapline she maintained. He had also stolen her food. He had begun to take a perverse pleasure in leaving her without food. To provide for herself she had secreted portions away but he always sought these caches out before he headed north to his trapline or west to the post. She built a cairn now and hid a portion of the pemmican there.

He noticed the mark on her cheek like a brand and joked about branding cattle, a conception of which she had no understanding. He noticed too her sideways glances towards the creek and, before he pushed off, he took a walk in that direction. He laughed and danced around her with the hide parfleche in his hands swinging it from a long hide lance. She fled to the bush and none of his searching uncovered her hiding place. Still he seemed delighted to have outwitted her in one way and sang to the skies as he pushed off down the river a quarter of a mile away.

She sat on a high rock and watched him disappear. The canoe she had paid for with her blood, and everything in it belonged to her but she was in no hurry. Even after he had eaten he would feel nothing, not even a faintly disturbing taste would warn him. In eight or nine hours he would be plagued by thirst and cold sweats. He would double over with pain. In the final delirium as he fought against death he might think he saw her sitting by the fire watching his pale face. He might cry out as he imagined that merciless hands were reaching into his bleeding flesh to draw out his still pulsing heart. He might wish that he had not . . .

Before Summer Comes
Marilynn Stratton

They always go to the cabin Easter weekend, because of Mother's delicate nose. Dad says the place has to be opened up and readied, before summer comes, but Rose figures the real reason is to clear the winter's accumulation of dead squirrels from under the cabin before the bodies thaw and begin to stink. One year, the dead squirrels were left until Victoria weekend and Mother's delicate nose was so offended that she wouldn't set foot in the cabin all summer.

Although Mother is the one with the delicate nose, she doesn't crawl under the cabin to hunt for dead squirrels. Rose inherits the job because Mother won't touch dead things and Mary Ann is too little to do it properly and Dad's stomach is too big. He might wedge himself under the floorbeams or trap himself in the cindercrete maze that supports the cabin, and they'll have to leave him there, like the dead squirrels, until somebody happens by to help. Nobody is likely to happen by Davis Lake at Easter.

They leave the city before dawn on Good Friday. Rose and Mary Ann squeeze into the middle of the truck cab, between Dad and Mother; Mary Ann sleeps, slumped over onto Mother's lap and she wakes up crabby when they stop for lunch.

They are almost at the Davis Lake turn-off when they see the sign on a farmer's gate: Pedigreed Collie For Sale - Cheap. Rose can't believe it when Dad gears down and turns into the yard. Mother protests; she doesn't like dogs.

Mother doesn't like goldfish or turtles or kittens either, but Rose is too excited to pay any mind to Mother.

"Lassie!" Mary Ann squeals, when she sees the big tan and white collie tied to the weathered clothesline post behind the farmhouse.

"The girls need something to look after, Fern," Dad says, "and a dog will be company for you when Mary Ann starts school."

"I don't like dogs," Mother says, flatly.

"You'll feel safer when I'm at work," Dad says, as he steps out of the truck to speak to the man standing in the doorway of the dilapidated farmhouse. Rose scrambles under the steering wheel and out of the truck behind Dad.

"Dog belongs t'my married daughter," the farmer tells Dad. "She raises collies, purebreds. This one's too skittish t'show. Has papers as long as yer arm. Thought I might get him t'herd cattle, but he's past it."

"Buy him, please, Dad," Rose whispers, hopping up and down on one foot. She walks over to touch the dog. He shies away, but his tail is wagging, so Rose squats in the gravel at the base of the clothesline post and waits. He sniffs her extended hand, cautiously, before he allows himself to be petted.

"Shy breeder, if that's what ya have in mind. I won't fool ya, he's useless. Just a house pet." Rose buries her face in the dog's ruff and wonders what a 'shy breeder' is.

The deal is struck and the dog is tied into the truck box, since Mother won't have him in the cab. Rose complains loudly, to impress the farmer. She wants him to know they are the kind of people who know how to treat a dog with papers as long as your arm.

"Its name is Lassie," Mary Ann announces, before they have gone half a mile.

"No way," Rose says. "Lassie's a girl. It's a boy dog." Mary Ann has no imagination; every collie in the world is

named Lassie. Rose wants a name that will mark this dog
from all others.

"Lassie!" Mary Ann screams.

Rose has just seen 'Breakfast at Tiffany's' for the
third time at the Roxy Theatre. Holly Golightly would be a
good name, or Audrey Hepburn, but they are girls' names
too, and Rose wants her argument to stick. "George Peppard?" she says, hopefully.

Dad laughs. "Who the hell is George Peppard?"

"Language," Mother says softly, through clenched
teeth.

"Lassie!" Mary Ann's bottom lip is quivering.

"Tiffany's a good name," Rose says. "It sounds
important, doesn't it, Mary Ann?" Rose can tell that Mary
Ann is gathering herself for another scream. "Lassie can be
his middle name," Rose says, quickly. "He'll have two
names, like you. He'll be Tiffany Lassie."

"Tiffany Lassie. Tinnaffy Lassie." Mary Ann tries the
fit of the name on her tongue. She says it, over and over,
mixing the syllables until Rose wants to punch her.

Dad ends it. "Tiffany Lassie's a fine name for a dog
with papers," he says, "but how about Taffy, for short?
Suits his colour."

They chain Taffy to a birch tree at the back of the
cabin while they unload the truck. Mother opens all the
windows to air the cabin and Dad splits firewood for the
cookstove. Mother gives Rose a damp rag and sets her to
chasing dust from the chair-legs and windowsills. Every so
often, when Mother isn't looking, Rose snitches a scrap of
bread or bit of cake and goes outside to feed the dog; she
says its name, again and again, gentling it and letting it lick
the crumbs of food from her hand. She catches Dad brib-
ing Taffy with food, too, but Mother never goes near the
collie. She is afraid of dogs, she says; they're dirty and
she's never met one she could trust. Dad says Mother was

bit by a dog when she was young and he's amazed she agreed to have Taffy on the premises. When Rose thinks about it, she doesn't remember that Mother agreed to any such thing. Dad did all the talking and it just happened.

After supper, Rose puts on dungarees and an old jacket while Dad removes the boards that cover the hole in the foundation of the cabin. Rose almost enjoys crawling around under the cabin with a big flashlight, although she always makes a few token complaints for Mary Ann's benefit. Mary Ann will be big enough, any day now, to retrieve dead squirrels and Rose isn't ready to give the job over to her. Rose slides through the hole, on her belly, and propels herself forward, digging her elbows and toes into the cold, hard-packed earth. She pretends to be tunnelling an escape from some terrible place where she's been held prisoner for months and months; she's lived on bread heels and brackish water; her velvet gown is tattered and her fine hair is shorn to a wiry stubble like Ingrid Bergman's when they burned her at the stake in 'Saint Joan.'

Every mound of dirt under the cabin must be searched and the flashlight beam must probe every hole in every cindercrete block. Whenever Rose finds a dead squirrel, she yells for Dad and inches backward—dragging the small stiff body by the tail—to the opening. She half turns and flings the corpse into the rectangle of light that frames Dad's workboots and trouser cuffs. Dad puts the dead squirrel into a cardboard box. Later, while Dad burns the box, Mother scrubs Rose's hands with disinfectant and makes her take a complete stand-up bath—in hard cistern water and carbolic soap—at the kitchen sink. While she is scrubbing Rose's hands, Mother always says, "You never know what the squirrels died of." Rose always tells her they froze to death, but she knows Mother doesn't believe it.

The next morning, Taffy escapes. Mary Ann and

Rose are still in their nightgowns, eating Corn Flakes at the kitchen table and looking out the window, planning their day, now that the dead squirrel job is done. They will wear old clothes and rubber boots and they will go for long walks. They will see how much ice has gone out of the lake. They will count all the familiar Davis Lake landmarks: the raft and the waterslide, stranded on the beach; the store and dance pavillion, their windows boarded over like sightless eyes; the stone chalet and the thirty-nine steps that lead to the fire tower hill. They will stroll up and down the deserted gravel lanes and make a game of remembering the names of cottages without looking first: Lazy Dazy and Bide-a-wee and Loafer's Den and Bonnie Doon and Spike's Inn. It won't really be a contest; Rose will win.

Mother is scrubbing the porch, in an old party-dress that she wears, sometimes, to do housework. It has a full circle skirt of huge orange floribunda roses splotched against a green background and Rose hopes it will get worn out and find its way to the dress-up box before she is too grown up to enjoy it. Taffy is dozing in the morning sun at the base of a birch tree, eyes closed, long nervous nose resting on his paws. The rusted chain that tethers him is coiled into a red snake at his side. His ears prick forward when Mother stops scrubbing. She lifts the scrub-pail and descends from the porch, heading for the dumping place at the back of the clearing. Taffy opens his eyes. Mother gives him a wide berth, but he stands up, on the alert. He stretches and shakes himself; his tail wags ever so slightly. Mother reaches the edge of the bush and swings the bucket. Just then, a gust of wind catches the floribunda circle. It billows and plumes; Mother drops the pail and grabs for the skirt, but it is too late. The whirling, circling cloud of green and orange flies up over her head. Taffy yelps and bolts. The chain snaps and he streaks—low to the ground—through a gap in the gooseberries and away into the bush.

Later, when Dad tells other people the story of how they lost their pedigreed dog, he will say that Mother's damn party-dress scared the collie right out of his wits, but Rose thinks Dad only says that because he never liked the dress anyway.

After Taffy runs away, Rose doesn't leave the yard; she calls and calls, all day, but Dad says it is no use; Taffy is too dumb to come when he's called. Dad tells her to put out food and water and hope for the best. After supper, Dad and Mary Ann dye eggs with the Easter-egg paints Mother has brought, but Rose watches out the window for Taffy. At dusk, she spots him in the bush. His coat is matted, full of burrs and twigs. He just stands—tongue lolling, nose raised to the wind—looking at the food and water dishes.

"Why doesn't he come for a drink?" Rose asks.

"Stupid, I guess," Dad says, "and scared and useless."

"The dishes are too close to the house," Mother says.

Rose is sure that Taffy won't run from her when she slides the dishes to the far side of the clearing, but he does. She goes back inside the cabin and peers out the window until the silver trunks of the birches melt into darkness. Once or twice, she is sure she sees something move in the yard, but Dad says it is only the wind ruffling the bare branches of the gooseberries. After Rose goes to bed, she hears Dad tell Mother that he will drive down to Uncle Willie's tomorrow for a coyote trap.

Rose is up and dressed at dawn on Easter Sunday. Taffy is lying in the bush near the empty food dishes. He springs to his feet and backs away when Rose rounds the corner of the cabin, keeping an exact thirty foot distance between them. Rose stops and leans against the cabin to think, pressing her back into the clap-board siding. Taffy lies down again and watches her.

Rose has seen a coyote trap, and it will break his leg for sure. She drops to her knees and flattens herself—face down— to the earth. She moves, ever so little, toward the dog. For an hour, she crawls toward him by imperceptible fractions of inches, talking gently to him all the while, her mouth and nose full of the pungent rotting smell of moss and mould and last year's leaves. The ground is uneven and rough; deadfall snags at her clothes and catches in her hair; her elbows and knees bruise on the frozen ground; her hands scrape against the straggly whisps of leftover snowdrifts. The dog doesn't move until she is ten feet from him. Then he retreats, wriggling backward on his belly. Rose stops moving and begins to talk to him in a rhythmic, sing-song chant. Taffy's tail brushes the dirt in nervous little sweeps.

Rose hears Mother and Dad and Mary Ann get up. She hears Mary Ann shriek as chocolate eggs are discovered under chairs and behind curtains. She hears the coughing sound of the cistern pump and she hears Dad chopping wood for the breakfast fire. She hears dishes clinking against the walls of the porcelain sink as Mother washes them. She hears the rasp of a wire brush on wood and she knows that Mother is scrubbing the porch steps with used dishwater. She hears someone beating rugs and she hears the whish of a broom on the stone slabs that make a path to the out-house.

When the high, cold sun is almost directly overhead, Mary Ann comes out and lies on the ground beside Rose, but she is no good at coaxing the dog: her voice is too loud, her movements too broad. Taffy backs away.

"Get lost," Rose says, never breaking the sing-song rhythm of her voice. "Get lost." Mary Ann's face puckers; she is getting ready for a good scream, Rose can tell. "Don't howl," Rose sings, "he'll run away." For once,

Mary Ann doesn't make a fuss.

Rose hears the truck motor and she knows that Dad has gone to Uncle Willie's for the coyote trap. When Dad returns, Rose has narrowed the gap to a mere five feet, but if she moves suddenly, or if there is an unexpected puff of wind, Taffy starts up and backs away and it takes another hour of crawling to regain the lost ground. Rose is hungry and tired, and her muscles ache from hours of stillness in the damp cold. Several times, Dad calls to her from the house, coaxes her to come in and get warm, to stop and have something to eat, but Rose will not be distracted.

When the sun drops behind the bony tops of the birches, Dad comes and stands by the side of the house. His voice is low. "We'll try the trap now, Rose," he says. "It's getting dark."

Rose stands up. Taffy doesn't move. Rose's legs are cramped and weak; they nearly buckle under her, but she holds herself stiff and tall until she reaches the porch. She sits down on the top step and watches Dad bind the jaws of the trap with electrician's tape. Mother comes out of the cabin with a piece of raw meat in her hand. When Dad starts across the clearing, Taffy turns and lopes a little way off into the bush. He stops and faces the cabin, head lifted to the scent of the meat. Dad pounds an iron stake into the ground and attaches the trap to it with a stout length of logging chain; he scoops a shallow pit in the dead leaves and lays the trap in it; he forces the jaws wide and fastens the spring. Then he scatters leaves over the trap and sets the meat on the ground. Rose leans against Mother's knees.

"It's only a dog," Mother says.

Dad walks toward them and Mary Ann comes out of the house. The four of them sit, silent, on the top step of the porch and wait.

It is dark when Taffy goes for the meat, and it is over before they know it has happened. The trap closes with a loud, nasty clang and Taffy leaps high in the air, a yelping ball of flailing legs. He comes down, free of the trap, and is gone.

Dad brings the trap back to the porch. There is blood on it, and clumps of golden fur, where the jaws have broken through the tape. Rose says nothing. She goes into the house and puts herself to bed.

In the morning, after they close up the cabin and pack the truck, Dad stops at the Davis Lake ranger station. He takes money from his wallet and Rose hears him ask the Ranger to buy some tinned dog-food and watch out for a big golden collie that has got loose.

Before summer comes, Taffy is dead. The Ranger telephones Dad, long distance, to say that he's shot the dog. He is tired of finding half-eaten fawns in the bush, he says, and local farmers are losing chickens. After the call, nobody says much. Mary Ann dresses her doll and Rose goes on with her Arithmetic homework. Dad reads his newspaper and Mother finishes peeling the potatoes for supper. But later, in the pantry, Rose catches Mother crying. Rose wouldn't have expected Mother—of all people—to cry; Mother doesn't even like dogs.

Print Dresses
Mary Riskin

In the dresser of this upstairs room there is hand-tatted lace that once was precisely tacked to necklines of dark dresses so that, when necessary, it could be snipped away and gently squeezed in a solution of pure soap flakes and warm water, then left to dry flat on a towel where the sunlight struck it. The sunlight and the soap have made it yellow.

In a lidded cardboard box in the closet, there are balls of brown string, collected from parcels and rolled newspapers and from the grasses and roads where they were once discarded. The ravelling of these brown strings would cross the yard and the gravel road, would wind through the ditch of Queen Anne's lace and into the rows of hollyhocks across the way, in the garden of my aunts.

I can see my aunts through this upper-storey windowpane: they are sitting in two canvas lawn chairs in the shade of their small green-shingled house and they're resting for a moment between the weeding of the vegetable garden and the making of the tea. The lazy nods and dips of their straw sunbonnets do not suggest the intensity of their conversation.

They want me to come out. I've seen them in my garden in the early morning when they supposed I was asleep. I've heard them rattle at my doors and windows. They did not intend, when they handed me the key, that I'd come in and stay.

I didn't intend it, either. There are things I should be doing, for my work, my home, for you. There are things I ought to be doing here as well, that I have not yet done.

Stacked on an upper closet shelf in this room, there are dozens of photographs which I have lifted, dusted, and returned. There are photographs of young and handsome men in suits and ties, of women with lace around their necks. There are people who, like my aunts and my mother, knew how to age with grace and self-respect and not a moment of wasted time.

There is a photograph of twelve young women in identical robes of white: some are kneeling, others standing, two sitting on carved chairs. The women are startlingly beautiful, their hair soft and flowing or caught with hairpins up behind their heads. This is the picture of a graduation class or the cast of a midsummer play: it's impossible to tell, just as I cannot be certain which of the women is my grandmother.

My aunts would be able to tell me, if I asked them. They probably hoped for that, that I would carry pieces from this house across the way and sit in the shade with them while they disclosed the past. Or that I would call from this upper storey window from time to time, bidding them into their mother's house to explain what I was holding. They would have argued between themselves, and even have called in my mother at some point, to settle the matter. They look for excuses to call my mother back, to draw her back to them. This is their way. They grew up as three.

One of my aunts has spied a weed in the flowerbed beside the lawn and she is kneeling on the grass to pluck it. The other aunt is watching her, or looking beyond her to my front door.

What they intended was that I'd discharge it all within a day or two, taking the things I wanted for our apartment in the city and packing the rest of it into boxes which they'd left in the woodshed for my convenience.

They assumed I'd clean the house from top to bottom in readiness for the agents and the movers. They are, my mother and my aunts, too old for such emotional and back-breaking labour as disposing of their mother.

Grandmother's bedroom is sparsely furnished and as tidy as she left it. All it required was a little dusting. The thin coverlet, quilted and nearly white, is folded and tucked to conceal the embroidered linen, to save the bed-clothes from dust and light. It's a single bed, austere and high, but I like it better than my double one which made it possible for a man to spend the night.

You spent the night ten times, perhaps eleven, before you finally moved in: you said it would be less expensive for both of us that way. You've spent more than you saved on gifts for me or the apartment, luxuries that no one has a need for, and the waste makes me cold.

On her dresser are the bone-backed brush and mirror which she used so dextrously, one in each hand, one hundred strokes through her thin grey hair each night. From her window, which faces away from the house of my aunts, she saw an open field and knew the spit of snakes in the tall weeds, the sticky cling of cobwebs in the trees. She knew them, but left them, too busy with this house for idle wandering: that was for children, the recollections of her own childhood serving up suggestions of blind man's bluff or hide and seek to bored daughters or, later, to her only grandchild. More often, aggravated by such a word as "boredom," she'd send them out to pinch suckers from tomato plants or to hang the wash, insisting on a hat to keep away the sun.

And silences. She expected that the house would be as silent as it is this afternoon no matter how many of us were in it, as she took her one hour's rest exactly with a black stocking over her clouded eyes to keep out light. And so it was.

I think that you would like to live here, for a while. You'd find this old house picturesque, if a trifle small, and would immediately set to work improving it with vertical blinds and bright, bold wallpaper. You'd find a place for a dishwasher and you'd cover the hardwood floors with acrylic, the roof with cedar shakes. Your radio alarm clock would go on the little painted table beside the bed. The table would have to go, eventually. So would the bed.

You'd ask me to stop winding the clock on the mantlepiece downstairs because the bonging out of the quarter hours would drive you to distraction.

My aunts have gone into their house. Even the exasperation of my being shut in here will not keep them from getting their tea by the appointed hour. With it, they'll have a biscuit each and plan their supper of aspic and bean salad and sweet brown bread, baked before noon and left to cool on wire racks on the kitchen table's oilcloth. They will wonder, as they set their table with linen napkins and plates and glasses (as their mother always did), what I am eating here.

At the beginning I ate nothing. There were only dead insects where the cornstarch and flour used to be and I wasn't hungry anyway. But then I found her well-used cookbooks that she'd made herself from empty scrapbooks, and her round script was steadier than I'd ever known it. I remembered: johnnycake with sweet apple jelly; a white sauce thick on soft macaroni; last week's buns steamed back into edibility. Beside some recipes she'd glued a black-and-white of the woman who'd shared it with her. Martha Beardsley (Pineapple Upside Down Cake, 1941), wears a black one-piece bathing suit and sits by a grey lake with one hand up to hold her damp hair away from her face.

My grandmother was not the cook that you are, with your pepper steaks and florentined eggs and kiwi fruit from the market. But she didn't waste a cent.

I scoop tea leaves from the cannister and wait for the kettle to whistle. Here by the kitchen door I can see out the front window and also out the back: it's a house constructed for people who watch from kitchens. The clock bongs twice: four-thirty. The office will be emptying of everyone but Jack, who'll have to do my work as well as his. And you'll be contemplating a game of raquetball with Harold, followed by a beer. The beer will make you amorous, and you'll remember I'm away.

In the pantry and then in the rootcellar, when at last I thought to look there, I found the sealed jars full of fruit and pickled meats, the flour and the sugar in large glass jars with rubber seals so tight that I despaired of opening them, cans of condensed milk and tubs of lard.

I've learned to use yeast again, and to soak the raisins in milk before I add them to the batter. I've recalled bread pudding. I wish that I had eggs.

I clean my clothes in the morning and myself at night, as Grandmother always did. I wash the dresses and the underthings on the scrubboard which I found beneath the sink. I leave them to dry on the wooden clothes rack in the bathroom.

I wash my hair in the sink, wringing the excess water out before I wrap it in a towel. Already it seems longer, silkier. I iron when it's not too warm. There isn't any urgency to that for her cotton dresses fit me, and she had several. Their prints, small and blue or mauve, suit me better than the things I brought with me from the city, and I've stowed all of them away in my suitcase which is in the front hall closet. I'd like to put it out on the verandah and let the aunts decide what to do with it.

My grandmother eludes me. I've looked for her as I swept her auburn corners, as I dusted her varnished wood. I've peered at the hand which held the pan and moved the flannel cloth, sought the fine grain of her wrist, but I haven't found her. I've stood at the foot of her bed when I rose in the morning and studied the indent in the pillow, but it does not belong to her elegant white head. She isn't here. If she were, I'd take her bird bones against my chest and say that she worked well, that there was a reason for it after all.

I see through the drawing room window that my aunts have been duplicitous. Your small green sports car is grinding slowly down their gravel, raising dust which they'll remove from furniture tomorrow. You've brought my mother with you and, in a gesture you'd never dare with me, you walk around to her door and gently help her out. She greets her sisters with two distant hugs and then all three of the women glance toward this house.

I turn away, the kettle boiling now. I know that they will invite you in for something from their table, at least a cup of tea, perhaps cold fruit and biscuits. They've been curious to meet you. And you, assured, will win them and give them reassurances. "She's a woman of her own mind," you'll say. "She'll come out when she's good and ready."

And all the time you'll be pitying their set ways, their narrow-mindedness, their silly printed dresses. You'll contemplate entire generations of women who never knew my liberty.

My grandmother is not here, but there's more of her here than I can clean away. In this drawing room, pale wood recalls darker wood, of pews, and hymnals, and Grandmother straight-backed and alert as she attended to the sermon.

In this kitchen is her stern look when a child asked for a second helping of dessert or an adult one of sherry.

The even seams of her cotton stockings mount the stairs (a neat darn near the ankle almost invisible), and in this room of hers are the drawers in which she kept her long flannel nightgowns and the spotless cotton undergarments.

I am brushing my hair before the mirror—eighty-nine and ninety. The teal-blue print hangs more loosely on me than it did before. She never filled her dresses, either— when I hear your rapping on the door. While you were drinking their tea, I made certain that the bolts on the door were fast, the sashes on the windows firm. My grandmother did not take security lightly.

I will come out eventually. For a time, until you've seen what I am thinking, I will come out to you. But in this house I've remembered why I feel revulsion when you rest your head on my belly and spill your gold, extravagantly, across the bareness of my skin.

I rummage in the top drawer for a hairpin. I know they're here somewhere. When you've finished knocking, I'll go down to pour my tea.

Breath of God
Clem Martini

It rained all of May and the first half of June, then July
baked dry as a cracker. I don't know which was worse.

Anyways, five days into summer break and the hot-
test day so far, I went into town for a swim and found
they'd closed the municipal pool for renovations. Calem
Sanderson was standing there as I read the notice and his
dalmation, Dagmar, bit Rufus, so I kicked it where it was
going to do the most good. "What did you do that for?"
Calem asked "They were only playing." "The trouble with
your dog, Calem," I told him, "is that he just doesn't know
when enough is enough." "And the trouble with *your* dog"
he replied "is that she isn't even a dog." And he whistled
up Dagmar and off they went. Figured he'd delivered
quite a zinger, too. It was about then that I realized it
wasn't going to be one of my more superior days, and
began to have some real dark suspicions about the rest of
the summer as well.

"C'mon Rufus," I said, "let's go."

Eventually, me and Rufus rounded the bend in the
road and crossed the texas gate that marks the entrance to
our place. Already you could begin to hear it, the soft
jingle-jangling of wind chime against wind chime against
wind chime. A couple more steps and we cleared the
Saskatoon berry bushes and the house sprung to view.

Flat land, big old clump of cottonwoods, red cedar
house set next to a small, dusty hill: that's all there is to
look at. It's not much, I'll tell you. And then the three

windmills out of sight on the other side of the hill that everyone talks about, turning and turning when it blows, which it wasn't for once. I remember one time Dad said he bought the place for the wind. I guess he must have, because he sure didn't buy it for the view.

Around town, Dad is kind of semi-famous for his feelings about wind. He teaches environmental design at the University in Calgary and he says that wind is just about the most important thing you can think of. "The breath of God" he calls it. Says it's "the closest thing we have on this earth to a manifestation of divinity." When he talks like that around strangers, I just want to crawl out of the room on my belly.

Around the house, all the way round the house, we have this strip of wind chimes he's collected. There're hundreds of them, from all over the world, draped over nearly every inch of the veranda. When the wind is down, like it was that day, they just dangle and twist, but the wind can come up pretty strong and sudden, and when it does they make quite a racket. If it's really blowing, some of 'em, the ones not built for hurricane-force blows, will bust like a fire cracker exploding. I'd say about once every two weeks the front porch will be littered with shattered pieces of glass and clay.

I left Rufus cooling under the cottonwoods and went inside. Dad's office looks down from the second floor onto the living room. Right away, as soon as I entered, I knew I wasn't going to get anywhere fast with him. He was crouched over his desk, hair mussed up and glasses perched on the end of his nose.

"Hey, Dad," I said and he called back, "Hey Sandra." I flopped myself down on the couch and kinda waited for him to glance in my direction to see what I was wanting. He just kept right on drawing and erasing and calculating. I could have waited a couple of days, I think, without much success.

"Pool's closed," I announced when it didn't look like he was ever going to ask. "Still working, hey?"

"Yup," he replied and lifted a hand to nab a different pencil.

"Going to be long?" I asked, casual-like, as if it didn't matter, and tugged a magazine out of the magazine rack. I don't know why I bother around our house: *The Saturday Evening Post*. I put it back.

"Fairly."

"I suppose you'd like it if I went back out to play, then."

He patted and brushed the paper like it was a favourite pet. "Wouldn't mind it," he allowed.

He was making it as obvious as possible that he wanted me to go out and play. The thoughtful thing to do would have been to get up, get out and let him finish his whatever. I peered out the living room window at the grass, dust, sun and no-wind.

"Dagmar bit Rufus again," I mentioned, hoping to draw him into the conversation with his familiar spiel about the Sanderson boys. "Real hard."

It didn't phase him at all. "I've told you," he said, "*not* to bring that chihuahua into town. She's just a mouthful for most of those dogs. Like waving a sandwich under their noses."

The heat rose off the porch and shook the countryside like a bedsheet: hills, trees, clouds, everything rippled outside. Inside, Dad's head crept closer to his papers with every moment I stayed. Really, it's no good talking to him when he's at his desk. I stood up.

"Okay, Dad. I'm leaving. I'm going out for a walk now."

"Good," he said, and his fingers floated over the desk like a butterfly, hovered, and dropped like a rock on an eraser. "Much better for you than lounging around the house, anyway." Then he finally looked up. He's got nice eyes, Dad does. Blue. His best feature, I think.

"Sorry, Sandy. Work," he said and shrugged. "I shouldn't be much more than a couple of hours, then maybe you can come back and we'll find something we can do together." And then he tossed me an eraser.

"Okay," I said, and tossed the eraser back. What am I going to do with an eraser? Sometimes he's really out of it. He waved, I waved, he went back to work, I went outside. The moment I set foot on the porch, I regretted it. I felt like a small, warm puddle of water being slowly evaporated. Rufus was lying in her favourite shady spot beneath the biggest cottonwood, looking comfortable the way only a dog in dirt can. I should have just let her be, it would have been the considerate thing to do.

"Up Rufus!" I barked. She opened an eye reproachfully. "Let's go," I called, and she scrambled out of the dirt.

"No girl, there're no biscuits," I explained for about the billionth time as Rufus (again!) snuffled my empty palm. I tossed the branch, she ran to maul it before returning it, and I wiped my hand against my leg. Dog spit. If God can make anything in the universe, why didn't he make dogs with bibs attached. Anyways, like I said, she loped into the brush, the dog spit dried on my leg and I turned and saw the car drive up the road to my left.

It's not unusual for people to take a wrong turn off the highway and end up getting turned about on the gravel roads down here, so it wasn't a big surprise when it slowed to a stop beside me. People are always asking directions. I was pleased too, because it broke the monotony of the day. Besides, it was some car. The window on the passenger's side slid down like a slab of dark ice melting. I looked in, trying to make out the driver.

"Hi, Mom. What are you doing here?" I asked. She just winked and grinned. "And there," she said, "hangs a tale. Hop in." When she saw I was hanging back, she added, "Just for a quick spin and a chat."

I drummed my fingers against the door and glanced back towards the house. "All right." The lock snapped up like magic and I climbed in. "But if Dad sees us, there's going to be trouble." I sat down and leaned back against the dark leather interior. The seat nearly swallowed me whole. I looked at my mother again. "You know that, eh?"

"Yes," she replied and calmly adjusted the rear view mirror. "Yes, I know that. Buckle up, will you honey." Then she turned the car the other way round and we headed in the opposite direction. "So this," I thought "is what a cruiser feels like." Dad says big cars like these are gas gluttons and only for people with nothing better to do with their money. I don't know. I waved and mouthed "go home" to Rufus as we slid away. She just barked and raced round in circles. Not the brightest breed of dog, Chihuahuas. Mom brushed a hand through her hair, smiled again, and tried to relax. "How *are* you?" she inquired like it was the most normal thing in the world for her to just drop by in some expensive rent-a-car.

"Good," I replied. "Just fine." She turned right at the crossroads. "And you're looking nice too," I said because along with the fancy car she had clearly put on a new dress and a lot of make up. Truthfully though, she was looking not so terrific. Her face was pale which looked even more out of place here in all the sun than it might have in Montreal, and experienced seamen would have had trouble unravelling some of the knots she'd gotten her hair into. I could just bet she was smoking again too. And she kept smiling frantically at me. "What the heck are you doing here?" is what I wanted to ask, but she was my mother after all, so instead I said, "Go ahead and say it."

"Say what?" she asked.

"How much I've grown. You always tell me."

"Do I? Well, it's true. And you have. You're turning into a real young lady." She took a left and headed for the hill. I glanced backwards to check out the rest of the car, and there, coiled on the floor, is this length of yellow, nylon rope. "Especially since I last saw you," Mom added.

"I suppose so."

"A real little lady," she repeated, and she slid a small package across the seat to me.

"What's that?" I asked.

"Open it."

It was so carefully wrapped, I was a little reluctant to just shred the paper. But when I did, I found a gold ring with a red stone. Because it was a gift from my mother, I decided it must be a ruby. She told me to put it on, and I did, and then she asked if I liked it. I answered that it was very nice, because it was. I didn't say anything more, though, because what do you say when someone gives you something that's worth more than most of what you already own?

We were approaching the 1-A Highway at this point. The 1-A is a two-lane highway that leads south and east into Calgary.

"Mom? Where are we going?" I asked.

Her eyes didn't leave the road, as she turned right onto the 1-A. "Just for a spin," she repeated.

I watched the kilometers slowly tick away. "Not again," I said. "Tell me you're not doing it again." She didn't have to say anything. I looked out the window in disgust. "You are so stupid some times."

"And that's exactly the kind of talk your father has taught you."

"Come on!"

"Tell me it's not the truth!"

I glanced at the back seat again. "The rope!" I said with a sudden realization. "I don't believe it. You actually brought it along to tie me up, didn't you?"

"Don't be ridiculous!" she snapped, then pursed her lips. "Only," she amended and altered her grip on the steering wheel, "if it turned out to be absolutely necessary. And only until I could deprogram you."

I stared hard at her. "Deprogram me!" I repeated incredulously, but what I was thinking was, "What kind of drugs have you been taking?" She must have guessed some of my thoughts because she continued, "Well, who can tell what your father has been saying behind my back? And don't tell me he hasn't been saying anything."

The car rushed on. We passed a farm, then a fence, then another farm. I counted from twenty backwards, then took inventory of the fillings in my teeth with my tongue.

"Well, Mother," I asked after a deep breath, "how are things with *you*?"

She studied me nervously for a moment, then ran a hand through her hair. She's been doing that a lot, I thought, to put her hair in such a tangle. "No so good," she said. "I'm lonely. The recession hurt the store. I've put on weight. Tried to get interested in aerobics, but just can't make it stick somehow."

"Maybe swimming," I suggested half-heartedly. "It's good exercise I hear."

She nodded. "Yea, but you've got to have a pool close by, and then there are particular hours for adults."

"Yes," I agreed. I understood how pool schedules could be difficult.

She pulled two long envelopes out of her purse and displayed them the way a magician displays the rabbit you knew was hid beneath the hat. Airplane tickets. I knew that.

"I've picked up a small place in Greece," she said quietly. "It's inland, but not far inland. An hour's drive from the coast. Wonderful, eh?" She raised her eyebrows hopefully at me.

"Wonderful," I echoed and traced a design with my thumbnail in the leather seat. "Who's looking after the shop?"

"I left it with Mary."

I shook my head. "And you wonder why the business is doing lousy. Mary? *I* could run the shop better than Mary. Geez, you give me the creeps sometimes. You're my mother, part of you is supposed to be in me. I hope for my sake that it isn't the real brainy part."

It was unfair, I know, and you would have thought I'd punched her in the stomach to look at her.

"I didn't mean that. I'm sorry. But look. Look. I'll go. Anywhere you want. We'll just . . . go, you know? Simple. But do you really remember what it was like last time you did this? We flew to Mexico, you didn't let me eat anything but Big Macs, you got sick, we both never set foot out of the 'hacienda' and two weeks later the police came and that was that. After, you lost your summer visiting privileges, I didn't see you at my next birthday cause of the tonsilectomy, and now I just hope you don't mind losing Christmas, because that's what'll happen when they catch us this time for sure." I brushed my hand through my hair. Now she had *me* doing it. "I never thought you'd do this again. Never."

She kept on driving but I could see her eyes were beginning to swim. "You don't understand," she said "You don't understand." I scouted out my pockets for kleenex but couldn't come up with anything except one way too old to use. "I worked hard after the divorce to get the business going. And it's doing okay. I mean, even in this recession, the banks are eager to lend me money. But courts don't review their decisions. They don't say, 'Gee, you're doing all right. Maybe you deserve more time with your daughter.' They don't do that. I am fit. I have stopped drinking. I am together. And all . . . " Her voice broke, caught and then broke again. She rubbed her nose with the back of her right hand. "All I get is three times a year? Christmas, Birthdays and summer? That's it? What's the point?" she concluded. The tears rolled around in her mascara, then slid down her cheek like ants on skis. "I'm so unhappy without you," she whispered. "I'm so unhappy."

I kept my hands in my pockets and fingered the kleenex. "Why," I asked, after some time, "don't you just, forget about me? Concentrate on the business. You know. Find other interests."

She blinked rapidly and then stared at me like I had gone crazy. The driver behind us gave her the horn, but Mom ignored him. "Is that your Dad?" she asked and then repeated it when I didn't answer. I said no, but she kept staring so hard that I had to turn away.

"Don't you love me anymore?"

Even with my head turned, I could still feel her staring.

I watched the countryside whiz past and felt that ancient kleenex. "Yea," I said. "Sure. I think I love you. I don't know. I guess so. I think . . . " The car behind revved up and tore past us. "I think I love you less than I did when we hung around together all the time, though. I think love has something to do with who you kind of hang around with most. And I . . . " I trailed off. "I hang around mostly with Dad now."

For a long time after that we drove in silence with Mom just blinking and staring hard at the road. Then, just before we reached the Calgary limits, she pulled a left without signalling into a farmer's driveway, then turned the car back for Cochrane.

Just before we came to the fence, I said, "You can let me out here." But she just shook her head and kept on over the texas gate. "No," she said. "No. I'll take you up to the house. Besides, I want to speak to your father." I didn't say anything about how Dad might not want to speak to her because I figured she'd know that as well as anyone.

So we pulled up in front of the house and Dad must have heard us coming because, before the dust settled, there he was.

"What the hell are you doing here?" he asked as soon as he laid eyes on Mom.

"I just came by to talk," she answered.

"I got nothing to talk about with you," Dad shot back, then turned to me. "Are you all right?"

"Sure, Dad, everything's fine."

"I just want to speak with you, Jim," Mom said again.

"I'm going to take Rufus for a walk," I interrupted quickly, "and leave you guys alone."

"Don't go too far," Dad told me. "This isn't going to take very long."

So, me and Rufus took the path that leads up and over the hill, and everywhere we went grasshoppers leapt up in front of us, bouncing off our chests and stuff. Dad says it's because of all the dry weather following the wet weather that there's so many, but I don't know; dry weather, wet, there's always grasshoppers. You know? Anyways, I didn't care for them so much, but Rufus went absolutely crazy—barking and snapping at them, which is the biggest reason I took off so sudden, because Rufus didn't come along until after the divorce and she's not too easy around Mom. I could see that whatever Mom had to say, she might not want Rufus running around her in circles like a mad thing.

So, we got to the crest of the hill and on one side were the windmills, still as statues, and on the other side, at the bottom of the hill, seated on a picnic table by the second biggest cottonwood, Mom and Dad. I held Rufus in my lap and put my hand over her mouth so she'd keep quiet, and between the two moving branches of that second biggest tree, I watched them. Mom was studying her nails, I think. I wasn't certain what Dad was looking at. Maybe looking for me to show up.

I keep thinking, then, that if the wind blew just a little, maybe the chimes would go at it, and they'd at least have that to talk about. But, of course, wind doesn't work that way, on demand, so they just kept sitting there, same as the chimes. Just dangling. And I thought about what it was like when they were together. It was a long time ago, I can hardly remember, really. Maybe I don't remember and only think I do. She wore her hair different, in long braids. He flew a kite with me once. We had potato salad on the grass of some park in some city out east.

Down below, my parents remained silent as ever. The branches parted and I saw them staring off in different directions, then the branches closed and they disappeared. I scratched Rufus under the chin and told her, "Never, never."

The Broken Globe
Henry Kreisel

Since it was Nick Solchuk who first told me about the opening in my field at the University of Alberta, I went up to see him as soon as I received word that I had been appointed. He lived in one of those old mansions in Pimlico that had once served as town houses for wealthy merchants and aristocrats, but now housed a less moneyed group of people—stenographers, students, and intellectuals of various kinds. He had studied at Cambridge and got his doctorate there and was now doing research at the Imperial College and rapidly establishing a reputation among the younger men for his work on problems which had to do with the curvature of the earth.

His room was on the third floor, and it was very cramped, but he refused to move because he could look out from his window and see the Thames and the steady flow of boats, and that gave him a sense of distance and of space also. Space, he said, was what he missed most in the crowded city. He referred to himself, nostalgically, as a prairie boy, and when he wanted to demonstrate what he meant by space he used to say that when a man stood and looked out across the open prairie, it was possible for him to believe that the earth was flat.

"So," he said, after I had told him my news, "you are going to teach French to prairie boys and girls. I congratulate you." Then he cocked his head to one side, and looked me over and said: "How are your ears?"

"My ears?" I said. "They're all right. Why?"

"Prepare yourself," he said. "Prairie voices trying to speak French—that will be a great experience for you. I speak from experience. I learned my French pronunciation in a little one-room school in a prairie village. From an extraordinary girl, mind you, but her mind ran to science. Joan McKenzie—that was her name. A wiry little thing, sharp-nosed, and she always wore brown dresses. She was particularly fascinated by earthquakes. 'In 1755 the city of Lisbon, Portugal, was devastated. Sixty-thousand persons died; the shock was felt in Southern France and North Africa; and inland waters of Great Britain and Scandinavia were agitated.' You see, I still remember that, and I can hear her voice too. Listen: 'In common with the entire solar system, the earth is moving through space at the rate of appoximately 45,000 miles per hour, toward the constellation of Hercules. Think of that, boys and girls.' Well, I thought about it. It was a lot to think about. Maybe that's why I became a geophysicist. Her enthusiasm was infectious. I knew her at her peak. After a while she got tired and married a solid farmer and had eight children."

"But her French, I take it, was not so good," I said.

"No," he said. "Language gave no scope to her imagination. Mind you, I took French seriously enough. I was a very serious student. For a while I even practised French pronunciation at home. But I stopped it because it bothered my father. My mother begged me to stop. For the sake of peace."

"Your father's ears were offended," I said.

"Oh, no," Nick, said, "not his ears. His soul. He was sure that I was learning French so I could run off and marry a French girl . . it was very hard to shake him."

"But why should he have objected to your marrying a French girl anyway?"

"Because," said Nick, and pointed a stern finger at me, "because when he came to Canada he sailed from some French port, and he was robbed of all his money while he slept. He held all Frenchmen responsible. He never forgot and he never forgave. And, by God, he wasn't going to have that cursed language spoken in his house. He wasn't going to have any nonsense about science talked in his house either." Nick was silent for a moment, and then he said, speaking very quietly, "Curious man, my father. He had strange ideas, but a strange kind of imagination, too. I couldn't understand him when I was going to school or to the university. But then a year to two ago, I suddenly realized that the shape of the world he lived in had been forever fixed for him by some medieval priest in the small Ukrainian village where he was born and where he received an education of sorts when he was a boy. And I suddenly realized that he wasn't mad, but that he lived in the universe of the medieval church. The earth for him was the centre of the universe, and the centre was still. It didn't move. The sun rose in the East and set in the West, and it moved perpetually around a still earth. God had made this earth especially for man, and man's function was to perpetuate himself and to worship God. My father never said all that in so many words, mind you, but that is what he believed. Everything else was heresy."

He fell silent.

"How extraordinary," I said.

He did not answer at once, and after a while he said, in a tone of voice which seemed to indicate that he did not want to pursue the matter further, "Well, when you are in the middle of the Canadian West, I'll be in Rome. I've been asked to give a paper to the International Congress of Geophysicists which meets there in October."

"So I heard," I said. "Wilcocks told me the other day. He said it was going to be a paper of some importance. In fact, he said it would create a stir."

"Did Wilcocks really say that?" he asked eagerly, his

face reddening, and he seemed very pleased. We talked for a while longer, and then I rose to go.

He saw me to the door and was about to open it for me, but stopped suddenly, as if he were turning something over in his mind, and then said quickly, "Tell me—would you do something for me?"

"Of course," I said. "If I can."

He motioned me back to my chair and I sat down again. "When you are in Alberta," he said, "and if it is convenient for you, would you—would you go to see my father?"

"Why, yes," I stammered, "why, of course. I—I didn't realize he was still . . . ."

"Oh, yes," he said, "he's still alive, still working. He lives on his farm, in a place called Three Bear Hills, about sixty or seventy miles out of Edmonton. He lives alone. My mother is dead. I have a sister who is married and lives in Calgary. There were only the two of us. My mother could have no more children. It was a source of great agony for them. My sister goes to see him sometimes, and then she sometimes writes to me. He never writes to me. We—we had—what shall I call it—differences. If you went to see him and told him that I had not gone to the devil, perhaps . . . " He broke off abruptly, clearly agitated, and walked over to his window and stood staring out, then said, "Perhaps you'd better not. I—I don't want to impose on you."

I protested that he was not imposing at all, and promised that I would write to him as soon as I had paid my visit.

I met him several times after that, but he never mentioned the matter again.

I sailed from England about the middle of August and arrived in Montreal a week later. The long journey West was one of the most memorable experiences I have ever had. There were moments of weariness and dullness. But the very monotony was impressive. There was a grandeur about it. It was monotony of a really monumental kind. There were moments when, exhausted by the sheer impact of the landscape, I thought back with longing to the tidy, highly cultivated countryside of England and of France, to the sight of men and women working in the fields, to the steady succession of villages and towns, and everywhere the consciousness of nature humanized. But I also began to understand why Nick Solchuk was always longing for more space and more air, especially when we moved into the prairies, and the land became flatter until there seemed nothing, neither hill nor tree nor bush, to disturb the vast unbroken flow of land until in the far distance a thin, blue line marked the point where the prairie merged into the sky. Yet over all there was a strange tranquillity, all motion seemed suspended, and only the sun moved steadily, imperturbably West, dropping finally over the rim of the horizon, a blazing red ball, but leaving a superb evening light lying over the land still.

I was reminded of the promise I had made, but when I arrived in Edmonton, the task of settling down absorbed my time and energy so completely that I did nothing about it. Then, about the middle of October, I saw a brief report in the newspaper about the geophysical congress which had opened in Rome on the previous day, and I was mindful of my promise again. Before I could safely bury it in the back of my mind again, I sat down and wrote a brief letter to Nick's father, asking him when I could come out to visit him. Two weeks passed without an answer, and I decided to go and see him on the next Saturday without further formalities.

The day broke clear and fine. A few white clouds were in the metallic autumn sky and the sun shone coldly down upon the earth, as if from a great distance. I drove south as far as Wetaskiwin and then turned east. The paved highway gave way to gravel and got steadily worse. I was beginning to wonder whether I was going right, when I rounded a bend and a grain elevator hove like a signpost into view. It was now about three o'clock and I had arrived in Three Bear Hills, but, as Nick had told me, there were neither bears nor hills here, but only prairie, and suddenly the beginning of an embryonic street with a few buildings on either side like a small island in a vast sea, and then all was prairie again.

I stopped in front of the small general store and went in to ask for directions. Three farmers were talking to the storekeeper, a bald, bespectacled little man who wore a long, dirty apron, and stood leaning against his counter. They stopped talking and turned to look at me. I asked where the Solchuk farm was.

Slowly scrutinizing me, the storekeeper asked, "You just new here?"

"Yes," I said.

"From the old country, eh?"

"Yes."

"You selling something?"

"No, no," I said. "I—I teach at the University."

"That so?" He turned to the other men and said, "Only boy ever went to University from around here was Solchuk's boy, Nick. Real brainy young kid, Nick. Two of 'em never got on together. Too different. You know."

They nodded slowly.

"But that boy of his—he's a real big-shot scientist now. You know them addem bombs and them hydrergen bombs. He helps make 'em."

"No, no," I broke in quickly. "That's not what he does. He's a geophysicist."

"What's that?" asked one of the men.

But before I could answer, the little storekeeper asked

excitedly, "You know Nick?"

"Yes," I said, "we're friends. I've come to see his father."

"And where's he now? Nick, I mean."

"Right now he is in Rome," I said. "But he lives in London, and does research there."

"Big-shot, eh," said one of the men laconically, but with a trace of admiration in his voice, too.

"He's a big scientist, though, like I said. Isn't that so?" the storekeeper broke in.

"He's going to be a very important scientist indeed," I said, a trifle solemnly.

"Like I said," he called out triumphantly. "That's showing 'em. A kid from Three Bear Hills, Alberta. More power to him!" His pride was unmistakable. "Tell me, mister," he went on, his voice dropping, "does he remember this place sometimes? Or don't he want to know us no more?"

"Oh no," I said quickly. "He often talks of this place, and of Alberta, and of Canada. Some day he plans to return."

"That's right," he said with satisfaction. He drew himself up to full height, banged his fist on the table and said, "I'm proud of that boy. Maybe old Solchuk don't think so much of him, but you tell him old Mister Marshall is proud of him." He came from behind the counter and almost ceremoniously escorted me out to my car and showed me the way to Solchuk's farm.

I had about another five miles to drive, and the road, hardly more now that two black furrows cut into the prairie, was uneven and bumpy. The land was fenced on both sides of the road, and at last I came to a rough wooden gate hanging loosely on one hinge, and beyond it there was a cluster of small wooden buildings. The largest of these, the house itself, seemed at one time to have been ochre-coloured, but the paint had worn off and it now looked curiously mottled. A few chickens were wandering about, pecking at the ground, and from the back I could hear the grunting and squealing of pigs.

I walked up to the house and, just as I was about to knock, the door was suddenly opened, and a tall, massively built old man stood before me.

"My name is . . . " I began.

But he interrupted me. "You the man wrote to me?" His voice, though unpolished, had the same deep timbre as Nick's.

"That's right," I said.

"You a friend of Nick?"

"Yes."

He beckoned me in with a nod of his head. The door was low and I had to stoop a bit to get into the room. It was a large, low-ceilinged room. A smallish window let in a patch of light which lit up the middle of the room but did not spread into the corners, so that it seemed as if it were perpetually dusk. A table occupied the centre, and on the far side there was a large wood stove on which stood a softly hissing black kettle. In the corner facing the entrance there was an iron bedstead, and the bed was roughly made, with a patchwork quilt thrown carelessly on top.

The old man gestured me to one of the chairs which stood around the table.

"Sit."

I did as he told me, and he sat down opposite me and placed his large calloused hands before him on the table. He seemed to study me intently for a while, and I scrutinized him. His face was covered by a three-day's stubble, but in spite of that, and in spite of the fact that it was a face beaten by sun and wind, it was clear that he was Nick's father. For Nick had the same determined mouth, and the same high cheekbones and the same dark, penetrating eyes.

At last he spoke. "You friend of Nick."

I nodded my head.

"What he do now?" he asked sharply. "He still tampering with the earth?"

His voice rose as if he were delivering a challenge, and I drew back involuntarily. "Why—he's doing scientific research, yes," I told him. "He's . . . "

"What God has made," he said sternly, "no man should touch."

Before I could regain my composure, he went on, "He sent you. What for? What he want?"

"Nothing," I said, "nothing at all. He sent me to bring you greetings and to tell you he is well."

"And you come all the way from Edmonton to tell me?"

"Yes, of course."

A faint smile played about his mouth, and the features of his face softened. Then suddenly he rose from his chair and stood towering over me. "You are welcome in this house," he said.

The formality with which he spoke was quite extraordinary and seemed to call for an appropriate reply, but I could do little more than stammer a thank you, and he, assuming again a normal tone of voice, asked me if I cared to have coffee. When I assented he walked to the far end of the room and busied himself about the stove.

It was then that I noticed, just under the window, a rough little wooden table and on top of it a faded old globe made of cardboard, such as little children use in school. I was intrigued to see it there and went over to look at it more closely. The cheap metal mount was brown with rust, and when I lifted it and tried to turn the globe on its axis, I found that it would not rotate because part of it had

been squashed and broken. I ran my hand over the deep
dent, and suddenly the old man startled me.

"What you doing there?" Curiousity seemed mingled
with suspicion in his voice and made me feel like a small
child surprised by its mother in an unauthorized raid on the
pantry. I set down the globe and turned. He was standing
by the table with two big mugs of coffee in his hands.

"Coffee is hot," he said.

I went back to my chair and sat down, slightly embarrassed.

"Drink," he said, pushing one of the mugs over to me.

We both began to sip the coffee, and for some time
neither of us said anything.

"That thing over there," he said at last, putting down
his mug, "that thing you was looking at—he brought it
home one day—he was a boy then—maybe thirteen-year-
old—Nick. The other day I found it up in the attic. I was
going to throw it in the garbage. But I forgot. There it
belongs. In the garbage. It is a false thing." His voice had
now become venomous.

"False?" I said. "How is it false?"

He disregarded my question. "I remember," he went
on, "he came home from school one day and we was all
here in this room—all sitting around this table eating
supper, his mother, his sister and me and Alex, too—the
hired man like. And then sudden-like Nick pipes up, and
he says, we learned in school today, he says, how the earth
is round like a ball, he says, and how it moves around and
around the sun and never stops, he says. They learning you
rubbish in school, I say. But he says no, Miss McKenzie
never told him no lies. Then I say she does, I say, and a son
of mine shouldn't believe it. Stop your ears! Let not Satan
come in!" He raised an outspread hand and his voice thun-
dered as if he were a prophet armed. "But he was always a
stubborn boy—Nick. Like a mule. He never listened to

reason. I believe it, he says. To me he says that —his father, just like that I believe it, he says, because science has proved it and it is the truth. It is false, I cry, and you will not believe it. I believe it, he says. So then I hit him because he will not listen and will not obey. But he keeps shouting and shouting and shouting. She moves, he shouts, she moves, she moves!"

He stopped. His hands had balled themselves into fists, and the remembered fury sent the blood streaming into his face. He seemed now to have forgotten my presence and he went on speaking in a low murmuring voice, almost as if he were telling the story to himself.

"So the next day, or the day after, I go down to that school, and there is this little Miss McKenzie, so small and so thin that I could have crush her with my bare hands. What you teaching my boy Nick? I ask her. What false lies you stuffing in his head? What you telling him that the earth is round and that she moves for? Did Joshua tell the earth to stand still, or did he command the sun? So she says to me, I don't care what Joshua done, she says, I will tell him what science has discovered. With that woman I could get nowhere. So then I try to keep him away from school, and I lock him up in the house, but it was not good. He got out, and he run to the school like, and Miss McKenzie she sends me a letter to say she will send up the inspectors if I try to keep him away from the school. And I could do nothing."

His sense of impotence was palpable. He sat sunk into himself as if he were still contemplating ways of halting the scientific education of his son.

"Two, three weeks after," he went on, "he comes walking in this door with a large paper parcel in his hand. Now, he calls out to me, now I will prove it to you, I will prove that she moves. And he tears off the paper from the box and takes out this—this thing, and he puts it on the table here. Here, he cries, here is the earth, and look, she moves. And he gives that thing a little push and it twirls around like. I have to laugh. A toy, I say to him, you bring me a toy here, not bigger than my hand, and it is supposed to be the world, this little toy here, with the printed words on coloured paper, this little cardboard ball. This Miss McKenzie, I say to him, she's turning you crazy in that school. But look, he says, she moves. Now I have to stop my laughing. I'll soon show you she moves, I say, for he is beginning to get me mad again. And I go up to the table and I take the toy thing in my hands and I smash it down like this."

He raised his fists and let them crash down on the table as if he meant to splinter it.

"That'll learn you, I cry. I don't think he could believe I had done it, because he picks up the thing and he tries to turn it, but it don't turn no more. He stands there and the tears roll down his cheeks, and then, sudden-like, he takes the thing in both his hands and he throws it at me. And it would have hit me right in the face, for sure, if I did not put my hand. Against your father, I cry, you will raise up your hand against your father. Asmodeus! I grab him by the arm, and I shake him and I beat him like he was the devil. And he makes me madder and madder because he don't cry or shout or anything. And I would have kill him there, for sure, if his mother didn't come in then and pull me away. His nose was bleeding, but he didn't notice. Only he looks at me and says, you can beat me and break my globe, but you can't stop her moving. That night my wife she make me swear by all that's holy that I wouldn't touch him no more. And from then on I never hit him again nor talk to him about this thing. He goes his way and I go mine."

He fell silent. Then after a moment he snapped suddenly, "You hold with that?"

"Hold with what?" I asked, taken aback.

"With that thing?" He pointed behind him at the little table and at the broken globe. His gnarled hands now tightly interlocked, he leaned forward in his chair and his dark, brooding eyes sought an answer from mine in the twilight of the room.

Alone with him there, I was almost afraid to answer firmly. Was it because I feared that I would hurt him too deeply if I did, or was I perhaps afraid that he would use violence on me as he had on Nick?

I cleared my throat. "Yes," I said then. "Yes, I believe that the earth is round and that she moves. That fact has been accepted now for a long time."

I expected him to round on me but he seemed suddenly to have grown very tired, and in a low resigned voice he said, "Satan has taken over all the world." Then suddenly he roused himself and hit the table hard with his fist, and cried passionately, "But not me! Not me!"

It was unbearable. I felt that I must break the tension, and I said the first thing that came into my mind. "You can be proud of your son in spite of all that happened between you. He is a fine man, and the world honours him for his work."

He gave me a long look, "He should have stayed here," he said quietly. "When I die, there will be nobody to look after the land. Instead he has gone off to tamper with God's earth."

His fury was now all spent. We sat for a while in silence, and then I rose. Together we walked out of the house. When I was about to get into my car, he touched me lightly on the arm. I turned. His eyes surveyed the vast expanse of sky and land, stretching far into the distance, reddish clouds in the sky and blue shadows on the land. With a gesture of great dignity and power he lifted his arm and stood pointing into the distance, at the flat land and the low-hanging sky. "Look," he said, very slowly and very quietly, "she is flat, and she stands still."

It was impossible not to feel a kind of admiration for the old man. There was something heroic about him. I held out my hand and he took it. He looked at me steadily, then averted his eyes and said, "Send greetings to my son."

I drove off quickly, but had to stop again in order to open the wooden gate. I looked back at the house, and saw him still standing there, still looking at his beloved land, a lonely, towering figure framed against the darkening evening sky.

Rat With Tangerine
Greg Hollingshead

The idea is to get from under the covers to the TV with a minimum of complication. The idea is to keep the grey winter sunlight closed out. The idea is to keep the morning's last dream rolling like a tangerine around the periphery of the long, quiet day.

The second quarter is over. In a prerecorded interview the coach is saying, "We're working as a team now. We're really going out there together and hurting people." Bill, watching this, hears the staple gun from the basement: his son Aubrey is building something. *Keep it down* Bill beams at Aubrey who beams back *OK Dad*, but the stapling continues. Results so far on Bill's telepathic career have been inconclusive. Shortly into the third quarter Diane comes in to fling open the drapes. *No* Bill beams, pushing his glasses up his nose, clearing his throat. Diane shrugs and returns to the kitchen. Conflict averted.

After the game one of those educational shows. "Hey, Aub," Bill calls from the top of the cellar stairs. "Come and see this." Aubrey emerges from the basement and joins Bill to watch a chimp talk American sign language with a lady psychologist in dark glasses. They're having a conversation, with subtitles.

"Who is this?" the chimp is asking, pointing with a limp hand at the show's host.

"A friend," replies the lady psychologist.

The chimp makes sarcastic kissing motions at him, then asks her, "When time eat?"

"What do you think, Ben?" she replies.

"Ben is uncertain. When time eat?"

During the commercial, Bill turns to Aubrey and says, "I thought language was supposed to be the last bastion."

Aubrey shrugs. "I guess you'd better get to work on that telepathy."

"Minds across the miles?"

"That's right."

It occurs to Bill that Diane has left the house at some point. "Where'd your mother go?"

"Primaling."

"They *are* getting closer."

Aubrey seems worried, as if he has something to say, but he goes back to the basement, so Bill walks over and opens the drapes. Across the street and down a bit there is a house he has never seen before. These new developments are really something. Bill walks back to the TV and watches an old Mary Tyler Moore, and then a drama about a student nurse who wants more than anything to graduate, but the other nurses treat her so heartlessly—in one scene they put a severed hand in her bed—that she has a nervous breakdown during which she swallows a number of small surgical instruments. Bill gets a beer and wanders downstairs to visit Aubrey, who is stapling chickenwire to a rhomboidal frame. Bill stands there with the beer in his hand. Aubrey is the first to speak.

"Bad news, Dad."

"Shoot," and Bill takes a big, staring swig. His last dream is just there at the periphery, a rolling tangerine.

"Wilson died last night." Aubrey is still working away twisting chicken wire with pliers. "He's the last rat, and it doesn't look good."

"Died premature, eh? Diets can kill?"

"Not so simple. They all lived long lives. But when I

dissected, the ones that could eat whatever they wanted, the ones who got really sleek and strong, were the worst diseased. And they all ate different things."

"Not wise to offer a rat a wide food choice?" Bill says.

Aubrey is running his fingers along the edge of a spruce slat as if he would like a splinter. "And why not, do you think?"

"You got me," and Bill is thinking, wouldn't it be nice to just crawl back under the covers and hello dreamland.

"I was thinking about 'disease'," Aubrey is saying, "like *dis*ease, you know? and if you consider what it must be like to live so confined—"

"I wouldn't worry about that. You kept 'em pretty comfortable, Aub. They had nothing to complain about, really, except maybe for a little itchiness in the bones, but that's understandable, right? Cooped up all day—"

"Never mind, Dad."

Bill goes back upstairs. He is feeling anxious. Halfway through the second period of a hockey game, a great desire for one of Diane's bread puddings comes over him. He beams *bread pudding* to her at her primal therapy group, or wherever she is. When the game is over he wanders into the kitchen and pokes around in the cupboards, but there is nothing exciting. Diane shops by pure habit, the smallest sizes. There are five or six jars in there of the same thing; three or four host fungus. Bill checks the sink for the roast that he has hoped would be thawing, but there is nothing. He wanders downstairs to the freezer for porkchops. On his way back he sticks his head in the workshop door at Aubrey but can't think of anything to say. He gazes at the porkchops, hefts them. "Porkchops," he says.

Aubrey nods.

Next there's a Victor Mature movie. Lotsa savanna. Bill is asleep in front of it when he hears the back door and voices. Diane has a way of talking at times as if her ego is lodged in her throat. Bill tiptoes into the kitchen not wanting to see who is doing this to her voice. He sits down at the kitchen table and beams *bread pudding* as hard as he can. An ordinary man with a fading smile—her ride to the primal class—goes past the kitchen window on his way down the back steps. Diane comes into the kitchen and she is still smiling.

At dinner Aubrey talks about his plans. One is an experiment concerning the effects of fluorescent lights on the daily life of caged mice. Bill suggests he make that the effects of *TV* on the daily life of caged mice.

"Irradiation study?" Aubrey asks thoughtfully.

"Sure, and on food. You know they're starting to irradiate fruit and vegetables now. Makes them last longer. 'Gamma Protected' they call it."

"I read that too," Aubrey says.

There is a pause.

"Diane," Bill says, "tell Aubrey what the guy at the party told you about the hookers."

"What guy? You tell him."

So Bill explains how big city hotels put blue lights outside to keep prostitutes away because they look like death under them. "Whereas everybody looks terrific under red. Hence red light district, get it. Same with food. People can't eat blue food. Put blue icing on part of a cake and people won't eat that part. Once I put blue food colouring in a guy's baked beans and he just about went insane."

"What about blueberries," says Aubrey, who is good at skepticism.

"Blueberries are purple." Blueberries remind Bill of raisins and raisins of the bread pudding that Diane has not felt like making. The tangerine is there too. "The point about TV is it sheds a sort of blue-white light. It's a blue world. I wonder what that does to people's, you know, outlooks."

"Maybe it makes them think they're under water."

"I never thought of that."

"You watch TV all the time," Diane reminds Bill.

"I know." He is the first to admit it. "I just might stop completely. I think I'm almost drowned." He tells Diane about the chimp talking sign language.

"So what are you saying, Pop," from Aubrey.

"Who knows. I'm brainstorming here. Diane, do you remember what I did after Aubrey was born?"

"You went out into the hospital parking lot and howled at the moon. I was never so embarrassed."

"That's right, and I wasn't even self-conscious. Boy, those were the days."

Aubrey has his hand over his eyes.

"In the drugstore the other day," Bill continues, "I overheard a conversation. One guy wanted medicine from the shelf and another guy was explaining how you can tell the quality by picking up vibrations from the packages. All you have to do is hold the different brands in your hands for a few minutes."

"The guy was a screwball," Diane says.

"There are more things in heaven and earth, Di."

"What's your point, Dad." Aubrey is tapping his teeth with his fork.

"The rats, Aub. Tell us about them again." Bill is on his feet circling the table, smacking his fist into his palm. "Diane, don't start doing the dishes. Why do you always start doing the dishes. Listen to this."

"You can both talk to me while you're drying." Aubrey agrees to explain again about the rats while drying. Bill sits on a kitchen chair with his elbows on his knees

and his face in his hands. As soon as Aubrey has finished,
Diane says, "People aren't rats."

"True, but they're mammals," Aubrey replies.

"Well they're not rodents." Aubrey and his mother
proceed to have one of their arguments.

"That's enough you two," Bill says finally.

"You heard your father!" Diane cries. "That's
enough!"

Fastidious as a maniac, Aubrey has been smoothing
and squaring the wet dishtowel along the oven door handle. When Bill looks again he is not there. A door slams.

Diane remains at the sink, scouring, and Bill sits
watching the muscles in her neck. He asks her about Mr.
Ordinary, what she wants to do. She shakes her head, sits
down at the table across from Bill, doesn't know, really;
the guy's married, two kids, one a diabetic, and so on. As
she talks she seems to become more and more confused by
the fact that the guy should sound so ordinary in the telling. They go over it, and over it. By midnight Diane has
gone to bed, and the house is still. Bill goes down to the
basement and offers Aubrey, who is shaping a water
trough out of tin with pliers, the use of the TV for his next
experiment. Aubrey accepts. Bill asks Aubrey what he
thinks about open marriage. Not much, judging from
Aubrey's embarrassed shrug, but kids are notoriously con-
servative. Bill and Aubrey carry the TV downstairs. After
that Bill walks around the house switching off lights, locking doors, turning down the thermostat. He opens the
drapes and stands in the darkened living room looking out
at the cold blue fluorescence of the street. It's snowing
again. And then he goes to bed, curling his body to an S to
fit Diane's, and falls asleep and dreams about a cold wind,
the front door slamming open, darkness, out of the darkness a white rat walking on hind legs down the hall to the
bedroom, tangerine held high in thin ecstatic paws.

Bugs
Nancy Holmes

It was raining the night I discovered the bugs.

In the dark, the old house smelled wet and musty. My little sister, a warm, sleeping solid, kept rolling into me as I lay rigid in bed listening to the rain hiss on the roof, the dank odour of our new home filling my nostrils.

I was squeezing my eyes shut, trying to blank out all memory of my first day at school in the new town. But instead of fading the ugly whisper grew louder until it rang like a shout in my head. "Dirty Bohunk" someone had said softly in my ear as I crouched over a bench in the crowded cloakroom pulling on my rainboots.

I was too restless to sleep. Around midnight I got out of bed and crept down the hall. The cold floor cracked loudly beneath my bare feet and I hurried to the bathroom, closing the door behind me before I searched for the light switch. I didn't want to wake Mom or Daddy: they would see my raw eyes and would ask what was wrong. I was too ashamed to tell them about the whisper in the cloakroom. As if they wouldn't have understood.

We'd only been living in the house for two days and I had trouble finding the bathroom switch in the dark. The damp smell of the walls was thick and stifling as if some-one were holding a dirty wash rag over my face. I found the light and I flicked it on.

Then I saw them. Thousands of crawling black bugs. A thin sprinkling of insects shifting all over the walls and ceiling. As soon as the light hit them, they sifted into the wall, swiftly poured into dark corners, behind the toilet and into the wooden trim around the door and window.

I screamed and by the time my parents arrived, the bugs had completely disappeared.

Daddy, tall and spindly in his long underwear, looked at me in disbelief when I described the bugs. I was aware of his bony limbs, a large expanse of hairy chest, his naked feet, white and gnarled, and was suddenly embarrassed to be in the small bathroom with him in his underwear and me in my nightdress. I clung to Mom while he inspected the walls and the corners, shadows making his thin nose and cheekbones sharp and elongated like some villain in the silent movies.

I buried my face in Mom's faded pink nightgown. Her large hands were warm as they held me and stroked my hair. She clucked and cooed, her voice husky with her accent, her breast full of scent: a mixture of yeast, cabbage and rose perfume.

Daddy sent me back to bed.

"I'll keep a lookout for these bugs of yours." He glanced at Mom, shaking his head slightly.

I slipped back under the covers and fell asleep immediately, as if I had absorbed sleepiness from my mother's soft skin.

Mom and Daddy thought I was having a nightmare and the bugs were a bad dream. Unfortunately as the days went by, the house revealed its infestation to everyone.

It was a cold, wet autumn and the house swelled up like a bloated body. For the insects, the humidity created perfect breeding conditions. The rotten eaves, sweating walls, sagging floors were riddled with bugs and soon everyone in the family had come across them in some chilly corner. The insects were extremely light shy, never oozing out of the walls unless the room was dark. And each night there seemed to be more of them.

Mom wanted to move.

"All my things! All my things!" she cried, gathering her cheap, colourful icons into her arms and sealing them away in chests jammed with mothballs; rushing from room to room, her long skirts sweeping, as she moved all her furniture several feet away from the walls as if the bugs were less likely to get at it there.

Daddy patted her arm and ignored her weeping.

"Anna, calm down. I will make the landlady fumigate the place."

Daddy wasn't Ukrainian at all: he was Polish. There is a difference, I've always thought, like the difference between the Irish and the English. The Ukrainians have a streak of Cossack violence. Every emotion is lavish and charged. My mother was sentimental, warm, open. She loved colour, sad songs, lots of good food, and boisterous weddings and funerals. Daddy was reserved and sober. He and all his relatives wore dark clothes and lots of them, as if always bundled up for a bleak Eastern European winter.

However, back then, in the early 1920's, "Bohunks" were Poles and Ukrainians alike. Our family was definitely "Bohunk" and our landlady wouldn't fumigate our house.

Daddy came home from work one night in a rage. His blue eyes were narrow and bitter.

"The bitch," I was shocked to hear him say. "The stupid bitch. Implies all the time I talk to her that *we're* dirty! That *we've* brought the bugs with us! This house is so infested it must have taken years for it to get this bad! Yet she has the . I'll prove it to her. I'll drag her here to see those bugs if I have to . . . to knock her out first!"

The ugly whisper of the cloakroom crawled into my head again. "Dirty Bohunk." I left the room where Mom and Daddy were talking loudly and angrily, not wanting to hear anymore about the landlady.

Her name was Mrs. Murray and she came to inspect

the house one morning when Daddy was at work and I was home sick although I think the cold was largely invention. I began to dream up excuses to stay home, thinking the kids at school, those with English names, were staring at me and whispering behind my back.

Mrs. Murray hadn't bothered to dress up to make her visit. I saw curling rags under her scarf and she wore a dingy, flannel housecoat under her rain gear. She had lovely round blue eyes with long black lashes but her face, perhaps once as attractive as her eyes, had deteriorated. Her skin was broken by faint blue and red veins; her lips were puffed with bruises. Years later I heard that her husband beat her and that she drank but I hated her with a simple purity the morning she walked into our kitchen, not even scraping the mud off her boots, her mouth pursed and smug as she informed my mother that she was the landlady.

"Well where are these bugs of yours?" Her voice slurred slightly.

Mom pulled up a chair for her, trying to explain the bugs only came out at night. Her accent became thicker with anxiety. Mrs. Murray pretended not to understand what she was saying.

Ignoring the offer of the chair, the landlady tramped into the living room in her muddy boots, took one quick look at the walls then returned to the kitchen, speaking to my mother in a loud, slow voice.

"No bugs here. You tell your husband that. Understand? No bugs here." Then she spoke more normally, noticing me huddled in a chair by the stove. "At least there weren't any before you moved in. You just keep the place clean, dear. Sweep the floors, wash the walls. You're living in town now, not on the farm."

Mom nodded Mrs. Murray out the door, twisting her hands and mumbling. As soon as the woman left, Mom burst into noisy tears and spent the rest of the morning scrubbing the floor which the landlady had streaked with mud. I went to my bed to read a library book, blushing every time I thought of Mrs. Murray—angry at her for saying my mother was dirty: Mom who even scrubbed the front door and who swept out the yard, Mom whose hands were perpetually red from washing and rinsing. I was angry with Mom too, for nodding so eagerly, for being so fearful. I ignored her when she came up to my room to offer comfort, company and hot tea.

Even then Daddy wouldn't move. He would make Mrs. Murray apologize, admit her mistake. He vowed to prove the existence of the bugs.

For a week he tore up floorboards, peeled off base-boards, drilled holes in the plaster and unscrewed light sockets, looking for evidence of the bugs: nests, eggs, droppings, dead shells, anything. Mom swept up after him, pleading, scolding, but he brushed her complaints aside even when he found no substantial proof.

Next he borrowed a camera and flash from one of his cousins, a pharmacist in Vegreville. It was a small, black box with an accordian-type front. We sat up til ten o'clock that night. It was like a holiday. Daddy was excited and nervous, shooing us away from the camera balanced on a tippy tripod; he fiddled with the viewfinder, adjusted the flash. Mom made us kids hot milk and cookies and kept saying "Hush" when we giggled or squealed in the dark, as if the bugs, who came out every night regardless of the noise level, would be scared away by rowdy children. I think she enjoyed herself that night; victory seemed imminent. She cheered and clapped when the flash went off and Daddy cleared his brow with a handkerchief, smil-ing proudly as we clamoured around begging him to take a picture of the family now that the business was over. I still have that photo—slightly overexposed, grey and grizzled like the weather that autumn. Mom looks unusually stern and we children are shyly disshevelled. I, the eldest, am tall and adolescently weedy, wearing a wilting aster in my hair which at the time I thought looked chic. The next day I wore one to school but after enduring the giggles of my classmates all morning I tore it out of my hair and threw it in the garbage.

That weekend Daddy and his cousin developed the pictures. They were failures. The white walls had reflected so much of the flash that the bugs were flooded out. Daddy wouldn't try it again—I suspect his pride was hurt that his photos turned out so bad.

By now Daddy was obsessed with the bugs. "Evidence" he went around the house muttering. "Proof." He refused to hire an exterminator with our own money though Mom suggested this frequently.

"It's the principle, Anna. The principle," he told her and I, thinking of "Dirty Bohunk," agreed with him.

Mom began to hate the house. On the farm she had coddled and loved her home. The kitchen had been filled with the warm, sweet weight of food smells—bread, cabbage rolls, doughnuts, poppyseed cake, sizzling bacon, fruity stuffs being preserved. Now she spent every day cleaning, cleaning, cleaning. She changed the sheets on our bed each morning, washed the walls, beat the rugs. I remember thinking resentfully that we always had potatoes and sausages for supper. And I remember Mom always looked tired.

There were arguments every night with Mom shouting, crying, pleading and Daddy murmuring or saying loudly, "That's enough, Anna."

One drizzly night I woke up from a fitful sleep. That day in the schoolyard the clannish groups of English girls were pointing at me and my new skirt, several inches too long. Mom always made my dresses long, in spite of my

protests. When she was a girl it had been a mark of growing up to be able to wear longer skirts. She couldn't understand that styles had changed. Even in my sleep I seemed
to hear a constant whispered titter that made me squirm.

I heard Mom moving around in the kitchen, in the
dark. I thought I heard matches being struck.

Daddy called out from the bedroom down the hall,
"Anna, come to bed. It's after one in the morning."

"Go to sleep. I'm busy," Mom answered.

I wondered if she were stalking the bugs, her old
enemies. Perhaps praying about them or damning them
with some old Ukrainian curse. After listening to Mom
shuffle around in the kitchen for several minutes, the rain
drumming on the roof put me to sleep again.

The morning broke clear, clean and wet like cold
water. I could hear sparrows chitter and clipping drops of
water dripping from the eaves and the trees. The sunshine
was bright and windy, flapping like a thousand bright
flags. The rain had stopped.

The house looked almost cheerful I thought, with the
sun making the water-stained walls nearly white.

I met Daddy in the hallway as we came out of our
rooms together. He nodded and smiled stiffly.

"Morning."

I remember thinking the sunny weather was making
Daddy uncommonly cheerful as he rarely did more than
grunt in the morning. I remember feeling very grown-up
because I was amused by my father.

I stepped into the kitchen, still smiling, and saw my
mother asleep at the table. The sunlight pouring through
the icy clean windows made the kerchief on her head glow
red and warm like blood. Her large, white arms were
wrapped around her face as she rested her head on the
table. A small, empty cardboard box lay beside her.

I wondered why she was asleep in the kitchen instead

of in her bed.

Then I saw the wall behind her. It dazzled white in the early morning sun. I began screaming.

Mom stirred and woke.

"Be quiet," she jumped up from the table and began shaking me. I gulped back my screams, shocked by her rough grip.

"Be quiet both of you," she shouted as my father started to say something, angrily. She turned on him, letting go of my arm abruptly, as if she had forgotten all about me, pointing at the wall behind her. "That's your proof. Your proof. You understand? Now get that woman and show her your precious bugs and get her to clean my house! Get my house cleaned!"

Mom's face was fierce and hot. I looked away and stared again at the wall.

It was covered with dead bugs. Each brittle black body was stuck to the wall with a thin pin. Hundreds of dead black bugs pinned to the wall.

I turned to my father, wanting him to say something sane, angry, wanting him to put his arm around me, to get me away from Mom who suddenly seemed violent and unreliable.

Instead his hands drooped at his sides and his eyes looked washed with age.

"I'm sorry, Anna. It's their stupidity. Makes me stupid . . ." he whispered hoarsely.

She opened her arms and he went to her. Holding him tightly, she looked over his sunken shoulder at me, her eyes stern and passionate, motioning for me to leave them alone.

I slowly walked out of the kitchen, leaving my father to his comfort. We moved a few days later.

Touching the Buffalo
Elona Malterre

Through the window Michelle could see her daughters. When they saw her car they began jumping up and down, clapping their hands. Michelle stopped the car in the driveway of the red brick two-storey which had been her home. Her daughters ran down the front steps, racing to touch her. She was out of the car, kneeling down, gathering both into her arms, kissing one daughter, then the other: kissing their cheeks, eyes, fine black hair, chubby fingers. She could taste chocolate. It was Saturday. She used to give them a treat if they cleaned their rooms on the weekend.

She looked directly into the small faces, round and cheerful as balloons. "I missed you so much," she said, pulling her daughters to her again and squeezing. She felt the beginning of tears. Wiping at them, she added quickly, "Go get your coats, girls. It's getting late and we have lots to do."

They ran back into the house, Michelle following with her thoughts: entranceway, plum carpet and beige, grass wallpaper; up stairs, the master bedroom and master bath, thick expensive towels monogrammed with her initials and Graham's. (Or had Graham thrown her towels out?) The girls' rooms, white colonial furniture and rose-coloured walls, Raggedy Anne dolls for decoration. Michelle had done the painting and decorating of the house herself, a house whose sounds—the whisper when the furnace came on, the flumping of awnings when the

wind blew, the swish of tree branches against the roof—
had become as familiar to her as the sigh of her daughters.

Now she had become accustomed to new sounds, the
sounds of her basement suite; water hammers clanging
through the pipes, strangers running water for their bath-
tubs, the closing of doors, and a woman's sharp heels hastily crossing a linoleum floor. When Michelle looked out
from the single window, she saw the black tires of cars in
the parking lot, bits of gravel embedded in the tread.

She looked around as she waited for her daughters.
"Tree-lined streets and manicured yards." Weren't those
the words the real-estate salesman had used when she and
Graham had bought the house? "Two-thousand square feet
of well-appointed elegance. Lots of room for a family to
grow."

She had given Graham the spruce tree in the corner of
the lot as a Father's Day gift two years after the girls were
born. She had planted it the night before he returned from
a business trip. The spruce had flourished despite what
Graham said about the location being too hot for it. It was
well over five feet high, bristling with dark needles.

Michelle's daughters reappeared calling "Bye,
Daddy" behind them. They were identical twins: Bonnie,
born three minutes before Brenda, each with ski-jump
noses and their father's impatient blue eyes. They'd both
had recent haircuts. Michelle used to braid their hair into
pigtails, which she tied with ribbons, different colours for
each child so the kindergarten teacher could tell them
apart. But ribbons and braids were a mother's skills, skills
Graham didn't have patience for.

Arriving at the car the twins began pushing each other
away from the passenger door. Michelle was surprised.
Bonnie and Brenda seldom fought.

"Mommy, I want to sit beside you," cried Brenda,
shoving at her sister. But they were the same size and

weight. Neither moved.

"No me," yelled Bonnie, shoving back.

"Girls! You both have to sit in the back seat. You know that."

"I want to sit behind you, Mommy!"

"No me."

"You can take turns. Brenda, you first. And make sure your seat belts are done up."

Bonnie, her face twisting into a grimace, started to cry.

"Honey, what's the matter?"

"Mommy, I wanted to sit close to you."

"You can sit behind me on the way home. Come on now, don't cry, Mommy's going to buy each of you a new dress. And we'll go to the museum too," Michelle said, pulling out a Kleenex.

At the mention of the museum, Bonnie stopped crying. "Can we touch the buffalo?" she asked, her blotched face suddenly bright with expectation.

"We'll see."

She made a turn into a parking lot where an attendant handed her an orange ticket. He looked a bit like Tony, the long sharpness of his nose and fleshy lips. "Thank you," Michelle said smiling, but without responding he turned and walked back into the white cubicle. She had thought about bringing Tony with her, telling the girls, but decided against it. It was too soon.

"There's an empty spot, Mommy. Mommy, you just drove by an empty place."

"I didn't see it."

"I told you it was there."

"I didn't hear you. I'll back up."

She parked the car, got out and pulled the seat forward so the girls could scramble out of the back. As

Michelle pushed the car door shut, both daughters reached for the same hand, knocking Michelle's purse to the ground. Its contents, a disordered collage of past, present and future, clattered on the asphalt.

"Must you grab? What's gotten into you today?" The fallen expression on the girls' faces made Michelle realize that she had spoken too quickly, too harshly. They saw her once a week. Eagerness made them clumsy and sensitive.

"I'm sorry, Mommy," Brenda said, bending down and picking up her mother's things.

"I didn't mean to get angry, but there's no need for shoving. There's enough of me for everybody."

"Daddy gave you this, didn't he?" Brenda said, slowly handing a sterling silver ball-point to her mother.

Michelle dusted off the bag with the flat of her hand and reached to Brenda. "A long time ago. Now come. I have two hands. Let's skip—like we used to."

Michelle had made the girls' dresses herself. Sewn from lilac-coloured cotton, they were decorated with pansies whose petals, braided into delicate purple clusters, danced around the girls' knees as they skipped.

Michelle, Bonnie and Brenda skipped past the glass and cement-fronted stores with Sale signs in the windows. Already merchants were cleaning out their stock for the next season's merchandise.

They skipped past the sandstone columns that circled the Bay. Once the biggest building in the city, the six-storey department store stood dwarfed by the straight-line structures that towered around it blocking out even the high sun of spring. Graham worked in one of those skyscrapers.

A couple dressed in blue jeans strolled casually in front of them. The young man and woman had their arms wrapped around each other's waists, the way Michelle and Tony always walked in the park.

"Mommy! Look at the pretty dresses those girls are wearing," Bonnie said, pointing at the store window where mannequins were wrapped in parrot bright clothes. They stood under a green striped lawn umbrella. Two other mannequins, a man and a woman, sat, knees touching, on a garden swing, the colour of the umbrella.

She and Graham used to sit like that on the wooden swing on her parents' porch, holding hands, talking about the future. But at some point during their life together, they had stopped talking, had withdrawn their fingers, and if they touched, perhaps when they passed a plate between them at the supper table, each would apologize. "I'm sorry," they would say, in the tone of people who had just met.

"Mommy. I can see it! I can see the museum!"

They reached the revolving glass door that was the entrance to the Glenbow Museum. "Okay, girls," said Michelle, trying to pull free of the fingers which gripped her hand.

"I want to go in with you, Mommy."

"I want to go in with you too."

"There's not room for three of us. You two go in together like you always do, and I'll follow right behind."

"No, I want to go with you."

"No, I do," Bonnie said, yanking on Michelle's arm.

"Would you stop that? You're not babies anymore that you have to pull on me. You can go through a door by yourself." Michelle ripped her hands from the girls. Immediately she relented. "All right, all right. I'll take you through one at a time."

"Mommy! Tell us about the Aurora Borealis. About how it came to the winter sky."

Inside the front door of the museum was the Aurora Borealis: an immense sculpture, images of moon and sun-coloured crystals rising as though frozen against mirrored glass; dawn-tinted lights and cascading water rising through the four-storey height of the building.

Michelle hesitated before she answered. Graham always said telling children about Gods and Goddesses was like saying babies came from under cabbage leaves.

"They're sparks from the swords of fighting Gods."

"No, not that. We want to hear the other story."

She began, "A long long time ago . . . "

"Even before dinosaurs?"

"Even before dinosaurs, the Dawn with her daughter, Aurora, came to visit Earth early each morning. But one day the God of the Frozen North was woken by their singing, and he carried Aurora off to his cave deep under the Purple Mountains. Dawn was heartbroken and she did nothing but sit and weep. We call the reflection of the moon on her tears the Aurora Borealis," Michelle concluded with an upward sweep of her hand in the direction of the sculpture.

"But Aurora sees her mother again," Bonnie added.

"Yes, in the spring. She comes out of the cave and Dawn stops crying, and they skip across the sky again, hand in hand. She and Aurora whisper their songs to the Sun so early in the morning that you and you," Michelle tapped the end of the twins' noses with her fingertip, "are still asleep."

"Can we go and see the buffalo now?" Without waiting for an answer, both girls raced over to the elevators, where they took turns punching the buttons until one set of doors opened. Michelle got in and they were carried silently to the fourth floor.

The girls showed no interest in the "Settlement of the West" exhibits. They knew better than to run in a museum, but they walked very quickly past the weathered Mounted Police cabin, and the grey, wooden-wheeled carts.

"I thought you wanted to visit the museum."

"We're going to see the buffalo," said Brenda, and the girls, holding each other's hand, continued speeding through the Indian section, past the buckskin vests decorated with red and blue thunderbirds, past the animal pelts, the weapons and the cooking utensils in the direction of the tipi and the buffalo.

A few months after the girls were born, Michelle had become a volunteer for the museum. Once a week she led children through the museum on a tour.

One day, a small Indian girl had lingered behind her classmates, who had gone on to another section. The little girl stood staring at the stuffed buffalo. Her hands rested on the red velvet rope which kept passersby from getting close to the animal.

"Can I touch him?" she asked.

At first, Michelle wasn't sure that the little girl had spoken. "Pardon me?" Michelle had to bend close to hear.

"Can I touch him?" she whispered.

Michelle looked at the buffalo. "Him?"

The little girl nodded her head.

"Why do you want to touch him?"

"Just a little pat. On the nose." The child looked at the floor. She wore red knee socks. One had collapsed in wrinkles around her ankle.

"But why do you want to touch him?"

"My grandfather . . . he used to say . . . that if you touched a buffalo's nose . . . you'd get your wish."

Michelle couldn't see the child's classmates or her teacher. "What do you want to wish for?"

The child's eyes were brilliant, as though she were on the verge of tears. "I can't tell you because then it won't come true."

Michelle looked around again. She lifted the red velvet rope. "Okay . . . but hurry!"

The child scooted under, reached a small hand out

and touched the buffalo's nose. She closed her eyes and silently mouthed some words, then scurried out from under the rope and looked up at Michelle with sparkling eyes. She then ran after the others in the direction of the RCMP cabin.

"No running, please." A security guard emerged from behind the tipi.

The look on the small girl's face stayed with Michelle, and that night at supper she told Graham and Brenda and Bonnie. "That's the silliest thing I ever heard of," said Graham. "Pass the salad."

"Mommy, can we go and touch the buffalo one day?" asked Bonnie.

"You'll do no such thing," said Graham. "Imagine what would happen to the things in the museum if everybody went around touching them. They'd be ruined in no time. I don't know why you insist on telling the girls these hocus pocus stories all the time. Pass the buns."

But the next time Michelle took the girls to visit the museum, she let them touch the buffalo. And whenever she took a tour of primary graders through the museum, she would look around, and if she couldn't see anybody, she would quietly ask, "Do you know what the Indians believed?" There would be a hushed silence. "That if you could touch the tip of a buffalo's nose, you would get whatever you wished for." She would then lift the red velvet cord from in front of the buffalo and allow the children to approach him. They would stroke the buffalo's long shaggy coat and his coarse tangled mane where it rose in a brown hump over his shoulders. Some would reach tentatively to his black varnished nose.

That was how she had met Tony. "Do you always do that?" he asked, appearing after a group of children had left.

"Do what?" She hadn't noticed him sitting behind the tipi. He'd been sketching some cooking utensils.

"Let the children touch him," he said smiling under a dark moustache, and pointing a torquoise-ringed finger at the buffalo.

"Children should be allowed to touch things," she said.

"You don't have to defend yourself to me," he said.

They had shared coffee and bagels in the delicatessen in Palliser Square across from the museum. Now he wanted her to leave with him for the West Coast at the end of the month. He had a place there. "Kind of run down but the girls can stay with us during the summer when they're not in school," he said.

Michelle saw Bonnie before she saw the buffalo. From the broken expression on her face, Michelle knew that something was the matter.

The red velvet rope around the buffalo had been removed and the buffalo now stood encased in glass.

Brenda knelt in front of the glass, her nose and palms flattened against the case. Tears streamed down her face and onto the glass.

"Come on, honey. Let's go." Michelle tried to take her hand, but Brenda pulled it away.

"We want to touch him!" she sobbed.

"You can't now."

"But why did they put this glass up? Why did they?" Crying, Bonnie knelt down beside her sister, and pressed her cheek and hands against the glass.

"Lots of things in the museum are in glass. To protect them. So dust doesn't get at them."

"But we can't touch him now!" Brenda screamed.

Michelle looked around her. Some people were standing by the tipi. "SSSSHHH. You're not supposed to shout in here. Let's go and see something else."

"But you promised!"

"I didn't promise anything. I said we'll see. And stop shouting."

"Mommy, we want to touch the buffalo."

"Brenda, please stop shouting! Bonnie, there's no reason for you to cry like that . . . Come on. You can't touch him anymore. Let's go look at something else. Please?" Michelle tried to lift Brenda off the floor, but her daughter let herself slide back down. Her chest heaved.

"No!"

"Let's go look at the geology section. You like the rocks."

"I want to touch the buffalo!"

"Come on! Mommy will buy each of you a new dress. A pretty blue one. Matching ones. With big ribbons." She grabbed for both their hands. But they withdrew them. Bonnie began to pound on the glass. Michelle grabbed the small fists. Then Brenda started. She smashed with her fists, but mostly she smashed with her heart. "Please!" she sobbed. "We want to touch the buffalo. We need to touch it. Please, Mommy, please."

Goose, Dog, Fish, Stars
Mark Jarman

There are black antlers, cashews, a clock made of pool balls. "You should meet Olofson," the young bartender says after a while. His eyes dark, the skin around them unmarked.

"Why not," says Hank.

Olofson wears a bleached workshirt, has a bit of a beard, weather-beaten cheeks. He looks to Hank like a longshoreman, maybe a sailor. Second generation Swede, raised by the docks of dark Ballard. "Give me something that will sneak up on me," calls Olofson. "Leave me handicapped." He waves a muscular arm around. The bartender pulls down a bottle of bourbon: Fighting Cock, the label says.

"This is basically nutritious," he offers solemnly.

Olofson nods, pale eyes closed, head moving like a blind man's. Behind them the coast guard pilots shoot eightball.

"Don't I know you from somewhere?" speaks someone.

"I don't know," Hank says softly.

"This tastes terrible!" Olofson the sailor cries, eyes still closed, drinking it anyway. "Well, how do you like it here?"

"It's interesting," Hank says. Locals seem disappointed by his replies. Is he to kiss the ground every ten minutes? Hank thinks of the frigates that once called here, holds heavy with stone ballast, timber, or the silk trade. He wonders if Virginia is sleeping. They had argued earlier about a guy she had slept with in Wyoming.

"She's bummed," grumbles one of the pilots at the tables. "Hasn't talked to me since I had that Cat run into the side of her trailer."

"Sure. Why not," his partner answers, studying the lay of the balls. A woman shrieks in a distant booth.

"Never did find that marriage certificate. Got the dee-vorce papers though. Those I need!"

At two a.m. the doors are locked but Hank and Olofson drink on, the bartender drawing them Red Hook gratis. The bartender reaches in a yellow box of Hav-A-Tampa Jewels, lights up a bomber and passes it across the bar to Hank. What the hell, Hank says, and has a toke. He imagines telling Virginia about it in their motel room.

"No clams this year," says the bartender in his smoke.

"Dead as doornails," says Olofson the sailor. "Took a backhoe to the beach. Zero. Nada."

"Oh," says Hank, feeling somehow to blame.

"Are you working right now?" they ask. The lights are dim, Los Lobos plays manic Tex-Mex accordion on the cassette deck.

"No. Not working." What had he been thinking of? Virginia. He feels sudden affection for her.

"It's bad right now."

"What is this stuff? Paint thinner?" asks Olofson, examining the bottle of Fighting Cock. "I think I've been damaged," he says holding his chest. He stares sadly at Hank.

"But you, you're both working?" asks Hank.

"Well, you know." They glance at each other. "This and that."

The joint is strong. It is cut with something, it makes itself known. Olofson lectures on about loss of the

clamming season to the peninsula, about blackmouth salmon, about money or *chickie-pull* as he terms it, and about
his dogpack theory of human behaviour.

"Think about it," Olofson the sailor says. "Like dogs.
It explains everything. Even the clams."

Dogpack theory, I'll have to remember this, thinks
Hank. The bartender touches his dark mustache.

"This one knows what we're talking about," Olofson
says, nodding safely. "Right? We're not rabble. Not everyone knows what we know." They study Hank.

It seems profound. Hank comes to believe that Olofson is the devil, in Port Angeles to talk personally with
Hank about his dogpack theories. Hank is laughing and
there are arrows in him: he is pinned to the bar at the knees
and elbows. He is St. Sebastian. Deer and antelope play.
He is in his white pants. They keep staring.

"He liked that joint now, didn't he?" says Olofson the
sailor. "I'm getting definite vibes from this one. He knows
what's what." The accordian wheezes to a halt, pale air
hanging.

Hank realizes they are after his ass. The handsome
bartender and the grizzled sailor. They have the wrong
man, he tells them. He can't stop laughing but the boys
don't find it so funny. Why me, asks Hank. There was
another, a dull servant with a broom. He pointed out Hank
as sympathetic, likely, alone. And Hank stayed late with
them, taking their drinks and smoke. Olofson flexes his
biceps.

"Did you hear the one about the goose?" Olofson asks
the bartender, pointedly not looking at Hank. "Seems there
was two guys, want this same goose. In the tussle the
goose got its head smashed in." His voice has anger in its
edges.

"Gotta go," Hank says. "Don't like the parable," Hank
says.

"He's gotta go," says the grizzled sailor to the bartender. "I guess he's not going to get physical." He seems disappointed. Hank finds the door.

"Watch yourself," says the bartender at the top of the iron stairs. "And whatever you do, don't say you're sorry. They all do."

Hank descends into the black alley. The door closes above. He walks warily to the front of the building, expecting cocks and knives under the skein of stars. He climbs up and crosses at the sidewalk. A dog howls by the quiet mill.

A black and white pulls out of the darkness of Front Street. For a moment Hank is relieved to see it. ID, says the policeman. Hank has none. "If you'll take me by my motel, I can show you ID."

The policeman runs his fingers over Hank's legs and torso. Hank gets in the back. He thinks about police shows on TV. This is not really happening. The plexiglass slams into place between them.

"Can we talk through this," Hank pointing at it, an odd echo with his words now.

"Yes, go ahead." Hank realizes the cop feels a confession is forthcoming.

"No, just wondering, you know." Hank has been drinking since the afternoon. It is now three a.m. Plus the joint. Things go around but he gets hold of it. The cop mutters at his hand. The radio crackles a reply.

"Why you interested in me?"

"Burglary. Not ten minutes ago. You fit the bill. Where you been?" The spine of the road bends.

"That bar."

"Closed an hour ago," counters the cop. Hank is wary of mentioning the two in the bar. Some alibi. He wonders about the two men: did they want to fuck him, or want him to fuck them? Just what is the etiquette?

"I know you from somewhere. Any record?"

"Speeding tickets, you know."

The tires hum uphill. The officer wears no hat. Hank studies the back of his head, his ears. Off in the distance squares change to triangles; the pull of perspective. Gravity pulls at Hank's face.

At the Flagstone, Hank steps inside to find the wallet in his other pants. Cheap-Eddie is asleep in his bed. Virginia is awake, hugs Hank.

"Where were you?" she asks. "I was about to call the police." Hank laughs at this, tries to explain what has happened. He cannot stop laughing or slow his babble. He feels basically he is crashing wings, bull in china.

Outside with the police, Hank articulates slowly, politely. Like two different people, Virginia tells him later. In the light of the parking lot Hank shows his Canadian passport, driver's license.

"You smoke?" they ask.

"What, marijuana?" Hank asks, trying to sound innocent. Is this a set-up engineered in revenge by the sailor and bartender?

"Come on. Tobacco."

"No. No. I don't smoke," relieved it is not about dope. A second patrol car bumps into the lot, carrying a woman and a man in the backseat. Their apartment had been broken into. They woke to see the burglar. A black policeman walks them past as Hank speaks with the first officer.

"Yes, that's him," they say.

The officers inform Hank that his age, build, beard and dark T-shirt all match the description. You have the wrong man, Hank insists, as he had to the men in the tavern. This is getting old. Hank talks and talks with them, giving them Virginia's California plate numbers, their

ID's, various numbers, names, addresses, cities.

"I'm convinced," says one uniform finally, the black man. Which way? wonders Hank, what does that mean? And then they leave, leave him to go inside the room with Virginia. Cheap-Eddie has slept through it all, dreaming of pieces of silver.

"I'll never sleep after that," Hank groans, lying beside Virginia.

"Talk to me," she says.

"What about?" Hank says.

"Talk to me," she says.

Hank passes out. She lifts and drops his arm several times but he is gone into whatever it is.

There is banging. "What the hell?" mutters Cheap-Eddie, blinking like a mole in his blankets. Hank opens the door. Two badges are held up. The older detective in a shiny suit that is hard on the eyes this early. You want to get dressed and we'll talk, they say. The mountains look pretty behind them.

Hank pulls on loose pants and a shirt, talks with them on the hood of Virginia's MG. Sunlight glares off every plane. Hank feels at a disadvantage; he is pale, shaky, unrested. The detectives have showered, had their coffee and breakfast.

"I know you from somewhere," one says. "You play ball?" Virginia brings a glass of water. Hank is touched.

"I talked with the police last night. You have the wrong guy."

"We'd like to hear it again."

The plainclothes seem to look down on the uniforms. The B & E artist has done any number of jobs and they want to nail him so badly you can smell it. Hank will do in a pinch. They want him downtown.

The older one in the golden suit tries to come on

tough. They have probable cause, he says. He has a lot of
laugh lines and his hair is greased straight back. He reminds Hank of a TV preacher. Or he played a guitar in say,
the Ventures. The younger detective is blown dry, in a
tasteful sienna suit. He seems apologetic and looks like
someone Hank used to know. It will come to him. Hank's
head feels a turn too tight. And what will the neighbours
think?

"Can we see that purse," the older one pointing inside
the MG. Of course it matches the one stolen, down to a
lipstick smudge.

"Been in Port Angeles before, Hank?"

Now Hank feels the MG's California plates seem
suspicious, as does the heavy flashlight given Virginia by a
worried brother in San Diego. As do the tools in the trunk,
ditto the tire iron, hank's socks, anything. They get to you,
thinks Hank. They say you did it, then you did it.

The detective rifles the purse, inspects Virginia's
bank book. The gold suit shimmers.

"They can't do that," she says to Hank. They do what
they want, thinks Hank. The veils drop lickety-split.
Things become evident.

"Are you working, Hank?"

"No sir."

"Not working huh."

They take Hank to the ghost car. "Call my brother,"
Hank says to Virginia. Cheap-Eddie has not shown his
face for fear it may cost him. "Call my brother in Victoria."

Hank is in the front seat this trip. They back onto the
highway, the older detective at the wheel. How easily it
happens, and what the hell is probable cause, wonders
Hank. I was weaned in the suburbs: aren't I exempt from
all of this?

"You keep your mouth shut some of the time. I like

that a real lot," the older detective says, as if reading Hank's mind.

Farther west the street is blocked off for the annual salmon derby parade. There is a naked woman at a window. There are barricades and bowlegged Kwakiutl and Quillayute Indians wandering booths of beargrass baskets. Dogs run in circles.

"You smoke, Hank?"

"No. You have the wrong guy."

"They all say that. No offense or anything. Last week it was a woodcutter slit a hobo's throat along the river. Same deal."

The ghost car pulls in an alley and Hank assumes he's going to get roughed up. The older one walked with his head bowed to a dumpster, peers in it, spits or tosses something, Hank cannot tell. Looking for evidence? Planting it?

"What's he doing?" asks the younger detective from the back.

"You're asking me?"

"This'll get him." He slips a pistol from a shoulder holster, levels the gun at the window and shoots it at the older detective. Hank jumps, his stomach paining him.

"Goddamit," yells the older man, "you firing those blanks off again? You didn't shoot it at him did you? Jesus."

"I was just showing him," says the younger detective sheepishly.

"Well we have to account for every goddam shell or the chief will have our ass in a sling. Every shell!" The older man fumbles in a small box, then throws the box at the man in the backseat. "The numbers better be kosher my man, or your ass is grass." He slams the car into gear, mumbling.

They back out of the alley fast and drive the one-way downtown. Snow-touched mountains move behind the

brick buildings, reminding Hank of Wyoming, of
infidelity. He can imagine the face she would make when
he put it to her. Some stranger.

"Been fingerprinted before, Hank?"

"Yessir, with the railroad. You have a computer,
right? Can't you feed me in and see if I'm clean?"

"Only works if what you're giving us is straight."

"Did you know this is the world's largest fishing
derby?" asks the younger detective. "Really super prizes."

"Whatever happened with that big blonde tart?" the
other asks.

"Oh her. She discredited her testimony, no one
believed a word. But I got a great deal on her Nova. With
the divorce she's selling everything, going to Alaska, get
away from it all."

"Well I tell you Anchorage is dogmeat," says the
older man. "Bumper to bumper with all the new cars and
money but nowhere to go. Terrible place for the family.
Dog eat dog I tell you."

This can't be happening, decides Hank. He begins a
gloomy meditation on chance, the greased passage from
wrong place, wrong time, to shit creek and lack of paddle.
If only he'd left the bar five minutes earlier, if only Virginia hadn't gone back to the Flagstone in a huff, if only
he'd quit school in grade eight and gone into Real Estate.
The real felon is likely in a sunny kitchen nook, forking up
scrambled eggs and reading of his latest exploits. Hank
feels peckish.

"I should at least get a breakfast voucher or something out of all this."

"Not from us," says the older man, grave as a fish.

Hank turns his eyes from the men and the mountains
to the Strait of Juan de Fuca, past the tottering canneries
and coast guard buildings, hears the thumping of a
freighter clearing Ediz Hook, watches oystercatchers and

curlews trot in the surf. Slime-green waves run in one after the other. One sneaks farther; the others follow. Dogpack theory. A heron seizes something in its dagger bill.

Hank understands this beautiful country has been made ugly for him.

He thinks of the couples moving on the sunburnt tides off Tongue Point, Cape Flattery; with their hooks and coolers of ice, searching for the main chance, the trophy salmon, the happy coincidence of bait to unsuspecting prey.

He thinks of the mix of currents and creatures, the pieces of the food chain. And over that sparkling blue stripe is Canada, the leafed islands just out of reach. Hank wishes to climb in a sloop with Virginia, drop the keel and become a dot on the horizon.

They lead him from the ghost car and he may as well be guilty for the way it looks. Tongues rattle, daughters drawn to fat mothers. A murmur of drums; the Port Angeles Rough Riders Marching Band And Colour Guard bleats, prances in the parking lot, warming up for the big parade. Dragoon hats, tiny fishscale skirts in light and legs, bosoms and thighs lifting to the sun. Batons hang forever. Much of life here seems to involve parking lots, understands Hank.

Flags full of stars droop everywhere. I hate marching bands, Hank realizes.

Inside the building few uniforms lift their heads. Another wayward one, no big deal. They talk, laugh at a joke about Dolly Parton.

"I'm cutting out for coffee," says the older one to the younger detective. "You finish up here, alright Jimbo?"

Hank is fingerprinted in the hall. A man brushes his teeth at the water fountain.

"Sorry if my hands are cold," says the little woman in a uniform of blouse and skirt. "Some of them say my hands are cold."

She rolls black ink on a glass surface, takes Hank's hands in hers. Each finger and thumb is rolled in ink and pressed to the paper forms, to the squares.

"Sorry dear, let's try your thumbs again. I can't seem to get them right. See?" She shows him the flawed impressions.

"Sweaty palms?" says the young detective. He rubs his palms together, then holds out a trembling hand, in imitation of a nervous prisoner. The detective is grinning. A joke, realizes Hank, a joke.

"Let's try again dear." She grabs his thumb.

Beyond the walls the band begins its anthem. Tuneless horns blat obscenely and drumbeats push hard through the blond wood of the hallway. Now the thing is starting.

Light
Bev Harris

One night Michael undressed Joan in front of the window in the door at the bottom of the stairs. He stood behind her, and set her before him just as she knew he would. He slipped his hand, hot, down inside her blouse and turned out her breasts—one, two, gleaming white under the light from the street lamp. The globes of light outside were hanging, shining, in the dark.

His chest was hot and Joan's back was hot too against it. Michael's fingers pushed her breasts to raise them. How soft, she knew, was the place where they curved away from his hand. Higher and higher and higher he pushed them toward the light until they shone all over. Wanting her to shine, every part, he unbuttoned her skirt and it fell to the tile floor. Her back bent like a bow, wanting more light. Michael's hands slid and played, up and then down. Her breasts leaned out to meet the two white globes outside, to glow with them.

Then Michael said, Joan, Joan, and she said Joan, JOan, JOAN, repeating her own name she didn't know why over and over. The sound of her name rose to the top of the hall, to the door at the top of the stairs and then returned to her. She took the doorknob, brass-cool, and twisted it. The door swung wide open, wide to the street, to the hanging globes of light and to the rows of lighted curtains blowing in and out on all the open windows, open to the light and to the summer night air. She was exposed, turned inside out, and glad, for all time had disappeared to a point. Time was pitched high inside her.

But slowly, gradually, it came down and she saw the door frame again and the silly muslin curtain in the window, the dust along the creases of it, the greasy string tied to the nails at the corners. And finally, the light hurt her eyes. Michael's hand was hot on her back again, and her legs began to shake.

Then it seemed to her so soon that Michael turned to face her and to say goodnight, I'll call you tomorrow. Joan sat down on the bottom stair. The stair was cool, even on that hot summer night. The rubber runner cooled her right through her pale pink skirt. She shivered when she heard Michael's car start up. She stood up and waved out the window in the door, parting the dusty curtain. Yes, he had seen her, he was waving back at her. With all time before him now he was the free one, sailing up the street, his hand smoothing back his hair from his forehead, his ring gleaming silver. He was moving the wheel in a great circle away from her and smiling, happy now, and free. See you, Joan said to him in the silence of the hall, and have a good sleep. She kept waving until she knew he had reached Sherbrooke Street and was home free.

It was past two in the morning and Joan was exhausted, skin sticking to skin. Feeling the ache between her legs, she sat down to ease it. The stairwell needed painting, lightening. What colour was it? It was a colour you could not describe. Joan ran a finger over the tile floor coolness at her feet. She didn't want to go up, but she couldn't stay down. So she checked her buttons and pushed a few straggling hairs behind her ears, readying herself for the climb.

But she heard the sound of a door opening upstairs and she knew it was Rosalee. Joan knew that Rosalee must have heard every last thing, every last sound. Rosalee must have heard because Rosalee lived for seeing and for hearing. She was an onlooker and a hunchback, a most holy hunchback. She rented Joan and Gil's front room that looked out to the street. It was Rosalee's door which had opened, Rosalee and her perfect hump. She heard everything that proclaimed itself in their household. But she never let on a thing. You could say that she stashed all their sordid secrets away in her hump and brought them out to gaze at, like dirty magazines, in the dark.

Joan heard her clip through the dining room with her tight little steps. She heard her go down the hall to the bathroom and close the door. Joan could not move. She pressed her mouth against the satin-cool wall. She sat very still, but she wanted to run. Where to? She thought of Michael. Perhaps she could have taken a taxi to Michael's apartment and begged him to let her stay. But, no, his mother was there, the flower-arranger, with all her dried stalks and dusty colours, her bits of brittle blossoms on the floor, her long-necked vases lined up on the dirty glass shelves. And the dead flowers, pink and blue and mauve, a large spray of them on top of the breadbox in the kitchen. She called them sprays, but they were so dry.

Joan heard Rosalee return to her bedroom and close the door. She seemed to do it emphatically as if she were sounding an all-clear. And yet, all the same, hardly breathing, Joan tiptoed up the stairs to the door at the top. Slipping the door shut, she entered the dining room and saw that Gil had left the lamp on the telephone table on for her, the way he always did when she went out for the evening. Was this gesture a proof of his thoughtfulness? He was so thoughtful. Or was it power, and calculated control? She knew that she would rather come in on all fours, feeling her way in the dark, fingering the dark turned wood of the table legs to get her bearings, crawling down the old flowered linoleum to the bedroom at the back. She would rather do that than to walk in there week after week as if nothing were going on. And if she caught her foot in the worn place in the Persian carpet, taking all the Coronation plates from the rail down with her, she might awaken the household to what she was doing. There, yes, there she could imagine them all standing around her in their night clothes—Gil's mother with her teeth out, Rosalee in her Viyella dressing gown, Gil holding up his pyjama bottoms with his left arm, Barbara in her pink baby dolls, Scotch tape holding her bangs flat. Joan could see them all looking down at her and shouting, "Get out! Get out!"

But she looked at the lamp, at the china dancing girl in her chipped skirt, frozen in her position of gaiety and hope. And she knew that as long as that light was on when she came in, it kept her there. She peered into Barbara's room off the dining room. She was asleep, her shoulders rising and falling in the old mahogany bed that Gil's parents used to occupy and that Joan refused to take. Could you make love where your parents did? Joan had wanted a new bed, but it hadn't made much difference in the end. Barbara treasured that bed and all the rest of her grandmother's musty things. But Joan had always hated them all, all the heavy and dark things. She had always wanted new things, light chairs that you could see clear through, that floated in a room, and modern pictures with splashes of red and orange, and lamps with big white shades that could light up a whole room.

Joan stood there and watched her daughter sleeping. Had Barbara heard her too? Had she been listening too, lying there on that dark old bed, listening to the sounds of her mother's name rising from the bottom of the stairs? What did she know? Rosalee was teaching her to sew on the old Singer treadle machine that Gil's mother had never allowed Joan to touch. What did they speak about, their heads bent over the black wheel?

Joan turned out the light above the dusty dancer,

walked down the hall and entered the bedroom at the back. It was a tall room with one narrow window in the wall that faced the alley. There was a card table under the window, a pale blue blind above it, two hard wooden chairs, one of which was kept by the bed for Gil's visitors. It was an airless room.

The moon shone on her husband's face, hollowing his cheeks. The bedclothes seemed to overcome him, the way his body had withered to bony angles. He slept clenched in a fetal position, as if mortally afraid. Afraid of what? Did he even want her to stay? The past had licked him up and left her only a long dark track down his side of the bed. He couldn't listen to the daily news, to current facts. Instead he quoted Victorian poetry: Here mystery and peace are wed in lonely union, while factual stars seem cold to our desire. "I wonder, Joan," he sometimes said to her, "how I came to arrive at this house."

Every weekday while Joan was at work, his mother came up from downstairs to get his lunch: jello, tea, more tea. Then they would take turns reading Anthony Trollope aloud. And every night before she went to bed, Rosalee came out to the kitchen in her dressing gown. Underneath it her hump was clean and sweet smelling from her bath. She would whisper to Joan, "Is Gilbert comfortable?" Joan said yes, but she didn't really know what Rosalee meant. She didn't know if he was comfortable or not, if he was happy or not. Everyone else seemed to know, but they asked her.

She slipped off her clothes and left them on the chair by the bed. She climbed in beside Gil and lay still. She moved her hands down her body, down her legs, touching herself everywhere. She looked at Gil's curved and bony back and found it hard to believe that he was once husky and strong and so in love with her. She lay awake most the night beside his bones, those bones in the flannelette pyjamas with the faded huntsmen on them.

The next morning Joan stood in front of the mirror in the bathroom pressing her palms hard across her cheeks, stretching her eyes open to brighten up her face. She ate her breakfast by the sink in the kitchen. Barbara was at the table with a bowl of cereal in front of her. She seemed to be dawdling over her breakfast, unwilling to eat it. Joan could hear some boys shouting outside in the alley. They were playing with a ball and the ball was thumping against the back door downstairs. Joan wondered why, if Barbara wanted to go, she wasn't eating up. Instead she was balancing the spoon across the bowl and then walking her fingers along it. And Joan knew that Rosalee would be coming into the kitchen soon. It was almost nine-thirty and Rosalee was punctual. The kitchen was hers at exactly nine-thirty to ten, though she rarely stayed that long. Joan stared up at the clock on the wall above her, its face the centre of a spiky sun once golden but now tarnished and flaking. It had been a wedding gift, one of the few new things they had put up. Her eyes followed the dusty cord that wound down the wall from the clock face to the sink, along the backsplash to the outlet above the counter. She wanted to pull out the plug, a childish gesture to try and stop time, to stop Rosalee from coming into the kitchen. Joan wondered what Rosalee would find to say to her.

"Barbara," she said turning her face to her, "will you hurry up? It's Rosalee's time. You could finish that little bit in no time if you'd get busy."

Barbara wore a bright blue top, boat-necked and sleeveless, tight across her chest. The bangs across her forehead were too long. Joan wanted to go over and brush them to one side with her hand, but she didn't move. Then she was startled to discover two new rises of breasts under the bright blue that she hadn't noticed before. When had this happened?

"It's horrible stuff. Look at it," Barbara said. Her face was sullen as she held the spoon out to her mother. "It's all mush. It's making me sick."

Joan glanced over at it. The bowl was full of soggy, ball-like wads, with a malicious dark spot in each centre. It was nothing that Joan could have eaten. "It's your fault," she said. "If you hadn't left it so long, it wouldn't be that bad. Now just get a move on and eat it. Rosalee'll be here any minute."

Barbara took a tiny bit of mush from the spoon with her front teeth and made an exaggerated grimace. Suddenly Joan was mad and yelled at her, "You're not going anywhere until you finish the whole thing!"

Barbara's face tightened and she turned her head to stare out the window which vibrated slightly each time the ball struck the door. But Joan had given her ultimatum and now she had to leave Barbara alone.

The doorknob to the pantry had been off for years because no one had gotten around to fixing it. Joan put two fingers in the hole, pulled the door toward her and stood inside, leaning against the ironing board to feel its coolness on her back. It was the only room she felt comfortable in. The smell of the cakes that Gil's mother left under the blue tin always welcomed her.

Joan set up the ironing board beside the pantry door so as not to get in Rosalee's way. Doing so, she heard Rosalee's door open and then each of her little steps down the hall to the kitchen. She spread a pair of her slacks out on the board and smoothed them down with the palm of her hand. They were red cotton, almost new.

"Good morning, Joan, Barbara," said Rosalee as she came through the door. She said it brightly. She carried her tray well out in front of her body, her head held high and courageous. She wore a tailored skirt and a white nylon blouse trimmed at the sleeve and collar edges with lace. The round brooch at her neck was a basket of dried flowers under glass. Rosalee prepared to set her tray down on the table, then changed her mind and put it down beside the stove. Her metal tray had three red roses on it; it held a teapot with a striped cosy, a china cup and saucer and a gleaming saucepan turned upside down on a china plate.

Joan said good morning and then looked out the window past Barbara. She could see the crumbling brick of the neighbouring duplex, so close she could almost touch it, and a clothesline heavy with grey sheets that blocked the sun. Grease stains spread upward on the wall above Rosalee's head. Rosalee stood near the window with her skinny arms folded across a neat leather belt, her grey hair woven with streaks of scant sunlight. To Joan she was a nun.

Her hump immunized her. She was exempt. Her hump placed her in a different category of humanity. It freed her. How old was she? how long ago was that picture taken of her as a pretty little girl under the tree in a yard, sitting with a black dog and a straight back. Had she ever known love? Only a girl of eleven or twelve when she had fallen off her bicycle, she had injured her spine and grown no taller. Rosalee had no way of making her own living so her brother and his wife supported her in Joan's little front room. They came each Sunday, tall, cool, well-dressed, and took her with them by car to the Presbyterian church on Kensington Avenue and brought her back again after lunch.

"It's going to be a nice day, I think," Rosalee said. Her chin was pointed to the scrap of blue sky. She upended her saucepan and walked over to the fridge where she put a white egg into her pan, a pure white egg.

She had a sixth sense about eggs. She could tell to the second when they were perfectly cooked and carry on a conversation at the same time. "I hope we got the worst of the hot weather over with last night," she said, turning to face Barbara and Joan. "It was so frightfully hot last night, I kept waking up with it."

Joan couldn't look at her or answer. She turned up the iron and worked on the red creases. Barbara was sliding her bowl back and forth across the arborite table top with her spoon. What did she want Joan to do?

"What about you, Joan?" Rosalee asked. The egg was beginning to jump in the boiling water. "Did you enjoy your bridge game last night?"

"Thanks, yes," Joan said. She was finishing up the pants and studying each pant leg like a road map. But she was trapped behind the board. Michael, now, she wanted to shout, come on over. Haul me out of here and never bring me back; if you loved me, you would rescue me. But Joan knew that he was still asleep in his apartment, his mother in her flower-dead room beside his. Then Joan was angry with him. And because she knew how ridiculous that was, she slammed the iron down hard on the board and the metal whined.

"It does you good to get out a bit now and then," Rosalee said. "Did you make out alright in all that heat? It was awful, wasn't it?"

"Yes, fine," Joan said and concentrated on folding the pants. They looked good on her. They had two zippers, one on each of the back pockets.

"And how is Gilbert this morning, poor man?" Rosalee asked it in a hushed tone, with reverence. What did she want Joan to say? That she loved him? That she would always stay there as long as he needed her? Say you love him, say you love him; they all wanted her to say it, but she had never said it. She couldn't say it. Of course she loved him. He was a gentle man and he needed her. She loved him, of course. But she wouldn't tell them. So she said, "Oh, about the same."

"Well," said Rosalee, "I thought I heard him trying to get up for breakfast with you and Barbara this morning. That was nice. He may be ill," she went on, "but he does consider his family, doesn't he? Poor man, he always tries his best, doesn't he?"

Doesn't he? Doesn't he? Joan nodded, but her eyes were snapping, she could hear them. Rosalee placed her warmed saucepan over the egg to keep it warm. "I hope he has a better day today," she said. "I hope he'll be able to enjoy a little lunch with you."

She went over to the fridge and put a bit of milk into the bottom of her china cup. She held her affliction like a sacred burden, like the earth itself was on her back so hard and so pure. She bore it all as a marvellous affliction. It seemed to Joan a marvellous and sacred exemption. For an instant Joan wanted to knock it off her, wanted to knock it to the ground. Her fist tightened around the handle of the iron.

But they were all shocked into stillness by a sudden smash. Barbara's bowl of cereal crashed to the floor. Milk and lumps of mushy grey splashed onto the legs of the chairs. And a piece of the dish flew through the air and landed right at Joan's foot. Rosalee said, "Oh." It was just a whisper spoken into her china cup, and she looked down into it as if it were the only thing in the whole world that wasn't broken. Then she arranged her dishes on her tray and prepared to leave. Though she was escaping, she looked lost, for where had she to go? She stood at the door nervously, her tray jingling in her slightly trembling hands.

"We'll manage," Joan said. "You have a good breakfast. We'll manage," she repeated.

So Rosalee said, "Good morning," hesitated in the doorway, and then was gone.

Joan faced Barbara. She was sitting with her chin down on her arms, forcing her eyes wide open to keep from crying. The tears that were caught behind them made her eyes glaze with an impenetrable light. The ball thumped again, thump and thump. Joan took the perfect red square she had made of the pants and set it, shining, on the counter. Then she said to her daughter in as light a tone as she could, "You can go." She released her.

Each step Barbara took down to the door made her rise higher.

The Rawleigh Man
Rebecca Luce-Kapler

No matter what life does to some people they remain
unchanged. Our Rawleigh man was like that. Ever since I
could remember he appeared once every month driving his
battered blue station wagon packed with jars of extract,
cans of spice and bottles of cleaning products. He shuffled
his hefty frame up our walk, his shiny grey suit crumpling
around his hips like old elephant skin.

"Morning, girls," he would say in his lazy voice when
my younger sister Sharon and I flew from the porch to
meet him. "I declare that you grow taller every time I see
you."

Then he would dig his hairy red hand into the depths
of his crinkled pocket and draw out four Mojos covered
with little balls of suit lint.

"Your mother home?"

Our fingers were already preoccupied in picking the
fluff from the waxed red and blue papers before popping
the soft white chunks of sticky candy into our mouths.

"Mom, the Rawleigh man's here," we hollered, following him into the house.

The only intrusion into this careful ritual occurred the
spring I turned twelve.

Things had begun as usual with the Rawleigh man
informing my mother of all the latest community news.

"Hardy's finally sold their farm," he said.

"They did?" Mom popped an extra potato into the pot
before coming to sit down at the table.

"Yep. Got a good price for it too." And he whispered a sum.

My mother nodded. "Farms are fetching good prices these days."

She pointedly eyed the pamphlets bulging out of his shirt pocket.

But the Rawleigh man could never be rushed.

"Saw Mrs. Smith today," he remarked. "She got her new chicks yesterday."

"I've got to do that this week," Mom told him. "What are your specials today, Jim? I know I need a tin of cinnamon."

"Mackinnon's are moving their cattle up to the summer range," he continued, running his fingers through his thinning hair.

"It's that time of year." Mom smoothed her apron with abrupt strokes of her rough hands.

The Rawleigh man looked around the sunny kitchen and took a deep breath of the cooking roast beef. His mouth watered so that he swallowed loudly.

"We got a special on drink concentrate." He pulled a wrinkled pamphlet from his pocket and smoothed it on the table in front of Mom. "Makes forty jugs. Come in handy at haying time."

"Okay," Mom agreed. "That in the lime flavour and a tin of cinnamon. And you better give me the orange concentrate too."

The Rawleigh man tugged a grubby receipt book out of his suit jacket and laboriously copied down her order.

"Anything else?" He turned the pages of the booklet pointing out a few bargains.

"Nothing I can't live without."

The Rawleigh man stood and hitched up his beltless pants before flopping back into the chair. His eyes tracked the scurried walk of a fly across the ceiling.

"Need fly paper?"

"Don't like the stuff," Mom replied. "Give me a swatter any day."

He loosened the steer's head slide of his greasy string tie.

"How'd ya like all this stuff you ordered for free and some other products besides?"

"Free?" My mother wrinkled her forehead and nervously rubbed her palms together at this unexpected turn. "You holding some kind of contest?"

The Rawleigh man cleared his throat. "I was wondering if you'd board someone for me, starting next week for a couple of weeks or so. She's coming out on Sunday."

"She?" Mom shook her head as she spoke. "I don't know. I'd have to know more about it, I guess."

"She's coming out by train from Ontario. I . . . she picked up the pamphlet and recreased the fold. "I back and forth a few months."

"Then you asked her to marry you." My mother relaxed and leaned ahead eagerly now that she knew romance was involved.

"Well sort of . . . not exactly," the Rawleigh man mumbled. "She asked me."

But Mom carried right on, not hearing his answer. "Of course she can stay here. And you want to pay me in products, is that it?"

The Rawleigh man nodded. He stood quickly. "And she don't know that I haven't a house."

"I'm sure she'll understand." My mother was sweetly diplomatic.

"Maybe so. But she thinks she's coming to live above some store of mine."

"Jim! For heavens sake! Why did you tell her that?"

The Rawleigh man stuffed the folded pamphlet back into his pocket. He sighed. "I never thought she'd want to come out here and marry me. And I kinda enjoyed pretending that I had a house and a store. Felt like I really did have it for a while."

"She's going to find out."

"Yup, I know. But not right away. See, I thought if she could grow to like me a little better first before I told her, she wouldn't mind so much." He cleared his throat loudly. "Then I could get us a couple of rooms at the boarding house once we was married."

"I can keep quiet," my mother reassured him. "And she's welcome to stay here."

The Rawleigh man pumped my mother's hand gratefully. With assurances that he would be back on the weekend, he left, forgetting to hint for a dinner invitation.

Late Sunday, the Rawleigh man brought out a thin woman with a pinched face and greying hair stretched into a tight bun.

"This is her," he said proudly, stroking a gaudy new necktie decorated with a painted palm tree. "Maggie MacKenzie." He put a big hand on the back of her faded paisley dress.

Maggie graciously shook my parents' hands but drew back quickly when she saw the dirty paws that Sharon and I held out.

The Rawleigh man treated the stiff little woman as if she were a china doll. I thought it was disgusting. And he had completely forgotten to give us our Mojos.

"I understand that I will be staying here while Jamie finishes the house," Maggie said primly as Mom handed her a glass of lemonade.

Jamie! I would never have used that name for the Rawleigh man. Jamie was for little boys or collie dogs.

"You're welcome for as long as you like," Mom promised.

"It's strange, though." Maggie put a thin claw on the Rawleigh man's fat arm. "I thought Jamie was already living in the house. I must have misread the letters."

The Rawleigh man coughed loudly, his large belly quivering with tension. "I was," he admitted hesitantly. "But I thought it should be fixed up for a lady."

"That is sweet of you." Maggie smiled thinly.

"Where did you live back east, Miss MacKenzie?" my father asked, balancing his lemonade clumsily on his lap. He hated tea-party atmospheres.

"I lived with my mother. She died last winter."

"I'm so sorry." Sympathy softened my mother's voice.

"God in His mercy ended her suffering," Maggie replied matter-of-factly.

Sharon yawned and wandered out to the kitchen and I followed. I could not stand watching our good old Rawleigh man continue to make sheep's eyes at the ugly woman he'd brought into our house.

Every evening that week, the Rawleigh man came and visited Maggie. When darkness fell, he would drive off to work on the store renovations. Everyone but Maggie knew that he went down to our south quarter and parked his car, pushing aside the boxes of extract and concentrate until his grimy old mattress was cleared.

The whole situation was driving Sharon and me crazy. During the day Maggie made our lives miserable by demanding that we fetch and carry for her.

"Can you see if your mother has washed my stockings? Bring them to me, there's a good girl. Can you bring me a snack? I'm not going down to dinner. The noise you two made this morning gave me a beastly headache."

Every hour it seemed there was something one of us had to do for Maggie while Mom made us curtail our louder games because of Miss MacKenzie's delicate head.

But she always recovered by evening. When the Rawleigh man arrived, we could hear them out on the porch swing and often Maggie's words would float right through the open window.

"But when will the store be done, Jamie? Can't I see it even if it isn't finished, Jamie? I'd like to make some curtains, Jamie."

Her whining voice grated. It seemed the only thing she cared about was that darned non-existent store.

As her visit stretched into two weeks and started on the third, Sharon and I had a conference.

"I can't stand her," I said. "This morning she was asking Mother if we couldn't be sent to visit relatives until she left. We're bad for her poor heart, she said."

"Is Mom going to do it?" Sharon's eyes widened at the thought.

"No, but she promised to keep us out of the house as much as possible. I don't think she likes it any more than we do." I twisted a long piece of my hair.

"And he doesn't even bring us Mojos," Sharon said sadly.

"We'll just have to do something about her."

"What can we do?"

"I bet if she knew that there was no store, she'd be gone in a hurry," I said.

"Are you going to tell her?"

"No. You are."

"Why do I have to be the one?" Sharon complained.

"Because you're younger and young kids are expected to do dumb things."

"Oh," she acquiesced.

That evening we were well hidden in the caragana bushes near the porch by the time the Rawleigh man carefully seated the skinny Maggie on the swing and then dropped his heavy body beside her.

Above us, we could see his arm creep around her bony shoulders.

"It's been good, these past two weeks, Maggie. I'd like to marry you soon."

We heard the swing squeak as she sat bolt upright.

"You've finished the store, Jamie," she squealed.

"Not exactly." There was a more solid squeak as he shifted.

"Not exactly? But we can live there? Can't we?"

"Not exactly."

I gave Sharon a nudge. "Now!"

She darted out of the bushes and onto the veranda steps.

"You don't really have a store, Mr. Rawleigh man," she breathed. "I heard you telling Mom that."

Maggie gasped. "You were listening you horrid child." She turned to the Rawleigh man. "Jamie? What's she saying?"

Sharon darted away and I followed. The two of us collapsed, giggling, into the haystack behind the barn.

When we returned to the house, the Rawleigh man was gone. Mom and Dad were reading in the living room, but Maggie was nowhere to be seen. Sharon and I waited for a moment, but nothing was said.

The next morning Mom simply told us that Maggie had gone to live in town, and by the end of the month things almost seemed normal again. The Rawleigh man came back to our house, shuffling up the walk, still wearing his grey suit and still telling Mom the news. But he never stopped to press sticky Mojos into our hands and he never ever told us how much we had grown.

The Curlew's Cry
J. Leslie Bell

Sheila stretched back on the couch, lit a cigarette, and looked at the unfinished letter to Neil which lay in the centre of the coffee table. There was something pitiful and inadequate about her letters at the best of times compared with Neil's. His often ran to six pages, full of details about old university friends, his jobs in the North Sea oil rigs, the characters he met in the Aberdeen pubs. By contrast, her letters, were niggardly and hastily written, dashed off, if she had a minute to spare in the lounge during the mid-afternoon lull. At the far end of the table was a cardboard box containing all the letters Neil had written to her since she had arrived in Canada. There were 48 letters in the box, 48 neatly written reminders of his dependability, his love, "the auld alliance", as he had put it. He would be here in one month. One month! She glanced at the letter again. There would be no point in finishing it now.

She had two days off and she was bored and hot and restless. She lit another cigarette and listened to the music which came from the apartment next door. The old man who lived there on his own played his classical records all evening. She enjoyed the music, although she only recognized one or two of the composers. She had seen his name on his letter box in the lobby: S. Sikirski. They had nodded to one another in the hallway but they had never spoken, thank God. She had no desire to talk to old foreign gentlemen about their troubles, the war, their back problems or whatever it was that old foreign gentlemen talked about.

Still, there was a vague feeling of security knowing that he was there.

She picked up her paperback and read a few pages and then put it down again. She went out to the balcony and leaned on the railing. The sun was just going down and its rays burned red on the surface of the river which she could just see between the gap of the two buildings across the street. Below, young couples walked and cycled towards the park. A man's deep, assured laughter drifted up to her. He had his thick arm around his girlfriend's narrow, tanned shoulders, locking her into his side. Sheila threw the butt end of her cigarette down at them and watched it twisting and swooping, drifting in the down draught away to the left, missing the couple by about twenty yards. The sun had slipped out of sight, leaving only a red haze in the sky. She stood there until it was dark, looking at the lights of the city, listening to the distant sounds of traffic until the iron railing became cold in her tight grip. Only when she went inside did she feel the pain and notice the two red horizontal welts on her palms.

The next day after lunch she walked to the park. She found an unoccupied bench under a clump of poplar trees and sat down and tried to read her book again but she couldn't concentrate. It was one of the books that Neil had recommended to her. It was by an emigre Czech author whose name she couldn't pronounce. She would finish it by the end of the month. She promised herself that. She would even finish the letter and give it to Neil when he arrived. It was very quiet in the park, save for the occasional jogger who went by, kicking up the red gravel. The sky was cloudless. Perfect. The sky over Scotland even now would be lowering and treacherous, with its shifting layers of grey and white and black. They had camped under that sky on Rannoch Moor; tramped under it along the banks of the Tay; sheltered from it in bothies and ruined Border keeps. Neil wrote of these things, these memories.

Remember the curlew's cry, he wrote. We lay in the tent holding each other all night. Listen to the curlew's cry, you said. I'll never forget that, Sheila. Never!

There was no curlew. We never heard a curlew. We never saw one.

. . . and the time in Lewis when we slept in the park and watched the Northern Lights.

There were clouds. Dense clouds. The moon and stars were covered by them.

And buried somewhere in one of those letters, a whispered refrain: "Why did you leave? Why did you leave?"

She closed her book and put it in her purse. She walked across the park, crossed the bridge, and walked down Memorial Drive and had lunch at one of the restaurants on Kensington Road. She had one beer and smoked five cigarettes, and then walked slowly home.

When she got back to her apartment Mr. S. Sikirski was waiting at her door. He was a very tall man with grey hair and a heavy grey moustache. In his left hand he was holding a worn leather briefcase. He stood there, very stiff and straight.

"I am very sorry to inconvenience you, Miss, Miss..."

"Laidlaw. Sheila Laidlaw."

He inclined his head slightly towards her. "I have been very foolish, I forgot my key. I have locked myself out."

"Is the caretaker not in?"

Mr. S. Sikirski shook his grey head. "I wonder if I could use your balcony. I could climb over. There is only three feet separating my balcony from yours."

Sheila eyed him dubiously, expecting for some

reason to see a muscle twitch on his face, or to see his hands shaking. He stood, unmoving, his eyes fixed on hers. Sheila unlocked her door. "You'd better come in." She threw her jacket and purse onto the couch and opened the French windows. "Be careful, it's twelve stories down. You'd better leave your briefcase here. I'll hand it over to you."

For an old man Sikirski was surprisingly agile. He braced himself with his right hand on the rail, and gripping the upper part of the window frame with his left hand, he pulled himself up. He teetered there for a moment, steadied himself, and then leapt over the three-foot gap, landing without a stumble on his own balcony. There was a glimmer of a smile on his lips when he turned around to face Sheila.

She smiled back at him. "Bravo." She handed him his briefcase.

He inclined his head again. "Thank you. You are very kind," He was about to go inside when he suddenly hesitated and turned around. "Miss Laidlaw, would you care to have a glass of wine with me and perhaps listen to some of my records?"

She was about to say no, but something about his stance checked her. It was as though he was standing in front of a firing squad, as though he had just refused the blindfold. Death or life. Yes or no. It is all the same to me, his pose seemed to suggest. She smiled again at S. Sikirski. "I'd like that very much," she said.

Mr. Sikirski's apartment, Sheila noted ruefully, was much neater than hers, but there was an unfinished quality about it, as if something was missing. In one corner stood a tall varnished bookcase lined with thick leather bound volumes with gold lettering on the spines. In the alcove opposite was a cabinet full of record albums, all neatly arranged. The cream-coloured walls were bare except for a simple wooden crucifix above a table with a solitary framed photograph on it. Mr. Sikirski showed Sheila to a chair and then went into his kitchen and poured out two glasses of red wine. He handed one glass to Sheila and then placed his briefcase on the table and carefully took from it several records.

He glanced at her. "I go to the library once a week. They have an excellent classical section." He took one of the records from its jacket and placed it on the turntable of his stereo and clicked the switch on. He took his glass of wine and sat across from Sheila. It was a piano solo that was playing. Sheila had to strain her ears to hear. The rippling notes sounded remote, almost as though they came from some other unseen place, imperceptibly rising and falling, then converging and moving away beyond earshot.

"It's very beautiful," said Sheila.

"Paderewski. He was my mentor." Mr. Sikirski sat very still, his head tilted to one side, his long fingers encircling his wine glass. As he spoke he did not look at Sheila. His gaze was fixed on some point over her shoulder.

He spoke quietly, distantly, like the music that was playing. He spoke as though there was no need for preliminaries, as if they had made a pact to dispense with small talk. "Before the war I taught private piano lessons. I taught in Lublin and Warsaw. I also taught here until I retired. I was never as great as Paderewski. I knew at an early age I would never be great, but I was a good teacher. That is how I met my wife. She was one of my pupils. She gave a performance in Wawel Cathedral quite recently."

"Oh, I didn't realize. I didn't . . . ."

"You thought I was perhaps a widower or a bachelor. No, we have been married for many years. I am waiting for her and my son." He made a motion with his left hand. "That is her photograph on the table. Her name is Maria and my son's name is Stefan."

Sheila looked at the picture. She was a young, fair haired woman standing on a snow-covered clearing in a pine forest. Beside her was a small, fair haired boy who was holding onto his mother's sleeve. Both their heads were turned slightly away from the camera, their smiles strained, as though they were peering into the sun.

"They will be here soon," Mr. Sikirski repeated. "Very soon. I have it on the best of authority."

"You must be very happy," said Sheila. She was looking at the photograph again. Only then did she notice that the woman wore the kind of high shouldered coat her mother used to wear during the war. The boy wore a sailor hat with a black band around it. She could guess that there would be white lettering on the hat denoting the name of a ship.

"Yes, I am very happy," said Mr. Sikirski, touching his wine glass to his lips.

It was getting dark now and the room was in half shadow. Sheila could barely make out his features. She couldn't take her eyes off the picture. A dying ray of sunshine touched it momentarily, illuminating the woman's fair hair, creating an aureole around her head; then the light was gone. She sensed that Mr. Sikirski was following her gaze. He answered the question that she could not ask.

"It has been forty-five years since we have met. I had to leave. There was no choice. Forty-five years, but they will be here soon. There is no doubt in my mind about that. It is a question of faith."

Sheila felt her hands suddenly trembling. She placed her glass on the floor and tried to light a cigarette, but she couldn't hold the match steady. She felt cold. Mr. Sikirski had just said something else but she hadn't heard. He was leaning forward slightly, one hand held palm upwards towards her. She did not need to see the expression on his face. She knew well enough what was there. She knew what she had to say.

"I'm sure they'll be here soon. I'd like to meet them when they arrive."

His voice was lowered to a whisper, but it was firm and assured again, merging with the music in the background. "Thank you. I knew you would understand." The chair creaked as he sat back.

He was asleep when Sheila finally left, his head slumped to one side. She took the glass from his hand and put it on the table beside the photograph of Maria and Stefan. As she passed him she touched his shoulder but he didn't stir.

White Mountains in the Moon
Betty Wilson

There's a ring around the moon tonight, but I can't remember if it's summer, fall or spring. Spring. Meadowlarks were singing when they brought me here.

A ring around the moon. Storm. Wind—? Or blessed rain?

Ring around the moon. Nurse was going to draw the curtain, but I begged, and anyway, the other's sleeping. Choking on herself. I don't mind it here except for that. That and the needles.

The moon's across my bed and I can make the coverlet white mountains in its light. White mountains in the moon! I saw them. Snowfall on the peaks.

They took me to the mountains, Jeannie and the man she married. (What's he called?) It was after Alfie'd—

Mountains in May. Aspens in palest leaf, and mist blue spruce trees up the slopes. Night. Snowfall in moonlight on the mountain peaks.

Alfie never saw them. Always, he said we'd see the mountains, but—

Is Alfie dead, or did I dream? Alfie. I mustn't call him that. He hates it. Mister. Mister Haythorne. Sand trickled in his grave before the preacher muttered dust to dust.

We crossed an ocean, and almost a continent, he and I before we stopped here on the wind-burned plains.

He said we'd see the mountains. But he never did. Merely half a day by car. He made the Rockies seem as far away as the cliffs of Cornwall's coast, but they're only half a day by car.

There's a ring around the moon tonight. Rain? Rain on the sand to make the wheat grow tall. Oh, we had harvests. 1915, the first year, and 1927, the year that Mister bought the truck. But he never understood machines. When it broke down he couldn't fix it. Someone told me, laughing, that he almost gave the thing away.

Perhaps this year there'll be a harvest, but I don't know how I'll plant the field. Horses are hard to catch, and the harness tangles of straps and buckles. Can I remember how it goes? Sweat-pad and collar. Hames and hame-straps, britching and belly-band. But the lines—I don't remember. Mister will— What am I thinking of? Mister's gone. I don't know where the horses are.

I wonder if the ducks came back? Alfie says the slough wastes two acres of our land that should grow grain. But I like the ducks and the frogs that sing there in the spring.

And what grain have we grown except for twice? Others. Parkers, Thomases. Even Pedersens, and they scarcely spoke a word of English for the first five years I knew them. Tractors and combines and—

If Mister understood machines— Who uses horses any more? But who am I to talk? The cream separator baffles me.

Am I talking to myself again? I must not do that. People will think me strange. The Thomas boy laughed at me. Forgot that he was in the house. I looked out to see our cows in Parker's grain and scolded Mister because he hadn't fixed the fence. Mister wasn't there.

There's a ring around the moon tonight. There was a ring around the moon the night before—

I hate the wind!

Mister'd been away all day and all the day before. Gone to buy seed grain and stopped for a quick one with the chaps.

I milked the cow and fed the calf and baby pigs. And waited.

Such a cloud! Green as rotten chicken guts.

Mister didn't come, but the cloud came up the sky. Supper. Salt pork boiled three times before I could choke it down. Never touched salt pork again.

The cloud like death, green death, rising, and rising overhead, until I was swallowed in lightning and wind, and the twisting cloud that ripped and dipped and tore the land. Deafening silence. Couldn't breathe. Then— Could a house be snatched up like that and flung against the earth?

The stove pinned me against the wall. A mercy that the fire'd gone out. After the rain, silence, and a burrowing owl calling and calling in the dark.

At first light Mister came, and others with him.

Mrs. Thomas took me home. Told me time and again that I'd been fortunate.

"Not even badly hurt! And there's little Mrs. Lakey dead, and two motherless children. And what's a man to do with motherless children? *We've* all got more than our share."

All but me. So when they had the house set up and patched enough to live in, I took the children. But never *my* children. Perhaps at six and eight it's too much to expect.

The father disappeared. Just walked away. We never heard of him again.

At school, the other children laughed at clothes I'd made the girls. Jeannie complained about our food, and it was poor. Others had roast beef and pie.

Before the Christmas concert, when she was ten, Laura asked me not to smile so much. My old false teeth were chipped. Gums like dirty brick.

We bought a Christmas tree that year. I can't remember how we managed it. Mister took walnuts and cut them into baskets with a hack saw. Cut his fingers doing it, and cursed, but they were fairy things, those baskets. I hung them on the tree with coloured darning yarn.

Pedersens had glass baubles on their tree.

As they grew older, the girls begged time to spend with neighbours, so between their visiting and school— It was dull for them at home. No games. Only my old tales, and the radio when we could afford to have the battery charged.

Jeannie was a pretty thing. I never said it, but I think I looked like that when I was young.

We'd never had a party in our house, but for her four-teenth birthday—

Mister went to town that morning, early. Things to be bought. Candles for the cake, lemons for lemonade, and Jeannie's present from the post office; the Eaton's parcel with a dress. He met some chaps. The party with no lemonade, no candles, and no dress had been over hours before he came.

The girls grasped him, each by an arm, and twirled him round and round, singing Here's Mister Haythorne now until his legs gave way. He thought it was a game.

Soon after that the boys began to come around. Jeannie married a fellow she met when she was hired girl at Thomases'. Rancher's son from the Cyprus Hills. I wish I could remember what he's called.

Laura? I wish I knew. Left at sixteen. There were letters at first. Said she was slinging hash in Regina. Slinging hash— I don't know what that means. How long ago? It must be years and years.

And so, we're alone again, Mister and I. The work gets harder year by year. When fences need fixing Mister sits beside the stove, and there's a broken window in the kitchen with cardboard nailed across the pane. And the floor— Lumpy knots in old boards. The table rocks because of them.

At hog-killing when Mr. Parker and Mr. Thomas helped—I tried to square the table before I called them in to dinner, but still it rocked. It shames me to see them laughing secretly at slopped-over tea.

It must have been last spring that Alfie drove the team to town to fetch some flour. The horse stood, unfed, unblanketed in a chilly wind. Takes strong arms and a steady hand to manage horses, cold and hungry. And he'd been with the chaps.

They said he'd landed head-first on a rock when the horses ran away. Children on their way to school found him, and the team and broken wagon tangled in the corner of a fence.

Sand trickled in his grave before the preacher muttered dust to dust.

Jeannie and her man took some days off spring work, and that's the time I saw the mountains in the moon.

Jeannie's husband asked me if I needed anything.

I told him that I had a bit put by. I did. $30 in a coffee can. I said I'd rent the farm to neighbours for a share of crop. Plenty to keep an old woman whose wants are few.

And so they went away, content.

People said the farm was overgrown with weeds, worn out, and wind-eroded. Nobody wanted it.

There was a cow, and the garden. But the cow crawled under Parker's fence and cut herself. After that she was no good for milk. Frost killed the garden in September. I saved potatoes, beets and cabbages, but they don't last forever.

Pedersens found me asleep. Wrapped me in blankets, picked me up and brought me here. The snow had gone and meadowlarks were singing.

The doctor's young enough to be my grandson. He says I have cornflower eyes. Cornflower eyes in leather, old and brown and wrinkled as my father's Sunday boots.

The nurses try to feed me, but I choke. And the needles hurt.

White-topped mountain— Gone. The moon has climbed the sky. If I move my head I still can see—a little of the ring.

If Winter Comes
Sam Selvon

It does have certain times in London, when a kind of blight descend on the boys. Everybody hard-up, and you can't get a ease-up from your best friend. And the point is, it don't happen in summer, when at least you have a little sunshine and a daffodil or tulip to console you, but in them grim days of winter when night fall on the city from three o'clock in the afternoon, and you looking all about in the fog for a friend to borrow a shilling for the gas meter.

But everybody cagey-cagey, men looking at you with suspicion from the time you appear in the distance, and some fellars, as if they have radar, could sense when a hard-up test on the horizon, and right away they begin to limp and cry big water, so that by the time you get near you realise it have a situation here that far worse than yours.

I mean, when a fellar like Brakes can't manage a borrow, you could imagine what the situation like. Because Brakes have a way, he would mamaguile you with all kind of sweet-talk, and hark back to the old days in the islands, and when he have the memories well-stirred, of a sudden he would come out with something like: "Lend me four shillings and five-pence ha'penny, boy—I in a jam."

Notice the sum he ask for. When Brakes making a tap he always asking for a particular sum as if he have something direct in mind.

But no approach was successful that season.

"These look like evil days," Brakes say to himself.

"What happen to everybody? I will have to think of something."

He had to put the old brains to work, because Mavis was after a coat that she see in a store in Oxford Street (the same place where Nina bounce some hats and cause havoc in international relationships) and this coat cost exactly 10 pounds. But as far as Brakes concern it might as well cost 500 pounds.

"Same reason I don't like to come window-shopping with you," Brakes grumble. "Everything you see you want."

"I must have that coat, Brakes," Mavis say, as if she didn't hear him at all.

"You know I ain't have a work now," Brakes say.

"If you love me, you would get that coat for me, Brakes."

Well I ain't fooling you, but woman really bad, oui. Mavis stick behind Brakes like a leech, until he had was to promise to get it for her before the next week out.

Brakes stand up by Tottenham Court Tube station pondering the situation when she left him. And the only thing he could think of is to get some fellars to take a hand in a sou-sou. That is a thing like this: about ten of you decide to give a pound each every week, and the 10 pounds would make the rounds of each person, and at the end of the ten weeks each one will have had 10 pounds.

But Brakes figuring on running a sou-sou where he don't have to put anything in. He planning to get ten fellars beside himself, and don't tell them is really eleven and not ten. And naturally he takes the first 10 pounds collected for himself. After that things would go all right until it come to the last week, when two fellars would be expecting to collect, "and by that time something bound to turn up," Brakes tell himself.

Well, he get eight of the boys and two English fellars,

and he went around like a landlord the first payday and collect the ten, and right after went and buy the coat for Mavis.

Mavis put on the coat and want to go West End right away. They cruise round by the Dilly, but everytime Mavis stop by a show window Brakes pull she away before she could say she want this and she want that.

"We haven't been to the theatre a long time," Mavis observe, wanting to show off the new coat.

"The most you getting is a walk in Trafalgar Square," Brakes say, feeling in his pockets and only clutching air, "to watch the fountains spouting water."

Well the weeks breeze by, and two days was to go for the last two fellars in the sou-sou to get the money, and Brakes wasn't nearer a work, much less the money.

He dress and went out in the last act of despair the boys resort to—looking for money in the streets. You don't know sometimes what your luck might be—you might spot a crumple-up pound note or a ten shilling somewhere on the pavement where people walking so fast that they ain't have time to look down.

Brakes have time—in fact his face rivet-down to the ground, but he reach to them side streets in Soho and the most he find is two safety pin. That wasn't a happy hunting ground, because it have a lot of tests does be liming there and if anybody drop a note or even a tanner by accident, you could be sure it hardly have time settle on the ground before a test ups it.

But Brakes wasn't thinking where he going. He collide-up with a fellar who was in a hurry.

"What is all the rush, Chippy?" Brakes say, recognising a shady Englisher who live by gambling.

"I am on something hot," Chippy say. "I am off to put money on a sure horse."

Brakes brain start to work tick-tock. "What is the

odds?" he ask Chippy.

"The odds are ten to one," Chippy say. He make to move off, then he stop. "Would you like me to put something on for you?" He pull Brakes to one side and talking in a whisper. "Meet me here by three o'clock if you are interested." And with that he takes off.

Well, by three o'clock Brakes hand Chippy a pound and remain sweating until the race finish. Praise the lord, the horse come in and Brakes see his worries over for the time being. All he had to do was collect the last hand and then pay off the two fellars.

The last man in the sou-sou was a Englisher, and as soon as he see Brakes he say: "Something fishy seems to be going on. I understand that this sou-sou thing is finished, and I haven't had any money. I have been looking all over town for you."

"Take it easy," Brakes say. "I have the money right here for you."

The Englisher lick his thumb and count the money. "It was a good experience," he say, "but count me out the next time."

After that, the only worry was Mavis. Brakes take a trip to the nearest public library and spent some time reading poetry before he went to pick her up after work.

"Did you manage to borrow money for the sou-sou?" was the first thing she ask him, because Brakes did tell her everything but she couldn't help.

"I bet on a horse and it come in," Brakes say.

"Where did you get the money to bet?"

"Well," Brakes start to fidget. "I had to get this money somehow. Anyway, don't worry." Brakes trying hard to remember the poetry he read in the library. "You know that nice poetry about if winter come, spring running a close second. It only have a few more weeks and then no more winter, and people won't need to put on any heavy clothes."

"What is all that in aid of?" Mavis suspicious and pull Brakes to one side of the pavement and stand up.

"Well, you won't need that coat any more," Brakes say. "I tell you, spring is just around the corner."

"What are you trying to say?" Mavis say impatiently.

"I sell the coat for a pound to get money to bet. It's quite mild now, you don't think?"

Though the day was really mild Mavis start to shiver as if she have ague.

"Sold my coat!" she say, holding on to her shoulders and trembling with imaginary cold. "Whay did you do that, Brakes?"

"I keep telling you about the poetry that say if winter come, spring racing a close second. Only a few more days and . . . "

Mavis ready to cry. "I haven't had a new coat for years. What will I do when winter comes again?"

Brakes ponder the question for a moment.

"Don't worry," he say brightly. "I will run another sou-sou and buy one for you!"

Hang out your Washing
on the Siegfried Line
Gloria Sawai

One Saturday in spring, when the brother was twelve and the sister nine, they climbed the ladder in the church tower to the belfry. The tower was dim except for a yellow square of sunlight far above where the tunnel opened onto the bell deck. It was dusty, smelling of old feathers and bird droppings.

The sister was first. The brother followed below. She knew, climbing in her pink and flaring skirt, why he wanted to be second. And soft slender pleasures curled about in the centre of her stomach. But as she stepped up on the wooden rungs, clinging with stiff hands to the bars, she scraped her feet hard against each rung, sending bits of dust and shrivelled bird droppings down on her brother's face, down on his upturned nose.

When they reached the top he shoved her with one free hand through the opening into the belfry and followed close behind. They lay on their stomachs, clutching with arms and thighs at the safety of the deck. Their heads leaned over the edge, their feet rested under the great iron bell suspended above. There was no railing. The height made them dizzy.

They lay quietly looking down on the church yard: the earth brown and wet, the carragana hedge sprouting bits of green, the small graves beyond the hedge, shabby in spring mud and winter's limp weeds.

From here they saw everything: McFarlane's brick house on the hill north of the church, the finest house in

Stone Creek, Saskatchewan; on Main Street, the Red and White store, Mack Gilman's Dry goods, Louie's new furniture store and undertaking parlour. South of Main Street, the Ukrainian houses, little clay houses in yards soon to be filled with rows of green vegetables and yellow sunflowers. And between these houses and the onion domed church to the east, the livery barn, where Doctor Long, old and very thin, shuffled silently each day to drink whiskey with Lars Holmgren.

"When I'm seventeen I'm going to leave this dump," the brother said.

"Why?" the sister asked.

"Why! Who wants to rot in this dump?"

"It's nicer than Graveltown. I heard some people from Graveltown are moving here next month."

"They can have it," he said. "It's a dump."

They heard an airplane somewhere to the north, saw its distant curve approach, watched it roar over Stone Creek.

"Take me to United States!" the sister yelled, aiming her voice with her cupped hands. She didn't learn until she was twenty that that country had a *the* in front of its name.

"Take me to United States!" she yelled again, louder.

"United States! Who wants to go to United States?" the brother said.

"Where do you want to go?" she asked.

He sat up, facing the bell. "Halifax," he said, "to join the navy and see the world.

If they ask us who we are
We're the RCNVR.
Roll along, wavy navy,
Roll along."

His voice bounced off the iron bell, filling the tower, spilling out into the yard below.

When he was thirteen he got a job cleaning the church. Each Saturday he was paid fifty cents to straighten hymnals, dust pews, change numbers on the little wooden board above the pulpit that told what pages the hymns were on. The job didn't include the altar, however. He didn't wash the starched white cloth under the vessels or the plaster face of Jesus standing in the altar's niche with outstretched arms. Only the women did that.

A few complained. Mrs. Carlson said that just because he was the preacher's son he shouldn't get special privileges. "It doesn't look right," she told Elvera Nelson, wrapping a jar of molasses in the Red and White. Elvera said the preacher's son was a wild one and needed watching. "As a matter of fact, I wouldn't be surprised if he wasn't in on that Walter Skogland business, and didn't Walter get two months in Reform School?"

But he kept the job for one whole summer, every Saturday flicking a limp cloth smelling faintly of lemons over the dusty pews. Each time he finished, he'd stand in his father's pulpit surveying his handiwork.

The morning Louie hauled Frank Schultz to St. Paul's the two children stood on the church steps and held the door for him. Louie and Sig Karetsky lugged the casket out of their truck, hugging each an end. They lifted it up the steps, Sig first, backing through the lobby, past the swinging doors, down the nave's long aisle. Louie told him, bumping against the pews, to watch his step. Sig said how could he with this thing right under his nose. Louie laughed and they set the grey box on metal stands in the chancel of St. Paul's, a few feet in front of the altar. Just beyond the arms of Jesus.

The news spread to the edges of town like spokes in a bike. "They've got Frank Schultz down at St. Paul's." By ten o'clock the other children had gathered: Mary Sorenson, Joe Lippoway, Andy Grimshaw, Abie Gilman. The brother stood beside the swinging doors in the lobby, holding an offering plate.

"A nickel apiece," he said.

"Highway robbery," Joe Lippoway said.

"Can you go in with someone?" Andy asked, who was ten.

"With someone! Why? Are you a little nervous, Andy? I believe Andy's a little nervous. Maybe you better not go in, Andy, if it makes you nervous."

"Who's nervous? I just want to be with someone, that's all. It's more fun if you're with someone."

"With someone it'll cost a nickel extra. A nickel apiece plus one if you go in by two's."

The sister leaned back against the varnished wall. "I know of a certain person who wouldn't think too much of this idea of yours, if he found out."

"Who's first?" the brother said.

"You be first."

"No, you go."

"I'll be next after you."

"No, I'll wait."

"Hell," Joe said, "I'll go." He threw a nickel into the brass plate and disappeared through the swinging doors. He was back almost immediately.

"It's Schultz all right. And is he ever dead."

Abie Gilman and Andy Grimshaw went in together. Three nickels clanged into the plate. Their stay was only slightly longer.

"Did you see his hands?" Andy asked, standing by the bell rope, his hair the colour of the rope. "Did you see how they were folded like he was praying?"

"Praying!" Joe said. "That's Louie's job. He's the one who gets them looking good finally. Did you ever see old Schultz with clean fingernails before?"

"He didn't get the thumb right," Abie said. "It was

sticking straight up. Louie should have tried to get the thumb to fold the right way."

When the sister went in with Mary Sorenson, she saw only the face. Bluish white like skim milk. Shiny as mucilage.

In the afternoon, during the service, they sat by the hedge, snapping beetles between rocks and making whistles out of carragana pods. The sun was shining, warm and orange. The air was pungent with the moist smells of upturned soil, crushed pods, and the cracked shells of beetles.

"Well, soon old Schultz will be galloping his way to glory. Flying through the sky to the sweet by and by," Joe Lippoway said, measuring a distant cloud with two fingers. Joe lived in one of the clay houses south of main street with his father, who spoke only Russian.

"I don't care if it rains or freezes. I am safe in the arms of Jesus."

"Okay, Lippoway, you can shut your mouth right about now," the brother said. Certain irreverences he would not allow.

"Yea, Lippoway, zip your lip," Abie added. Abie was a Jew and had no dealings with St. Paul's, except on burial days. But he was a Jew and felt a certain respect for holy places.

"I understand the Communists in Russia hardly believe in anything anymore," the sister said, her neck stiffening against a bough.

When the mourners gathered at the grave, the little group watched from behind the carragana hedge. With six men and three ropes the casket was lowered into the newly carved opening. The family stood together at one end, their bodies leaning in a dark unity toward its edge. The preacher stood at the other end, holding a spade. He looked thin standing alone by the open grave. He spoke the words clearly but in a high voice that rose in the air like little streams of smoke.

"From dust thou came.
To dust thou shalt return.
From dust shalt thou arise again."

When she heard her father's words, the sister crumbled a lump of dirt between her fingers and wondered why Frank Schultz had suddenly become a thou. Up until now he'd only been Frank, a farmer six miles south of Stone Creek.

When Joe heard the words he made small flapping gestures with his crook't arms as if he were flying, but no one was paying attention to him now.

Abie seemed to hear a different voice. A quiet voice from an ancient flame. Take off your shoes, Moses. The ground you stand on is holy ground.

One afternoon in fall she caught him smoking. He was sitting on the ground behind the garage nearly hidden by Russian thistles. First she saw the wisps of grey rising from the thistles and the red spark of his cigarette. Then she saw him sitting there, leaning against a rock. She stood and watched, strong in the righteousness of her sex.

"So. Here's where you keep yourself," she finally said. He jerked the cigarette out of his mouth. "I didn't know you smoked." He held the glowing object down by his knee.

"So? Now you do."

"Well, isn't this interesting. I guess Dad would find it quite interesting too if he knew about it."

"Make sure you let him know then," he said, raising the cigarette with a flourish.

"I didn't say I was going to tell him. I only said that if he knew he'd find it very interesting. That's all I said."

"Well, if he'd find it so interesting I think you should tell him. I think you should go right now and tell him." He snuffed out the cigarette and sat straight up. He picked up a thin stick, placed it on the end of his nose, the tip resting on his forehead. It was a favourite trick of his. Only he could do it because of his odd-shaped nose.

"You think that's quite clever, don't you, balancing things on your nose like that. I suppose you think the girls at school find it very smart and clever when you balance pencils on your nose like that and get them to laughing."

"Do you know anyone else who can do it?" he asked.

"I should hope not," she said and turned to leave.

"Hey, wait a minute. Have you ever heard this song before?"

She stopped, stood there among the swaying weeds, and listened to her brother sing in that curious new voice of his that she detested.

"Hang out your washing on the Siegfried Line
If the Siegfried Line's still there."

"Certainly I've heard it. Mr. Nelson sings that when he's mowing the grass."

"Do you know what it means?" he asked.

"No."

"You really don't know what it means?"

"How should I know what it means?"

"Well, I guess you don't at that, do you? I guess you haven't heard what that song's all about, have you? That," he lowered his voice significantly, "is the dirtiest song in the English language. A very obscene song."

"What's dirty about it?"

"I'd never tell." He leaned back against the rock and slipped another Sweet Caporal out of its cellophaned package.

"What can be dirty about hanging out your wash on the Siegfried Line?"

"O. You said it."

"I said what?"

"The dirty words."

"You mean those are the dirty words?"

"That's what I said." He flicked a match against a rock, bent his head into the weeds, out of the wind, and lit the cigarette, inhaling deeply.

"What part is dirty—hanging out the wash, or the Siegfried Line?"

"O. You said it again."

"But you said it first."

"I did not. I sang it. Singing's different. It's like quoting."

"Well, tell me what it means then."

"Me? Never."

"Does it mean the same as what Walter Skogland tried to do to Rattray's cow?"

"I'd never say. You wouldn't get me to talk about anything like that."

She stood in the weeds and looked at him.

"So. You said the words, didn't you." He raised his head smoothly, easily, sending a delicate ribbon of smoke curling into the prairie sky.

He didn't forget. When she stood by the kitchen sink in a white apron, washing the supper dishes, he crept up behind her and whispered the song in her ear. When she climbed the stairs to go to the bathroom, he stopped her on the landing, nudged her, winked lewdly, and sang between closed teeth:

"Hang out your washing on the Siegfried Line

If the Siegfried Line's still there."

In the bathroom she sat on the toilet, her panties curled around her ankles, her heart pounding.

Once in the living room, where her father was kneeling in front of the door, hammer in hand, repairing a hinge, her brother, sprawled on the brown sofa, hummed the song softly under his breath. She left the room, trying not to hurry, and asked her mother in the kitchen if there was anything she could do to help.

Later he told her. "You really thought that was a dirty song, didn't you? You were scared I was going to tell, weren't you? Ha."

"Oh, really. Wasn't that a smart thing to do now? Weren't you smart and clever to think of something like that." She ran, furious, across the alley to Sorenson's.

When he was fifteen he got Sig Karetsky's old job working for Louie.

"Do you think it looks right?" Mrs. Carlson asked Elvera Nelson, when she heard the news. "The preacher's son working for Louie like that? Won't people think it's kind of fishy? I mean it could cause talk." She sat at the kitchen table, nibbling on a piece of shortbread.

"What's a mystery of me is why Louie would hire him. There's one that needs watching," Elvera said from across the table, her elbows sunk in little folds of fat.

But he went to work every Saturday, leaving the house at nine, whistling down the driveway.

One morning in June he forgot his lunch. His mother picked up the brown bag from the kitchen counter and told his sister to take it to him. She combed her hair, preened in front of the hall mirror until her mother called her to stop fussing over herself and get started. She slipped on her new blue sweater, examining herself again from different angles in the hall mirror. She was going downtown to bring her brother his lunch.

Outside, the sun was pouring down, shining on the purple blooms of lilacs, stippling the young leaves of car-raganas. It flecked the wings of a meadowlark perched on a fence post, spread over weeds and grass onto the gravelled driveway where it soaked into the little crevices between the stones, warming the sleek backs of ants and beetles. There was no space anywhere without the light.

At the end of the driveway her father was kneeling beside the car, fiddling with his tool box. The sun spilled out over the car's slick top and down on his greasy tools. It shone warm on his curved shoulders and smooth grey back.

She walked past the lilacs to where her father knelt by the blue car. He looked up. "My. Aren't you spiffed up this morning," he said. "Are you going to a wedding?"

She held the brown bag out in front of her. "Not a wedding. He forgot his lunch. I have to bring him his lunch. That's all."

She opened the gate and walked across the alley. At Sorenson's she stopped for a minute to watch her friend Mary do a backbend under the clothesline, her body curved against the earth, her hair streaming.

"Where are you off to?" Mary asked, upside down.

"To Louie's. I'm bringing my brother his lunch. You knew he was working for Louie, didn't you?"

"Well, I guess," Mary said, her back circling the grass.

She walked down the sidewalk edged with dandelions and Russian thistle, past Nelson's, through the vacant lot to Main Street. She stopped in front of Gilman's, where Abie was sweeping the sidewalk in front of his father's store. The straw of his broom gathered dust, gravel, crushed candy wrappers, guiding them over the sun-warmed cement into the narrow ditch on the curb's edge.

"Where do you think you're going?" he asked.

"Me? Oh, nowhere special. My dumb brother forgot his lunch and I have to bring it to him. You know he's working for Louie now, don't you?"

"Of course." He continued sweeping, tufts of yellow

straw swirling over the concrete.

At Louie's she walked across the oiled floor, past lamps and sofas, to the office at the far end. She opened the door. He was sitting on a wooden chair, his feet up on the desk, staring at the ceiling.

"Is this all you have to do?" she asked.

"All! Don't you know Louie's gone? Who'd answer the phone if I wasn't here? Who'd take care of things?" He picked up a yellow pencil, held it by his ear, ready for any important message.

"It doesn't look like much of a job to me."

"Some jobs take muscles. Some take brains." He laid the pencil on the desk blotter and fussed about in the drawer with a box of paper clips. She looked at a closed door across the room.

"Is that where you keep them?"

"When we've got them."

"You don't have any today?"

"Not in there."

"Well, here's the lunch you forgot." She set the bag on the desk and turned to leave.

"Hey, wait a minute," he said. "You might be interested in that shoe box." He pointed to the shelf beside the desk littered with old magazines, an ashtray, and a white shoe box with Captain's 4.98 written in black on one end.

"Why?"

"Oh, no special reason. I just thought you might like to know what's in that box. But I guess you wouldn't be interested after all."

She walked over to the shelf and grabbed the box. She opened the lid, lifted up a gauzy sheet of tissue paper. She saw it for less than a second, smaller than her hand, veins blue under the white skin, tiny fingers curled tightly like the claws of a kitten. She felt a ragged lump in the centre of her stomach, sharp and hard as frozen dirt. She shoved the box back on the shelf.

"Why did you do that? Why did you do such a stupid thing as that? What a stupid thing to do!"

"What did I do? I didn't make you open that box. You're the little Pandora who grabs the box and puts her nose right in."

"Why is it in a shoe box?"

"What's wrong with a shoe box? Any smaller they flush them down the toilet."

"Oh, you're really something, aren't you. You really think of marvellous things, don't you. Brilliant and marvellous. It must make you very proud to think of such marvellous things. Well, have a nice time eating your lunch, that's all I have to say."

She fled from the room, past the sofas, lamps, and caneback chairs, out the front door. She ran past Gilman's, cut across the vacant lot to Nelson's, past Sorenson's, and across the alley. She didn't stop until she reached her own yard and leaned against the gate, her heart pounding.

Her father was still working on the car. He was lying under it on the gravel, hammering away at something. She saw only his feet, twisting under the bumper.

She ran to the house, through the kitchen where her mother was chopping walnuts, into the living room.

She sat on the piano bench and paged through ragged song books. She looked up at the photographs that littered the piano's top. A picture of her grandparents on their Golden Wedding Anniversary, standing in front of a poplar tree, holding a cake. One of her cousin Algren on his Confirmation Day, standing on the church step, holding a scroll. One of her and her brother, when he was five and she was two, sitting in a chair together, holding a ball.

She turned some pages to her next week's lesson and played the first six bars of *Minuet in G*.

"Ketchen's," she said. "Remember?"

"Ketchen's?"

"Yes. The chickens—don't you remember?"

"Oh. *Ketchen's.* The chickens in the kitchen at Ketchen's."

"The flies, don't forget."

She lay on the high bed, rested her head on limp pillows, pulled the green blanket up to her chin. He sat in a chrome and plastic chair beside the bed, holding a pair of sunglasses by one stem.

"Our father took us to very strange places sometimes," he said, "but none as queer as Ketchen's." He twirled his sunglasses, perched them on the end of his upturned nose. "I wonder if they still keep their chickens in the kitchen."

"They didn't keep them there. They just walked in. Don't you remember how hot it was, and they left the door open, but they didn't have a screen?"

He let his glasses slip off his nose into his hand. Then he said, "And everywhere you looked, flies. The light cord hanging from the kitchen ceiling. Remember that? I thought some wind was twisting it, but it was flies crawling all over the cord, covering the whole cord."

"The peach sauce, don't forget."

"I thought it was pears."

"No. Peaches. Remember? Mrs. Ketchen asked if we'd stay for lunch, and Daddy said he'd be delighted. And you started gagging. She served the sauce on plates, flat dinner plates, and you didn't know how to eat it. Your peach kept slipping all over the plate and you started laughing. Remember? Then Daddy cut it with a knife and told you to use your fork."

"Ketchen's," he said. "It's funny. He still thinks about those awful places. He actually misses those dry and dusty places."

A nurse, plump and middle aged, her clipper hair tidy under a white cap, walked into the room, carrying a trayful a tiny paper cups.

"Here's a little something for pain, honey, and to help you sleep when your visitor leaves." She laid the cup on the bedside table, turned to leave, then stopped, her neat head framed by the wooden panels of the door and the bronze crucifix shining above it.

"Listen, honey, the doctor wonders if you've had any luck yet."

"Luck?"

"With your bowels."

"No luck."

"Patience," the nurse smiled. "It will come." She turned again to leave. They listened to her brisk steps down the corridor.

"That's all that matters now. They don't care about my eyes, ears, nose, throat, feet, hands, or heart. Only my bowels."

"How did it go?" he asked. "How was it?"

She turned over on her side, scrunched the pillow up and lay back again. "Do you remember the summer in Stone Creek when I worked at Silver Cross? You were still working for Louie I think. One morning I was picking peas in the hospital garden. I was on my hands and knees in the dirt when I heard a woman screaming. And I remember thinking as I pulled those pods that when I grew up and had babies I wasn't going to do that. I was going to be poised the whole time, maybe just grit my teeth a little. When it was over I'd ask the doctor if he'd like a cup of tea or something. I'd be real cute about it."

"And were you?"

"Are you crazy? I bawled and roared. I yelled at them to stop it. Stop the whole business, I'd changed my mind. But when it was over. Lord. It was lovely. The doctor held her in the palm of his hand. She was all bloody red, sleek and shiny. And I shouted hallelujah like some Holy Roller."

When he left she turned over on her side, reached for the tiny paper cup on the table, swallowed the green pill. Everything's green here, she thought, as she sank into the pillows . . .

A bench presses hard against the dark and twisted sore between her legs. She tries to move her thighs, to lift the aching from the wood's hardness, but her thighs cling to the bench. The baby is tucked under her blouse out of the wind. She hears its small sucking noises, feels the gums biting her breast, tiny fingers pressing back and forth rhythmically like a cat's paw. The boat glides silently over the black water.

Across the deck her brother leans against the ship's railing. He's wearing sunglasses and he's alone. Where are the others? Andy and Joe and Abie and his cousin Algren, and the rest, who laughed together on summer nights under the lamp posts? He leans against the railing, looking down on the black water.

Their father is kneeling at the forward end of the ferry trying to fasten a sheet of loosened tin to the prow. He clutches the tin with one hand. With the other he rummages through the tool box, searching. He can't find the right tools. The tin rattles in the wind like the old Imperial Oil sign on Main Street on a dusty spring night on the prairie.

Her brother looks out on the sea and on the passing islands. He's enjoying the scenery, she thinks, but doesn't seem to notice their father kneeling at the ship's prow. She wants to tell her brother to look at his father now. Notice what he's doing. Observe how he's fastening the tin, how he's trying to repair the boat. She wants to tell everyone:

That's what my father does—he repairs things, mends things, doors and carburetors, people's sorrows. Her father bends over the tool box. His thin hair rises and curves like threads of smoke in the wind. Her brother gazes out to the edges of the sea. She wants to tell her brother to turn around now. She wants to tell everyone to turn around and pay attention.

She tries to pronounce the right words for this, but they're stuck somewhere down beneath her bowels. Maybe it's the baby pushing on her belly, pressing down on the grey and purple bruise between her legs. Maybe she can't say the words because of this.

Or maybe she had already said them. Maybe, without realizing it, she had said, "Open your eyes and look around and see what's going on." Only they hadn't heard, no one had heard, her brother hadn't heard. They weren't listening . . .

One morning in August it happened. While the sister was dialing in Toronto, the brother was leaning back in a leather chair, in his twenty-fifth floor office in San Francisco. He was looking up from a yellow legal pad on the walnut desk in front of him, gazing out of wall-sized windows to the ocean, watching ships in the harbour. From Rio de Janiero, Yokohama, Hong Kong. He was staring at the ships and at the sun's brightness on the ships and on the water. He was thinking of Manchuria.

When the telephone rang he raised the receiver to his ear and poised a black pen over the sheet of yellow paper.

"Daddy just died," the sister said. "He was killed in a car accident," she said. "He was knocked down by a car on Spadina Avenue. He's dead."

In Manchuria it was 9 p.m. Outside of Mukden, old Chinese farmers were squatting in the barley fields. After a long day of work they were smoking their pipes lazily under the slanting rays of the sun, the smoke rising silently above the barley as they emptied their bowels into the fields.

"No," the brother said. That was all the brother said. For a long while he sat in his leather chair in San Francisco, touching the telephone.

But he didn't see the telephone, or his hand resting on it. He didn't see the wall-sized windows, or the harbour, or the sun glittering on the water. He didn't see the light pouring through the windows into his office, spreading over the green carpet, reaching into the farthest corners of the room. He didn't see it, but it was there, moving over the leather chair and himself sitting in the leather chair. Glowing on his arm, on the telephone, on his hand touching the telephone.

Then he saw it.

He saw the yellow brightness of it.

And the brightness rolled off an iron bell and poured out on a prairie town. It spilled down on Main Street, pressed against the buildings on Main Street, against himself in Louie's new building where he sat in a wooden chair holding a pencil near his ear. It pressed against him—his chest and eyes—until the tears came wet and shining on his cheeks.

Then the yellow brightness drifted out into the street. It mingled with the dust in curbs. It rose in swirls above the town and lost itself in glimmering waves over the prairie.

The Angel of the Tar Sands
Rudy Wiebe

Spring had most certainly, finally, come. The morning
drive to the plant from Fort McMurray was so dazzling
with fresh green against the heavy spruce, the air so
unearthly bright that it swallowed the smoke from the
candy-striped chimneys as if it did not exist. Which is just
lovely, the superintendent thought, cut out all the visible
crud, shut up the environmentalists, and he went into his
neat office (with the river view with islands) humming,
"Alberta blue, Alberta blue, the taste keeps—" but did not
get his tan golfing jacket off before he was interrupted. Not
by the radio-telephone, by Tak the day operator on
Number Two Bucket in person, walking past the secretary
without stopping.

"What the hell?" the superintendent said, quickly
annoyed.

"I ain't reporting this on no radio," Tak's imperturb-
able Japanese-Canadian face was tense, "if them reporters
hear about this one they—"

"You scrape out *another* buffalo skeleton, for god's
sake?"

"No, it's maybe a dinosaur this time, one of them—"

But the superintendent, swearing, was already out the
door yelling for Bertha who was always on stand-by now
with her spade. If one of the three nine-storey-high buck-
etwheels stopped turning for an hour the plant dropped
capacity, but another archaeological leak could stop every
bit of production for a month while bifocalled professors

stuck their noses . . . the jeep leaped along the track beside the conveyor belt running a third empty already and in three minutes he had Bertha with her long-handled spade busy on the face of the fifty-foot cliff that Number Two had been gnawing out. A shape emerged, quickly.

"What the . . . " staring, the superintendent could not find his ritual words, ". . . is that?"

"When the bucket hit the corner of it," Tak said, "I figured hey, that's the bones of a—"

"That's not just bone, it's . . . skin and . . ." The superintendent could not say the word.

"Wings," Bertha said it for him, digging her spade in with steady care. "That's wings, like you'd expect on a angel."

For that's what it was, plain as the day now, tucked tight into the oozing black cliff, an angel. Tak had seen only a corner of bones sheared clean but now that Bertha had it more uncovered they saw the manlike head through one folded-over pair of wings and the manlike legs, feet through another pair, very gaunt, the film of feathers and perhaps skin so thin and engrained with tarry sand that at first it was impossible to notice anything except the white bones inside them. The third pair of wings was pressed flat by the sand at a very awkward, it must have been painful—

"The middle two," Bertha said, trying to brush the sticky sand aside with her hand, carefully, "is what it flies with."

"Wouldn't it . . . he . . . fly with all six . . . six . . ." The superintendent stopped, overwhelmed by the unscientific shape uncovered there so blatantly.

"You can look it up," Bertha said with a sideways glance at his ignorance, "Isaiah chapter six."

But then she gagged too for the angel had moved. Not one of them was touching it, that was certain, but it had moved irrefutably. As they watched, stunned, the wings unfolded bottom and top, a head emerged, turned, and they saw the fierce hoary lineaments of an ancient man. His mouth all encrusted with tar pulled open and out came a sound. A long, throat-clearing streak of sound. They staggered back, fell; the superintendent found himself on his knees staring up at the shape which wasn't really very tall, it just seemed immensely broad and overwhelming, the three sets of wings now sweeping back and forth as if loosening up in some seraphic 5BX plan. The voice rumbled like thunder, steadily on.

"Well," muttered Tak, "whatever it is, it sure ain't talking Japanese."

The superintendent suddenly saw himself as an altar boy, the angel suspended above him there and bits of words rose to his lips: "*Pax vobis . . . cem . . . cum*," he ventured, but the connections were lost in the years, "*Magnifi . . . cat . . . ave Mar . . .*"

The obsidian eyes of the angel glared directly at him and it roared something, dreadfully. Bertha laughed aloud.

"Forget the popish stuff," she said, "It's talking Hutterite, Hutterite German."

"Wha . . ." The superintendent had lost all words; he was down to syllables only.

"I left the colony . . ." But then she was too busy listening. The angel kept on speaking, non-stop as if words had been plugged up inside for eons, and its hands (it had only two of them, in the usual place at the ends of two arms) brushed double over its bucket-damaged shoulder and that appeared restored, whole just like the other, while it brushed the soil and tarry sand from its wings, flexing the middle ones again and again because they obviously had suffered much from their position.

"Ber . . . Ber . . ." the superintendent said. Finally he looked at Tak, pleading for a voice.

"What's it saying," Tak asked her, "Bertha, please Bertha?"

She was listening with overwhelming intensity; there was nothing in this world but to hear. Tak touched her shoulder, shook her, but she did not notice. Suddenly the angel stopped speaking; it was studying her.

"I . . . I can't . . ." Bertha confessed to it at last, "I can understand every word you . . . every word, but I can't say, I've forgotten . . ."

In its silence the angel looked at her; slowly its expression changed. It might have been showing pity, though of course that is really difficult to tell with angels. Then it folded its lower wings over its feet, its upper wings over its face, and with an ineffable movement of its giant middle wings it rose, straight upward into the blue sky. They bent back staring after it, and in a moment it had vanished in light.

"O dear god," Bertha murmured after a time. "Our Elder always said they spoke Hutterite in heaven."

They three contemplated each other and they saw in each other's eyes the dread, the abrupt tearing sensation of doubt. Had they seen . . . and as one they looked at the sand cliff still oozing tar, the spade leaning against it. Beside the hole where Bertha had dug: the shape of the angel, indelible. Bertha was the first to get up.

"I quit," she said. "Right this minute."

"Of course, I understand." The superintendent was on his feet. "Tak, run your bucket through there, get it going quick."

"Okay," Tak said heavily. "You're the boss."

"It doesn't matter how fast you do it," Bertha said to the superintendent but she was watching Tak trudge into the shadow of the giant wheel. "It was there, we saw it."

And at her words the superintendent had a vision. He saw like an opened book the immense curves of the

Athabasca River swinging through wilderness down from the glacial pinnacles of the Rocky Mountains and across Alberta and joined by the Berland and the McLeod and the Pembina and the Pelican and the Christina and the Clearwater and the Firebag rivers, and all the surface of the earth was gone, the Tertiary and the Lower Cretaceous layers of strata had been ripped away and the thousands of square miles of black bituminous sand were exposed, laid open, slanting down into the molten centre of the earth, O *miserere, miserere,* the words sang in his head and he felt their meaning though he could not have explained them, much less remembered Psalm 51, and after a time he could open his eyes and lift his head. The huge plant, he knew every bolt and pipe, still sprawled between him and the river; the brilliant air still swallowed the smoke from all the red-striped chimneys as if it did not exist, and he knew that through a thousand secret openings the oil ran there, gurgling in each precisely numbered pipe and jointure, sweet and clear like golden brown honey.

Tak was beside the steel ladder, about to start the long climb into the machine. Bertha touched his shoulder and they both looked up.

"Next time you'll recognize it," she said happily. "And then it'll talk Japanese."

Eva and the Apple Tree
Catherine Simmons

He sat in his apple tree, knees pulled closely to his chest, watching the fierce roll of clouds and the blossoms which fluttered brilliant against the moving grey. Waldor, arms wrapped about his legs, squatting in the last moment of spring's white light. The wind gusted, flipping up the leaves of his tree. Their undersides flapped silver. Then he heard the screen door slam.

"Waldor. You're a dink."

The wind carried white blossom petals across the sky, and swirling, they fell at his wife's feet. Her hair rose in the storm's energy.

"You are, Waldor," she yelled. "A big weiner, Waldor."

He watched her churn across the lawn, one cloud streaking over her then another, until she stood at his tree's base.

"Waldor, listen. This is the 1980s. That means I'm not cooking dinner while you squat in your damn tree like some kind of monkey king."

Sometimes the wind blew hard filling her mouth with air and blossoms, changing the volume of her voice.

"Waldor. I'm talking to you. I am not going to cook dinner alone."

Waldor watched Eva silently. Anger put energy into her body which intrigued him. Her round arms grew pink and solid; they flushed and pulsed. And her thick thighs tightened, her body growing heavy with grey energy.

"Get down and help. Now!"

She was not a fat woman, no, but the plump round-ness of her arms, of her heavy legs, showed that she thrived on food. And he knew that it was hunger, more than him, that was making her angry.

Eva's teeth clamped together and she moved forward, took hold of a branch and started to swing it. "You goomba. You scum bag. Get down from your tree and help me."

Waldor watched the thick grace of his wife's arms pushing the branch; Eva's arms dappled with fat raindrops, framed by apple blossoms. Eva's arms that held him in the night.

He unravelled his legs from his chest. "O.K.," he said. "I'll get down."

So she stopped swinging the branch and extended her arms to help him.

"You're a twit," she said as they walked to the back door, rain on their backs. "You always wait to see how mad I'll get."

"You have a very bad temper, Eva, when you're hungry."

"I'm not hungry." And Eva slammed the screen door.

So Waldor said he would make dinner; he would cook a nice meal to make his wife happy. Eva read to him from the paper while he stirred the white sauce, offered to make him a drink while the fish broiled.

"You know what?" Eva rattled ice, banged the fridge door, her movements strong and careless. "I know you like me shaking you out of your tree; that's why I do it."

Waldor looked out of the window at the spring pud-dles releasing stars of light. Eva handed him his gin and pink lemonade, her heavy fingers ice-damp. "You think of me as your cave lady; as your big bulging goomba. So that's what you get."

"Cave lady," he said moving to her, pressing against her body so that she moved her arms to encircle him. He pushed into the hug, his hands feeling for the thickness of her upper arms. And Waldor's fingers moved in her dappled flesh, flowed in the center of her warm life. Eva's life which fed his.

"The cat wants in," Eva said releasing him. "Lazer's been out in the rain. Dumb fart."

Lazer was at the kitchen window looking in. Waldor watched Lazer's mouth open close open close; Lazer rushed in as Waldor pushed on the screen. A wet cat. An unhappy cat.

"We'll have wine tonight," said Eva scraping a kitchen chair across the floor. And she heaved herself onto it, then, arching her pudgy toes, stretched to the liquor cupboard. Her breath was short as she slid bottles about with her heavy arms.

"Dinner's ready, Eva."

"O.K. Take this." And she thunked to the kitchen floor.

Waldor watched Eva eat, watched her sniff each bite fully, heavily, before bringing it to her mouth. And he listened. Feeling wine in his belly, the warmth of his wife's knee against his thigh, Waldor listened to Eva as she sniffed and chewed crazily. He heard the sounds which gave him security.

"Good food," she said. "For all the hours you spend in your apple tree doing nothing you're a good cook."

"Eva. Most people do things to avoid thinking. So I think in the tree. And I'm watching from the tree."

"I know, you goon." Eva stood and rubbed her thick cheek against his. "I'll start the dishes if you make coffee."

So Waldor measured ground coffee aware always of Eva's movements, her body filling the whole kitchen like

the scent of fresh apple peels. The hair on her bare
forearms held the light as she reached, fell into shadow as
she turned, banging the saucepan against the counter.
Eva's upper arms a warm pink. Then, with billowy thighs
dappling, Eva left the kitchen. Waldor heard the bathroom
door close, heard the fierceness of his Eva's long-lasting
stream.

They took a very long time with their coffee and
liqueur so that twilight had fallen when Waldor poured the
last of the pot into their mugs. The spring storm had passed
and the sky framing Eva's face ebbed violet. Waldor liked
where Eva sat at the table with the kitchen window behind
her, the sky always changing around her head.

"Feel like a game of gin rummy?" Eva's fingers
moved over her empty glass becoming fluid in the half-
light.

"Sure."

"More Brandy first though. You want more of your
green crap?"

"Yeah. Thanks. But it's not crap; I like the mint. And
the colour."

So, with thick fingers curling about the bottles, Eva
poured.

Waldor brought the green liquid to his eyes, looked
through the glass to his Eva. Eva underwater, her face
drifting, changing. "Cheers," he said lowering his glass.
And he saw that directly behind Eva was the full whiteness
of the rising moon. A searing arc circling her face from
jaw to jaw. "How strange," he murmured.

"What?" Eva's mouth formed an O, the silver light
casting her lips in a milky warmth. Eva's head perfectly
framed by the full moon, the white light bringing a delicacy to her face. And in the silence of the moon's glow,
Waldor saw a fine-featured Eva. Lunar dust powdered her
angles and he began to know that she was magnificent.

"Waldor, what in hell's your problem?"

"Eva. Eva don't move. It's the moon." Eva his wife, glazed by the moon's pollen. She must embody the mystery and magic and strength of women always.

"So what about the moon? Quit staring like that."

"But Eva. With the moon behind you like that, you're an ancient goddess. You're the Virgin Mary. I can't explain. It's like you are all women." His Eva. Her face waxing white and strong.

"You dough-brain."

"Eva. Don't talk that way." His voice felt strong; he was powerful in his assertion.

"Waldor. Drink the green stuff."

"But really. You must feel a glow. I see it now; you're special, Eva."

"Waldor!"

"Eva, you have a halo."

She turned, looked out the window and the physical effect of the moon was gone, but his vision was not. It was stamped onto the back of his eyes forever.

"It's just the moon, Waldor. No big deal. Now quit being such a weiner. O.K.? Let's play cards."

"Eva!" His body hardened, he was aware of the heavy veins in his hands, of the darkness of his voice. "Don't call me names like that."

"Waldor. Remember me? Your cave lady. Huh?"

"Eva. Never. No—you're the essence of women. Now listen. Stop using those words, stop having such a rotten self-image. Really, Eva. My darling. Be calm. Then I'll get the cards." Waldor heard his power and thought again of his wife's delicacy.

Eva looked at him. But she did not speak.

"Now," he said, "I'll get the cards."

Waldor left the kitchen and, in silence, watched his wife from the hallway. The moon was above her head now and the sky behind her bled a heavy purple, but Eva's features remained soft. Her full lips he saw, moved gently, as though she were talking to herself. And he knew that her thoughts were beyond his comprehension; she wore a halo, she embodied all women.

And from the hallway Waldor saw their cat Lazer, feet tucked beneath his body, streamered eyes staring. Lazer staring at Eva. Waldor, standing squarely, watching cat and wife, knew he was right. For cats knew about special things. Cats recognized the wise and the ancient. Lazer yawned and carelessly licked a paw, twisted himself and began cleaning his tail.

Waldor brought the cards to Eva and dealt. They played three hands and three times Eva smashed her cards on the table with eleven-card gins.

"You poor poop, Waldor, playing against Eva the lucky one. You stand no chance."

"Eva. Stop using those stupid words. That kind of language doesn't suit you. Now listen." And Waldor, taking her thick fingers in his palm, said "It's not luck, Eva. It's a sign. You have wisdom." Waldor looked across the kitchen for the cool confirmation of Lazer's unwavering golden eyes. Lazer, the cat, was sleeping.

"Waldor. Cut the sap."

"You'll feel it soon, Eva. Don't worry, you're bound to feel it soon." Waldor passed a cloud of a touch over Eva's knee and felt sunlight on his fingers.

"You goon. Quit touching me like that."

"You're lovely."

"Enough of this crap. I'm going to bed. You've spent too much time in your apple tree."

Waldor stood, stretched and flexed his muscles. He felt good, strong. He watched Lazer soft-pad after his Eva.

While Eva slept, the moon scattered light on her face and Waldor traced the silver lines with his forefinger. His goddess, his Eva.

Eva mumbled, her heavy lips moving.

"What is it, my darling?"

She opened her eyes to the strange light. "I said cut it out, you weiner. How'm I suppose to sleep with your hands all over my face?"

His blood surged, pulsed hard in his heavy chest. "Eva. You are not to speak like that in this house again." He sat squarely in the bed and held her shoulder hard. "And I mean it."

Eva rolled tenderly toward him. "Yes, darling," she said. And softly fluttered her lashes in the spring moonlight.

Waldor sat, legs extended, knees apart in a garden chair on the deck in the tree. He was reading "Alberta Report." Waldor paused from the article on the Prince and Princess of Wales to survey his workmanship. He was pleased that he had spent his summer hours building this deck, doing something useful. Waldor sipped his martini and went back to his article on Di and Charles. He wondered how he could have wasted so many hours before, simply staring at things from the tree branch.

Waldor looked closely at a photo of Princess Di; did she dye her hair? He looked at his watch, sniffed the air and smelled the late summer scent of ripening apples. Then he became angry. It was past six and he ought to be smelling burning charcoal, not apples. Eva was late lighting the barbeque tonight. He had to admit it was she who brought his Calgary tree to bear edible fruit, his warm woman Eva, but really, she was getting slack.

Waldor continued looking at the photographs until he heard the light thud of the screen door, and silent moments later, felt Eva's full hand on his foot.

"Waldor."

"Hi Eva. I'm hungry." He looked down at her, saw sunlight flash golden about her head and butterflies flitting here and there about her shoulders. But even with all the sunlight, Eva's hair wasn't very blond; maybe she should dye it.

"I'm not surprised you're hungry, Waldor, it's late." And she smiled at him. Every time Eva smiled, round red apples fell from the tree. That caused her to laugh which caused more to fall. So, tumbling and laughing amongst falling apples, Eva began collecting the fruit in her apron. She became breathless and pink-cheeked, her apron heavy.

"Eva. Have you forgotten that I'm hungry?"

Eva stopped laughing; the apples stopped falling.

"I'm sorry, Waldor. I've brought you a picnic. It's too nice out to eat inside." Eva smiled and apples fell from the tree.

Reaching down, Waldor pulled up the small wicker basket Eva handed him. Then he moved his garden chair and made room for his wife on the small deck. She took his hand and sprang onto the branch, her movement tossing a wind of butterflies and the smell of warm fruit.

"This is o.k.," he said.

"Yes. Hand me the basket, please."

Eva brought out a white tablecloth which they spread over their knees. It was a very small basket, but from it Eva pulled eight stuffed vine leaves, deep fried squid, black olives, green olives stuffed with pimentos, shrimp and anchovies, haggis, yorkshire pudding, cornish game hen, yogurt, two pounds of cheddar cheese, a quarter pound of fetta, roast lamb, a box of crackers, two hard-boiled eggs, a Big Mac (his favorite), three bags of ripple chips and a bottle of apple cider. "Just for you," she said. Waldor peeked into the basket: it was still full.

Waldor ate and ate. Eva munched on apples from the tree. Good thing, he thought, remembering Princess Di's slender arms. She crunched too loudly, though. And Waldor drank his apple cider until it was almost dark and Orion appeared in the sky. Orion, the Giant Hunter: Orion who dominated the heavens and ignited Waldor's mind with tales of power and wonder, with the desire for something unique in his life. He continued drinking his apple cider while the Big Dipper turned towards them. Finally Waldor held the full bottle to Eva, "Wouldn't you like a sip? Just a sip?"

"No thank you," she said and smiled at him in the heavy half-light. They heard the soft thud of falling apples.

So Waldor sipped on into the night. Eva was quiet, she rarely spoke and never moved. And in the mystery of her presence he did not care to speak. It crossed his mind that he had planned on seeing the 11 o'clock news, but instead he became quite drunk. Then he held Eva's hand.

That night she made a hammock in the tree for him. Before he slept, Waldor watched the Northern Star slide from one into two, and as two they pulsed until he nudged them back to one again. Eva breathed sensuous cotton sighs into his ears and he moved his hand to caress her breast, but could not tolerate the flap of butterfly wings nor the thunk of falling apples. For with every thunk he knew that she was smiling, perhaps laughing silently, and he was insulted. Sex with him was no laughing matter. And his tenderness towards her became anger. He turned away from Eva and in summer's darkness applauded his strength in ignoring her.

In daylight Waldor dozed in his tree, but it was a restless doze. It was autumn. That he knew. The leaves were orange, they were gold; they were dying. The apples were dead. And it was cold in the hammock at night. He had slept through the first frost. Waldor farted in his tree's branch, threw a mush apple onto the deck below. So he knew it was autumn. He also knew he was getting fat. He was fat. Too many picnics. And apples made him sick. Most of the picnics Eva brought him lately had been apples and more apples; she was intent on having him eat apples. So he had not wanted to eat yesterday and ignored Eva when she came out with the picnic. She simply handed him a fresh red apple. "You have to keep up your strength. Your power, you know." And she laughed. Then she sleepily padded about under his tree picking up the brown slimy apples which had fallen.

Waldor scratched his right armpit. So he knew two things: it was autumn and he was fat. But he did not know why he felt yesterday the way he had. Waldor farted again. And he remembered Eva falling yesterday, her body sagging heavy and loose to the earth from slipping on a mushy apple. "Get up this minute, Eva. Get up. You're a disgrace. It's terrible to see you lying there like that," he yelled. "What's your problem?" Her arms billowed into the appled ground and, for a moment, like a flash of sun between storm clouds, he felt joy watching her body churn energy to rise. She struggled, her arms grabbing a branch, pulling her weight. Her round arms. Her heavy pink arms framed by slowly flickering butterflies.

"Get up, Eva. Right now. And I mean it," he yelled but his mouth opened closed opened; he could not yell because those were not his words. Had never been his words.

And he had to turn, could not bear to watch those arms shaking the branch because he wanted very suddenly and very intensely to have those arms help him down from his apple tree.

Even now, he could not doze for thinking about Eva's arms. He was angry too, for he was certain that Eva had seen his weakness. Waldor scratched himself and threw another brown apple onto the deck, watched it splat, then closed his eyes. He curled up tightly, the dead apple tree leaves rattling with his weight.

The screen door thudded. He heard Lazer meow. He heard the last apples dropping. He knew Eva was at his tree's base. Waldor opened his eyes.

Eva said, "Wanna bite?"

Waldor shook his head. "I've had enough apples."

"So why the hell don't you get down and make us some dinner?"

Waldor watched his wife, waiting.

Waiting for the Rodeo
Aritha van Herk

WARNING: DO NOT COME TO CALGARY. THERE IS NO CRIME, NO MONEY, NO DISEASE. THE CITY HAS BECOME COMPLETELY CONVENTIONAL AND SHOULD BE AVOIDED. BY ORDER OF CALGARY CITY COUNCIL. SIGNED, MAYOR RALPH KLEIN.

Tip did not consciously decide to ignore the posters, the newspaper ads, the radio and television bulletins. She was going to Calgary and she went, without much consideration of the consequences. That was the way she travelled; when the moment came, she followed it. If she had been one to listen to horror stories, she would never have gone anywhere. Every city had its drawbacks, its white-gloved commissionaires and fungus epidemics, its travelling magic shows. Audiences watched magicians like hawks; if they could detect a trick, the magician's apprentice was allowed to saw the magician in half, a ritual accompanied by goatish shouts and bellows. Too, Tip had once contracted a bad case of the staggers in Regina and had only been able to pull herself out of it by flying to Amsterdam and walking the cobblestones for a week. That had given her a bad scare and she never wanted to see Saskatchewan again. But it didn't stop her following her life's lust—to live in every Canadian city substantially enough to flaunt its markings in public. Everyone else wore their armbands and tattoos with a tribal loyalty; they only travelled when they were looking for trouble or because there was a rash of work.

For the last five years Calgary had been swollen with outsider markings, so much so that it would have been hard to find a native, but now, Tip knew from the television, the streets were empty and the wind howled down the glass coulees without ruffling much more than cement dust. Everyone had played Monopoly, tossing their dice on the sidewalks in front of the buildings they were gambling for. But the game had tired and the players packed up their Chance and Opportunity Knocks cards and went west, leaving behind the hopscotch outline of their chalked dice squares.

Tip always ran with the climate; when a city boasted a high suicide, divorce, and amputation rate, she was one of the first to move there, knowing that it would be a hot spot, a pride place to live. But now the deterring ads yearned her toward Calgary. She had never stopped there, only passed through on the TransCanada. And her life was getting predictable; it might be more fun to play in an unfashionable city. Most of all, she wanted to evade plot.

Tip owned a rusty U-haul for her moves. She never actually unpacked it, just pulled it up on the sidewalk in front of her crash. She had shoved all the stuff to the back and lived in it a few times when she hit a city with a housing shortage. It held the masked and intermittant objects that she had collected, had narrowed her eyes and imagined a future use for. She towed it behind her Ford.

Tip arrived in Calgary two weeks before Rodeo. As an economic joust, she decided to turn her pennies in. She went to the bank and asked for penny rolls. The teller brought her a dozen.

"Oh, that won't be enough."

"How meny dew yew wand?"

"A hundred." Each roll held fifty pennies.

The teller squinted. "A hunderd?"

"Yes. I've been saving them." For four years, she might have added, chunking them into her ten piggy banks, clinking them into empty mayonnaise jars. Now they waited, fat and heavy, to be emptied; for the plugs, the slots, the lids to release their copperbrown stream. Tip anticipated the ritual, shaking each container onto a heap on the floor, kneeling to count by fistfuls, rolling them into the brown cylinders. It was an afternoon's occupation and by the end of it her hands would be greenish, she would roll the last fifty and fold the ends down with satisfaction. She saved it up for herself the same way she saved the pennies, caching them in her piggy banks once a week or when she sorted her purse. She was never one who said to the cashier, "Oh, I have two pennies." She took them home for deposit in her own poor box, surreptitious pleasure in their accumulation.

She waited for a rainy afternoon, then bundled in an old woolen sweater with frayed wrists, she began to heap the pennies, tipping them into a noisy pile on the floor. She stood to cascade the piggybanks empty, rattle them from a satisfying height. Then, on her knees, she began to count and roll. Occasionally, she would stop to add the accumulating cylinders—fourteen, thirty-seven, fifty-five, sixty (she stopped for a cup of tea and streaked black across her face), ninety-two, and finally one hundred. There was still a small heap left and she separated it into piles. Eighteen, she would have to get more rolls. One hundred and eighteen rolls, fifty-nine dollars. She rocked back on her heels and stroked the neat cylinders with her palm. She would turn them in, all that extra weight shed, and use the paper bills to entertain a day. She divided the pennies between three plastic grocery bags and scrubbed her face and hands, feeling that she had completed her move, that she was settled.

The bags were so heavy she had trouble lugging them into the bank and she set them down on the teller's counter with a terrific clunk. The teller scowled. "Yew cand hand doze in all ad onze."

"Why not?"

"We don wand dem. Dere's doo many."

"What am I supposed to do, drag them off and bring them back two at a time?"

The teller shrugged.

"You're a bank, you're supposed to take them." Tip began hauling rolls out of the bags, slamming them down on the teller's desk pad. "Twofoursixeighttentwelvefour-teensixteeneighteentwenty—"

"Hew many are there?"

"Hundred and eighteen—twentytwotwentyfour-twentysixtwentyeightthirty—"

"All ride. Slew down." She counted, then re-counted them and put them back into the grocery bags before hauling them one at a time into the vault, wincing. When she returned to her computer stool she looked at Tip as if she were part of a hold-up. "Yeh?"

"You haven't given me the money. Fifty-nine dollars."

"Oh yeh." She opened her drawer and reluctantly extracted four tens, two fives and nine ones, crumpled and well-circulated. Several of the ones were criss-crossed with scotchtape.

"Don't you have any new money?"

"Newp."

Tip folded the bills once and tucked them into her hip pocket. She felt light as the dust that the wind was blowing across the parking lot in front of her feet.

To compound her re-location, she hung all her clothes up in her new mirrored closet and began to sort them, moving the hangers in a complicated chess of different seasons and occupations. Play clothes, work clothes, dress-up clothes, costume clothes, evening clothes, sexy clothes, maneuver clothes, impractical clothes, wornout but loved clothes. Then she re-sorted them according to their function. Pants, jeans, skirts, dresses, suits, blouses, ties, scarves, belts, sweaters, t-shirts, underwear. And then, began to tear them from their hangers, hold each considered item up for her critical eye; keep it or pitch it? It was hard for Tip to get rid of clothes—they had a past, they lacked the safe anonymity of pennies. Sorting clothes was unsettling; once the pile of hangers lay flung beside the pile of clothes to be discarded, she had doubts. Would she never wear that purple velvet again? Were those silk slacks really splitting at the seam, couldn't they be mended? The pile lay on the floor while she speculated, sometimes returning an item to a hanger and place in the closet, sometimes flinging even more onto the pile. Until she was utterly sick of the process, swept the bundle up in her arms and carried it down to the car wanting to be done with it once and for all. But then had to scan the yellow pages searching for where to abandon it: Goodwill, the Salvation Army? And thinking of that, had to consider consignment shops. Would someone else actually pay for her old clothes? She reviewed her discards again. She could take them to an amateur theatre; they must need costumes. The clothes wrinkled in the back window of the car while Tip tried to make up her mind. Finally, she stuffed them into the nearest clothing box in the nearest shopping center, not caring how wrinkled or stained they would get or who would parade them on the streets. And driving away, she saw in her rearview mirror the leg of a pair of red pants executing a limp kick out of the box's chute door.

    She had worn those pants when she was the magician's apprentice, when she stood behind him on the stage after he seduced the audience by conjuring rabbits and scarves and flights of paper birds, after he sawed her in half. He had insisted that she wear red pants, that she wear red pants with a black scarf, that she conceal within her pant legs the accoutrements of his trade. They were filled with pockets, huge expanding pockets, and driving away, Tip was worried that someone would try the pants on and discover themselves the magician's apprentice without any real wish to follow that profession, without agreement or their own volition. But she had to get them out of her life, until she discarded them she would always be reminded of her role as his sidekick, the cantor to his liturgical exercises. The job had paid well, but night after night she grew increasingly tense as time for the concluding act drew near. His finale was to place her in a kind of pine coffin and saw the box in half, all very realistically, the saw rasping at the wood, the crumbs of sawdust flying so that the audience, certain of the act's authenticity, thrilled to be watching the terrible demise of what they took to be an endless stream of magician's girls (all tarts who had no life beyond magic), watching for a trickle of blood to appear on the floor under the coffin (which was always balanced each end on a straight-backed chair); they held their breath as the magician finished his laborious work, would knock the two halves of the coffin apart and wave his hand, whereupon Tip was supposed to spring up, the two halves of enclosing wood falling away from her red pants, her sexy bosom. The truth was that the coffins (a new one delivered by the local coffin-maker every day) were slightly larger than they appeared, so that she could tuck up her legs and curl herself into a ball in one half of the coffin; but every night she watched and listened to the progress of the saw so close to her ear, her unseeing eye, that the job began to wear on her. One night, unforgivably, right before the magician's finale, she stole the gate receipts and ran away, changing her name, her hair colour, her way of dressing so that he could not trace her. She even gained weight and consciously altered her walk. Magician's apprentices are not allowed to quit their jobs. They know too much. If he found her she was in trouble. And now he had. So the red flag of her discarded apprentice pants signalled both relief and worry. If he happened to see them walking down the street on a body's legs, he would know she lived here in Calgary now; on the other hand, they cast a sinister light on the rest of her closet and she was glad to abandon them to thrift shops and second-hand dealers. She wanted no reminders of her failed vocation.

Next, she had to learn money machine etiquette. When she first came to Calgary, she barged up without waiting her turn, looked over people's shoulders and was surprised when they turned and snarled at her. The rules were unbendable. You came up while someone was using the machine. You stood exactly three feet behind them, directly behind them so that they could use their back as a shield, and if they glanced over their shoulder at you, you looked away into the distance. You were no machine thief, you had no intention of watching them punch in their number and then bashing them on the head in order to steal their card and commit computer crime, emptying their programmed and helpless accounts of their programmed limit.

While break-in artists left polite lists of what they had taken (for insurance purposes) and homeowners left a chicken in the fridge for hungry break-in artists, the elaborate ritual of money machines was played out 1900 times an hour all over Calgary, customers brandishing their punch-in cards, their key numbers cleverly memorized (one street in from the back door, the fourteen stations of the cross, subtract the last digit of my birthdate from the first), all following the indelible etiquette of the money machines, protocol as rigid and unyielding as the plastic and metal consoles it was performed for, an elaborate punctilio. Tip tried to ignore rules but the behavior proved infectious and she averted her eyes with as much disdainful courtesy as everyone else. "Who, me? I'm not trying to see your number. I'm just waiting my turn." Nobody knew where the money came from although everyone used the money machines and everyone had a different limit, seemed to have a different monetary designation. Trading numbers and cards had become a gambling racket—you threw yours in the pile to see if you could come off with a higher limit. Even better, the money that the machines doled out was always crisp and new, a pleasure to riffle between the fingers. Money machines were illegal down across the line.

Still, Tip needed a job. The most prevalent occupation in Calgary was that of doorman. Most places had at least one doorman; high class places two or three, a head doorman, an under-doorman, who stood a few steps in front of the head doorman, and a street doorman, who stood at sidewalk level. They were all dressed in top hats and tails, with gold-headed canes across the arms of the head doormen and whistles around the necks of the street doormen. The whistles were to summon rickshaws. The doormen, whose primary employment was staying on their feet, were always yawning, huge molar-displaying yawns that would crack a normal person's jaw, but the doormen were used to it. The problem was that the yawns were contagious, and if you passed a doorman you were sure to catch yourself in the middle of a yawn half a block farther. It got so that people would avert their faces when they passed, all the doormen saw were the backs of heads and determinedly walking bodies. Of course, when you came out of a cave at eleven o'clock at night, pitch black and raining hailstones, there were no doormen around, they were all in the back gambling or trying on each other's uniforms. The biggest union issues were changes of colour and cut for the tailcoats.

The big event came. Rodeo, when the city went naked, resulting in a carnivale levelling, everyone stripped of status and design. As compensation, the animals carried the people's clothes; there were cats with feather boas around their necks, horses wearing buffalo greatcoats, dogs in t-shirts. Because their hats and tailcoats were essential to their duties, the doormen kept those on, although they discarded shirts and pants and shoes, and were able to yawn just as effectively in semi-uniform. During Rodeo Tip got a job as a necromancer, using her magician's apprenticeship as experience. Curled inside his wooden coffin she had indeed felt herself close to the dead, even wondered if she should try to get closer. She sometimes thought what would happen if she remained stretched flat in the coffin, if she lay with her hands folded across her breast and her eyes lightly closed, with her legs neatly stretched, knee to knee and ankle to ankle under the incipient scrape of the saw, if magic would really happen, if the toothed blade would caress its way through her body without noticeable harm. That recurring idea was what made her decide to run away from the job. Some night she might be tempted to try it and would end up as titillation for the diseased audience.

Necromancy was a good racket down six-gun alley; everyone needed to communicate with their dead, not so much because of the future but because of the present, which was as close as most of them could come to imagining the future. All Tip had to do was persuade them that the voice coming from the ceiling was the voice of their own particular loved one, and with some artificial smoke and red lighting, a heavy and pervasive incense, most people were quite willing to believe that their mother, who had had a soprano voice in real life, would have a raspy contralto in death. The answers to their questions were easy to devise. Falling in love had become unfashionable, and most people's questions had to do with careers and jobs. There was no predictable plot. Tip dressed in an old wedding gown minus veil and train and wrapped a tie-dyed scarf around her curly hair. She put on some half granny glasses for disguise and made sure that she was wearing tennis shoes and that the dress was easily torn off. If the magician stumbled onto her, she wanted to be able to run.

When she wanted to Rodeo dance she went to the Brass Ring. Like everything else in Calgary, you had to know how to get in. You could hear the music, you could see bodies moving through intermittant windows, but you could not find the door; there was no door, you entered through a complicated series of inter-connecting under-ground passages and back alleys which let out onto a box alley that was always carefully watched. This was no place for hunters or pickups but for real drinkers and dancers, people who wanted to move to the inspiration of alcohol in their bloodstreams and the music—all of it old and hardly heard or remembered by the young. The average age was forty and the bouncer made an attempt to keep everyone under thirty out. Tip slipped him a twenty and got in that way; found herself a table in a dark corner on the lower level and waited for the morning, watching the people thump the brilliantined floor, watching the bodies work their way closer as the night wore on; she danced too, with the lean bandannaed men in wrist and neckline tans, uneasy with the nakedness required by Rodeo. All the music that the headphoned jockey played was from the fifties, Tip's mother's tunes. For Tip, this was a better memory exercise than the machines in the arcades. This was human, noisy, sweaty, the determined bodies writhing or leaning over each other, the broken strobe, the massive bouncer flexing his arm across the door, the table girl's ferocious seating plan, pointing out tables with a six-gun; if you moved without her permission, she'd shoot, hit a hamstring or a funnybone with narrow-eyed deliberance. Everyone was terrified of her pointed bouncing breasts and her choppy walk, her levelled finger. All the bouncer did was watch the door, she didn't need muscle.

The Brass Ring filled you up, satisfied you. When you hit the cool air of the alley at four in the morning, you were high, strung at a pitch that could keep you vibrating for hours. When you went home to sleep the dancing went on and on in your ears. Tip went to the Brass Ring every night after her red-light necromancies, danced and danced until her breasts fell from bouncing, ran all the way home and high-kicked inside the door before she put her earrings in the fridge and fell fast asleep, not even hesitating to dream about the magician she knew was pursuing her.

Every night during Rodeo the hot-air balloons puffed their way south, south-east above the city; a house, an ice-cream cone and a propane tank among the striped and shivering coloured globes. They floated and duffed, rose and fell. Tip watched for them, the slight hiss that they gave to the air, their implacable float. All of Calgary's dogs hated them, perked their ears and twitched sleeping tails and growled, dived under chairs or ran to windows and barked, tore madly after the balloon's wake or burst through screendoors into their human's houses. During Rodeo dogs scanned the sky before going outside, anxiety on their muzzles, their raised and pointed noses. The balloons began to fly longer, all day and all night, glowing teardrops hanging above the city in darkness, the balloon-ists as a dare beginning to detonate fireworks from their baskets, lighting the sky in unpredictably celebratory

purples and greens. The dog population of Calgary went
crazy, neurosis and psychosis increasing until they refused
to chase cars or cats, refused to water hydrants and instead
spent all their time eyeing the transfixed sky. The balloon
baskets carried groups of laughing people having cham-
pagne breakfasts and cognac lunches, tossing pennies into
the sky for luck, renting a feather bed basket in order to
become a member of the hot air club, piquency to
lovemaking in the air that did not exist in the hotels and
alleys below. Tip fell in love with a balloonist, even
though he never removed his leather goggles and aviator's
helmet, mainly because she wanted him to teach her his
trade. His eyes behind the brown circles were kind, were
preoccupied, and when he was on the ground he was
always looking up, wanting to hiss his way to the mare's
tails of clouds that streamed above the city.

One night in the Brass Ring with her aviator, Tip saw
the magician. He was in disguise but she knew it was him,
she recognized his mustache. At first she froze, then com-
forted herself that he would not recognize her. But of
course he did and came toward her table, even though the
table girl pointed her pearl-handled six-gun at him. He
held up his palms, "I know these people," and she spun her
gun around her forefinger and walked away.

"I've missed you," he said to Tip.

"Haven't you found a replacement?"

"She's not as good as you were." He smiled.

Tip was starting to sweat. The balloonist looked at the
ceiling, he didn't notice. "I've got a new job."

He twitched his mustache and smiled again. "I
wouldn't mind," he said reasonably, "if I could get back
the pants that I had specially made for you. They were
expensive and I think they'd fit the new girl."

"I don't have them anymore."

The magician looked thoughtful and drew at the blue

silk bandanna that was knotted around his neck. It came undone and at his gentle tugs grew larger and larger until he held up a new pair of apprentice pants, blue this time, the pockets even more capacious than those of the previous pair. "I'd like you back," he said. "I'd teach you my tricks and you could eventually take over."

Tip shook her head. "There's no future in it. I'd always be your apprentice." The balloonist stood up to go to the can and the magician dared to lay a soft white hand on her knee.

"It's more secure than Calgary. Come now, my dear. Hanging out with balloonists and doormen? Not your style is it?"

"I like it fine. Better than being sawn in half every night."

He ignored that. "I've added a couple of trunk escapes to my repertoire. You'd be perfect."

"What do you do? Stick swords through it?"

"See?" he said gently. "You know the trade. Clever girl." His hand vised itself over her knee. "Come on now, without making a scene. You know you were meant for me. Besides, the gate receipts . . ."

Tip had no weapon and the aviator must have encountered a lineup at the urinal. She stood up, the magician's hand squeezing her arm.

"No funny stuff now," he said happily.

Tip shook her head. They climbed the stairs, moved toward the edge of the dance floor which was right by the door. A greying cowboy lurched against them and turned to slur, "Hey sweetie, wanna dance?"

"Yes," said Tip. "Please." The magician had to let go. The cowboy steered her onto the floor of naked bodies and began to jive, spinning Tip around. She could see the magician by the door looking patient. There was only one exit.

"Please," she said to the cowboy, "I'm getting dizzy."

He swung her into a slow, belly-rubbing waltz and as they turned around the light-pinpointed floor, she worked him deeper and deeper into the crowd. At the end of the waltz she kissed his cheek and slithered to the floor, began to crawl towards the dark warren of tables. She knew without looking that the magician was starting to scan the crowd, check heads. She knew that in a few seconds he would act, would invade, if he had to, the whole of the Brass Ring, would either begin to perform or threaten: the tables would start flying through the air, the d-j's record would begin to spin backwards, the wind would begin to blow. Tip peered from under the edge of an askew tablecloth. One of his best tricks was making his apprentice disappear. Maybe, in the storm he was bound to create, in the energy he would have to unleash, she could make herself disappear. She chuckled suddenly. It was the old rule. If you guess how he did it, the apprentice got to saw the magician in half; the apprentice became the magician. Tip knew the story had to come from somewhere, it had to be possible. She held her breath and concentrated.

When does a magician's apprentice know that she has absorbed her master's knowledge? If she knew, there might be more rebellions, more magicians sawn in half for inflamed crowds. When apprentice becomes magician history hesitates. It's a rare occasion; most apprentices never dare to try. Tip squeezed her eyes shut and willed herself to disappear. When she opened them, she was floating above the table she had been hiding under and the Brass Ring was in an uproar. The magician was flinging bolts of lightning from his palms. Half the crowd thought it was part of the floorshow and the other half thought the situation was serious. The bouncer, who was closest to the magician, had grabbed him, only to find himself flat on his back in a corner with a lump on the side of his head and a chair leg bent around his wrist. There were screams, laughter, and Tip saw her pre-occupied balloonist lose both his goggles and his flying helmet to an unseen hand. She almost giggled but caught herself in time. Putting on his knowledge with his power made her see the indifferent strength of his illusion.

She stayed where she was and watched the turntable trail into silence, the confused jumble of the people on the dance floor, the lights going up to expose the stained walls and the empty glasses. The magician scanned the crowd for Tip, and then all his strength waned. He felt he had better sit down. She had escaped. He hadn't expected her to usurp his power, hadn't expected her to have the nerve to revolt so thoroughly. He was angry but he was also impressed. He knew enough to retreat gracefully.

He stood, bowed to the titsy table girl who strode up and levelled her six-gun at him. "You're supposed to stay at the table I give you," she said. "Those are the rules." She cocked the hammer of the gun.

"Would you like a job? I need an apprentice," he said.

She shook her head and pointed her gun toward the door. He looked at her and nodded and as he moved away, from his fingers drifted hundreds of tiny hot-air balloons that bobbed and swung in the draft of the room and its bodies, as though he were wishing Tip well.

The music began again.

The day after Rodeo ended, Tip took her fifty-nine dollars and went downtown to look for an object to add to her U-haul collection. Her necromancing was over and now she planned to become a hot air pilot under the tutelage of her preoccupied balloonist. The dogs had returned to their occupations, the doormen to yawning and the people to clothes. An Indian slept on a bench on the Stephen Avenue Mall and a window washer performed his tenuous ballet high against the side of a golden-mirrored building.

Tip looked up at the chartreuse sky, down at the dusty sidewalk. She had found the blue silk pants with the capacious pockets folded into a neat square in her mailbox. What if the magician returned? She stopped in front of a gun store. Inside were racks of shotguns, velvet cases of pistols, knives in leather sheaths. She went in and fingered a double-bladed throwing knife, then shoved it back across the counter at the clerk. "I don't think I need it," she said. As she pulled the wooden door shut behind her, she saw the half-effaced sign stencilled in gothic script on its glass. ALL STORIES   ND. The rack of twenty-twos in the window winked at her.

She would stay here, live in Calgary and wait for next year's Rodeo.

Notes on Contributors

Editor:

Fred Stenson has published one novel, *Lonesome Hero*, and two books of non-fiction. His short stories have appeared in *Saturday Night*, *Chatelaine* and in the 1984 collection *Three Times Five*. He was born in Pincher Creek, Alberta and lives in Calgary.

Contributors:

J. Leslie Bell was born in Glasgow, Scotland. He has published in various literary magazines including *The Canadian Forum* and *Queen's Quarterly*. He won the *Calgary Herald* short story competition in 1985, and the Alberta Culture short story competition in 1986.

Shirley Black is a native Calgarian. She was runner-up in the 1984 *Calgary Herald* short story competition, and placed second in the 1985 *Red Deer Advocate* short story contest. She has also been published in the *Alexandra Reader*.

Cristine Bye was raised on a farm near Coronation, Alberta and now lives in Calgary. She is a feature writer for the *Calgary Herald*.

Joan Clark moved to Newfoundland a year ago after living in Alberta for 20 years. Her most recent novel, *Wild Man of the Woods*, was runner-up for the 1986 Canadian Library Association Award. A forthcoming novel, *The Moons of Madeleine*, (Viking) takes place in Calgary.

Caterina Edwards was born in England and raised in Alberta. She has published one novel, *The Lion's Mouth*, and many short stories in literary magazines and anthologies. Her first play, *Terra Straniera*, was produced professionally in 1986.

Bev Harris lives in Calgary and teaches composition at Mount Royal College. Five of her short stories were published in *Three Times Five* (NeWest, 1984).

Greg Hollingshead has taught English at the University of Alberta since 1975. A collection of his stories, *Famous Players*, has been published by Coach House Press. "Rat With Tangerine" first appeared in the *Prairie Journal of Canadian Literature*.

Nancy Holmes was born in Edmonton and now lives in Calgary. Her poetry and short stories have appeared in several journals including *Descant*, *Quarry* and *Dandelion*. Her poetry will be featured in NeWest Press's anthology *Ride Off Any Horizon, Vol. 2*.

Mark Anthony Jarman, born in Edmonton, is a graduate of the University of Iowa Writers Workshop. His collection of stories *Dancing Nightly in the Tavern* won the Writers Guild of Alberta short fiction award. He has recently published a collection of poetry, *Killing the Swan*. "Goose Dog Fish Stars" is reprinted by permission of Press Porcepic.

Ruth Krahn was born and educated in Edmonton, Alberta. Her stories have appeared in *Dandelion*, *Fiddlehead*, *Grain* and on CBC's *Alberta Anthology*.

Henry Kreisel was born in Vienna in 1922 and joined the staff of the University of Alberta in 1947. He is the author of two novels, *The Rich Man* and *The Betrayal*, and of *The Almost Meeting*, a collection of short stories. In 1986 the

Government of Alberta awarded him the Sir Frederick Haultain Prize for significant contributions to the Fine Arts.

Rebecca Luce-Kapler was born in Ponoka, Alberta and now lives in Whitecourt. She has published a number of short stories and won the Michener Medal for Excellence in the Fine Arts from Red Deer College in 1983.

Elona Malterre grew up on a farm near Balzac, Alberta and now lives in Calgary. She has received awards in poetry and television script writing competitions. She has a novel forthcoming from Dell and Seal.

Clem Martini was born in Bowness, Alberta and lives in Calgary. He writes short stories and plays. "Breath of God" won second prize in the 1984/85 Alberta Culture short story competition.

Shirlee Smith Matheson grew up in Lacombe, Alberta and now lives in Calgary. Her forthcoming books include *Youngblood of the Peace* and *A Girl Called Alien*. She has received awards for her short stories and historical articles.

W.O. Mitchell was born in Weyburn, Saskatchewan and has lived most of his life in Saskatchewan and Alberta. He is one of Canada's best known novelists, playwrights and raconteurs. His works of fiction include *Who Has Seen the Wind*, *Jake and the Kid*, *The Vanishing Point*, *How I Spent My Summer Holidays* and *Since Daisy Creek*.

Cathy Reininger was born in Peterborough, Ontario and moved to northern Alberta in 1978. In Alberta, she began writing articles on natural history for several periodicals including *Heritage* and *Western Producer*. She began writing short stories in 1984.

Mary Walters Riskin lives in Edmonton. Her fiction has appeared in such magazines as *Chatelaine*, *The Malahat*

Review and *NeWest Review*. Her first novel, *The Woman Upstairs*, is to be a 1987 publication of NeWest Press. "Print Dresses" was first published in *The Malahat Review*.

Helen J. Rosta was born in Alberta and lives in Edmonton. A collection of her short stories *In the Blood* was published by NeWest Press in 1982. One of her stories "Hunting Season" was produced for television and aired on CBC. Another story "This House" won the Flare Fiction Competition.

Gloria Sawai was raised in Saskatchewan and presently lives in Edmonton. Her short stories have appeared in *NeWest Review*, *Grain*, *Aurora 78*, *Best Canadian Stories* (Oberon, 1982), *Three Times Five* (NeWest) and *Short Stories by Canadian Women* (Oxford). She is also a playwright.

Diane Schoemperlen was born in Thunder Bay, Ontario and has lived in Canmore, Alberta for the past ten years. She has published two books, *Double Exposures* and *Frogs and Other Stories*. She is currently working on a novel with the support of a grant from the Alberta Foundation for the Literary Arts.

Sam Selvon, originally from Trinidad, lived in England for 30 years before moving to Calgary in 1978. His awards include two Guggenheim Fellowships and an honorary doctorate from the University of the West Indies. He has written many novels, short stories and radio plays. His novel *Moses Migrating* won the Writers Guild of Alberta award in 1984.

Catherine A. Simmons was born in and lives in Calgary. Her first published story, "A Man's Home Is", appeared in the Fall, 1985 edition of *The Dinosaur Review*.

Marilynn Shirley Stratton has been an Alberta resident since 1966, and has lived in Calgary for the past eleven years. Her short stories and poetry have been published in *Prairie Fire*, *Blue Buffalo*, *Glass Canyons*, *Western People* and *Western Sportsman*; her work has also been broadcast on CBC Radio's *Alberta Anthology*.

Merna Summers was born in Mannville, Alberta and now lives in Edmonton. She is the author of two collections of short stories, *The Skating Party* and *Calling Home*. The latter received the Writers Guild of Alberta prize for short fiction in 1982.

Jan Truss lives in Water Valley, Alberta. Her novel *Bird at the Window* was the first winner of the Alberta Search For A New Novelist Award in 1973. Her novel *Jasmine* received the Ruth Schwartz Award, Children's Literature, and was runner-up for the Canada Council Award.

Aritha van Herk was born and raised in central Alberta, and now lives in Calgary. Her novels include *Judith* (1978), *The Tent Peg* (1981), and *No Fixed Address* (1986). She is co-editor of *More Stories From Western Canada* and *West of Fiction*.

Rudy Wiebe was born in Saskatchewan and has taught creative writing and Canadian literature at the University of Alberta, Edmonton, for the past twenty years. He has published, among other books, seven novels and three collections of short stories. *The Temptations of Big Bear* won the Governor General's award for fiction in 1973.

Betty Wilson grew up at Grassy Lake, Alberta and currently lives in Edmonton. Her novel *Andre Tom MacGregor* won the Search for an Alberta Novelist competition, the Beaver Award and the Gibson Literary award in 1977. It has been translated into Russian.